CLOAKED MAGIC

THE MIDLIFE MAGE COLLECTION

DAPHNE MOORE

L.A. BORUFF

INDEX

Bliss: drug created by magic. A key ingredient is destroyed innocence. Dealers have found human children to be an abundant cheap supply.

Brandon Sauer: a fetch

Caladrius: (CAL ad ree us) a changing kin that can appear as human or bird. Gifted with the ability to heal.

Ceri Gault/Ceridwen Alarie: Mage.

Changing kin: generic term for the kins whose gifts involve shape shifting.

Chaos magic: loose clumps of magic that are easy to manipulate but have a tendency to dissipate.

Crixus: a very old Goblin.

Custom Keeper: a svartalf who coordinates important ceremonies with the wishes of the participants, trying to preserve custom as much as pobbile

Daoine sidhe: (deen-ya shee) a kin claimed by the DayKing. Gifted with the ability to charm and persuade, generally considered very attractive.

Dara Gault: Ceri's college age daughter.

Darius: deceased goblin associated with Crixus.

DayKing: one of the creators. Aspected to the day and light. Also called Marduk.

Death: physical embodiment of concept of death.

Diego: gatekeeper for the House of Mists.

Dominion: Worlds native to each kin. All the dominions have gates or thin places that lead to earth, which is humanity's dominion.

Dragon: A generic term for the kins who have at least one form that has wings, four limbs, and scales.

Drake: an associate of Johann Schmidt's. Presumed to be a dragon.

Dreg: A bliss addict who has mutated and degenerated from their original kin.

Enkimmu: Kin that gains control of others after drinking their blood.

Eoin: daoine sidhe, member of Rhys' triad.

Erebite: (eruh-BITE) one of nine beings formed from the Chaos that preceded the dominions being created. The nine agreed to 'sleep' in human forms, their power quiet until given time to mature, which would exceed a human lifespan. So reborn endlessly, still sleeping.

Escaped Energy: Noir, black dog: when enough chaos magic is concentrated in an area, it can spontaneously take on physical form from images in minds in the area. Noir was sustained by Ceri, while the black dog eventually dissipated and the energy went back to a neutral state.

Esther (Schmidt?): Johann Schmidt's wife. A mage. Deceased. Also descended from the mage clan Sisitu.

Evan Keller: an athlete with academic problems. Ceri is his English teacher.

Fé: (fay) a general term for several kins, who have a deep seated need for transactions, physical or emotional, to be balanced somehow.

Fetch: a kin able to take on the appearance and

memories of other beings. In childhood, they can immerse themselves and become a perfect copy of their donor. The process is called imprinting.

Gaius: Raphael's son. An Enkimmu.

Geas: a magic that forces a certain course of action, such as obedience to orders from a specific individual.

Giselle: a servant in Nick's home in the svartalfar dominion.

Goblin: a warrior kin enslaved by the Daoine Sidhe.

Godhome: dominion where Tiamat and Marduk live.

Guardian: a magical construct that protects the House of Mists and prevents Raphael from leaving the dominion. Sentient and loves stories.

Gunther: a svartalf.

Hjalmar: a mage in the svartalfar dominion.

Henry: Human child. Inhabitant of House of Mists.

House of Mists: name of a dominion.

Ilani: teenage inhabitant of House of Mists. Unknown kin.

Jack Holmes: Liz's father

Jimmy Gault: Ceri's son in high school. A mage of unknown paternity.

Johann Schmidt: ruler of the central Ohio supernatural community because everyone is afraid to cross him. Believed to be a fé. Also called Lou. True name Lugh.

Katie: an awakened erebite.

Kin: term for the different kinds of supernatural peoples. Most are claimed by the DayKing or Night-Queen, but a few are independent.

Lilim: (LIL im) a kin who feeds on emotional or life energy. Has the ability to project emotion and change the emotional states of those around them. Typically one of the better organized kins and usually found in groups. One of the sources for vampire folklore.

Liz Holmes: Jimmy's human girlfriend.

Lotus: an apsara, and Johann Schmidt's trusted assistant.

Mage: human able to see and use magic. The effects they can create are called will workings.

Mary: Liz's fetch.

Morgan/the Morgan: chief of chiefs of the Daoine Sidhe. Rules with an iron fist.

Nick Damarian: Ceri's svartalfar almost boyfriend. Metallurgist who works for government think tank. Also called Sigiward.

Nia: A woman who works with Johann. Certified as an EMT.

Nimaya Sharma: yaksha. Priya's foster mother.

Night Queen: one of the two creator beings. She is aspected to the darkness and night, the moon is her symbol. Also called Tiamat.

Noir: (nwar) tiny chaos dragon.

Nunamnir: A shapeshifter who becomes a sea monster. Lives in the sea.

Odette Keller: human mother to Evan Keller, a well-connected lady.

Oni: (OH nee) one of the giant kins, found in East Asian human folklore.

Priya Sharma: A yaksha high school student.

Queen Zarah (surname unknown): Ruler of the lilim.

Raksasha: (RAHK shuh suh, RAHK shuh suhs, RAHK shuh see (for a female)) Kin with illusion and shapeshifting abilities. Often called assassins.

Ramki Sharma: yaksha. Priya's foster father.

Raphael: ruler of the House of Mists. An Enkimmu. Also called Asmedaj.

Rhys: Leader of the daoine sidhe in the central Ohio area

Rusalka (pl rusalki) (Ruw-SAA-LKaa, Ruw-SAA-LKee) water spirit, forms water into shape of human body to interact. Very concerned with politeness.

Santo: troll, employed by Johann Schmidt.

Signy: a svartalfar, Nick's cousin.

Sisitu: name of the mage family Ceri Gault is descended from.

Solveig: a servant in Nick's home in the svartalfar dominion, Giselle's granddaughter.

Svartalfar: (SVART ul far) kin whose gift is in working metals and mining. Found in northern European folklore.

Tara O'Brien: a young daoine sidhe.

Tatiana: a teenage inhabitant of the HOuse of Mists. Of the changing kins; she shapeshifts to a wolf.

Thin-blood: term for a person whose parents are from different kins, or who is of primarily human descent.

Thomas Pryce: lilim. Leader of lilim organization in central Ohio.

Therese: Raphael's sister. Kin unknown.

Thrall: in svartalfheim, a servant or slave.

Triad: group of three daoine sidhe. Members of that kin prefer to function as members of a triad.

Tristan: a servant in Nick's home in the svartalfar dominion.

Troll: a giant kin; reputed to eat anything- or anyone- who isn't a troll.

Tuatha: (Tew ATH uh) an extinct kin, one that had no allegiance to the creators.

Ulrich: a svartalfar. Nick's nephew.

Una: daoine sidhe, Rhys' sister and member of his triad. Known to have manufactured Bliss.

Unbodied: the creature that rises when a strong-willed person refuses to accept their death. Incorporeal, they eat life force, preferring sentient beings. Human folklore refers to them as ghosts.

Vasily: rusalka. Leader of the central Ohio rusalki.

Vinaya: yaksha. Priya Sharma's foster mother.

Vittorio: troll employed by Johann Schmidt.

Ward: protective magical construct, created to defend an area from intrusion.

Wolf changer: generic term for the kins who shapeshift into a wolf.

Xerxes: a goblin associated with Crixus.

Yaksha: (YAK Shuh) a kin who controls plants and fertility. Some are benevolent, some are mischievous. Found in Indian folklore.

UNFAZED

PART ONE

THE HEAT LAY on the students and me like a layer of half-melted taffy, sticky and unpleasant. The fan and open windows didn't touch it, and the elderly high school building only had working air conditioning in the administration and science blocks. Fancy that.

This late in October it should've been nice and cool, but we were experiencing a colossal heatwave. The trick-or-treat and party costumes would likely be even skimpier than usual.

Priya, a new transfer student, shook her head. "Why are commas and semicolons so complicated, Mrs. G?" Her words lilted, which made her accent pleasant and enchanting.

I smiled at her. "You just have to practice a little more. You're doing well."

She widened her brown eyes at me and made a face, standing with her tablet tucked against her waist. She was the last student I was working with today.

Soothing her worries about the test on Monday had taken more time than it should've, but she understood the material.

When she left, I consulted the list I'd made for closing up the room. Details slipping had dogged me for years. It had worsened enough lately I'd begun fighting back with checklists. The little things seemed to be what always got me. I couldn't even really blame this on being middle-aged. I'd always been forgetful... though it *was* worsening.

There were moments when I wished my Friday afternoons didn't include tutoring teenagers in grammar and writing, but you do what you've gotta to make a living. True, I could manipulate magic, but all that talent had ever gotten me was hunted. No making gold from straw for me. Teaching not only paid the bills. It also kept me safe.

I checked that I had my car fob before I locked the room, then set off at a good pace down the hall, hoping to avoid anyone calling my name for a volunteer opportunity. The vice-principal was like an evil jack-in-the-box, ready to jump out of nowhere with extra work clenched in her damp fists.

The coast was clear. Outside the school doors, my old beat-up, bright blue Malibu gleamed like a hope of escape in the parking lot.

My son, Jimmy, went to school here, and I usually gave him a ride, but he'd gotten one with his girlfriend Liz instead today so they could get ready for the football game later. Important stuff. Since they'd started going out, he'd gone to all the games to support her cheerleading.

A couple of the other teachers were staying even later than I was. Their cars sat in the parking lot, looking sad and lonely, but I was free! As an added bonus, I had a little extra time to shower and get myself ready before my sort-of date.

We were going to a Halloween party. I even had a costume I'd bought in a fit of whimsy—and my daughter's encouragement—at the Ren Faire.

I started the car and swore before I threw it into reverse. The gas gauge read way too close to empty. I'd forgotten to fill it this morning. Once again, I would have to support the local extortionate prices at the gas station down the street.

Gossamer strands of loose magic tangling through the air reached out for me as the tank filled. The world was full of it, but only those who perceived it could use it. The movement of putting the pump nozzle back into the cradle helped me shoo them away. I wanted them, every moment, so much it sometimes hurt.

But I knew better. The last time I truly called the magic, I'd ended up in a dungeon—and not the kind in romance novels. Even if I would risk capture for me, I wouldn't risk my kids.

Once in the car, my hands tightened on the steering wheel, and I inhaled deeply. The magic tangled and fizzed around me, wanting to be let in. I kept it out with the determination of long practice. There were days when I was weak and sifted a little so I could use it for a tiny bit of will working, but not today. I was going to be going out on a date, and I didn't want to smell of magic, not at all, in case any of the *many* kins were around.

While this world was humanity's territory, humanity's home, it touched on all of the other dominions. Almost like a crossroads, and so the inhabitants of other dimensions often traveled here, finding thin spots in the barriers between their dominions and ours. Thus, legends of elves and vampires and so many other creatures sprang up behind them. Together, they were the kins, humanity's brothers and sisters, each kin with their own gifts. The lilim, famed for their looks, could influence emotions and feed on them. Daoine sidhe were strong, attractive, and deadly fast. Fé created illusions more real than reality.

Humanity's gift was to manipulate magic to create whatever effect we desired if it lay within the strength of will of the mage. It only manifested in a very few of us. The kins, who could tell when magic was being, used hunted mages amongst the humans. All kins wanted us as servants or slaves. Magic was a powerful and frightening talent and our hunters found it incredibly useful—once we were controlled. I'd escaped after being taken, and now I hid in plain sight. Calling myself a thin-blooded lilim—human enough to have none of their emotion-influencing abilities—gave me the opportunity to monitor what the various factions were doing. If a hunt came to town or suspicion drifted in my direction, my family and I would be gone in moments.

I pushed the memories back and headed for home. My house was nestled in the depths of a housing development that had seen better days long ago. Small lots, weather-beaten exteriors, and elderly vehicles predominated. But it was mine.

Liz's tiny orange car was already parked on the street. My son's girlfriend was a tall, blonde athlete and one of the sweetest girls I'd ever met.

Introverted and quiet, Jimmy had inherited his good looks from his father but his personality from me, poor guy. I had no idea what Jimmy had done to catch her attention.

Both were in their senior year. A bit late to it, Jimmy had only just started looking at colleges, despite my constant nagging.

Dara, my daughter, had flapped out of the nest so fast she'd almost ignited her feathers. She was taking a semester off of college. I wasn't sure what the allure of a bartending career was, but she seemed to enjoy it right now. She was beyond listening to my advice at this point. All I could do now was hope I'd succeeded in teaching her to be a good—and also competent —adult.

The basement door had been left open, as per the house rules when they were down there. The faint whiff of incense and hum of low voices confirmed their presence. They'd be leaving for the football game soon.

In my room, I stripped out of my sweaty work clothes, peeling off my bra with a sigh of pleasure. I'd have to put on another, but for the moment, it felt so good.

After showering, I considered my costume. A puffy, white-sleeved, low-cut shirt, front-lacing brown corset, and a wide ankle-length skirt in vivid emerald— I'd even bought shoes to match. Dara had helped me pick it out—a happy memory. She was busy enough that we didn't see each other too often. Not enough by far.

The corset, made of tan leather, whispered under my fingers, soft and supple. I wanted to look good, but I didn't want to look quite *that* available.

When I'd mentioned that, Dara had rolled her eyes. "It's not that low, Mom. You look great!"

Oh, why not? I put it on, tugging the blouse a little higher, and applied some makeup before posing for myself in the mirror. Well, all right then. I did look nice. My naturally red hair held some gray strands now, but I'd dyed it black when I'd escaped and gone into hiding. The ensemble would've looked better with my hair it's natural color, but at least the creamy blouse flattered my freckled skin.

Banging on the front door brought me careening back into the living room, the skirt swishing around my ankles quite satisfactorily.

When I opened the door, instead of being the date I was looking forward to, the handsome face of my visitor knotted my stomach with annoyance.

"Oh," I muttered. "You." Bleys was the representative of the lilim who dealt with thin-bloods like me, or like they thought I was.

Some of the kins interbred with humanity, though the children were almost always less powerful or entirely lacking in the kin's power. Lilim accepted those children and made extensive use of them. It was much better that they think me a non-magical lilim offspring than what I really was. If they knew I was a mage...

My claim of being a thin blood put me under the purview of the lilim, not Schmidt, the fé who claimed this territory. I'd gone to him to get a new identity when I'd arrived in the city, and while I'd liked his subordinates, he'd annoyed me to the point of madness.

The thin-blood lie explained any minor slips of knowledge I might make, and Jimmy had been fathered by one. It meant he couldn't be a mage, but that was better for him. Dara hadn't inherited the talent either, though her children might.

A consequence of the lie was that I had to pay a portion of my salary to the organization of lilim in the area and be available to run errands for them. In exchange, they were supposed to protect me from predators in other kins. Like the changing kins, there was a new pack of werewolves in town.

Normally, they confined their hunts to those who wouldn't be missed, but they also preyed on humans who found out about the kins and had no protector. I had no wish to be their prey.

I shivered and covered it with a huff of unfeigned annoyance. "Bleys. I've already paid my monthly tithe. What are you doing here?"

His perfectly arched brows shot up as he took in my appearance. "Are you going to let me in?"

Sighing, I opened the door enough for him to enter.

"You look lovely, Ceri." He strolled into the living room. "The costume suits you."

I tensed as steps thudded on the stairs. Please don't come up, please don't come up...

Liz emerged from the basement, already dressed in her cheerleader outfit, and hurried for the door. Bleys's eyes were fixed on her, and I could almost see his gears moving as he watched her move—young, pretty, and enthusiastic.

Jimmy followed her, flicking an annoyed glance at Bleys.

Liz did a double-take as she took in my outfit. "You look really nice! I forgot what time it was, Mrs. G. We have to get to the field. Is it ok if I come here to shower after the game?"

"Sure. They're traveling again?"

She nodded. Her parents were entrepreneurs who spent a lot of time away from home. She had standing permission from them and me to stay here in Dara's room. It helped alleviate her anxiety.

Liz and Jimmy ran out the door. Bleys's eyes remained on her in a way I really didn't like.

"My son's girlfriend. Don't even." I glared at him. Lilim were like psychic vampires, consuming emotional energies. Far too many of them chose to use sex as a primary feeding method.

"Very nice." There was amusement in his glance and a purr in his voice. "You both look like a dream."

"No, Bleys." While he was low status in the city—hence, him riding herd on thin-bloods—Bleys at least understood no meant no and had only tried once to use the emotion influencing powers on me. It had ended badly. Nowadays, I refrained from assaulting him with my heavy bag, and he didn't try to mess with my head. That relationship worked for us.

"The new boss is throwing a party tonight and wants everyone to show up so he can meet them. Mandatory, Ceri. Ten sharp. I'll text you the address."

I bit my lip. "I've already made plans."

"Bring your date too, if you want. Just show up." Bleys shrugged. "There's going to be a billion people there, but I don't suggest you start your relationship with the boss by ignoring orders. He doesn't seem the forgiving type."

That would attract attention I didn't want. I'd have to let Nick know plans had changed. If it was like other lilim gatherings, the people would be pretty and the food good, and if we exited quickly, we should be fine.

"Fine," I grumbled.

"Thanks so much, Ceri!" His mocking voice faded as he strolled out of the house.

I straightened and poured two glasses of wine as I waited for Nick to arrive.

Nick pulled up a half-hour later, just as the sky began darkening. He waved as he got out of the car, which was parked precisely parallel to the curb. He was always punctual. I'd never known him to be late. He worked for an Institute that contracted with the federal government as a metallurgist. He didn't look the part, though. He was in good shape, tall and thin with lightly grayed, brown hair. No glasses.

"I've already poured a glass of wine for you," I said. It was an old joke between us. I had one or two brands I liked, and I always ordered them. He'd taken to ordering them for me at restaurants before I arrived, since I tended to be late. I laughed at him as he mimed shock and sipped.

"Sorry." I drained my glass.

Surprise flitted across his face. "Bad day?"

"Trying. Just found out I need to show at a work function. Another costume party." The grimace on my face welled from someplace deep within me. "Mandatory. We can meet up and go to the other party after?"

He gazed at me, and then his eyes shifted to my

wine glass. I looked down to find my fist was clenched on the stem.

"I would like to go with you if it's bothering you this much, Ceri."

It warmed my heart, but when he said Ceri, I missed my real name, Ceridwen. Ceri was close, but I'd never liked it much. The rest of his statement caught up with me...I'd only heard that tone rarely from him, but it was determination. We'd be here hours, discussing it to death, if I tried to dissuade him.

"Do you have a costume?" It was the first step to giving in. If we were just in and out, he should be safe. Nick was solid and average and quiet. Not the lilims' preferred meal. And Bleys, while an ass, would help get him out if one of the nastier lilim decided to bother us.

"I have a mask. I'll say I'm an actor." He smiled at me. The smile said the conversation was over and done with. I sighed. I liked his stubbornness, except when it was directed toward me.

Shaking my head, I put the glasses in the sink. "Fine, thank you."

"Bets on where Liz will end up after the game?" Nick gave me a wry smile as I sat next to him on the couch.

"No bets. She gets nervous when she's home alone."

"She's going to college?"

I nodded. "She's deciding which one suits her best,

and getting Jimmy to apply for himself, which is more than I've succeeded at."

"He's a good kid. Some people just aren't as well organized."

I eyed him. "I bet you fold your socks, and I know your books are in alphabetical order on the shelves."

"Yes. Doesn't mean I don't understand disorganized people." His eyes twinkled as he watched me rise.

I held out my hand. "Let's go."

The address was in an old-money suburb, a large house next to a golf course. Probably cost more than I'd make in a decade. Stone-built, it was enclosed by a tall stone wall as well. The gate across the driveway had swung back, and Nick drove us in. The driveway curved farther and farther into the property, shaded by old trees and landscaped within an inch of its life.

Cars that didn't fit on the extended parking area sat on the plush, velvety grass, waiting for their owners to leave. Like weeds, they were more akin to my car than the expensive sports cars parked in the driveway.

Jack-o'-lanterns grinned on the ground, and orange fairy lights and silvery spiderwebs decorated the trees and plants. Hardy autumn flowers, asters and mums, bloomed in fanciful pots situated on the grounds. A flagstone path led to open French doors.

Early as we were, most of the lilim in the city had already gathered inside. It looked like a model and actor convention. Overly pretty people wearing expensive clothes. It turned out being beautiful and able to make people fall in love—or lust—was good for the bank account. Who knew?

Worry clenched my gut as Nick's sleeve brushed my arm and he took in the room. I set my phone alarm for five minutes and hurried to the door. Then, I spotted Bleys and veered toward him.

"These are your coworkers?" Nick sounded bemused.

Oh, I hoped he didn't ask too many questions. "Second job, and they aren't educators. I just have to show up for a few minutes."

Bleys met me halfway, glancing at Nick, brow furrowed. "Good. This way."

For his sins, Bleys did try to shelter thin-bloods from the predatory, full-blooded lilim...who were *all* in the house. He kept a hand on my arm, leading me to the side of a clean-shaven blond man of average height.

He didn't look as scary as he must've actually been to keep this many lilim in line. Lilim followed the strongest, which meant he'd beaten their old leader. Susan, a woman whose cruelty had been legendary, had vanished from public view a few months ago. I didn't want to know what had happened, although I could easily guess.

"Mr. Pryce, this is Ceri Gault. She's one of the thin-bloods who serve the family."

Shrewd, penetrating blue eyes met mine, and I fought the urge to step back. That bright intelligence came across as threatening. Luckily, my outfit hid the sudden outbreak of sweat.

"Pleased to meet you." His voice was low, though rather pleasant. "And your guest?"

Nick extended a hand. "Nick Damarian."

Pryce's interested gaze at Nick made me even more nervous. My text notification pinged. Perfect timing.

"Oh, no, we need to go!" I frowned at the phone, grabbing Nick's hand as I backed up and bowed slightly. "Jimmy needs a ride to the urgent care center."

Poor Jimmy. As far as they knew, he was one of the unhealthiest children ever. That lie and a programmed ping had saved me from so many awkward situations. Prevarication was my friend. "Pleasure to meet you," I called as I turned and beat tracks.

The eyes on my back pursued me to the door, and I worked to keep my knees tight to prevent them from shaking.

"Do you want to visit for a bit before the kids get home?" I looked up at Nick's face, my voice shy. "I'd like some time to recharge before going to the other party."

Nick smiled back at me as we worked through the bodies toward the door. "Of course. I'd love a break."

Heat rose in my cheeks as I glanced away, into the sea of people in the yard. It had been a long time since I took a risk like this. We made our way to the door and departed, avoiding more groups of lilim and thin bloods as we trekked to Nick's car.

Once we were in the car, he turned to me. His tone was very quiet as he said, "There's something I need to tell you."

"Yes?" This sounded a little serious. What could he need to tell me right this moment?

Nick took my hand and gazed into my eyes. "I think you're aware that the world has room for lots of different...kins. Since this party establishes that you know about them, I have to say I hope never to see so many lilim in one place again."

My muscles stiffened, and my voice chilled, despite my best effort to remain casual. "I might be." How had this slipped past me? Was he a thin-blood or even a full-blooded kin? Why had he waited so long to tell me? *How* did I let this happen? I had to get out of here. I pulled my hand back and out of his.

He stared at my hand now in my lap and grimaced. "I'm not entirely as I appear."

"Illusion?" I couldn't stop the ege in my voice.
"Yes."

Damn it. "What kin are you?" Anxiety dampened my palms. I liked him, and I wanted to continue as friends, but that largely depended on what he said next. I sincerely hoped he wasn't a troll. Though I was fond of him, I was also superficial. I didn't want a meat-eating giant around my kids. Or me, for that matter.

"A svartalfar."

Oh. Okay. Uh. I groped for what I knew about them...metalworkers, which made sense. He was a metallurgist, who worked for a local think tank. I'd never seen or met one before, to my knowledge. This wasn't so bad. And if he thought I was an ordinary human he would've hidden this from me. But I should've been able to see past his illusion.

It was his turn to ask questions. "Are you a remark-ably restrained lilim or a thin-blood?"

"Thin-blood." I lied automatically. I couldn't keep the laugh out of my voice, even though I'd have to think long and hard before I told him the truth, if ever. I wanted to see his true appearance, to make sure he was telling me the truth, but didn't want to risk a spell to give me truesight. Especially not here.

Little shivers of anxiety fought with memories of Nick going back years. I'd known him for *years*. He'd always been kind, and we'd been friends for a long time before he tentatively suggested a date three months ago. We'd only dated twice since then as I worked past my anxieties. It had taken me nearly two decades to learn to trust men, even a little, after my husband handed me over to the kins in exchange for money and status. And the first one I take a chance on turns out to be a kin. Seriously?

It was a very quiet drive.

When we pulled up at home, Liz's little car was already parked in the driveway. My worry spiked and made me get out of the car quickly. They'd left the game early, which Liz would only do if injured. Something was wrong.

Nick trailed me heading inside the house. I paused on the porch, magic scraping at me, demanding and thick. It had an edge that I had last felt a long time ago when enemies had come for me. Magic wasn't sentient, but I had a low level of foreseeing that warned me if I might need it. A deep sense of foreboding weighted my stomach.

I frowned. This close to home, I accepted a trickle of the power and used it to turn on my alternative vision, truesight. It would let me see what was real and what was not as I hurried through the front door.

Jimmy sat on the couch, unusually far from Liz, staring at her and frowning. She had her leg elevated, her ankle and knee wrapped in bulky elastic bandages.

Liz flashed Nick and me a thousand-watt smile. "Hi! It looks worse than it is."

Beneath the smile, truesight sketched an unformed face beneath hers, a lanky body expanded to match her athletic form. Holy crap. A fetch had copied Liz's shape.

CHAPTER 2

ADRENALINE TURNED my joints to jelly as my thoughts scattered like rabbits startled by a lawn-mower. Fear for Liz, fear of what the fetch meant, though not of the creature herself, made it hard to breathe.

Fetches were a kin blessed, and also cursed, with hyper-elastic minds and forms. Human folklore said that they were a death warning, the duplicate telling you the end was nigh but that myth had grown from fetches being used to replace people the kins wanted to take. Even the kins had hesitated to just swipe the rich or powerful, so they'd left substitutes. And they still followed the practice to this day, obviously.

I'd learned the truth about fetches from the one who had duplicated me when I'd been captured eighteen years ago. I found her after I broke free and took her with me and my daughter, knowing she was as much a victim as I. We still stayed in contact. She'd moved and become a school bus driver in Alaska, near a large fetch community.

A quirk of that kin was that the younger the fetch, the more malleable they were. Many fetches tried to live quietly and hidden since their children were regarded as valuable commodities by the powerful. Once a young fetch imprinted upon a person, they were that person until the original died. So, kill the original and the child fetch reverted to its own form, ready to be reused. A creative owner could question many prisoners with a single fetch child ...and why care if the experience scarred them or drove them mad? The poor fetch children often killed themselves within a year, helped in their method by all the knowledge they'd acquired from the people whose memories they'd absorbed.

Even when forced to give up a child, fetches charged a premium for their sacrifice. The fetch in front of me had cost someone steeply, and I needed to find out what had made Liz that valuable.

Then, I would find her and bring her back before her captor decided to kill her.

The truesight granted by my magic didn't waver as I made my way to my shabby green recliner and seated myself. Jimmy watched me, half rising, and not-Liz clasped her hands together between her knees and shifted forward.

"Are you feeling well?" she asked. Even having known a fetch who'd copied me, I thought the mimicry was uncanny. Perhaps because the impression was so recent.

A rustle next to me reminded me of Nick's presence. I turned to him, and another truth met my eyes. His skin was darker than any human, a flat black more like spilled ink than the multifaceted tones of human skin. His face, framed by ash-blond hair, was similar to the illusion he wore- the cheekbones a little sharper, the eyes set more at an angle.

With silver eyes full of concern, he crouched by me, one hand resting on the arm of the recliner. "Ceri?"

I turned my gaze back to the fetch. "Did you replace Liz at the game?" I tried to keep my voice even, as it wasn't the fetch's fault, but a little of the worry and anger bubbled around the corners, melting the words. This would reveal me, but I didn't care. Memories of fear and anger, of when I was taken to be broken, shoved me to the cold place where I could kill if Nick betrayed my trust. A fetch child would be easy to contain as long as I kept her separate. She would feel the affection I hoped Liz had for me. "I *see* you, fetch."

Nick drew in a breath. "There's something pertinent that you haven't told me, either," he whispered.

He didn't sound happy. He sounded downright snappish. Only mages could see true. He knew what I was now, for better or worse.

I couldn't find any fucks to give at the moment.

Jimmy's brows drew together. His hands clenched

as he stared at the fetch, mouth tight. He was good at staying silent and gathering information before he spoke, like me. "This *isn't* Liz, then. I wasn't completely sure, so I wanted to wait until you saw her. What do we do?"

The fetch shivered. Her eyes—wide and blue—darted from me to Nick to Jimmy.

I stared at her. "Do you know why they took her?"

The fetch nodded vigorously, her blond ponytail bouncing. "She's a mage. Like you."

Liz was a mage? I was o-for-2 at this point on not knowing when someone was *other*. I would have sworn it wasn't possible. She had none of the signs. I'd seen faint traces of them in my children even though they only carried the potential to pass it on to their children. I didn't even see that in her.

Jimmy stared at the fetch. "Mom. I know what a fetch is. Is Liz dead?"

I shook my head hastily. "No, I don't think so." Of course, I couldn't know if that was true.

The fetch looked on the verge of tears, lips trembling as she glanced at him. She'd feel Liz's feelings for him, too. Even if her current identity was stolen, the being sitting on my couch was still a child. I had to remind myself of that.

"Oh, God." Jimmy paled. He looked away from me, shoulders tensed, body curled as if he were expecting a blow out of nowhere. "Mom, you said the kins smell when you do the magic, and that's why you don't. Does that mean they could smell a spell on a human even if that person didn't have any magic themselves?"

Worry sent a cold chill down my spine. "Yes, Jimmy. Is there a reason for that question?"

He inhaled then raised his chin. "I did a ritual I found in one of your books to clear Liz's mind and help her focus so that she'd pass the essay test today." The words burst out of him like a long-delayed flood. "I can do magic too, Mom. Look."

He twiddled his fingers, and the sight confirmed the feathery sensation as the magic in the room moved in a subtle flow around his hands. It was a small shift, but it answered him, pooling in his hands. A prickling sensation crossed my arms as he manipulated it, and a pale flame flickered on his palm.

"I know you worry. That's why I didn't say anything until now." He met my eyes, his other hand clenched and white-knuckled. So young. My baby.

The concealment of his abilities hurt, but pride flared in me—he was a mage! And fear—I wanted him to be safe, not a hunted commodity. Each emotion fought a brief battle inside me. And confusion—his father was a lilim, how had he manifested as a mage? He must mostly be my son, and that thought eased an old, old wound.

I got up, walked over, and hugged him. "It's easier to learn if you talk to people. Is there anything else I should know before I go to get Liz?"

The cat was out of the bag for the fetch and Nick.

I'd deal with it later. Grandfather had told me to kill any kin-member who found out what we were and bury them deep to avoid being enslaved. I didn't want to kill Nick or the fetch. There must be another way. I just had to find it.

Jimmy closed his fingers, and the light winked out. His words came out in a rush. "Dara can do it, too. Dara put a spell on you a month ago so you wouldn't be so stressed and scared and angry all the time. But it made you forget things even more. And we couldn't figure out how to take it off. We tried, over and over. So, we warded it instead, to keep the kins from seeing the spell."

Even more mixed emotions stampeded through me. Pure rage that they'd messed with my head joined the hurt, fear, and pride. They had risked so much. We needed to run *far* away, so I could train them how to hide and get it through their thick heads. We needed to conceal ourselves and run if discovered. Standing and fighting, however attractive, had never been an option while they were younger and seemed foolish to me even now.

"You do have a lot of problems." Nick's calm, measured voice made me want to bang my head on the wall.

I faced him, caught up in hope that Nick wouldn't turn from my friend into my worst nightmare. Because I needed help getting Jimmy and the fetch someplace safe, along with Dara. A plan was forming in my mind for finding Liz.

First, though, I needed to examine the spell and ward they'd hung on me. Why hadn't I noticed it before?

Gazing down, sharpening the truesight to a level I never used because of the headaches it gave me, subtle sparks sprang into focus. They orbited me irregularly, head to foot.

They'd built this ward over the spell, hiding it, a beautiful and powerful piece of work. The magic of it swirled around my hand when I ran my fingertips over the surface of my arm. It felt like my own life force. No wonder I hadn't noticed it passively. It hid the magic. I could work at least minor magic and not risk anyone seeing it. That could be handy. Very handy.

My children were brilliant. They'd worked out a way to use magic to hide magic. It shouldn't be possible. And I was still absolutely furious at them for concealing all of this and spelling me without my permission. Talk about needing consent. I leveled Jimmy with my best mom-glare. "Did you put the ward on yourselves, to hide?"

"Yes." Jimmy nodded, still eyeing me nervously, expecting wrath.

The ward clung like a plastic wrap when I tried to lift it, tangling on me and itself. Tugging, I reinforced my grip with more magic, feeling the ward's resilience. A tough, flexible ward.

"How did you figure out how to do it?" Nick asked.

I ignored the prickles of Jimmy trying to see what I was doing as he explained. "Dara went to the library and checked out books on magic. We practiced in the basement when mom was grading papers. Afterward, we just looked at the books in Mom's library." His voice sounded distracted while his attention focused on me.

Those books lived in a locked cedar chest. I was going to find out how they'd gotten past the ward I put on it. I didn't like feeling incompetent.

My money was on Dara being the instigator and architect. She was far too sneaky for her own good.

I concentrated on the orbiting sparks. Despite my best effort, hurt welled inside me, almost breaking my focus. My children had hidden their talents from me, used them on me even.

Though they'd tried to help me...I'd damaged them with my fear. I faced it even as the ward shone like a lure to work more magic.

Clenching my fist, I caught one of the sparkling motes and crushed it. The magic tore under my fingers, disrupting a portion of the spell. As I watched, the mote reintegrated, though much smaller.

The damn thing even regenerated. Whichever of my children had done it, had real power. No wonder they couldn't get the underlying spell off. I didn't have the time to finish doing this right now. I had to find Liz before they started getting down to breaking her mind and spirit. Later, when I had my head again, Jimmy and Dara were going to catch hell.

And then help me remove the calming spell they'd put on me, which would potentially be punishment enough.

"Why hide it from her?" Nick asked.

"We didn't want Mom to worry. You're awfully accepting, Mr. Damarian." Jimmy's brow had furrowed, as it always did when he suspected patronization. My son's temper wasn't as well controlled as it needed to be now.

"Because I'm one of the predators you should be afraid of." Nick's level voice carried a chill, quiet menace. "I'm of the kins, and you never knew."

My son left the couch, backing away from Nick and the fetch.

Crackling fire appeared in my hand.

"Ceri, do you think I'd hurt him?" Nick didn't shift his gaze from Jimmy.

I didn't, actually, but still. "Why did you threaten him?"

"He needs to be less confident. Overconfidence will get him taken even if they can't see his magic." He turned to face me. So strange, the face I could see underneath the human visage I was so familiar with.

The fetch—I couldn't call her Liz—looked at us uncertainly from the couch. Her tone was tentative as she asked, "What's going to happen now?"

"We need to find Liz." Harsh and clipped, my

voice rattled in my ears. I gentled it. "Tell me about the person or people who bought you from your clan. Where did they take you so that you could take your impression from Liz?"

Her lips trembled. "The man who came was tall, and dark-haired. He wore expensive clothes, and he seemed very nice." She looked from me to Jimmy with wide, scared eyes. "I liked him. I showed him my ball, and he said it was the prettiest. Grandmother told me that I was going to be a human girl all my life, and that I'd be happy with my new family because they loved the girl. Plus, I'd still see my real family when they visited at night. Then the man took my hand, and we got in a shiny red car. He took me to a place with lots of trees, a park or maybe a small forest. At first, when he left, I was all alone. Then Liz came. She was a little scared, and then I became her. And I drove home in her car, to here."

She rambled just like Liz did when she was nervous. Liz was smart, but under stress she sounded like a young kid.

"Do you know who took her, from her memories?" Nick asked, his voice quiet and kind.

"She was blindfolded the entire time. I didn't see who brought her or who waited for her either."

"Do you remember the name of the man who spoke with your grandmother?" I held my breath. I knew most of the kin community by name.

"Bleys."

Oh, dear heavens. Lilim had taken her. I had to get to her as quickly as possible. I knew the exact techniques they would use to try to make her pliable. My skin crawled with the memories prickling in my mind and making me sweat. Lilim would bludgeon her emotionally until she gave in completely to what they wanted.

The thought that Bleys would pay for a fetch substitute to have Liz for himself was laughable. Fetches were expensive, and he had no reason to care what a human teenager's parents would think if she simply disappeared.

"Jimmy, go into Dara's room and get me some hair from Liz's brush. Nick, please move the furniture back to the walls." I paused, looking at the fetch. "You aren't Liz. We can call you Mary, if that's okay. Do you like the name?"

"It's our middle name. Yes, that's fine." She hobbled off the couch as Nick shoved it back. The injury was real. Liz would be injured when I found her. Or had she been taken before the injury? Ugh.

Nick frowned, then picked her up and carried her to a kitchen chair before grabbing a bag of frozen peas. She put it on her ankle with a grateful smile.

I tracked it all in a blur, pulling to mind a locating ritual intended for objects. People shed hair. Liz certainly did. I cleaned it out of the vacuum all the time. So I'd follow the trail of shedding until we found her.

Bleys would not be a happy lilim if the trail led to him before I found Liz.

I settled on the floor, stealing a cushion from the couch for my backside. The full skirts of my costume pooled around me, a sea of green on the beige carpet. Jimmy plopped down beside me, dropping the handful of hair into my waiting hand. Liz had long thick hair, and just pulling it out of a brush made for a decent-sized handful.

I elongated the hairs, twisting them around one another, and then pulled the green pendant from around my neck. I wrapped the hair around the stone.

"You're using crystals?" Nick's voice sounded amused.

I ignored him. Liz liked that pendant and had borrowed it for junior prom last year.

Her personal energy still permeated the hairs. If only I'd ever studied locating people properly. Hiding from them had always been my priority.

I inhaled, clearing my mind, feeling the silky streamers in the air around me and Jimmy. My need had called them, thick as a knot of scarves.

A single strand would be enough. Accuracy was needed for this, not power. Coaxing it into the stone and hair, I set my will to find the hair that matched the strands, as fresh as possible.

Doing that while keeping the truesight burned. I wasn't used to channeling power, since I spent most of my time hiding mine. I ignored the discomfort as the ritual clicked into place. My will and the magic merged, forming a whole that answered my desire.

Will-working had its dangers when it focused on living beings, and humans were the most at risk. I'd learned painfully over the years to blur minds because I didn't want to injure people more than I had to, but it was difficult and tricky for me.

Apparently, not for my children though.

I couldn't simply want to find Liz. My magic didn't work that way. The connection through the strands of hair gave me a bridge, something to tangle my desire to find her on.

Jimmy sprang to his feet and offered me a hand up.

The pendant tugged in my hand, insistent, swinging to the west. I headed for the door with Nick close behind me. "Is it safe for them to be here alone together?" Nick sounded curious.

It was good of him to remind me. Maintaining spells played hell with my focus. I'd forgotten what I intended to tell Jimmy and Mary.

"You think Jimmy might do something to Mary?" I stopped and met my son's eyes. Worry and hurt lived in them along with the hope I could fix everything. I didn't need to be a mind reader to know his expressions and what they meant. "Jimmy, don't go anywhere. Don't answer the door and keep Mary with you. She was never going to hurt you. They are nonviolent. She's very frightened and she can't change back to her real self unless Liz dies. So get used to Liz having a twin. You should start packing, we're leaving as soon as I get home. Text your sister and let her know, too. I can't split my focus from searching for Liz."

"Leaving?" Jimmy's jaw dropped, fear and upset vying for supremacy in his face.

"I can help you pack. You never fold your clothes right." Mary made a face as she studied Jimmy's features.

His responding expression was a mix of annoyance and surprise, seasoned with curiosity. But not malice.

She had Liz's memories. Jimmy was a good-natured person. After a little more talk he'd be trying to find out about what fetches were, and they'd probably become friendly if not friends.

Nick put his hand on my arm, the touch firm but light. "Why don't we use my car, it's all-terrain. You'll leave your transmission behind if you go off-road."

He had a point. I followed him out the door to his black pickup truck. Nick slid into the driver's seat. The crystal twirled and shifted to the west. I guessed that cleared up whether or not Nick was joining me.

THE SOFT AND squishy seats in Nick's truck were much more comfortable than the ones in my car. I belted myself in and held the pendant in front of me. It served as a visual cue for him—I didn't need it since I had the itchy tug within me, strong and uncomfortable.

I was so tired, the sensation similar to a long workout but with no end in sight. Showing how weary I was would be a bad idea. Weakness gave people ideas. It made them reckless. I didn't need anyone to be reckless tonight.

The pendant swung as he took us north, moving slightly but always pointing in the same general direction. It didn't seem like Liz was moving. That was good, at least.

"How well do you know this area?" If I guessed his logic, he was headed for a westbound state route that was much less likely to dead-end before we'd found how far west we needed to be.

"Decently." The pale greenish light of the dash illuminated his face. His expression was strained, a little sad. A quick glance in my direction showed eyes without the usual quiet humor lurking there. "Ceri, even with all this, I value your friendship. Please don't run without talking with me first."

"I'll..." Gazing away, biting my lip, I struggled, caught between two wishes. "I'll try." I wanted to trust him, but all of my life lessons had taught me something very different.

I liked him, as well. In fact, I'd hoped maybe we could be more than friends, but I didn't think that could happen now. Trust had to walk with caring, and my trust was huddled in a ball, tucked up against a wall. Crying.

Fields and farms edged the west side of the city, seasoned with stands of trees, some large enough to be called small forests. I chafed at the necessity of the circuitous route. The magical tether sank into me, scratching at my insides. It would become more uncomfortable as we got farther away, a negative indicator.

Not that it was any fun now.

He turned at the next road when the pendant bobbed south rather than west, following the curves of the old country road. The car jounced and whined. The next county over didn't have the money to maintain these less traveled roads.

Trees surrounded us, cutting off the harvest moon.

This patch of forest made me uneasy, made me want to run away.

Nick grimaced. "Can you dispel the ward that's trying to push us out?" he said.

A repelling ward was easier to resist if we knew why we felt repelled. Emotional wards like this one were far less effective when I was aware of their existence.

"Can you stand it? I don't have much reserve left." My voice caught on the words. I didn't like admitting it.

"Yes. Ah, well, it'll make us both irritable when we catch up with the girl."

The stone and the tether tugged west again. I took slow, deep breaths to ease myself past the sharp pain in my gut. "Slow down."

The car crept along, and a hidden drive came into view.

The scratching and cramping from the tether rolled through me hard and strong. Weariness made me bow my head for a moment, and my nerves stung from the constant flow of magic. I didn't like pain, and this was worse than arthritis on a rainy day.

Nick pulled over and parked in a small, clear area. "We'll walk from here so they don't hear us coming."

"Yes." As right as he was, I wasn't sure how far I could really walk. Not with this magic eating me up inside.

He ghosted into the trees. I did a double-take then

shook my head and started walking on the driveway, leaving the dark woods to Nick. I didn't want to risk a twisted ankle tonight. The cooling air puffed around me, and I couldn't see the stars. Clouds were piling up, making the sky look like a storm was finally coming. Of course, me being outside, searching for a missing girl, was the best time for it to pour down rain.

Perhaps a quarter-mile farther down, the road split. I followed the pain right and then spotted a familiar car parked where the trees thinned to nothing next to a field. I knew that silhouette.

Bleys stood by the car, using binoculars to survey the field. Why was he here? Why had Liz been brought *here*? Lilim lived in expensive areas, normally. Unless this was a place where no one would report her screaming.

The depth of the slow, cold fire that rolled through my gut and chest startled me, fueled by an anger at the betrayal that shouldn't have surprised me. He was what he was. And he would tell me everything he knew.

The anger helped with the pain, and I drew in the magic recklessly, infusing myself with speed and strength. I'd pay later when all of this was done, but I would see it finished.

I moved, swift and silent, grabbing his shoulder and slamming him back against the sturdy oak that had been sheltering him.

He squawked, dropping the binoculars and shoved

at me. Against my greater strength, he stiffened, gazing down and focusing on my face. "What the hell? Why are you here?"

"Where's Liz?" I slammed him against the tree again.

"Ceri, this is a mistake," Bleys said.

The world narrowed to Bleys's face, and not in a good way. Red fringed him.

"Don't lie. You have one more chance. Who... has... Liz?" I emphasized each word by slamming him into the tree with each syllable. Leaves drifted down from its shaking limbs.

"I don't know!" He hissed the words. "I see the door move, but I don't see them come out, and I can't get past their ward. That hurts, Ceri. Stop shaking me!"

"He sounds like he's telling the truth. Do you have a way to tell?" Nick's calm voice soothed the burning anger a little. He stood next to me, though I hadn't noticed him until he spoke.

I used a simple magic developed when Dara was a toddler—useful when raising children and subtle to boot. It was amazing how easy it was to call out to magic tonight, since the air was already electric with the incoming storm. Magic gleamed around me. It would sparkle brighter if his words were true. A lie would turn them dark.

I hadn't thought to use it on my kids for years. If I had and thought of the right questions, so much might be different. But why would I ever have thought to ask my children if they planned on using magic against me? I hadn't even known they *had* magic until tonight.

"Did you take Liz from the game?" I snarled.

Bleys shook his head once. "No. She was brought to me, and I was told to take her to a rendezvous point and make her calm. It was a kindness. A troll had taken her, and she was hysterical." Bleys grimaced. "When the fetch came in, I saw it was a high dollar transaction that no one knew about, and I decided to follow so I could tell Pryce and maybe get a boost. And maybe find out so I could tell you later if something happened. I know the kid likes her, it's hard to miss."

The glitter didn't darken. He was telling the truth. I'd outed myself for nothing. Damn it. "He speaks the truth." The words fell like stones. I didn't relax my grip, and I used my other hand to pull his cellphone from its case, in his coat pocket.

"Pockets are normally for just my use." Bleys's insouciant tone was contradicted by his expression.

"Not tonight. If you're quiet, I'll let you live for the next few hours, Bleys. Don't push me." Again, anger leaked into my words, making them sound hollow and strange in my ear.

I didn't get this angry anymore. Once, when I was young, but I thought I'd learned that lesson. No fool like an old fool.

I sucked in my breath as the pull intensified. The magic wanted consummation, to no longer be trapped in a spell, neither free nor static.

Pinned against the tree, comprehension spread across Bleys's face as he put two and two together. "Ceri, did you make a good choice when you told us you were one of ours, a thin-blood? It looks to me like you might have hidden talents."

"This would be the point where you decide whether you wipe his memory or if he dies." I heard the hush of the blade being drawn. I glanced over my shoulder. From somewhere about his person, Nick had produced a knife. It didn't gleam in the small amout of light by Bleys's car, so it had to have been made of a dark metal. "I'll help if needed." His tone was exquisitely serene.

I stared into Bleys's eyes. Fear flickered there. I didn't like him much, but I didn't think I could kill him. Fire danced inside me as I pulled more magic, and a sob forced itself out as I reached for Bleys's memories, blurring the last few minutes. He fell to the ground, expression blank.

"Do you think it will take? I heard that mind magic often doesn't last. That it fades quickly." Nick looked at Bleys piteously.

Shivering, rubbing my arms, I shrugged. "If it does fade, we'll discuss the alternate method."

Several deep breaths later, while trying to soothe the pain, I stepped into the field.

Halfway to the trailers, next to the ward etched into the earth, a truck hit me from the side. Or, at least, it felt like one. I flew to the side, half-stunned, rolling, and trying to get up. I couldn't catch my breath.

An enormous wolf rushed me. Huge jaws snapped, and I screamed when its teeth sank into the arm I threw up to defend myself. It was hard to focus my will when I was this hurt and so afraid. Focus was one of the first lessons the world taught to mages.

The lesson I learned when the first kin who caught me tried to tame me.

Never again.

I opened myself to the endless flow of magic, just as I had when I was a small child, before Grandfather warned me not to do it. Back then it burned, the pain like no other.

This time, it was a pain mixed with pleasure that was like sex and chocolate and a glass of cold, white wine after a very long day at work. It comforted, exhilarated, and buffered the pain as the wolf of the changing kin ripped his claws across my abdomen.

The pain wasn't completely hidden, and the agony pulled a scream out of me. But it left enough solace that I could still focus my will on him, and call the unborn lightning dancing in the sky.

Its cry hurt my ears as the bolt struck nearby, a painful flare of light. Tears streamed down my face from my abused eyes, and I coughed. The air stank of burnt hair.

Blood trickled between my fingers as I tried to hold the skin of my stomach together.

I turned and saw that Nick had killed the other changer. After wiping his knife on the grass, he crouched beside me. "Do you know any healing magic?" he asked.

"Sadly, no. Will you help me up, please?"

"I don't know if you should be moving, Ceri." He shouted, startling me. "Stop hiding! She's hurt, and I will see your trailers melt if you don't bring some help!"

Metal and fire were svartalfars' friends. They could work both of them using only their wills, and made weapons and armor unmatched by other craftsmen. Flickers of heat shimmer wreathed Nick's hands. I'd never heard him so upset.

The ward rippled as people crossed it. Liz was with them, dressed in a long nightgown, apparently under no duress. Priya, the student I'd tutored earlier today, stood next to her in a similar outfit. An older man and woman hovered behind them.

All but Liz looked to be of Indian heritage. Offhand, I wasn't familiar with most of their kins. I knew about apsara, who were mostly entertainers and concubines. That knowledge came from dealing with Lotus, the woman who worked as administrator for the fé who ruled the area. Unlike her, the people here didn't live and breathe sex appeal.

I'd never heard of an apsara appearing as anything but a person in the bloom of youth, actually. Why was I thinking about apsara? My mind was wandering, and I felt floaty. That probably wasn't good.

The older gentleman's eyes grew wide as he stared at me. *"This* is the mage who put the spell on Liza." He spoke with a pronounced accent, softening Liz's name with an additional vowel.

I didn't correct him.

Nick had fallen into a deceptively casual but ready stance, the knife's tip inclined down.

"She should go to a hospital or a healer." The older woman's firm voice sounded comforting like my mother's had. My head was spinning. I wasnt doing too well.

"We can't explain the injury there. Do you have any healers here?" Nick still sounded angry. "You're yaksha. That's one of the things you do."

Yaksha were Indian nature spirits, but I'd never heard of them being able to heal as an ability. My skin cooled, and the pain receded more. All to the good. The pain could take off.

"A healer comes," the old man replied.

"I'm so sorry, Ms. Gault," Priya whispered.

"She's going into shock." Liz hovered next to me, her hands shaking. "We should elevate her feet. I got my first aid badge."

A giggle tried to bubble up. Liz was an eagle scout, even, but I didn't think scouts covered surgery in their merit badges. Using my stomach muscles also seemed a bad idea at the moment. What was happening? I was losing track.

"Good idea. They're claw marks, but they didn't actually get to the intestines." The old man peered at my abdomen. "She should last until the healer can get here."

"She'd better." Nick's growl sounded odd to me, his voice rough. "The girl is here of her own will? You didn't force her to stay?"

"Um, I am," said Liz in a tiny voice, "Mr. Damarian."

"Get a sheet so we can lay her on it and move her inside." The older woman ordered, brisk and efficient. "Priya, Liz, get us one from the linens."

I clamped my hand on Liz's as they lifted me. I would not pass out. I would find out what was going on here.

I BREATHED THROUGH THE PAIN, staring at Liz. "Are you okay? How did you end up here? Do you know what happened?"

"I'm okay, Mrs. G." Liz squeezed my hand. The girl's grip strength was better than Jimmy's, for sure. "I didn't really believe Jimmy when he said he put a spell on me. But then I wrote the paper, and it was easy! When I turned it in at school, Priya took me aside. She told me her family really needed some help. So I said yes, but I didn't know all this would happen!"

The spell certainly hadn't helped with run-on sentences in speech. Liz remained a smart, pretty young woman, and as gifted with magic as a tree stump.

Tears dripped onto my hand. Priya was also crying. I hoped this didn't turn into a remorse party. I didn't have the strength to soothe everyone right now.

I stifled another gasp as they tilted me to carry me into the mobile home.

Liz continued, "But I wasn't able to help them because I only had a spell on me. So I guess you can help?"

This was *not* the situation I had expected.

"What is going on?" I stared into her distressed face. She was crying, from stress, I thought. I couldn't focus on that. The pain bit into me as they moved me across the yard and into one of the trailers.

They settled me on a bed in a tiny room, nudging Liz out. Nick didn't budge from my other side, and Liz hovered in the doorway. It was like being treated at a teaching hospital.

"We are yaksha. We come from India, all of us who live here. After my wife and I emigrated, we discovered after we bonded to the land here that it was losing its ability to sustain us. So we sent for aid. Our family sent Priya, who, while young, is most sensitive to magics. She saw Liz shining with a spell full of power, and she —and we—assumed Liz was a mage. When she consented to help, we set the plan in motion." He gazed over at Liz, who looked down at her toes with a sheepish expression.

"When first the energy from the land began to fade, we pooled our money and made an agreement with the fetches to take one of their own to replace a mage if ever we found one. When Liz agreed, we took up our option on the fetch and sent her so that the human family wouldn't suffer for their daughter's loss. Then we found out that Liz wasn't actually a mage. Finally, we contacted Lotus, the seneschal for the prince here, and she told us that there is a rule stating that a mage cannot be snatched within the bounds of these lands."

"Then you're lucky she isn't a mage. Schmidt, the 'prince' here, is an ass." The words drained me, but I couldn't resist the cheap shot.

The elderly man bowed his head. "But you *are* a mage. Will you aid us?"

Three anxious and hopeful faces gazed at me. I could resist them as easily as anyone asking for help, even though I swore at myself for doing it. "Liz. Didn't you think that we would notice you'd been replaced?"

She looked guilty. "I thought that I could switch places with the fetch on weekends so she could go to school and finish up there and I could be here, and then we could switch, and I could do whatever they needed every once in a while."

Reclined, I couldn't bang my head against the wall.

"You do realize that this means that Jimmy and I are going to have to leave the city, right?" I flicked a glance at the yaksha couple. "While Schmidt, the 'prince' may have this rule, people are likely to try anyway and simply deliver me or Jimmy to another place. Even though I'm injured, I will defend myself."

"We would be willing to hide you if you wish. Or hire you. I know we made an egregious error."

I didn't really want to work for Schmidt. Or Pryce,

the new lilim leader, who would be my other choice if I stayed here. If I had the option, I might be willing to do it for these people. I didn't like fé or lilim, but these yaksha hadn't tried to screw me over... yet. If I did work for them, and Schmidt's rule actually was enforced, I'd need to move out to this area, but I wouldn't have to quit my job, leave my students, and rip up all of the roots we'd grown. Besides, I was so tired.

"I'll do it. Let's get the contract together. I'll see what I can feel here from the field so I know what I need to do. Please bring me some of the dirt from outside, where I bled on it, and put it into one of my hands, even if I don't answer you. I'm going to scout using my magic. Liz, text Jimmy, give him this address, and confirm he and the fetch—we're calling her Mary —should come here right now. He can use my car."

The older woman murmured, "I'll find out what's keeping our healer." She left the hall.

While Nick and the old man—Ramki—were working on the contract boilerplate, I shut my eyes and meditated. It helped with the pain, leaving my body behind as I reached out, relaxing into the sting and flow of the magic.

The land energy here felt wrong on a basic level. Like water trickling out of a pipe clogged almost shut by mineral deposits, a thin flow with a harsh rasp to it.

What was wrong?

I floated on the currents, swimming upstream, seeking the source of the magic and the blockage. I bumped into something solid and slick. It stung me like a thousand bees, and I backed away, examining it visually rather than by the feel of the flows.

The land magic had made a barrier to keep something contained, something that caused pain with even the most glancing contact. I moved closer, straining to see. Something horrible was buried or hidden there.

The rush of the currents became a murmur. *Heal this abscess.*

Bodiless me swallowed, feeling every nonexistent nerve on alert. The magic rarely spoke, but when it did, only a fool didn't listen. *Blood to cleanse? I don't have much left...*

Infuse your magic in other's blood as a proxy. Cleanse this. A sharp impatient flip of the currents swatted my back like a cat being tapped on the nose.

Okay... My answer was weak, and the sense of hearing a voice vanished.

I reoriented myself. The location in the real world was just off the road, several miles from the trailers where my body lay. Like an oyster making a poisonous pearl, the land magic was draining away and accreting around what was hidden there.

I'd need to go there physically. I couldn't leave it be because it could keep growing until the land felt the barrier was sturdy enough. As Ramki had said, yaksha bonded to a particular place. No wonder they and Priya looked so thin. They were starving.

Scouting, stretching my awareness, I couldn't see

anything living in the area. There were no guardians to prevent me from dealing with this problem. The current of energy swept me back to my body once I no longer fought it.

I'd been warned long ago that magic was seductive and once I started really using it, I wouldn't want to stop. Even though I felt burnout from the unaccustomed strain nibbling at me, the endorphins from using the power masked the pain. If I was lucky, I'd last through this final task.

"Let me in." Bleys's voice. They must have let him into the warded area when they retrieved the bloody dirt from outside. Fear gripped me. If my lilim liaison had thrown off the mind magic so quickly, I might have to kill him, and I was so weak.

Bleys stepped into view. Lines of weariness bracketed his mouth, and a few leaf fragments stuck out of his hair.

Nick said, "Keep out of the room. You're filthy, and she has open wounds. Are you responsible for the shifters attacking?"

"No." Bleys regarded me, wearing a tired, quirky smile on his face. "Are you willing to listen to a different job offer?"

"I'm not going to found a captive house, thanks." Mages who surrendered to the kins and served generationally were called captive houses. It was not a compliment.

"Pryce offers full benefits, dental, and two weeks'

vacation as a new hire. You'd be an employee, able to quit if you want."

Sounded way too good to be true. "Mm. So other people paying tithes can pay my salary?"

Bleys had the grace to wince. "It's tradition. And you were the one who lied. If you hadn't said you were a thin-blood, a tithe wouldn't have been asked."

I stared at him, hurting and tired. "You've already told him, haven't you?"

"Yes. But the offer is for employment, not indenture, and he *does* take no for an answer. He might continue to woo you, but what businessman wouldn't?"

I shook my head at him and gave up on reality, dozing to escape the pain. A few shushing noises had the trailer quieting except for the low moan of the wind and the whispers of the remaining leaves in the trees.

Waking to gentle fingers probing my abdomen was less than pleasant. My eyelids were too heavy to move, and I felt hot. "Definitely is going to need stitches," said a stranger's voice, male.

"Then start. I'll cover it until payment arrangements come through," Lotus's voice replied. Why was she here? Schmidt's administrative assistant shouldn't be involved.

"Good." Jimmy's voice sounded scared. "Is Mom going to be okay?"

"She'll be fine. Why don't you join Liz outside so your mother can rest." Nick's voice was gentle but firm.

My son's voice was equally firm. "She needs to go to the hospital."

"No, the healer will be able to take care of her. If you're going to stay in the room, you two need to be quiet and stay in the corner, out of the way." Lotus's voice left no room for argument.

Another moment of black consumed me. When I opened my eyes, a stranger was sewing up my stomach, which was blessedly numb.

"You're going to need to rest for a couple of days." The stranger, a man with white feathers mingled in his hair, started packing his tools away. A caladrius. Romans had called them healing birds, but the truth was they had two forms, like most of the changing kin. They had the ability to heal with a touch. I hadn't known any lived in the area. Most didn't leave their dominion. They had not been treated well by humans when they were discovered. "You lost a fair amount of blood. There are no perforations, and it's been cleaned, so I don't expect infection, but you need to take it easy."

He strode out. I turned my head to look at Lotus. "I made a contract with the yaksha. But Jimmy and Dara will need protection as well."

My daughter was hard to protect, but I'd find a way.

"Would you have a problem with Jimmy working under contract for Schmidt?" Lotus stooped next to me.

It felt too easy. I would go along with the suggestion for now, but I was ready to grab the kids and run.

They couldn't prepare for everything I could come up with.

"Not until it's been thoroughly reviewed by a neutral lawyer, no."

Lotus smiled at me, her dark eyes merry. "But of course. We've been trying to find a new mage, and everyone knows that you and Schmidt don't get along. Your son and Schmidt will get along, I think. They have similar senses of humor."

I winced. She had me on that point. "Where is Dara?"

Jimmy's voice drifted from the next room. "She texted me she was okay. She said she didn't want to leave right now. I let her know to call you later."

Annoyance and relief washed through me.

"I'll go, let you rest more." Lotus rose. "Nick, call me before the two of you leave, please."

A few hours later, I touched my stomach. I could move now and made action follow thought by swinging my feet off the bed.

"Whoa, wait!" Nick's hand cupped my elbow, steadying me.

I shook my head. "No, I need to fix this now. There's a place where something bad has been dumped, and the land is trying to encyst it. I need to fix it."

His protests weren't effective enough to stop me. "You're barely able to walk!"

I snorted. "Luckily, I don't need to run a race. But I need to be near it, and I need you and the yaksha with me. You to lean on, them to help me."

"What will you need?" Ramki asked.

"Blood and life to purify. To rejuvenate the land. I've shed a little too much tonight to do it all on my own."

It had come to me while I slept. My blood could be the purifying crucible for the taint, and I could charge theirs with my magic to serve as an additional source. It should work. Otherwise, they'd have to wait for me to recover. I didn't think the old couple had that much time left. This was dire.

While I hadn't performed magic often, I'd read about it compulsively. I'd practiced where I could, when it was safe and secret.

Nick texted someone and then carried me to the car, and the others followed in a different vehicle to the place I'd seen.

The rural highway had a small turnaround point close by, edged by trees. The brush tangled around them, so I stepped carefully as I left the pebbled area. Priya walked next to me, hands hovering to steady me if needed.

An aura of pain and misery rolled over me when my feet touched the grass. Priya stumbled and gagged. "What is that?"

"The psychic remains of sacrifice, I think." It was hard to keep my voice even. I'd never felt anything like this—an unclean aura of power like streaks of fire on my skin, a whining, evil rasp in my ears, something scraping across my feet as if the ground had teeth and was trying to chew my skin off.

So much pain swirled around me, the magic tainted with it. What had been left here?

"Bones." Nick's answer hissed between his teeth.

I hadn't realized I'd spoken aloud.

I smelled ash and dirt as he cupped his hands, and the earth shivered beneath our feet. Ivory and grey bones, stained with old dirt, scraps of clothing, all rose to the surface of the earth, impelled by his will.

"Ah, this was the dumping area." A world of regret flavored Lotus's voice. "I didn't know there were so many. While you work, I'll call people in to see them buried."

"You knew about this?"

She pursed her lips. "We knew Bliss was being produced nearby."

I stared at her, horrified. Bliss was a drug used by the supernatural community. The process to make it required the sacrifice of innocence, harvesting the pain and fear of children or higher animals. Its use was forbidden in all the places I'd lived, though that didn't stop its trafficking.

Lotus stared at me, full mouth tight. "We found the place where they made it but could never find where they hid the bodies of the kids they used. Now we know."

"They aren't resting." I whispered the words, hearing fragments of light voices on the breeze.

"They'll be taken to a place to rest where their sorrow and pain will be sung away and they can sleep." She frowned. "And I'll try to find a way to give their parents closure as well, though we can't risk them being buried without safeguards now."

I turned to face Nick. "I need your knife."

He unsheathed it and gave it to me, hilt first.

"Please come here. I'm going to shed your blood and charge it with my magic so you can regenerate the magic here while I transmute the cyst."

"How much blood?" asked Priya in a tiny voice.

My laugh was strangled. "Only a little. Blood holds a lot of magic. And I need to shed mine to fix the wall around this place and clean it."

"How about I draw the blood?" Nick asked. I noticed the knife wobbled in my grip. "Or can this wait?"

"No. It needs to be cleaned." The old couple had aged even as I watched while Priya became even thinner. Nor could I stand the thought of the trapped fragments of children bound here.

It was now or never. Once I collapsed, I'd lose my nerve and never come back here. I really didn't like pain.

Nick drew the knife blade lightly over their arms,

enough that a line of blood rose. Drawing my hand over the line of blood on Priya's arm, I forced the prickles of normal magic down, and the line of blood sparked with light like a line of rubies. I repeated the same process on the older couple.

"Just stay here. Don't leave." My voice wobbled. Frowning, I noted that Nick had drawn his own blood.

He raised a brow. "Just in case?"

"What, a wandering vampire comes through?" The sarcasm helped steady me, since vampires didn't exist. I tapped the point with my fingertip. It was so sharp I didn't feel the pain until after the blood welled out. I knelt and braced myself then lowered my hand to touch the ground, establishing a connection for the tainted magic to pour into me.

I choked as the torrent poured into me like the worst of sewage and cemetery, death and rot and filth. The magic howled, twisted and foul, scraping me inside with dragon claws and teeth. A scream burst out of me as I struggled to filter it, to force it back into the neutral energy it should've been.

There was so much. More than I could encompass. It felt like my skin would rupture and inflate like a balloon, then explode.

Nick's firm hand pressed on mine, and the flow of magic lessened. "I'm a creature of the earth. I can slow it for you. I can't clean it, and I can't hold it for long."

The breath of respite showed me the way, and I grabbed the magic within, twisting it into a will-working. I could use this magic to restore the necessary magic, once the pain lessened enough to think.

A spark flared within me, causing chain reactions to start, and the magic began to flow out of me. I panted, leaning against Nick, and more of the magic flowed into me to repeat the process. When I drained to the last, he caught me before I fell face-first into the bones.

One last task, though pain rasped through me, the ribbons of magic slipping through my clumsy mental fingers. It required almost no energy from me, only manipulation. Pain... I called the magic I'd stored in the yaksha's blood, aspected now to them, and joined them to this new magic. The cyst had been converted with the rest, but the power in the land was changed enough that I wanted to be sure they were nourished.

Nick rose, holding me in his arms.

I opened my eyes. The older couple had changed, the white hair and wrinkles washed away. Priya all but glowed.

It was done. Even if I was so drained I couldn't move a finger. I could still perceive the ribbons, so the burn out wasn't complete.

"How about we try again for a nightcap. When you're feeling better? Maybe a week or two? In a less exciting moment." Nick whispered and carried me to the car.

I laughed, then winced from a stab of pain. "I think that's a wonderful idea."

PART TWO

CHAPTER 5

ONE WOULD HAVE THOUGHT a high school
cafeteria would be the last place to find magic.

Wrong.

The normal lunch monitor was out sick, and it was
my turn to do substitute lunch duty. Thankfully, it was
more entertaining than I'd thought it would be.
Leaning against the wall to ease my aching feet, I
watched threads of magic ripple through and around
the students talking, munching, and flirting in the final
minutes of their lunch period. It interwove with their
quicksilver emotions and bodies in a tapestry of ghostly
color and motion.

My grandfather had told me magic was insentient,
only a force, but I knew better now. Over the graves of
murdered children, on the night of Samhain or
Halloween or whatever you chose to call it, the land's
magic had spoken to me.

After being ordered to purify a festering knot of

magic, how could I have said no? Leave tormented ghosts to their fate? Not happening.

Cleansing it had cost me. It was January now, and I could do only minor magic without pain. About two weeks ago, I'd tried something more powerful, and the twinges warned me off of completing the spell. The knowledge that I was a sitting duck was nerve-wracking.

Humanity's supernatural gift was our ability to manipulate raw magic, though only a few of us could use it. Grandfather had said we needed to be able to see it to use it, and most couldn't...and many who *could* denied the ability, like I'd been doing for years. Those of us who embraced the power called ourselves mages, and if we made ourselves conspicuous, we were hunted by the other supernaturals living in our world.

I'd been prepared to run and hide again, taking my protesting children, Jimmy and Dara, with me, but a clan of yaksha, a supernatural people associated with nature, had stepped forward as my protectors. Their gratitude for my help in making the magic clean again made them do it, but their claim was only as good as the ruler of this territory's permission. Johann Schmidt kept the supernatural peoples, the kins, in line over most of the state of Ohio.

He kept his contracts. He'd made one with my son for his services, and I wondered if that was the only thing keeping the three of us safe. There were others who would want to take us, country-wide. My son's contract was the best of a bad situation. I would've rathered that he remained secret, but at least now he was with someone who wouldn't abuse him.

A tray clanging to the floor brought my focus back to the here and now, my eyes darting in the direction of the sound. My gaze passed over my son, Jimmy, and his girlfriend, Liz, sitting at one of the tables.

He and I generally ignored each other at school. The mutual agreement spared Jimmy the embarrassment of acknowledging that one of the teachers was his mother.

Liz, on the other hand, smiled and waved at me. A cheerful girl, encountering the supernatural world and seeing me nearly gutted by it hadn't diminished her cheer at all. In the months since the incident, she'd helped the fetch, who was now her twin, by watching streaming shows with her and explaining points Mary missed in her secondhand knowledge, and in return hoped Mary would write all her papers.

It worked for them. I turned a blind eye, mostly.

I'd spent the time recovering, teaching, and watching warily for outsiders to come for us. Dara had decided to use her savings to backpack across Europe during the winter, saying off season should be cheaper. She'd promised to call or text the moment she felt threatened, even if there wasn't much I could do at this distance. Like mother, like daughter—Dara lied a lot. There hadn't been a peep out of her since she left two weeks ago. She had sent a few messages, but they were short and rather terse. I'd have to deal with that relationship soon, or it would be permanently damaged.

Near the embarrassed teenager picking up the tray, the new hire for the catering company that supplied lunch paused. Our eyes met, hers a tawny brown, huge in her triangular face. She'd attracted a great deal of attention from the boys, her outstanding looks a lure they hadn't the experience to deal with other than by posturing for her notice. She was also a thin blooded lilim, sent here by her kin's leader, Pryce, reason as yet unknown.

I'd posed as one of them for nearly two decades unnoticed, a woman whose heritage was too far back to have their emotional manipulation abilities. That had to be embarrassing for their previous leader if she was still alive. She hadn't been seen since Pryce took over a year ago.

I glanced at the clock. One minute left for my lunchtime. There were only two more periods in the day, thank the stars. The teenage chatter rose and fell in waves, both comforting and annoying, like a warm but scratchy blanket. I liked routine and normalcy. The current uncertainty was not to my preference.

The tinny bell tone pinged through the building. Students rose, starting a concerted shuffle towards classrooms, with slow eaters resentfully emptying their trays and banging them on the trash cans.

The lilim had maneuvered in the crowd until she was close enough to touch me. Her name tag read

Frances and her expression was intent, those big eyes fixed on me. If she wasn't careful, she'd end up with frown lines.

"Please contact Mr. Pryce as soon as you can." Her breathless voice drew a melting glance from a boy running late. He flinched under my raised eyebrow and hurried on his way.

I nodded to the lilim and headed off to my classroom. *As soon as I could* would be the twelfth of never without some stated reason to do so.

My room was quiet, with a lacy pattern of frost covering three quarters of the classroom windows. The delicate white spirals obscured a glorious scenic view of the parking lot. All in all, I preferred the ice to the regular view.

The room always reflected the weather; blazing hot when it was warm outside, freezing when it was cold. I put on the sweater draped over my chair and got to work.

I had a prep period before Senior English at the end of the day and was using part of it to make a lesson plan for Mary, Liz's fetch. As well as composing a note to her telling her not write Liz's papers for her, however much Liz wheedled.

A flicker of motion caught my eye through the icy windows. Something had moved quickly, too quickly to be animal or human. An icy finger ran down my spine at the risk to the people in the school, but I'd long since created a protective ward around the building and grounds.

It wasn't paranoia when they really were out to get you.

I'd created the wards when I first took the job, sixteen years ago. Before the town woke up, I'd paced them out at dawn and dusk, twining the ribbons of power into a thick tightly woven braid sunk deep in the earth. One outlined the building, and the other larger ward outlined the grounds and athletic field.

Now I fed them a flick of magic and they shone in my sight, my magic causing pain and harm to anything that planned harm to the school or those within.

A howl echoed in my mind, angry and spiteful, as the magic drove whatever it was away. I'd check again after class to make sure it hadn't lingered. It shouldn't. Wards hurt when aimed against a target. Ones as old and strong as mine could kill.

I settled in my chair and opened my laptop. Lesson plans didn't write themselves, and a planning period was a precious resource.

Too soon, the bell rang, and the students wandered in. Several students had opted to wear their coats to class. A smart choice.

What a day. With my attention divided, monitoring the wards to see what trouble might be waiting outside their bounds, my students were unwilling to pay attention to even the risqué bits in *Hamlet*. The chilly temperature of the room didn't help, either.

I should've gone into teaching science. Their rooms had proper climate control.

During the communal rustle of books and clothing as the students got ready to leave at the end of class, I called out "Remember. First drafts for your paper are due before school starts Monday morning. They don't have to be perfect, but they have to be there."

Groans went up but they kept moving, happy to be gone. The last class on Friday afternoon was a hard gig.

Evan Keller paused as he went out. Tall, blond, and an athlete, he'd found my class difficult, especially the part where he didn't receive the special treatment his mother and coaches tended to demand.

"Mrs. G. Can I have an extension on the first draft deadline? I've had some problems..." He let his voice trail off hopefully.

I shook my head and infused my voice with patient encouragement. "Like I said, it doesn't need to be perfect, and you still have this evening and the entire weekend. You can do it."

He huffed out a breath and reached into his pocket. I would've bet good money a contraband cell phone lurked there but didn't want to deal with it this late. Easier to pretend I hadn't seen.

A moment later, Priya Sharma paused at my desk and offered me a note and a shy smile. The rich brown of her skin that wasn't covered by a puffy red coat had turned a little sallow over the past week. She was a member of the yaksha family who'd made themselves my protectors. Their powers affected the fertility and growth of plants and animals, humans included.

Not the most spectacular offensive ability, but they got along with most of the kins. Priya had confided she was interested in practicing medicine.

This was her first experience of winter, and the cold was hard on her. I accepted the note, nodded my thanks, and began packing my own things, just as happy to leave the building after a long day.

When the room cleared, I opened it. *Ramki and Nimaya need to see you as soon as possible.* It was written in Priya's neat but hesitant hand. *It's very important. But they didn't want to call. Or text. Or email. Or have me explain it in this note.*

Priya was coming along nicely in the sarcasm department.

My wistful plans for a glass of wine and a book when I got home fizzled. Ramki and Nimaya were fiercely independent beings, the de facto leaders of the yaksha in the area. Only fear of death for them and Priya had made them deal with outsiders originally. It hadn't gone very well in the short term. They'd decided to find a mage, but they'd mistaken Liz for a mage because she'd had active magic working on her. Jimmy had put it there to help her pass a test.

Of course, our sweet Liz had been more than willing to be kidnapped and replaced so long as someone else did her homework and she could still see Jimmy.

The strategy had gone off the rails immediately. I'd still managed to fix their problem, and they'd retreated back into isolation with the happy assurance they'd been right to seek out a mage, the rest of the details swept away. I'd promised them my services. Since then, even though they were supposed to be my protectors, they called on me for emergencies. On occasion, the hardest service was keeping a straight face.

Their ideas of emergencies were not necessarily typical. The yaksha kin as a whole were, however, knowledgeable about goings-on in the city and Priya's family passed the gossip on to me.

The classroom phone rang as I was finishing the day's paperwork. I picked up to hear the office secretary announce, "Odette Keller," as she transferred it.

Oh, geez. She didn't even give me a warning. I should've ignored the call and run for the hills.

Evan's family were big donors to the school and expected kid glove treatment for their children. "Good afternoon, Mrs. Keller."

Mrs. Keller proceeded to inform me that I would be giving Evan an extension on his rough draft.

Hmph. This lady had another think coming. I was all out of special favors to give. All out of fu... well, anyway. I wasn't budging.

I was polite, but I didn't cave. They were doing him no favors by expecting he would always be given special treatment. He was smart enough to go to college, but with his current habits, he'd fail by the end of the first semester.

After letting me know about her good relationship with the principal and a veiled threat to my continuing employment, blah blah, Mrs. Keller hung up on me as the clock ticked over to four. I rolled my shoulders to dispel the irritation and tension. The extra stress was unwelcome, but if I gave an inch all the influential parents would try to walk all over me.

The haze of sunlight through frost told me I'd be able to get out to the yaksha's place with a little light left. It was a tricky drive when the roads were icy, and they were sure to be after dark. I'd manage, but this would've been much less hairy tomorrow afternoon, in the bright afternoon sun.

I grabbed my coat and bag and headed for the parking lot. The assistant principal, Amy Griswold, nicknamed Grizzly by the students—not without cause —ambushed me as I went past the office.

"Ceri. I'm so glad I caught you." Her bright lipstick-framed smile showed far too many teeth. Oh my. She wore a shaggy brown cardigan that did *not* help keep her nickname out of mind.

I cursed my luck and stopped. "Oh? What is it?" At least I sounded pleasant, even if I didn't feel it.

"Zander Daniels had to take medical leave as of today. That leaves the drama club without anyone to direct the play, and they're rehearsing all next week, with the play in two weeks. I thought of you since you did the directing before we took on Zander." Her smile broadened. Oh, geez. She was laying it on thick.

Ah, yes. The headache of running the drama club. I would've felt guilt had it not taken me *years* to unload it on him.

"When will he be back?" I shifted from foot to foot. Time was in short supply, the thin winter sun heading further to the west and darkness coming early this time of year.

"We don't know yet." Amy's voice swooped down with practiced sadness. "It was sudden, and apparently it's serious. I think you would need to be prepared to take them all the way to opening night and beyond."

So much for any free time in the near future. On the other hand, the kids had already invested weeks of rehearsals into the production. Darn it, darn it. "Okay, I'll do it. What's the play?"

"The Crucible."

Stars save me. Not the biggest box office hit. It was hard enough to bring in an audience but even more so than usual, the only attendees would be the families of the students on stage. That wasn't ever easy for them. "I have a copy of the script at home, so I don't need a new one. I'll see you later."

Her heels clicked a rhythm in my head as she walked jauntily down the hall, having relieved herself of the responsibility of dealing with the drama class to a total chump.

Tap-tap-tap. Cru-ci-ble. Cru-ci-ble. Tap-tap-tap.

Frick!

I sucked in a deep breath and hurried toward my car. At least it was Friday. I would get a little time to gird my loins before wrangling the actors.

First, though, I needed to go and see Priya's family. Given their personalities, the note had an urgent undertone I couldn't ignore. Not that I would even if it wasn't urgent. I just might've waited until tomorrow.

Being capable of bending reality with my will, shaping it to my desire if I wanted it badly enough, wasn't all it was cracked up to be. I was a high school teacher because that actually paid the bills. In the world of the kins, which I inhabited, mages who didn't have protectors either hid or were enslaved. I'd hidden for most of my life, but now I was in the open. Exposed.

I'd agreed to work for the yakshas because my alternatives, Johann Schmidt or Thomas Pryce, were unacceptable to me. I'd permitted my son to contract with Schmidt because I'd been assured of his safety.

Too bad for me, close proximity to Schmidt might lead me to try to murder him.

Both Pryce, the leader of the lilim faction in the area, and Schmidt, the leader of the whole area's magical community, lilim included, were willing to bide their time. Good thing I knew enough to be cautious and ready for an attack. The yakshas weren't powerful in terms of aggressive abilities, but they did live in Schmidt's territory, and he had outlawed taking mages who had a protector. Therefore, the yakshas claiming to protect me also put Schmidt's protection over me, in theory. We would see. Normally his word was pretty good.

However, after cleansing the magic on the yaksha's land, I'd been nearly gutted by a wolf changer, then overstrained my magic. I could do small amounts of magic but trying to do any that required true power brought on blinding headaches. I'd been stretching my magical muscles and resting alternately for almost three months, and the headaches hadn't eased. So, at the moment, I preferred using mundane medicinal and technological means to solve problems whenever possible.

I hoped they only needed help figuring out how to reconnect to the internet. That had been the reason for the last *urgent* visit.

Since Halloween, my life had become interesting in the *may you live in interesting times* sense. I sighed. With the kids almost grown, I had thought I could look forward to quiet.

THE COLD AIR slapped my face as I hurried out of the building. Geez. I would almost have rather been actually slapped. This chill was bone rattling. My whole body shook as I fumbled for the fob in my pocket. I finally got it and pulled it out, unlocking the door as I hurried, practically diving for the car. As my hand touched the door handle, a voice breathed in my ear. "Boo."

I jerked upright and back, cannoning into a strong body, my head impacting his jaw. I saw stars for a moment from the shock. He staggered back, then laughed. "I'll award a 'D' for situational awareness, but an 'A' for reaction time." He fingered his jaw, silver-gray eyes alight with amusement.

My heart pounded fast enough to warm me against the chill. "Nick. I swear if you do that one more time..." I let the threat trail off.

"You'll kiss me?" He waggled his eyebrows in mock lechery.

"No, I'll smack you." Adrenaline fading, my lips twitched to answer his smile. As a svartalf, one of the kins who had inspired the legends of dark elves in northern Europe, he was probably much older than I was. As a result of that and most of that long life spent stalking and hunting game when he wasn't smithing, Nick was quiet and easy to miss, and took ruthless advantage of it to sneak up on me. It was a quirk I could've lived without, but as a reward for his patience as we tried to ease into a relationship, I put up with it. "Why are you here?"

"I figured your *me* time started as soon as you left work, and I had a present for you." He pulled a small package from his coat pocket and handed it to me.

Tall and wiry, his graying brown hair ruffled by the chilled wind, he appeared average to attractive. Beneath the illusion of an average, human appearance, he was striking in both features and coloring, ink-black skin and white blonde hair. The silver eyes remained the same.

The package, heavy for its small size, intrigued me. I pulled the tissue apart. A silver cuff bracelet lay in my gloved hand, inset with lapis lazuli. The vivid blue streaked with green made me catch my breath. The piece was extraordinary. Far too extravagant for my casual boyfriend to give me. "Nick, I can't accept this." Even I could hear the wistfulness in my voice.

"Ceri, you'd take flowers, right? The stone was one I found and cost nothing. I mined the silver long ago and worked it recently. The only cost is my labor. Less than a dozen roses." He tugged my coat sleeve up and slid the beautiful cuff onto my wrist, unclasped. "Clasp it and think of a word while you do it."

In a moment of weakness, I did. I didn't think I owned another piece of jewelry quite this gorgeous. How could I say no?

He tried to undo the bracelet, and it didn't move. "Only you can take it off. Just think of the word while you undo it. It's silver, so it'll be easy for you to put a magical effect in it. I made it for you. If you don't want it, no one else will ever have it."

"Nick...." I tested, and it did unclasp when I thought of the word. "It's too much. And it's called *will working*, not *magic effects*." I made air quotes around his phrase, smiling at him. He really was cute.

"I was inspired. It was made specially for you." The pride in his voice was unmistakable, though he was trying to downplay it.

I glanced down at the bracelet. Nick wasn't the kind of man who would expect anything in exchange for a gift. I could see him destroying it if I didn't accept, not out of spite, but because it was intended for me alone.

It was strange but lovely how the thought warmed me. "Thank you, Nick."

"Enjoy your *me* time. I'm going to the office and

doing paperwork this evening." Nick grimaced. He worked at a lab that contracted with the defense department. He went by Mr. Damarian even though he could have required Dr. Damarian.

I squeezed his arm before looking down at the beautiful bracelet again. "I'm off to Priya's house. Her parents sent a note, they need me to visit."

"Let me know what the great emergency is. I don't know how you survived the great router failure incident in December...or that a boy asked Priya on a date and she said yes, catastrophe in November."

We both chuckled. They did seem to misconstrue the whole emergency concept...often.

Nick continued with careful casualness, "Would you be interested in waffles tomorrow morning? I'm open for breakfast."

He knew I loved waffles, even if my waistline didn't. I'd add some extra walking time to make up for it. "Sure. Text me where."

I hopped into the car, cranking it up to warm. It'd take far too long for the heater to get to full blast. I watched him stride to his pickup, parked on a street next to the parking lot. My almost-boyfriend, mostly because of my trust issues. I suspected his patience came from long experience, svartalfar was a long-lived kin.

Tiny snowflakes powdered the windshield as I drove, the grey skies and leaden clouds warning of more to come. Priya's family lived in a small, wooded area beyond the outskirts of western Columbus. The roads narrowed and began curving, so I slowed down. A thin layer of slush had already formed on the road, enough to make it unpleasantly slick. It was full-blown ice in places, despite the county's attempt to brine the pavement.

Flickers of darkness hung in the tree branches like strange Christmas ornaments past their season. Since just after Halloween, I'd noticed chaos magic manifesting in the area as I drove to see Priya's family. Searching for signs, I'd found them in other places around the city, taking forms that fueled reports of paranormal sightings from regular people. None of the kins wanted provable sightings. Many were old enough to remember the days of mobs with pitchforks and torches and preferred as much subtlety as possible.

The road wasn't getting any better, so I slowed even more and took a moment to smooth out the unruly wisps of chaos magic fluttering in the air as I turned to go down the hidden driveway toward the yaksha family home. Chaos magic by its nature was more likely to dissolve, hurrying it along didn't take much effort. Using it on the other hand...I wished I knew why it was showing up all of a sudden.

A man wearing a long dark frock coat wavered into being in the middle of the road only feet in front of the car. I could see the snowy drive, trees, and iced-over bushes *through* him.

I slammed on the brakes and skidded on the ice,

twisting the wheel so that he wouldn't pass through the car— or worse, me. Encountering one of the unbodied was dangerous.

An unbodied was born...er, created when someone —it didn't matter what their kin was—refused to accept that they had died. No one but the unbodied were sure what happened, but the universe warped around them, and they came into being with the memories and emotions of the body that had died. Incorporeal, they differed from ghosts in that the unbodied ate energy, life energy by preference. Preferably humans.

Crap.

Even as I hung onto the wheel, I called up a ward, something to protect me from his—its—touch. I stole a little life from the vegetation all around me to prevent his theft of mine. Plant life energy was more diffused and taking it caused far less harm than taking an animal's.

The headlights lights went out, as well as the dashboard display.

A hand reached through the windshield and tried to touch my face, and the ward crackled, preventing the contact. This close, I could see he had a strong face. He might have been handsome if his expression hadn't been distorted with anger and malice. The unbodied hated the living, jealous and angry we had what they'd lost. They were intelligent, but it was hard to communicate with them since their rage drove them to attack sooner or later.

How on earth had he manifested here so subtly? I hadn't felt a trace of him in the area, except for the possible flickers outside my classroom window. I stifled the impulse to try to negotiate with him. The only bribe or payment they took was life force, and I wasn't going to start killing animals or people to feed him.

Hoping against hope, I pressed the starter button, but nothing happened. As I expected, he'd drained the battery. The car had stopped mostly off the road, at least. I'd heard something grind and then an ominous clunk when I came to a halt rattling over rocks.

Wonderful.

The unbodied vanished from sight.

I craned my head around looking frantically for him, but I couldn't detect him with either my eyes or my magic. He'd gone wherever they went when they weren't manifested. No one had ever gotten an answer to that question.

The argument whether they should be considered a separate kin or not was ongoing—they were created from humans and kin who had died and then manifested. They shared abilities and powers, like kin, but they weren't born into the unbodied state.

He'd looked hungry. My temples ached. I needed to get behind the yaksha's protective wards. They'd drawn them at the edges of their property, rooted in the earth's magic. Based on my prior experience with the ward, the unbodied wouldn't be able to pass them.

Without permission, I had barely managed to pass through.

The problem was that unwarded humans lived in the area as well. Heavier snow now splattered on my windshield. I really didn't need that.

I called Nick before I got out. I didn't want distraction as I power walked and jogged the rest of the way.

He picked up on the second ring. "Hey, Ceri. What was the emergency?"

"I'm not there yet. An unbodied manifested in the drive up to their property. And now the car won't start."

"Are you all right?" His voice sharpened.

"I'm fine, the car isn't." That was an emergency.

Amusement crept into his tone. "And you want me to come out and make it better? Did you send the unbodied on its way?"

"It vanished. I'm going to head behind the wards, but car repair and backup to get the unbodied would be nice." If he'd been here, I would have batted my eyelashes. If I'd had my full power, I wouldn't have needed backup, but it was what it was.

"Does that mean I might get invited to your me time this evening?" Even more amusement and a trace of wistfulness. He really was cute.

I hemmed and hawed playfully. "I could see my way to sharing that bottle of wine with you if you fix the car. How soon can you come out?"

"Soon. I'm still at work. It will take forty-five

minutes or so to get out to where you are. And yes, I can drive the unbodied off if it's still there. Since you've been having headaches, it might be better if you stay behind the wards unless I need help."

The calm confidence was sexy. Nick was a svartalfar warrior and artificer. I'd seen the results of him fighting once, a changer brought down in seconds when Nick was only armed with a knife. I wouldn't have asked him to come out otherwise. Priya was safe behind the wards, but she wasn't protected if she needed to get groceries, run errands, or go to school. "I'll walk the rest of the way to the Sharma's place. It's a better place to wait. The yaksha have permanent wards. And the people who live there need to be warned."

"You have a personal defensive ward up?"

"Yes." I drawled the word. It was sweet of him to ask. The worry in his voice warmed me. "I'm not stupid. It was the first thing I did when I saw him. He tried for a touch, then vanished."

"Call me when you get there." I raised a brow at his commanding tone but decided to let it pass. He was driving out to fix my car, after all. I owed him a solid.

"I will."

I grabbed the boots on the passenger seat and put them on, leaving my work shoes in the back. The tree overhanging the edge of the road dumped snow on me as I forced the door open. Freaking frak.

Concentrating on my ward against life consumption, I squeezed out of the car. How had the darn car gotten so messed up by a simple turn off the road? I had no idea.

The wind stuck cold fingers through my coat. I hadn't planned on walking far, so it was too light for the weather. I thought about grabbing my emergency blanket from the back but didn't want to take the time to fish it out from under all the crap in the trunk. I wanted to get to the safety of the wards. My breath plumed white as I hurried down the drive. After the first slip almost set me on my butt, I slowed, careful to set my feet purposefully each time so I didn't slip on the ice.

After several chilly minutes, the trees cleared and the small field with its little gathering of trailers came into view. Six trailers, five single and a lone double-wide, all arranged in a circle with their doors facing inward. A small parking area lay below the circle, in the direction I approached from. The ward stretched just outside the parking area, in a circle that contained all the trailers and a good portion of the field. It covered the kin in the area, but not the humans, all living not-far-enough away.

Stepping carefully, I hurried toward the Sharma's doublewide, and the door opened before my first knock was complete.

Priya, now wearing a crimson shirt that came almost to her knees and puffy green pants, peered over my shoulder. "Where's your car?"

"About half a mile down the road. There's an unbodied on your drive. Warn the people in the other trailers not to go out. Nick is coming, and he should be able to drive it away." I spoke between shivers and teeth chatters.

She took my coat and hung it up as I stepped in. The small living area was as I had seen it before, with the addition of an elaborate clay pot on the counter. The workmanship was beautiful, its ornateness out of place in the plain furnishings of the trailer.

Ramki and Vinaya, the couple who looked after her and had requested I come, peered at me. "An unbodied?"

"Yes. Your wards are strong enough to keep it out, but people shouldn't leave unless they can fight it."

Vinaya smiled at me. "It's good you're concerned, but the others who live here don't leave the wards. They're too poor to afford an illusion, and not close enough to human appearance." She fiddled with the plant. "Mary will be over in a moment." Mary was living amongst the yaksha now.

That explained why Priya hadn't run to warn anyone. They wouldn't be leaving anyway.

"What do you need?" I asked.

They, like Priya, were a little sallow, but still seemed healthy. Vinaya indicated the pot, standing and gesturing me over. A tiny grip of green appeared in its middle, vivid against the rich dark earth.

"We need you to forge a connection between our

little one and the energy of this land, as you did for us."

I tried not to stare at her, but it was hard. I wanted so much to ask about their method of reproduction, as plant-based beings, how did they create this little one? Good manners stopped me. Some things were better kept private.

Luckily, while the difficulty of cleaning the land magic near here was what had strained me, wards and connections like this were simple. They were among the first magics learned, the base on which the greater will workings stood.

I called my magic, detected the little sprout's magic, which was very like the adults'. I wondered if the tiny plant was sentient at this stage, as I easily connected its magic to the lands. I'd hoped they wouldn't need intervention to connect their children, but at least they'd been able to, ah, conceive without help. Up to this point, they hadn't even had that. Perhaps tweaking the will working further would establish them as completely independent.

A throb of pain warned me I was doing too much. I retreated from the trance and glanced at my phone. Almost an hour had passed. "Connected and congratulations."

I smiled, the headache clearing away. The doting way they stared at the sprout was incredibly sweet.

A haunting wail split the air, reverberating in my ears. The unbodied. And I'd forgotten to call Nick when I got here. "Oh, no."

I RUSHED OUT WITHOUT A COAT, inhaling sharply as the cold bit into me. My inner eye was still open, and beyond the greenish haze that marked the ward, among the trees, a firefly light glimmered blue and white. It wove a pattern in the gloom, moving so fast the light blurred in a line. Nick was fighting the unbodied.

Another howl, like fingernails raking the chalkboard of my soul, sent new goosebumps to join the ones already called up by the temperature. I stopped at the edge of the ward, calling up my own defenses against the life drain and the cold.

A plume of mist drifted by me. I turned to find both Priya and Mary ready to charge through the ward.

Both young women stared at me when I shook my head. Silent rebellion wrote itself on the air, teenagers ready to charge into a complete unknown that would kill them.

"No." I bit the word off. The ward shimmered, its complexity glowing green to my inner eye. The girls glared at me, trembling on the verge of running through the protective energy.

I grasped a strand of magic, avoiding the bits of chaos magic that tried to twine with it, and called fire to burn around my hands. Even a tiny wisp could look impressive when it appeared from nowhere. Gritting my teeth through the stab of pain in my head, I held a hand up, red and yellow flames dancing around it. "It will kill you. Nick will try to save you, and that'll give it a chance to kill him. I'm going to cross to help him. If either of you sets a toe past the ward, there will be severe consequences." Hopefully, the fire on my hands was intimidating enough to convince them to do as I said.

With a hard stare at the girls, I stepped through the ward's energies. As insurance, I tweaked the web of protection and made it physical. I'd studied it enough on my visits and had already worked out what I needed to do. A bonus was that it didn't require me to use any magic to maintain it.

Priya cursed as she hit the wall I'd created and bounced back with a curse. I didn't know where she'd picked up those kinds of words.

Oh, man. The cold air was like shards of ice in my lungs, so cold it burned. I wrapped the flames around my body for warmth and bolted down the drive before I thought how insane this decision was.

Cloud cover made my vision uncertain, so I headed toward the moving light, stopping when forms moved in the shadows of the trees, and I backed into the middle of the road. A gust of wind shook snow on me from the branches above as I shifted my concentration to summon a small ball of light. I didn't want to hit the wrong person. Or be hit.

Snow crunched as Nick and the unbodied swirled through snow and around trees, changing positions in a complex series of strikes and parries. Several trees bore darkened patches on their trunks, where the unbodied had stolen some of their life. It couldn't have been here long. The damage was too slight.

Snow flew as Nick shifted his footing, dodging a strike. He was at a disadvantage since he needed to consider his footing, as opposed to floating above the snow as the unbodied did. Smart and deadly, the unbodied was taking advantage of the terrain, forcing Nick into deeper snow.

The translucent figure of a man had tears in his coat, exposing his pallid skin and the Victorian clothing beneath it. The edges of the wounds shimmered with the same colors that wreathed Nick's knife. Despite the difficult footing, Nick moved with easy grace, passing the knife from hand to hand to strike.

He was more coordinated than I was on my best day. It made sense. He was a svartalfar. Many of them survived from a time when swords and armor and shields were used every day, although he'd refused to tell me his age.

The only sign of effort was the cloud of foggy breath he trailed. Poor guy was breathing heavily.

Nick stumbled. The unbodied took advantage of his momentary vulnerability and tore his ragged nails at the air. Nick threw himself backwards, the blow passing just above his head. I'd gotten the rhythm of their fight, and what Nick needed was defenses, not another attacker interfering in this deadly dance. Especially not one whose crowning achievement was a yellow belt in karate.

I reached out for more strands of magic, even though the ones I already held had given me a throbbing headache.

Nick rolled in the snow, scrambling to his feet, limping now. He needed a stronger defensive ward, so I twisted the surrounding magic around him. As I wove the strands of magic, warmth trickled across my mouth. Wiping at it hurriedly, I looked at my hand to find it stained red. My nose was bleeding from the strain of doing the will work so hastily.

The fibers of chaos magic swirling in the air, composed of all colors and none, twining with my magic, even though I hadn't pulled on them. An abrupt burst of power dazzled my eyes, the wards on Nick and me flared like a sudden dawn.

The unbodied shrieked in rage, lunging in my direction. I flinched, but didn't try to run, trusting my ward to stop it. When it worked, the unbodied's face stretched with rage, mouth gaping large enough to swallow me whole as its cohesion lessened.

It was only a face now. Its eyes were a gateway to hell, shining with an unearthly light. I suppressed a shiver as the rage poured from its gaping mouth.

From behind, Nick carved it in half with a neat and precise strike. I watched him through the diffused unbodied. Had the unbodied depended on that lack of cohesion as a defense?

Nick's knife blazed. The light ran over and around the unbodied almost as if the glow were consuming it. The misty face writhed and twisted around something that looked like a solid bar of magic. Had he forged the knife or had there been a mage like me involved?

It would've been convenient for an artificer to have a mage available.

I shook off the thought. Nick was a friend. He'd proved himself. I needed to stop reverting to paranoia. Even if most people *were* out to get me. I dismissed the flames as he strode to my side, favoring his right leg and frowning. He pulled a handkerchief from his pocket and handed it to me. "I had it handled. Your nose is bleeding. You've been pushing your magic too much, again."

"You're not my mother, Nick." My tone was breathy, the adrenaline not yet faded from the unbodied's charge.

"This is where I make a comment about a paddling.

Take it as you will." He was limping. His mouth was set with pain and the chaos magic covered him like an opal veil.

That couldn't be healthy. It might cause the injury to heal wrong or even mutilate him. I called it to me, reaching out to hover my fingertips an inch from Nick's chest. The chaos around him flickered, then contracted and bunched near my hand, forming into a tiny dragon. I kept my arm still, continuing my summons, and the small shape winged to perch on my wrist.

Sometimes chaos magic took on a form from the imagination of its viewer, i.e. me. Usually it dissipated in a few minutes, back into wisps of potential. Contact with me would give it stability and more time in this shape.

Also, it was adorable.

Nick stared at the dragon in awe. "That's... That's impressive. And scary. Not an illusion either. What did you do?"

"I called it to me. The chaos magic surrounding you formed it. I think the chaos grabbed bits of the unbodied as it dissipated to build a permanent shape upon." I frowned. There was so much I didn't know as I often groped my way around practicing my magic. I'd spent almost twenty years hiding and not using it or will-working. It frightened me how easily it came to me now. Almost as much as how easily I could injure myself going beyond the basics with will working.

My son and daughter were mages too. How would their ability shape their lives, for good or bad?

There'd been no one to teach me after my grandfather died when I was in my early teens. I'd gone to distant relatives who knew nothing about the kins, and even at that age I'd learned to keep my mouth shut. Since then, I'd learned what I could from the few books I'd scavenged over the years. The same for my kids. I'd thought they hadn't inherited the gift, but they'd hidden it from me to keep me from worrying.

Flicking the familiar anxiety away, I examined the tiny dragon, as it became more real with each beat of my heart. Fascinating.

"Did it take this shape from you?" I asked.

"No. The only dragons I'm familiar with are much bigger."

The cold sent another shiver through me. Nick must've noticed. "Let's go and get warm," he replied.

I steadied him as we walked down the drive.

"Are you guys ok?" Priya shouted, braced against the ward at the edge of the little parking lot as if she were a mime. I knew Nick couldn't see the ward, only the results. I waved and nodded.

A smile flickered across his face. "An invisible wall?"

"Yes." I couldn't help the tinge of pride in my voice. I'd kept her safe.

The tiny creature stroked its head on my arm. I squelched in the mud. The flames I'd summoned had melted the snow around me and my boots were soaked. Nick wore his usual light jacket and work boots.

"Wait to fix the car?" he asked.

"Yes. No one comes here. Nobody will bother it." I gave him a wry look.

"I'll drive," he muttered. His truck waited across the road from my car, the driver's door open.

His emergency stop had been much neater than mine. Maybe it was a good idea for him to maneuver this snow in his own vehicle.

"What happened?" I asked.

"It tried to jump me in the cab. I swerved and jumped out, so I had room to move." He grimaced and slid into the truck. I hurried around the truck, mindful of the ice, and waved again at the girls before hopping in.

As he drove the short distance to the ward, I continued to ponder the little beast. The chaos magic had faded into the steady thrum of a living aura. No wonder there was so much odd and outré happening recently—the magic, influenced by minds, could create things both winsome and, well, not so nice. It made me sad to think of the dragon fading away.

I only knew of one source of this kind of magic in the area. A girl I'd met once, briefly. She was either a guest or a prisoner of Johann Schmidt. I'd met her when Jimmy had driven out to work and I'd stayed for his shift, avoiding his boss.

If she was the source, she needed to learn to reign

in the magic she emitted. We couldn't have little magical dragons floating around all over the place.

The two girls waited for us in the parking area. Nick stopped before the ward, and I got out. It was simple and quick to change the ward back to its original parameters, enabling him to drive through. The girls caught sight of the dragon and crowded close as soon as the ward was down. Mary cooed at it, and reached out, looking to me for permission to touch it.

I nodded and she stroked its head.

Mary was a fetch, one of a kin whose young could take on the shape and memories of a single person. The kin sold a few of their children to protect the rest. Mary had copied my son's girlfriend Liz. Liz had been mistaken for a mage back when the yakshas were desperate. I'd helped sort it out, and when Mary ended up needing a home, the yakshas had taken her in.

I felt bad for her. Her family couldn't take her back. When a child took on the appearance and mind of an outsider, they were no longer considered a fetch by their people. While Ramki and Vinaya were willing to homeschool her, she was much more interested in academics than they were. Though I'd spoken with certain contacts to get Mary identification papers so she could go to school, I hadn't yet made any progress.

Nick parked and joined me. Both girls gazed at him with big, wide eyes. With his illusions in place, Nick was an attractive but forgettable man of mature age, not one that they'd ever expect to see with a knife in hand battling a monster.

They knew what he was, but they'd never actually seen him fight.

Vinaya opened the trailer door wide and asked, "Would you like some chai to warm up?" She squinted at the dragon on my finger. "Is that safe for you to bring in, Ceri?"

Yaksha. Calm as plant herders could be.

Chuckling, I moved the dragon to my shoulder so I could use both hands to steady Nick as he climbed the two steps into the trailer.

Nick smiled at her as we entered. "Yes, please. Chai would be very nice."

"It's safe," I assured her. I didn't think the little creature would survive long, but it seemed to like me, so I'd keep it close.

Nick massaged his leg while the warm smell of spices and milk mixed in the air. The seasoned milky tea hit the spot. As we drank, Vinaya glanced at her mate. "There was one other thing."

Wait for it...

"Yes?" I took another sip. Her chai was delicious, better than a restaurant's. It warmed me from the toes up.

She drew a long breath. "There's a meeting tonight of the heads of the various kins. It's going to be in conference room A at the Regency. Johann contacted us since he doesn't represent us. There is a..." she rubbed her forehead, face intent.

A triumphant flicker crossed her face as she remembered the word. "He called it a ghost hunter. A ghost destroyer, maybe, coming. Priya said that he is a human who has a television show. His name is Lucas Wheeler. He's heard about all the odd happenings currently going on. All the sightings of weird things and the incidents over the past couple of months. So he's coming to investigate. Johann didn't sound happy when he called. I know you like humans, being one yourself, and prefer to prevent any unnecessary killing. I'm pretty sure that that's what the consensus is going to be since that's an easy way to deal with it." Her brown eyes were concerned as the words tumbled over each other like rocks rolling in a rapid stream.

Johann could be ruthless when he was protecting his territory. I didn't expect much consideration for life from the kins. They were inhuman and sometimes inhumane, and never pretended to be human except in a cosmetic sense, and while I had formed relationships with a few, I didn't delude myself.

Many of them came from a time when life was cheap.

Though I was annoyed to find out about something this important so late, it sounded as if the meeting had been thrown together in a hurry. Maybe that was why Pryce had summoned me. Hmm.

The death of a human to protect Vinaya's friends and her family wouldn't bother her in the least. This was a courtesy that she paid me, telling me about the meeting.

"Do you mind if I go as your representative? Since I'm technically protected by you?" And that way, I could make my voice heard.

"That's what I thought you would want to do. We don't mind." She turned her gaze to Nick. "Will you be attending? Johann had said that he wasn't able to contact you."

He sighed and looked down at his chai. "Normally I avoid politics, but I think this time I'm going to attend. At least Ceri will make the meeting interesting."

"If you're going to be seeing Mr. Schmidt..." Mary's soft voice broke into the conversation. "Would you be able to ask about my documentation? I've been studying with Priya, and I want to go to college. But I can't go if I don't have any identification. I thought that he said that he would attend to it, but I may have misheard. Could you remind him? Lotus says that he's very busy right now, but I need to apply for financial aid and colleges, and the deadline is the fifteenth of next month."

Yet another way Johann Schmidt was a pain in my butt. Mary, as the fetch of my son's girlfriend Liz, had no official identity until one was made for her. Johann was the best source for those, and he charged a premium for it. It'd taken me five years to pay off the papers for myself and my children. I had no idea how

Mary's would be paid for. I'd been hoping the yakshas would be able to split it with me. Technically, it was totally their fault, and they should've paid for all of it, but they didn't have a lot of money. "Yes, I'll ask him." I'd also check in with my contacts to see if any of them had found a cheaper avenue for legitimate looking papers.

Mary looked relieved and leaned back in her chair, sipping her chai. As a fetch, she still appeared identical to Liz, but their personalities had started to diverge. Mary was studious and introverted, only drawing Liz's extroverted ways about her when she had to. When a fetch first took over a personality, they tended to act *very* similar and it was difficult for Mary to force the change to happen faster, but she was doing her best.

Given that circumstances were forcing me into Schmidt's presence, I made a mental note to ask if he had a way to confine the power leakage from Katie. She leaked chaos magic. I had no idea why. I had only discovered the connection when I drove to Schmidt's to pick Jimmy up when he'd run too late. Another teenager in appearance, but I'd discerned the magic leaking from her in the few minutes we'd spent together before Jimmy appeared. If this problem continued, the powers that be might find themselves murdering one curious human after another. Which *would* be noticeable. Another topic for the upcoming discussion.

I was going to have to make a list at this rate.

"Thank you for the information and the tea," I said after draining the last of my cup.

"You're most welcome." Vinaya glanced at the pot and smiled.

Nick accompanied me out the door. As soon as he opened it, the dragon launched into the air and sailed over to land on Nick's truck. I was gonna miss the little guy when he dissipated.

"I suggest we carpool, since I'm going to the meeting, and we shouldn't take the additional time to fix your car." Nick glanced at me with his eyebrows raised in question.

I considered, but it was an easy choice. I was bone tired, and my temples were throbbing a staccato rhythm.

Uh-oh. Something felt bad. I sniffed hard and sighed. Liquid bubbled down my nostrils. I bent forward in time for red drops to splatter down to the snow instead of my shirt. I sighed, pinching the bridge of my nose and fishing around in my pocket with my other hand for a handkerchief. I'd taken to keeping one on me just in case of this exact fiasco.

"Sure. Thanks for the lift." I sounded nasal and ungracious.

Nick laughed and shook his head.

With my head flung forward, I allowed him to take my hand and lead me toward the truck, so I didn't have to look up. I really had no idea why it was good to throw my head down during a nosebleed, but that's what the interwebz said to do, so that's what I did. The little dragon landed on my shoulder right before I slid onto the passenger seat.

In the cab, belted up, my mood lightened. Nick driving didn't infringe on my independence whatsoever. He knew the way to the Regency, and I didn't. Plus, his truck and all. It wasn't like I was going to walk there with my car out of commission. That annoying part of my brain that demanded independence was starting to bug me.

The snowfall intensified as he drove with calm confidence. I snuck a sideways look at him as I fought drowsiness. The heat blasting from the vents relaxed me. "What exactly is unusual about this hotel?" I asked in an attempt to wake myself up with conversation.

"It's one that caters to a specialized clientele." Nick flicked his turn signal and maneuvered around a slower-moving car. Not that we were exactly speeding along in this mess.

I pursed my lips at him. "I knew *that*. I was asking what more you knew about it."

The corner of his mouth curved in a smile, but he kept his eyes on the road. "It's run by a pair of oni. They came here from Japan oh, in the sixties, I think. They opened the hotel in the seventies, long before I came here. The original pair are pretty old. I believe their children run it now. Being big and muscular really helps in making sure that your clientele behaves."

I could believe it. Oni were much larger than

humans and many of the kins, often with horns and fangs. Many used an iron club as a weapon, mashing those who opposed them to paste. It made the hotel a good place to hold a meeting that might get tense with many factions of the kin present.

"Do you know why the daoine sidhe have their headquarters downtown in a human hotel? Since it's the exact opposite of this meeting place?" I asked.

He chuckled. "To discourage fights. The Regency is a place that can actually *contain* a fight among the kins, which is why councils are held there. If people need to sort things out, they get sorted out at the meeting."

"I didn't know you had the right to sit on the Council, but that does make sense now that I think about it. You're the only svartalf in town, aren't you?" Did he even want to sit on it? It sounded like a headache.

He shrugged. "Participation is more a 'you must be this tall to ride this ride' kind of thing than population. I don't often choose to attend, because most of the items that are discussed don't interest me. They don't call council meetings very often, anyway. Only for matters that impact the kins of the area as a whole."

He glanced quickly at me, then returned his attention to the road. "But since you're attending this one, and you're feeling poorly, I find myself suddenly interested in the current topic."

Happiness at his concern warred with unease at his knowledge of my weakness. I didn't want to be dependent. That way lay cages and servitude. I had a damn good reason for being skittish about dependence, but I had to find a way to trust him. I could be cautious, but trust was pivotal in a good relationship.

"Just as long as you remember that you're the back up." I wiggled my fingers.

The little dragon snorted at being disturbed.

Nick laughed as we both looked at the little guy on my hand.

The Regency lay to the north of Columbus, in an undeveloped area mostly composed of trees. The grounds surrounding the building were immaculately kept, and the winding road leading to it had been recently plowed and salted. Only a dusting of snow lay on it, and no ice. The faint tracks of other vehicles shone under the truck's headlights.

When we pulled into the parking lot, I discovered that the Regency was a large building, not unlike a chain hotel. Its isolated setting was the strangest part of the scene. The building looked like it belonged along a highway.

Nick and I got out of his vehicle and headed for the door. Chaos magic drifted and glittered in the clear air. There were lots of magic users inside, for sure.

I walked with my arm crooked across my chest. Tiny claws dug into my coat sleeve with each motion, the dragon clinging with surprising strength, its wings tucked flat against its body. In that pose, it could've been a snake from above.

Once inside the light and warmth, I turned to the counter and blinked. The woman who stood behind the counter had skin a lovely shade of rich bluish-purple, with tusks covering half her lower face. It wasn't the skin color that made me blink twice, and not the tusks, not really. It was the fact that she was somewhere over 8 feet tall. The blinking third eye in her forehead was also unsettling.

I caught myself and kept from looking startled at the lady's appearance.

With a nod and a pleasant smile, she said, "No illusions here please."

"Oh, of course. It's habit." Nick let his trickle away. His true appearance was always a spectacular sight. He was tall, muscularly built, with night-dark skin and long silver hair kept in a braid that fell somewhere south of his butt. The knife at his waist lay now unconcealed.

Still blinking that third eye, the woman peered down at me. I tried not to let it look like I was craning my neck upward.

"Mr. Damarian," she said. "I don't recognize your companion?"

"This is Ms. Gault. She's a mage associated with the yaksha population, representing them as their protected."

She cocked her head at me and gave me a *very* condescending smile and in a sickly-sweet voice said, "I'm very pleased to meet you." Turning back to Nick, her voice went back to normal. "We typically have a no pets policy, but I'll relax it if you pay a security deposit." Her voice remained level. "The meeting is already underway in conference room A. You know the way, correct?"

"Yes." Nick tapped his foot while I pulled out my credit card.

The woman looked at my card with a snarl in her lips. "Child, *you* are the pet. I'm not worried about a manifested little dragon." The kins looked down on us mages. I'd always known that. It was obvious. But this was a bit much!

I sputtered, the protests and defenses of me and my status rolling through my mind too fast for actual words to come out. I pulled my hand back as Nick yanked his wallet out of his back pocket. "How much?" he snarled.

"It'll be a hundred dollars, scaling up if there's any damage. If there isn't, it will be refunded at the end of the night."

"Fine," I grumbled, unable to keep the grumpiness out of my voice at this point. *Pet* indeed. Nick pulled a crisp hundred dollar bill out and waited for a receipt, which she wrote out in long hand.

Transaction done, Nick headed down the hall, stopping a few feet away to wait for me.

"I need to make a quick stop in a washroom to get the blood off." I had standards. Besides, some of the kin here probably liked the smell.

He nodded and looked toward conference room A. "You do that, I'll let them know you're coming."

There was more chaos magic shimmering around in the bathroom. Like gnats or mayflies. The dragon reared up, spreading its wings, and took flight, eating a few wisps. It stayed whole, and I quickly scrubbed my face. Did feeding it mean it'd stay around longer? I hoped so. "Eat up," I muttered as I grabbed a handful of paper towels.

After I was done drying, it—no, he, I'd decided on the drive his name would be Noir—landed on my shoulder. Noir was heavier now, more solid. Feeding him did work.

He curled up like a cat, head tucked against my neck, while I repaired my makeup. I let my hair down to cover him, brushing it forward. Better that than nothing. People would've also noticed my shirt squirming. After a long deep breath, I walked down the hall and into the conference room.

The sheer beauty index in the room hit me like a bat to the face. The daoine sidhe, renowned for their icy beauty, had sent a female representative.

Pryce, a lilim, bore a heartbreaking handsomeness that didn't hide the calculating brain behind it.

Nick even featured and well done him. He was stunning amongst the gorgeous.

And then there was Johann, a stark contrast with greasy hair, acne -scarred skin and a paunch. Given he was a fé, I didn't believe his appearance wasn't an illusion for a second. Apparently, he was exempt from the rules.

"Ms. Gault. It's good to see you." Pryce's quiet voice broke the momentary silence. He squinted and smiled. "Does the dragon have a name?"

Well, crap.

PINNED BY THE ATTENTION, I concentrated on not gulping. "His, ah, his name is Noir." I had no idea why the name had appealed, but it suited him. The dragon poked his head out from my hair, and he twisted to look at me, eyes shining like inky jewels.

Johann rolled his eyes. "Of course. Imagination has never been your strong point."

How nice of him to comment on my answer to another person's question. He never failed to annoy.

Stepping into the room was rather like entering a zoo cage, with a bunch of beautiful predatory creatures all staring at me, trying to decide whether or not they were ready to take a bite. A weak part of me took comfort in Nick's presence, especially given my weakened state.

I'd met Pryce once before. Charisma radiated from him, drawing the eye and attention, even if you didn't want to look at him.

Next around the table was an auburn-haired woman with gray eyes and an unreal beauty that stole the breath. A daoine sidhe, a child of the day court, though child was hardly an appropriate word for this woman, who was new to me.

It was strange having someone different here. The daoine didn't generally delegate power. I would have expected to see Rhys, the current leader in the area, known to me only by description. Though I'd heard gossip he'd stepped back from some of his duties while trying to find a way to rescue his sister from the dominion of the House of Mists.

I shivered. She'd been involved in making Bliss, the drug of choice for the supernaturals, but the legends I'd heard about that place made Hell pale in comparison.

The next was a man I'd missed in my initial evaluation of the room. Seated far back in his chair, inconspicuous, I guessed him to be a rusalka. Not least because a mist rolled around him, thinning as I watched. The humans had the rusalka folklore down as them being primarily female, which wasn't true in the least. The easiest way to describe a rusalka was water demon, though technically they weren't demons at all.

Creepy? Absolutely. But not demonic. Their bodies were made entirely of water, but magic helped them achieve a humanesque shape. Their power grew from drowning living things. The more they drowned, the more powerful they grew.

Lovely.

Like Johann, he was not beautiful. The flesh of his face was pulled tighter than an elderly actor trying to regain their youth. His skin gleamed with a liquid sheen, like a skull painted with liquid make up. He regarded me with eyes like black pits.

Finally, Johann Schmidt. Since I'd seen him last, his aquiline nose had become more crooked, as if it had been broken several times in the past month. He grinned at me, his teeth uneven and yellowed.

None of it real. He was a fé, illusion his power to call. It said something about him that he'd chosen this appearance.

"Who invited you?" In contrast to his appearance, his voice was mellow and pleasant.

"The yaksha appointed me their representative, since they couldn't come." I walked to the chair furthest from all of them and sat, the rusalka my nearest companion. Yeesh. I ignored the urge to shiver.

The oval conference table shone golden in the bright light. Made of heavy wood, it appeared massive and heavy enough that it would be difficult even for a troll to lift. Several wooden chairs remained empty. Noir hopped to the arm of my chair as Nick settled himself beside me.

All eyes had moved to the tiny dragon. I tried to pretend he wasn't there as he twined his supple neck around my finger.

The rusalka leaned forward as avarice lit the daoine sidhe's pale gray eyes. Fear and anger rippled down my spine as I fought to keep my expression neutral. I hated being looked at as a thing, and the dragon was a manifestation of my being and the chaos magic. Even more of an object from their perspective, and proof of my power.

Perhaps I should have let him fade, but his beauty called to me.

Thankfully, Pryce's expression didn't change, but Johann's brows climbed up his broad forehead like two caterpillars.

The daoine sidhe tore her gaze from the dragon and then frowned at me. "Introductions, Schmidt."

"Of course. Ceridwen Alarie, this is Ariana mac Diarmud, the representative for the daoine sidhe." He nodded to the man at my side. "This is Vasily, for the Rusalki. I believe you know Thomas Pryce, and of course we're well acquainted." His voice dripped innuendo.

That son of a bitch. He'd introduced me under the name I'd had him bury all those years ago when I first came here. The name I'd shared with the husband who'd sold me and our daughter to the lilim kin when he'd discovered I was a mage.

"Alarie? Wasn't there an incident, a clan of lilim dying in a fire, and..." Ariana trailed off, glancing from Pryce to me.

Pryce didn't turn a hair. "It's not a unique surname, though unusual, to be sure." My heart pounded in my chest. If they found out about all of that, who knew what that would mean for me, yaksha protection be damned.

Schmidt cleared his throat. "Ceridwen is a mage, under yaksha protection."

Ariana gave a musical chuckle. "That's rich. How will they hold her? Threaten my garden with mites? Blight my grass?"

Schmidt arched one eyebrow. "Ask me to back them up, since I made an edict against poaching personnel a long time ago? You should make sure you know the rules in my territory, Ariana, so you don't accidentally break them." Still mellow, his voice darkened with menace. It was odd, Johann wasn't usually this overbearing out of negotiations. It was as if he were seeking to provoke the daoine sidhe representative. I'd heard there had been troubles between them in the autumn. Maybe he wanted a reason to fight.

In the silence that followed, I spoke. "I go by Ceri Gault here. Please address me by that name." My voice was sharper than I intended, and Vasily glanced at me, something stirring in the black pits that marked his eyes, like a monster just under the water's surface.

A brittle pause, then Johann continued, "This is Nick Damarian. You're all acquainted, correct?"

Nick hadn't taken his eyes off Ariana since she spoke. "Yes," he said in a voice as dark as his skin.

"To return to the matter under discussion, what is the best way to dispose of Lucas Wheeler? He's scheduled to arrive in Columbus in the middle of next week." Johann set the tips of his fingers together and regarded all those at the table, one by one. "I am open to receiving suggestions but remember that mine is the final say in this matter."

I'd done a search on the man and his show, Wraith Stalkers, on the way here before the phone reception had cut out. Information was power, and I needed power in this room.

Vasily lifted his hand up and said, "I can drown him." I would've expected his voice to gurgle or sound watery, but instead, it was a friendly baritone. As if he were volunteering to bring the chairs to the family BBQ.

Arianna shrugged and picked up her tablet. "Flip a coin. Killing is easy. Buying him would be fairly simple as well, and then we could use him as an asset. The show has high ratings and could be used to direct attention as we prefer."

I noted to myself that an asset for the daoine sidhe was not an asset for anyone else. Also, that if one of the powers here spoke for not killing him, why had Nimaya told me the human was in danger?

"Killing him and the crew would be wasteful, not to say, noticeable." Pryce folded his hands on the table and looked around at the factions in the room. "Moreover, as my peer has stated, we can make use of the show and the man as an ongoing method of disinformation and a money-making tool. Investment would be minimal. After fifteen minutes interacting with

Wheeler, he'll gladly do whatever I suggest. His crew follows his lead."

Lilim or daoine sidhe fighting for an asset. Both would prefer him dead than belonging to the other kins. That was why the yaksha had told me.

"What was your plan when coming into this conference?" Nick asked, eyes on Schmidt.

Greasy hair shifted on his ratty t-shirt as Schmidt shrugged. "Fatal fentanyl dose. Then put the body with the drugs in a hotel room."

"That seems hasty." Pryce's smooth voice soothed me...not at all.

Johann frowned. "I've researched him. Wheeler is actually competent at what he does. That's the last thing we need here given the current situation. He's a skeptic, but he wants to believe, and we have plenty of real activity going on. Digging will uncover things we want to stay buried. He can't make us public if he's dead."

Controlling my flinch was difficult. Killing as a first solution was unlike Johann, which meant he was deadly serious.

He still caught the slight motion and smiled at me. "Not to be rude, but could you let me know where you got your little friend there? And when? And who has seen it?"

The dragon preened under his gaze. It extended wings like gauzy shadows.

"It formed earlier this evening. Nick, the rest of the

people here, and I, are the only people who've seen it." No need for them to know the girls saw it, too. I scratched the little guy between the wings. "There was an unbodied hunting near the yaksha territory. Nick took care of it."

"You never disappoint, Ceridwen. Informative as ever." Johann considered the dragon.

"It's because I care." I bared my teeth at him in an unfriendly smile.

He turned his attention to Nick. "An unbodied?"

Nick nodded. "Yes. Definitely an unbodied. A mercenary I think, since they don't typically linger where they can't feed, and Ceri had gone behind the yaksha wards. He couldn't attack until after she came out, and they're not typically known for patience."

He hadn't told me that. Annoyance flickered in me.

"I had heard about a contract on you." Johann regarded me with secretive brown eyes. Too bad I hadn't heard about a contract. "Do you have any suggestions on what to do about this human? You're the closest to human here, so you should speak for them."

This was the opportunity I'd been waiting for. I wasn't going to waste it asking about the contract. There'd be time for that later. "I suggest approaching him and convincing him that what's been happening is all faked. It fits in with his mindset and doesn't involve casually murdering someone. Or raping their mind. Then he'd leave and we could go on with our lives."

A faint snort of laughter from, of all sources, Vasily.

"Murder keeps people quiet, though. And provides decorations."

Ariana's nostrils flared with distaste. Pryce sighed.

I chose to ignore the comment. "Why don't you give me a couple of days to do this. After all, he's not a threat until he broadcasts. Drastic solutions can be applied if he gets proof and if I fail."

"True." Pryce nodded, his eyes meeting Ariana's in a clash like swords. "It does save the strain of contention over a potential asset."

Her answering smile cut like a razor.

"Keep in mind that the fentanyl solution is the one that will be employed if you fail, Ceridwen. The man's life is in your hands. Have a nice day." The curve of Johann's lips could not even charitably be called a smile.

The dragon hissed at him. Everyone froze, including me. It would make life difficult if it echoed my emotions that obviously. Not cool, little dude.

"It's manifested enough to make noise?" Johann walked to my side. The tiny dragon, still perched, flapped its wings at him, stirring a faint breeze.

"You need to control your pet better." Ariana spoke and for a moment I thought she was telling Nick to control me. My anger spiked, but her eyes focused on the dragon. "This will cause many troubles if it's loose. Can she control it? I could."

"I remind you that Ceridwen is a mage, with all

that entails," Johann replied dryly. "Of all of us, she can contain it best."

I wondered at his defense, but it seemed best to appear as if I had the situation under control. Stroking my hand down the dragon's back, I moved him to my lap, out of sight. He cooperated, nipping my fingers until he settled in a position he liked.

"So, on the topic of the human, we are decided? No drowning?" Vasily asked.

"No drowning." Johann nodded at me. "Ceridwen has a week to let us know if she succeeds or fails."

I made a protesting noise, which he ignored. No pressure—I needed even more time, and I wasn't going to get it.

Assent echoed around the table. Ariana rose and nodded to Johann. "Goodbye."

"Sit down." Johann's voice rang like the crack of doom. He stared at her until she settled back in her seat. Then he rose. "I bid you all good evening." And left. Wow. Power move.

A glance at Ariana's expression chilled my blood. Witnessing homicidal rage often did that.

There was no way Johann had provoked her like that unintentionally. He was probably trying to avert an incident, to focus her on him rather than on her obviously forming plans to take me from the yakshas, in violation of his rules. Less effort than the conflict that would break out when she broke his rules, and he had to punish her and the other daoine sidhe. Again.

On our way out of the building, I tapped Nick's hand. "You didn't make any suggestions."

"I would only suggest something I didn't want Schmidt to do. He's not a big fan of mine." He squeezed my hand. I let mine linger in his for a moment before I pulled it away.

I t was a brisk walk back to my car from the safe spot we'd left Nick's truck. Ice and snow crackled underfoot as we approached it. The dragon had fallen asleep, so I'd zipped him into my coat, tucked against me so the contact would sustain him. Above, the sky was clear and flecked with stars, and our breath puffed tiny clouds as we spoke.

A patina of ice and snow layered my vehicle, and we scraped the windshield. Nick tugged his gloves off, placing his palms on the now clear area. "It would be better if you bought cars made of something reasonable, rather than plastic."

"Says the man who drives a steel box. Can you fix it?" I crossed my arms, tucking my hands under my armpits in a feeble attempt to keep them warm.

He shot me a grin. "Yes, but plastic is just a pain to deal with."

I stared out into the dark as he worked, trying to ignore the freezing cold. The hair on my neck did that prickling thing that said danger was near. I opened myself up to all my senses, using my natural abilities to seek out potential threats.

Shadows moved wrong in the moonlight. The breeze tended from the west, moving the branches in that direction, and these scraps of darkness moved to the east. "Nick, incoming!" I screeched.

He spun away from the car, knife flickering into his hand.

At the sound of my words, attackers broke their cover of illusions and darkness. Humanoid, but gaunt and withered, their limbs twisted and gnarly.

Dregs. Supernatural creatures almost lost to their addiction to Bliss. At least these opponents were still alive. Addicts who had degenerated physically, becoming warped shadows of their former selves. For hire to anyone who gave them their drug of choice.

Johann had driven out the production of Bliss, one of the few things I gave him credit for. The filthy drug was manufactured in part by destroying innocence. In the minds of the Bliss makers, human children were cheap and plentiful sources.

Yanking the surrounding ribbons of magic close, I called light and fire to me. Noir took flight straight up. The power manifested as bright light, illuminating the mass of malformed shapes. Their claws and teeth gleamed wetly in the light.

Despite knowing what they were, I still hesitated to let the fire loose on them. My pause lasted only until the swarm closed in on me, their fetid smell like decay and rot. A ragged claw scored my arm with a quick, bright shock of pain.

Hands clamped on me, dragging me up and away from Nick, scoring my skin. Noir swooped, slapping his wings in the face of one of the dregs, pushing that attacker back. My blood flowed down my arm, shockingly warm in the cold. The first technique the kins employed against mages was fear and pain, to scatter their will. I'd lived long enough to learn to focus through it, to use fear to sharpen my will working.

The fire roared out in a circle from me in a tidal wave, engulfing my surroundings. The sudden heat baked my mouth dry, but it did its job. The fire ignited the dregs who held me, and I dropped to the snow, my coat smoldering even though I'd protected myself from the blast. Screams tore at my ears as the dregs burned next to me, some collapsing, others trying to run.

The stink of burning flesh made me retch until I had to back out of the pile of burned dregs. So many of them, all now dead. My head ached, and when I licked my lips, I tasted blood. A sudden weight hit my shoulder, my little dragon's head stroked against my cheek. He wasn't *that* heavy, but I was frikkin' exhausted.

Nick maneuvered around the pile, holding his hands out. His silver eyes caught mine, full of worry and sympathy. "Drop the fire, Ceri. Let's get you home."

My headache peaked an hour later as he drove us home in my car. Noir sat in my lap, comforting me. I didn't ask how Nick would get back to his truck, the pain in my head too intense. It narrowed my world to a pin pick, occupying all of my attention.

In a distant dream, Nick picked me up and carried me into my house and then to my bed. With gentle tugs he took my shoes off. He pulled an old blanket from the linen closet and wrapped me in it after he removed my coat.

I barely registered the pillow dipping as Noir settled beside me.

"I'm going to clean up those cuts," Nick whispered in my ear. "Just relax, everything's taken care of."

The sting of disinfectant woke me from the drowsiness that swept over me. "Nick?"

"Yes? I'll be done soon. Just need to make sure they all have antibiotic cream on them."

Such a sweet man. "The contract is why they attacked us, isn't it? How do I find out who's behind it?"

"You could talk to Bleys. He's a lilim, and they're tapped into all the gossip. I'll try to find out tonight while you sleep. You've done too much, Ceri." He finished applying antibiotic cream and started applying Band-Aidsband aids and bandages to the deeper cuts.

I sighed. "I should have stayed hidden."

He chuckled, his voice deep and rich. "No, it was killing you day by day. You're happier now, I think."

He was right. Even if my head hurt, I felt more alive.

Nick settled down onto the knotted rag rug at the side of my bed. "Go to sleep. I'm here, and I'll let your son know what's going on when he gets here or wakes up."

A responsible adult. I let exhaustion overcome me, grateful for the refuge from pain.

I WOKE to the delicious aroma of frying bacon. The throbbing in my head had settled to a bearable level, for which I was grateful. Sitting up, I grimaced. Going to sleep still wearing all my blood- covered clothing, including a bra, had not made for a sweet- smelling me or clothing that didn't look like it had gone nine rounds and lost.

The shadowy dragon's cool nose brushed my knuckles. I glanced down, and it nudged my hip before it waddled up the bed and collapsed on the pillow, tucking its head under a wing.

An immediate shower was called for, and then I'd see if the clothing could be salvaged or if it was too ripped and bloodied. I slid out of bed and Nick called from the kitchen area, "Get your shower in, there's plenty of time before this is ready."

Svartalfar noses were almost as sensitive as their hearing. A snicker popped out of me—such a delicate hint on his part. He wanted me to have a shower as much as I wanted one. A sprig of hope bloomed in me as I turned on the hot water. The fact he'd spent the night hadn't roused reflexive anger or fear. There was hope for starting a relationship with him. My inner demons weren't protesting this morning. How nice.

The two others I'd tried to build a relationship with had run afoul of the deep well of anger I'd created when I was on the run before Jimmy was born. Risking discovery, I'd created a construct in my mind, where I could dump emotions that got in the way. But when I'd created it, I hadn't put in a way to let them out. They occasionally seeped out, flaring up at times, always when I grew close to a man.

And therapy wasn't an option, for obvious reasons. Mandated reporters hearing about kidnapping, drugging, coercion and worse would go to the police immediately. Or put me on a psych hold, since I lacked proof. Neither was an option I could afford. Perhaps enough anger had trickled out that Nick wouldn't be exposed to a savage fit of temper and run. I probably should warn him about my inner demons at some point. At least give him a heads up.

Steamy water streamed over me as the smells of oranges and mint from the soap and shampoo soothed the worry.

When I came out, scrubbed and changed, my hair in a stubby wet braid, Nickkki had plated bacon, scrambled eggs and toast, with butter and black raspberry jelly on the table. He'd already started on his portion, which was twice the size of mine.

"Lavish." I settled down and started eating.

Noir perched on the side of the table. Nick dabbed jelly and butter on another plate, then placed a spoonful of eggs, a slice of toast and a strip of bacon. The dragon carefully dipped the toast in the jelly. I hadn't noticed he had delicate forelegs in addition to wings that he kept tucked against his chest.

Why would he eat? The dragon was made of pure magic.

As if he read my mind, Nick said, "You need it, so he needs it. You expended a lot of energy yesterday. Do you feel better?" His hair combed back but not yet dry indicated Nick had taken advantage of the guest bathroom.

How had he gotten a change of clothes? Did I want to know? Savoring the scrambled eggs, light and fluffy and cheesy, I decided not to ask.

I splurged, spreading the toast with jam. My waistline could deal with it. "The headache's mostly gone. Are you willing to help me save the lives of Wheeler and his production crew?"

"Of course. But keep in mind that if Wheeler isn't willing to be saved, what happens later is not your fault." Nick's calm gaze met my own.

The toast took a quick trip back to my plate. He was right.

I shivered. There were days I felt I had to keep

reminding myself that I *was* human. Not that humans were above killing, but the bloody-minded casualness from some of the kins about violence bothered me.

Nick continued, "I'm worried about these attacks on you. Dregs are cheap to hire. An unbodied? That costs a premium and requires specialized skills. It almost looks like two different attempts, one to kill you and one to frighten or capture. The dregs weren't really trying to hit you. It looked like they were trying to herd you." He tapped his fingers on the table. "Though the unbodied could've drained you and left you too weak to resist another creature picking you up..."

I swallowed. "I killed them for nothing?"

The dragon paused in his delicate nibbling of jam and toast to stroke my arm with his head.

"No, you killed them to defend yourself. I would have, but you acted faster. You need to rest from using your magic until you heal. The strain can kill you. I've seen it happen."

"How many mages have you known?" I squinted my eyes at him. There weren't a whole lot of us around.

"A few. Some were wild. And no, I'm not going to tell you how old I am." He tempered the words with a smile.

Nick reached for a slice of my bacon, and I swatted his hand. "What's key is that whoever offered these contracts has apparently decided to ignore Johann's territory and edicts."

He nodded. "Which makes them powerful, stupid, or both. But they would see you as a prize, you know that. You need to be more careful, Ceri."

"I know. But I don't want to go back to living in hiding. We can't, now that Jimmy is outed too, and Dara. Both of my children. I'm hoping that since these initial attacks have been repelled successfully that there won't be many more. Or that Johann acts. He's not one to put up with people violating his rules. If there's one thing he's good for, it's protecting what he considers his. Jimmy working for him means he's under his protection."

"Yeah. And it would be better if you were too. The yaksha just aren't powerful enough to drive off people hunting you." Nick regarded me. "What did Johann do to upset you so much?"

I spread my hands, one still sticky with jelly. "It's hard to articulate. I don't trust Johann. I don't much trust his contracts. I don't trust his words." It was more a feeling I had about him. A sense of danger.

"But he's a fé. They're bound by their words." Nick's brows dipped.

It was a good thing I trusted this guy. I told him the truth. "I don't believe that he's a fé. He poses as one, but he doesn't feel like one."

To my surprise, Nick didn't laugh at me at all. He reached over, his expression thoughtful, and served himself more scrambled eggs. "Your intuition tells you that?"

He respected me enough to take me seriously. Very good. "It does. And my intuition is generally pretty good."

"What does your intuition tell you about me?" He smiled at me and winked so I nearly snorted in my orange juice.

"That I can trust you to be in my home when I'm asleep. Which is a huge thing for me. A big step." I reached out with my non-jellied hand, and he took it, carrying it to his lips. The silver bracelet gleamed in the morning light.

"Anything else?" His brown eyes were warm as they drifted over me.

Flustered, I tugged my hand and he let it go. "Maybe? I don't know. I want to, but I'm not sure."

He sighed and ate more eggs, moving the subject to a more stressful but less flustery subject. "What's your plan to keep Wheeler alive?"

"I'm pretty sure that the cameras or whatever they use to film, have metal in them. And you manipulate metal. If they have a catastrophic malfunction while they're filming, that would be good. Also getting in contact with whomever Johann's lawyers are and making sure that no trespassing signs are posted on his land. If Wheeler shows up there, having a letter ready to tell him that he can't record in the area."

Nick looked at Noir. The little dragon finished the food on his plate and sidled toward the jelly. I moved it next to my plate and got a dirty look for my efforts to keep him out of the sugary food.

I sighed. "Yes. I know that the manifestations have crept out of that area. But at least the areas where it's highly likely he'll see something will be concealed. As for the rest—I don't like using mind magic. Unlike lilim, I don't like to just change people's' minds and emotions for my convenience. But if the alternative is him dead, I will."

"It's not a bad plan. But it presupposes that you know where they're going to be and when they're going to be there. I can't exactly sabotage their equipment from across the city just by thinking about it. You know I need to see it or touch it, Ceri. Svartalfar, not mage."

Crud. It was a good idea, but most ideas were good at first. "Good point. Do you have any suggestions on how I could find out?"

"Perhaps Bleys?"

I grimaced. Bleys was the lilim who had been in charge of monitoring me and collecting my tithe to the lilim clan when I used to pose as a thin-blooded lilim. Not a bad man, but I preferred to avoid lilim when I could. I had too many bad memories where they were the stars.

On the other hand, Bleys actually had a decent number of connections in a variety of endeavors. The show coming here had stirred up quite a bit of interest from ghost hunting enthusiasts. He might even be a fan. It seemed the kind of show that would appeal to him. He liked laughing at skeptics explaining away the truth.

I grimaced. "You're right. I'll text him. He'll want a favor, though."

"Just make sure you hammer out precisely what the favor is before you agree," Nick said, carrying our plates to the sink. "Since you're feeling better, I have some leftover work that I have to be at the lab to finish. Give me a call if you need me. Let me know when you finish with Bleys so we can work out a firmer plan."

Back at the table, he leaned over, and his lips brushed my cheek. I leaned into the caress, and he paused, his brows raised questioningly as he glanced at the couch, the question in his eyes both amused and hopeful.

My cheeks heated. Nick always called up a mix of confusion and desire in me, tempered by wistfulness. I didn't want to hurt him, but I wasn't sure if I could handle being really physical with him. Or anyone. It hadn't gone well in the few relationships I'd had before.

A wry smile quirked his mouth in answer to my blush and he headed out the door.

Regret smacked me as the door closed. I pushed it aside and texted Bleys.

Do you have schedule information for stalking-wraith episode being filmed this week?

During the wait for his answer, I started grading

assignments. I'd only gotten a few done when my phone chimed.

Not that I can share. Pryce said if you want the information to call him. Bleys helpfully followed up by texting the number.

Nice. And ugh.

I regarded my phone as if it were an angry snake, then sighed. I had no choice. Pryce had boxed me into the conversation. At least he hadn't demanded a personal meeting. That was a good thing.

He picked up immediately. "Good afternoon."

"Mr. Pryce. I'd like the shooting schedule if your organization has it."

"We do. What is your offer?" He sounded as pleasant on the ear over the phone as he did in person. Even if I didn't like what he was saying. Or him.

"A starting price would be helpful." I snapped the words, cursing myself for getting involved in all this mess to begin with.

"I'd like an honest account from you of what happened on the day of the fire. The day a secret holding facility burned to the ground and a lilim family lost tremendous standing. The day you escaped with an infant and then absconded with the expensive fetch meant to replace you, leaving your spouse in a most awkward position, since he could no longer access your inheritance."

The statement floored me. "*Why?*"

A pleasant chuckle answered me before he spoke

again. "I like to know facts. They are in short supply for that incident."

I bit my lip. "And you'll give me the information I want?"

"You have my word." Oh, he was too damn smooth.

"And there will be no retaliation for that event?" That was a big potential problem.

"None from me. Nor will I pass this information on without informing you first." Calm and cool, his voice. That fire happened nineteen years ago. Why in the world did he care?

He'd *inform* me. Hmph. "No. I want to know who you're going to pass it on to with at least a day's notice. *And* to be able to veto passing it on at least once." This was a high price to pay, but if he didn't get it from me for this payment, he'd think of another reason to know my inner secrets.

He was silent for a good three seconds. "Agreed."

That promise was as good as I was going to get and better than I'd expected.

I swallowed as rage poured into me as I tried to shove it back into its prison. It went reluctantly, painfully. My throat hurt. Fear for my relationship with Nick mixed into the general anger. I didn't want to drive him away. "Okay. I'd been taken to the place for the, ah, *treatments* to make me more trustworthy."

Memories crowded into my mind. Treatment was a nice, clinical word for what had happened. Aching exhaustion, lights beating through my closed eyelids night and day. So hungry I'd have eaten whatever they'd brought, my throat cracking with the need for water. Even when I knew it was drugged.

They'd pinned my arms and legs pinned so the joints hurt no matter how I shifted. A lilim stayed in the room with me while I was blindfolded, playing games with my emotions. Unwelcome hands on me, all over me.

I'd cried and agreed to do whatever they'd wanted, just so they'd bring Dara back to me. I'd slept, her tiny body snuggled next to me, knowing I'd obey just to keep her with me. Even if I couldn't keep her safe. Shame scalded me at that memory. I'd given in. I'd relented.

Then, the day I woke vomiting, with my breasts tender, I'd realized I was pregnant. A baby to be born a slave, like me and my daughter. Rage had given me the strength to gather my will, pulling the ribbons of magic to call fire and smoke from thin air. Forcing it into the hall, a searing choking wave. Shouting and screaming in the halls. Pure chaos, and not the magical kind. Just panic.

The doors had opened at my will. It'd been the only time I'd been able to force a lock. Running through the empty compound, into the street, hiding and running, my daughter on my hip and my son in my belly. I'd gotten us free.

Any price had been worth that.

I wasn't proud of the thefts I'd done afterward, but

I'd sent money anonymously to the stores when I eventually got a job.

"I understand what the treatments entail. Details aren't needed." His voice held a hint of unexpected gentleness.

"Two months in, I figured out I was pregnant." I said it baldly. "They'd let me have Dara with me in the holding cell, rather than taking her away, since I was, quote *responding well* to the treatments. The shock when I knew I'd gotten pregnant gave me the focus needed to grab her and run. I went to the house to grab what money I could, and my fetch was there. She was a victim too, so I persuaded her to run with me. It wasn't hard to convince her. She didn't like my ex."

He hissed a breath in through his teeth. "I see. Did you ever see the lilim involved in the conditioning?"

"No. They took precautions." My voice was flatter than the great plains. I didn't want to relive that time in my life, coping with flashbacks and withdrawal from the drugs they'd used was bad enough. A surge of anger poured over me, and I gritted my teeth. I picked up a magazine from the end table and began shredding it, methodically destroying it as I cradled the phone to my ear with my shoulder.

It fell to the floor.

"Ms. Gault?"

"I'm still here. There's nothing more to tell. The rest is history that has nothing to do with your people." I couldn't help the curtness of my words. It took everything in me to squeeze them out. The anger resisted being pushed back down.

"Very well," he said matter of factly. "The crew is already in the city. Tuesday will be two separate day shoots, each at a different location. I'm sending the details to your phone now. There will be a night shoot on Wednesday, in an isolated area near where Schmidt lives. That would be the area where they'd be most likely to see unusual activity."

"Understood. Goodbye." I hung up without thanking him, considering the price he'd made me pay, and continued shredding the magazine. It felt good. I continued through the rest of the magazines, in hopes that it would vent the overflow and not pour out on Nick when I saw him next. I had to vent what I couldn't contain. To calm myself down.

The dragon watched me. When I was done, the floor was covered in shreds, I was sweaty with effort, but I did feel marginally better. The little chaos creature pounced on the shreds that fluttered to the floor. He rolled in them, and the shreds clung to him, even when he shook himself and his wings.

My laughter may have been semi-hysterical but watching him brought a gush of cleansing amusement. I had two classes worth of grading to do, the Crucible to reread, and wards to reinforce. The wards would come first, since I was alone. I didn't relish the idea of dregs or an unbodied in my home if they found a crack.

I closed my eyes, the better to see fine details with

my inner eye. Noir glowed next to me, magic and flesh. I tucked the surprise at his increasing physicality away to be considered when I had fewer distractions. The bracelet gleamed with the magic that concentrated 'in the clasp. I turned my gaze outward, to the edges of my property. I'd anchored the wards with my blood, painted on stones I'd buried when we moved here. The lines shone, steady but lower powered than I liked. I wove ribbons of magic into it. The wards detected intent, rather than the kind of creature that passed it, which was how Nick had passed it even though he was of the kins.

I was glad I'd gone that route. In the past, I would have shunned him based on that and lost a good friend.

When I was done, my ward shone pale blue and flickered with red. I'd added a jolt to drive the ill intended away, rather than simply barring their passage.

Housekeeping on a whole 'nother level, that.

I called Lotus, the woman who handled most of Johann's administrative work, while I swept up the paper scraps. She was an apsara, a kin concentrated usually in modern India, but she and her family lived in Columbus and charged Johann a premium for her services. I'd never had any troubles dealing with her, thankfully.

She told me she'd email the legal papers to me and set the trolls on posting signs.

Unfortunately, the place where the show planned to film didn't belong to Johann.

Nothing to be done about it. I had other matters to attend to as well. Halfway through the grading, my doorbell chimed. The security feed showed me a courier in uniform, waiting with a box. He'd passed the wards. I examined the box as well. No magic from any kin permeated it. Nothing to compel me to drop my wards, or step outside.

After signing for it, I carried it to the coffee table. The dragon, draped on the couch, stirred sleepily.

Within, another box sparkled. It was gift- wrapped in silver, glitter-covered, gold, metallic paper, with a blue velvet bow and a plain white card with script printed on the front.

Because human life is precious.

It was signed by Pryce. I had no idea how to take that. He was so confusing.

Within was a thumb drive with the entire itinerary of the show while it was in the city.

This *was* important.

I texted the shoot locations to Nick. One was close to Johann's home, where a ghost had allegedly been seen. If it had been an unbodied, none of the humans would have made it out alive. It had to have been some- thing else.

Nick replied a minute later.

I'll go there today and scout it. Will let you know what the terrain is like. Keep

grading. Complete with little fox emoji wagging a finger at me.

I settled back into the couch and Noir crawled into my lap. He extended his head, much like a cat asking for a scratch. I obliged.

Yes, Nick could tramp in the snow and cold while I graded papers. I sighed in relief. Anger had stirred, a little, but nothing like had happened before, when I drove men away screaming.

I'd shred a library if that was what it took.

Johann lived an hour and a half away. Part of the agreement when he hired Jimmy was that my son would be given transport when road conditions were bad, as they had been. Santo, a troll who worked for Johann, drove Jimmy here in bad weather. I'd gotten used to him, but the thought of my son riding with a reformed man-eater was only slightly better than him being in an accident by himself.

As if on cue, Jimmy slammed in. "Hi, Mom."

I set my pen down and grinned at him. "Hi yourself. Done for the weekend?"

"Yeah. Can Liz come over?" He headed straight for the fridge, then came back with a cheese stick and cola.

"Yes, of course." His girlfriend had an open-ended invitation, but Jimmy tried to remember to ask, which was sweet. "Is your homework done?"

He sighed heavily. "Not yet. Santo said I didn't need a diploma to work for Johann, you know? And full time pays a lot."

It must've been nice to know everything and not worry about the future. I missed that from my teenage years. I sighed, trying to think of a neutral answer that wouldn't ruffle his feathers, then decided to state the issue up front. "Only if it's what you want to do exclusively for the rest of your life. If he fires you, where are you then?" I raised my eyebrows.

Jimmy stared at me and snorted.

"Yes?" It took effort to keep the edge out of my voice.

"Running from mage hunters?" He raised an ironic eyebrow, in clear imitation of Johann.

I moved Noir out of my lap and got up and paced, still a little jittery.

"Mom?"

"Hmm?" I didn't look at him as I paced off my nerves.

"Why is there a little dragon on the couch?" Jimmy stared at Noir, who stared back and stretched his wings.

I couldn't help but grin at the little guy. "He followed me home, so I've decided to keep him. Back to the point, on the run, you still need skills to earn a living. And Johann already agreed not to interfere with your schooling. I'll only put up with so much blackmail, and I won't have your chance at a good future endangered."

Jimmy sighed, then gave me his quick, shy grin.

"For an evil overlord, he's ok. He said the same thing you just did."

That was hard to swallow, even as the mischievous gleam in his eyes melted the anger away. His sister Dara had the same trick. I missed her, but she'd decided that travel was her way to be safe. The farther she was away from here, the safer she was for the moment. Once she was home, I'd teach her as well as Jimmy more about their magic.

Noir hopped off the couch and waddled over to Jimmy, who stooped to pet him, a foolish smile curving his mouth. "Liz'll love him."

Indeed.

SUNDAY MORNING, before I had a chance to start worrying, Nick texted me. **Need to do some preparation. Are you and Jimmy available?**

Jimmy had finished his homework and spent most of the night watching movies with Liz. He could sleep in the car.

Yes.

His reply came within seconds of sending mine, as if he'd had it ready to send as soon as my affirmation came through. **Meet me at Cheese and All at One. The reception is poor where we're going.**

Cheese and All was a diner near Johann's property. Since Jimmy had started his job, I'd been there twice. The food wasn't bad, but I didn't think that was the reason for the rendezvous.

Chasing Jimmy out of bed and into the shower took

the better part of an hour. Noir settled on his lap in the car and both of them went to sleep as soon as we started moving. He and Liz had been up far later than they'd promised. Again.

Nick's pickup waited in the parking lot of the restaurant. He leaned against the door, sipping a hot drink. The smell of coffee hit me as I got out and left Jimmy slouched in the passenger seat, snoozing. He'd zipped Noir into his coat at my request and had his arms cradled around the lump.

"What are we going to be doing?" I asked.

He grinned at me, his expression more wry than normal. His eyes seemed tired. "We're building a blind. The crew is in Columbus right now. I've got a friend watching them and keeping me updated. The crew has looked over the site—the place where the show's going to shoot the segment on ghosts has all their tracks. I scouted in the woods around the clearing, and I found other tracks—the crew is being observed by people with very good woodcraft. I can't tell what they are, but I'm treating this as a hazardous situation. So we're going to build a place where we can spy on the filming that's separate from the house that Johann has on the hill. That will be observed by anyone with half a brain, and surely a production team with a show this popular knows a few things."

This was genius. "So, a hunting blind kind of thing?"

Nick looked a little proud of himself, as he should

have. "Yes. That's why I asked you to bring Jimmy. He needs more exercise."

I swallowed a nervous laugh. "This will be fun."

Building the blind meant working in the chill for several hours with Jimmy complaining nonstop. He still did the work, but after a while I started fantasizing about gags.

Noir perched on one of the bare branches, moving occasionally and dislodging snow on top of us. The cold didn't seem to bother him as much as I expected it might. He just liked being cozy inside our coats.

"Why are we doing this? Just drive ten minutes and get Santo or Vittorio and this would be done in a snap." The whine in Jimmy's voice was pronounced.

Nick patted down the edge of the blind. "Because I don't know who the spies are in Johann's camp. Even with loyalty, he's going to have at least some, even if they spread the info he wants them to. Whatever is stalking the show is very good at what it does, and I'm not going to chance your mother being killed or captured because someone spoke the wrong words to the wrong person."

Jimmy's eyes narrowed. "We have our magic. Mom could drop anyone coming for her."

While his certainty was flattering, we needed to work on his overconfidence. But not today. I was freezing and had been fantasizing about hot coffee for an hour.

"We're done?" I directed the question to Nick.

"We're coming back to man it tomorrow morning, right? Since the shooting will be at night?"

"Just about. That's the plan." He squinted around. "Do you see the house from here?"

"Yes," I replied.

"I've semi cleared a path to it starting here. If we have to run from here, this is the best way to reach it. It has the fewest barriers. Because we'll be running as hard as we can."

Adrenaline skittered through my veins as I nodded. "Got it."

Nick walked to the place he'd indicated, and the brush seemed lighter there, though it wouldn't exactly be fun to run through. It sure would beat being dead, though.

"Coffee?" I asked.

"Let's go."

Noir hid under Jimmy's legs when I ordered. Caffeine and warm liquid improved my mood considerably, but Jimmy was uncharacteristically quiet on the drive home, obviously thinking.

As I pulled into the driveway, he spoke. "Mom, are we really in danger?"

Ah, the young. "We always are, Jimmy. But I don't want twenty -plus people killed because I was unwilling to face danger. With Nick helping, I think we'll be fine."

"I want to help." For all his complaining today, he would do the right thing. He was a good kid.

"You can come along if you're here. But school comes first, so get your homework done early."

His eye roll was epic as we went into the house.

O n Monday, after drama rehearsals, I settled on the couch with my Chinese food and checked submissions for the papers. As expected, Evan Kelly did not turn in his first draft. I'd gotten a message from the office that his mother had requested a conference as soon as possible.

In between work, the school play, and trying to keep people from being killed, I was swamped. She was gonna have to wait.

A saving grace for the play was that most of the kids knew their lines. They weren't as good about hitting their marks, though they were a little better than some groups I'd worked with in the past. The previous director had done a good job. I felt as if a giant hand of stress was pressing me like a grape, leaning until I was just wrinkled skin and pulp. I only had two more days before Wheeler arrived and every passing moment brought more stress.

Enjoying the crunchiness of sweet and sour chicken, I sighed. Evan Keller. That kid hadn't submitted his draft at all, *and* I'd allowed late submissions.

I set a small clump of rice, a piece of pineapple,

and a bit of chicken on a paper towel. Noir sniffed the chicken then ignored it. He ate the fruit and rice.

Jimmy was due home in another hour. He'd texted me he needed to finish a task Johann had given him.

There was going to have to be a discussion with Johann about working on school nights with Johann the next time I interacted with him. I could acquit him of malice. He did support education. But firm limits needed to be set where emergencies warred with Jimmy's grades.

Chewing on a pepper, I checked the local news on my phone and froze. I tapped the story as I swallowed hard, no longer enjoying the bite. In vivid color, a group of frightened teenagers ran from a huge, black, dog-like animal. I skimmed the story. It had happened close to where the shooting was to take place. One of the teens had used his phone to record the chase after he climbed a tree.

The dog looked like nothing that should be in this world. Glassy black fur, red eyes, teeth almost as black as its pelt, saliva that burned into the dirt—and it had vanished while chasing them, as if the energy creating it had run out.

Wonderful. Johann had been asleep at the switch. His people should have suppressed this long before it hit the news.

As if the thought summoned him, my phone rang. I glanced down at the screen. Johann.

"Hello?" I answered in a sour voice.

"I assume you've seen the news. I'm calling to ask if you can come by and see what you can do to strengthen the wards. What Drake and I have set up does not seem to be stopping enough of the energies Katie sheds." Johann's tone was clipped and distracted.

A smile curved my mouth. I'd wanted to use Johann's line for years. "Certainly. And at that time, we will discuss my fee."

I shoveled more chicken into my mouth, grabbed my key fob, scribbled a note for Jimmy, and headed out, Noir beating me to the car.

DARK STRANDS OF MAGIC, flickering with opalescent light, filled the windshield. I could see the road through them, but the mass was so distracting I had to pull to the side of the road. It was like driving through a whiteout snowstorm. I zipped my little dragon into my coat, and he chirruped sleepily.

The constant slither of silky, black ribbons of magic couldn't be blocked, intruding on normal sight. They wrapped around me, almost tangible when I got out of the car. Johann's property was buried in it. I waded forward, like walking through water.

The ward they'd set up wasn't far from my stopping point. Most kins didn't perceive magic other than their own talents, which was good. Otherwise, they'd have run screaming to get out of the seething mass of chaos magic within the ward. As I walked down the private road, the subtle, moonlight gleam of it beckoned me. To the inner eye, it glimmered white, streaked with metallic gray, cutting through the dimmer colors of the ambient chaos. The ward blended two people's magic in a lattice work so fine I would not have been able to see the gaps. Beautiful workmanship. Most kins could make wards of one type or another, but I'd never seen anything like this.

It might've even been able to imprison my magic, but I didn't think it could be affixed to a living being. Its roots sanksunk into the earth and its top reached for the sky, overarching and creating a sphere to contain the energies within.

The ribbons of chaos magic, apparently infinitely compressible, wormed through the gaps I couldn't see, making the ward look like dark seaweed grew all over it. A lovely and dangerous sight.

The length of the ribbons on the wall remained constant, perhaps a foot or so. Magic flaked off of them constantly in small globes that fluttered in the air, often joining other bits of magic in a collection like a swarm of bees. They drifted away from the ward in all directions.

As I approached, dodging bits of magic, the dragon struggled out of my coat and flew ahead of me, snapping at the bits and swallowing them. It gained mass as I watched.

I hurried forward and tapped its nose. "Stop that. You'll get too big."

It eyed me with its dark opal eyes, then shrank back to its original size.

How did it do that? The more I found out about this little thing the more I realized I didn't know.

Traces of Jimmy's magic crackled around the weedy chaos magic but hadn't penetrated down to the ward.

"Why did you park down the road?" The low voice surprised me as I leaned forward to examine the ward, searching for a way my magic could evade the chaos ribbons.

I jumped, turning.

Johann and an unfamiliar man stood a few feet to my side. I hadn't heard or seen their approach while I concentrated, meaning they'd both moved very quietly.

"Thank you for coming. This is Drake." Johann gestured to the ward. "The ward is partly his magic. Can you perceive the issue?"

I turned my attention back to the ward. "Yes. I can see Jimmy tried to work on it. Is this the task that kept him from his homework?"

"Yes."

I shot Johann a bit of a glare. "I understand the emergency, but his homework is important. If he's still here..."

"He is."

I flared my nostrils. "Then tell him to start working on it while I work on this."

Still giving them a bit of a severe look, I turned my attention to Drake. He was a big man, taller than me by at least a foot and lean and muscular. Given his name, either he was a dragon, or I was intended to think him one. Dragons came in many shapes and sizes, but only a small percentage were able to assume human form. They were the most threatening of their kin, which started at dangerous and proceeded from there. Thousands of pounds of predatory scales and teeth and claws didn't normally make for good neighbors. I hoped he hadn't seen the nose pat.

My little dragon shifted on my shoulder, resting a foreleg on my ear and spreading its wings.

"Peace, little brother." Drake's voice was quiet and low. "She's safe with me."

Did dragons evolve from chaos? There were so many types...and I should be concentrating on the task at hand, not wondering if Drake had been really a tiny chaos dragon when he was born...or formed. Whatever.

"Why are you here?" I spoke quickly, smoothing the little dragon's tail.

"Drake will walk with you and take care of any issues so you can concentrate on fixing this. Jimmy did his best, but he couldn't figure out how to plug the leakage."

I nodded, turning back to the ward. I needed to teach Jimmy so many things, soon. How to ground his magic, how to see patterns in working—I hadn't before when I thought he hadn't inherited the talent, and he'd said he wanted to wait and see how he did by himself when I offered two months ago. I was going to need to insist.

Drake's large, quiet presence promised extreme violence to anyone who interfered. Good. I wanted to get this done and to get back home. I had to be up early.

Gingerly, I threaded my hand through the strands of magic, shivering a little at the silky texture. I was doing too much. I'd be lucky if the burnout was short, but this was an emergency.

The ward chilled my fingertips, rough and unyielding as stone.

Searching with my inner eye, I perceived the pinpricks as a part of the design of the ward. Their magic had woven together, yes, strong and unbreakable, but it had not merged. They were both unyielding and dissimilar, creating tiny gaps as they layered together.

Their magic could hold the brunt of the energies back. What it needed was something that could function akin to grout or spackle, spread thin throughout. Unlike those items, it would also need to merge with the structure already in place. If I could coax the standing magic into mixing with mine, it would gain the needed fluidity to spread and cover the gaps. I needed the source to not be the magic already within me. I didn't have enough. I didn't want to use the magic floating freely in the air. Using chaos to hold chaos seemed a losing bet.

I blinked, then turned to Drake. "Did Johann or you lead in making the ward?"

"Johann." Oh, good.

"Can you give power at a distance, or do you need contact?" I squinted up at the big guy.

"Contact." The man needed to learn to use his words with non-dragons.

"I need you to feed power to me so I can alter the wards to better contain the chaos."

He stared at me in calm stoicism.

"Are you willing to do so?" Good grief I had to lead him to the answers.

"Yes."

I gritted my teeth, no less annoyed by the flash of amusement I caught in his dark eyes.

He approached and put his hands on my shoulder, gentle as the brush of a butterfly's wing. I turned under that light touch and reached out for the ward, connecting myself to its structure.

"Now," I said.

I was unprepared for the howling blizzard of power that rushed through me, chilling me to the bone. Cold, ancient, abundant. I stitched my shattered concentration back together and mixed my magic with his, shaping the storm into a more supple form, tempering it. Then I let it flow into the ward, spreading further and further, seeping into the cracks and enclosing the chaos magic within the ward. I didn't try to push magic back into the containment, just stopped the flow outward.

Even with Drake contributing the majority of

energy, I was drained when the magic met with itself after passing along the whole of the ward and sealed the containment entirely. Breathing heavily, white mist hanging in the air, I murmured, "Done."

"And well, very well," he said. "I don't sense any more coming out."

"I tied it into the ward, so it should be stable, but I can't guarantee how long it will last. I've never done something like it before.

"Still better than it was. Johann and your son are inside." He motioned toward the house. I braced myself.

When we entered the house, the heat kissed my face with a welcome burn. That cold had settled into my bones. Jimmy had fallen asleep on the couch, his laptop lay open in front of him.

Johann sat reading a leather-bound book in an armchair. "Is it done?"

"Yes. I want to talk to Katie." I wanted to know what was going on. I'd had to push through all the seething magic contained within the ward. It was blindingly thick. I didn't know how Jimmy could stand it.

"What kin is she, Johann? She can't be human, and if I know what the problem is, I might be able to help. Her, I mean. You'd get my bill, of course."

Johann sighed. He looked...tired. "I was afraid you were going to say that. Katie...have I mentioned human languages lack in certain matters? Her physicality is human."

I waited a moment. "And?"

"Her...soul, for lack of a better term...is an erebite."

If only I had the vaguest idea what that meant. A small smile curved Johann's lips, a rare real one that reached his eyes, at my confusion.

"Not taught at remedial mage school, Ceridwen? There are nine erebites, each a creature of primordial chaos and vast power. They had strong opinions on how things should be run...wars were fought. In the end, they agreed to be bound to human bodies, their power sleeping, reborn endlessly in a dream."

"Why wouldn't they wake?" I was still confused.

"The humans would need to mature enough to wield their power. Since humans die so fast, they'd never mature enough. An elegant solution, yes?" If anything, Johann looked even more tired.

"I guess you could call it that. What happened?"

"Someone, somehow, managed to find an erebite and awaken it. Katie's the result, the human portion is thankfully dominant. So I don't have to act." His mouth set in a grim line, he met my eyes, all humor gone. There was no mistaking his meaning; she must be a terrible threat

"I'll see if I can help." While I felt shaken, I also didn't want to abandon the teenager I'd met without even trying.

Johann inclined his head. "You're a brave woman, Ceridwen. She's up this way."

I followed him up the stairs. He knocked on a door, then opened it when a young woman's voice answered.

"A visitor, Katie."

I stepped in. Katie was thin, almost fragile in her appearance. Large eyes dominated a triangular face framed by brown shoulder length hair. She was perhaps twenty, though I would've estimated her as younger if she were human. She smiled at me, looking away from the video game she'd been playing.

"Can you control your leaking at all?" I asked.

She shook her head, fine dark hair flying around her thin face. "I've tried. It's like controlling breathing. You can only hold it for so long, then it just kind of seeps out."

I considered as more magic swirled around us. She was like a glacier constantly calving little icebergs. Seeing the process gave me an idea. I drew magic in from the world to do my will working. I had my own, but the line between it and my life energy was fine, and what little training I'd gotten as a child had been to never, ever use it. Too easy to kill yourself with a will working.

She did the opposite. She didn't seem to draw in at all, but she leaked magic everywhere. If she could pull it in—or I could do a working to enable her to pull a portion of it in—it would help the problem.

"Johann, do you have any type of necklace with a strong chain and silver coin?"

"Yes. Do you need the coin pierced?" While he was definitely a toad, Johann was quick on the uptake.

"Yes, thank you." I approached Katie. "I can do a working to help you suck some of the magic back in, like breathing in rather than constantly exhaling or holding your breath. Are you comfortable with that?"

She considered, her narrow face thoughtful, then nodded. "I think so. Why do you want a silver coin?"

"If I put it on an object that contacts your skin, the working will function. If it leaves your skin, it'll stop. That will allow you to control it. I don't want to do something that might hurt you later and not be available to fix it. And having autonomy over your own power is good too."

Her smile wobbled for a moment. She sucked in a deep breath. "You're the first to think of me making my own choices. Thank you."

Johann returned with the coin. He dropped it in my palm, small and heavy. I squinted at its side. The head of an emperor gazed into the distance, with words in abbreviated Latin below.

"I was thinking a silver dollar," I said weakly. "Not some ancient coin that's probably valuable."

"This will be purer and easier to hang your magic on." He shrugged. "Wasn't doing anything in its case anyway."

I cupped the coin between my hands. Breathing on

it, I wove the ribbons of chaos and linked their magic to the act of breathing, a subtle draw inward of magic with each inhale. The strands of my magic and the chaos magic mixed and wrapped around the coin, sinking into it, the silver, a matrix the strands could twine around and root themselves in.

I stopped. The working closed around me, drawing magic into my store with each breath I took.

Smiling, I offered it to her.

She held it cupped in her palms. With my inner eye wide open, I watched her closely.

There it was. The magic flowed into her as easily as out and drawing it in didn't increase the outflow, which I'd also worried about.

"How do you feel?" I asked cautiously.

"Good. Is it working?" Katie lifted her eyes to mine. "It feels kind of great."

"Yes. The net outward flow is much less." Oh, this was great. It didn't completely eradicate the problem, but it helped.

"I wish I'd asked you earlier." Johann handed me the chain, and I threaded it through the coin, rooting the working in the chain as well.

"It might've been better if you had. But it's unlikely I would've come. Jimmy and I need to go home now, he has school, and I have work. I'll be sending you the bill for these services tomorrow." I smiled at him cheekily, looking forward to what I might charge him for this.

"If you're willing, Drake can drive you so you can

sleep on the way. He can make his own way back." Johann's tight smile echoed mine. "I'll send you the bill for that, and you can take it off of your final invoice."

I considered. "If he swears that he means no harm to me or mine, by the treasure he's gathered, then yes."

Drake, standing in the door, laughed. "I so swear. And well played."

THE EVENING of the night shoot, I cut the school drama rehearsal short, framing it as a reward for their hard work. They had been improving, though the girl playing the sheriff staggered drunkenly all over the stage in her later scenes. I didn't change it. I liked the humor it added to a stone-serious play.

Jimmy had watched the rehearsal, finishing his homework on his tablet. He'd insisted he wanted to tag along. Given that Liz hadn't been by in several days, I figured he was trying to protect us both.

If only he could protect me from the parent-teacher conference coming on Monday.

It was still light as we walked to the car. Fat white flakes of snow drifted down, and I sighed. The last thing we needed was more snow.

Jimmy remained quiet for most of the drive. We'd compromised on the music. Jimmy and I both liked folk music. An old labor protest song with guitar accompaniment entered its third minute.

Fast falling snow made driving tricky, but I could afford to glance at my son from time to time. Jimmy fiddled with his seatbelt. His longish curly hair fell over his eyes, and he slouched in the seat as much as the seat belt would permit.

I waited. Jimmy wanted to say something, something difficult for him, and he was working up the nerve to do it.

"Mom. Why did you hide all the magic stuff for so long? Now that people know, everything is a lot better. Johann's really nice. He's worked with me a lot, and he pays more than anybody else's after school jobs put together even if I can't really say what it is. And for you, nothing bad has happened. So why were you so scared?" The words came out in a rush, Jimmy's tone wavering between triumphant and worried.

Another mile passed as I weighed my words. The words that sprang to my lips would not have been either helpful or kind, so I bit them back. "What happened this time was a miracle. In the normal run of things, when a wild mage is discovered, they're taken—as in kidnapped—by whatever kin found them. The other kins are scared of mages, and so they find ways to control us. We're both more powerful than they are and much more fragile than they are. And the kins have had a long time to work out ways to manipulate us. One of the common approaches is hiring a lilim to use their emotional control abilities. Inflicting pain is the default. They'll use whatever lever they can to break their victim. There are many ways to take away your ability to focus your will. Once they have you, there are also ways to condition a person to make them obedient."

Exhaling, I rolled my shoulders. It had taken a great effort to keep my voice even. Driving was not the time or place for crazed bursts of anger.

Jimmy snorted, the sound full of scorn and self-confidence. "Like I'm going to want to work for somebody who hurt me?"

Possibly I should have beaten him as a child. Or something. He really didn't get it. I'd sheltered him too much. Hidden us too well. He thought like a human.

Around us, the light had dimmed with an early winter sunset, the cloud cover hastening the night. "I hope you never find out. It's worked on *many* people over the years. That's why there are captive houses—mage families that have been kept by various kins for so long that they've become generational servants."

"You mean slaves." Jimmy bit out the words.

"Yes." Maybe I should've been blunter.

"Why haven't you done anything to get them free? The wild mages all uniting to do it?" From the corner of my eye I saw Jimmy staring at me, his expression appalled.

The laugh that escaped me was too seasoned with bitterness. "Because I got Dara and myself out of that exact situation by the skin of my teeth. I don't like your boss. He took advantage of me when I was desperate. But I will grant that he is as honorable as he can be and still hold his territory. And he'll protect you. Otherwise, we would be gone from here."

"Even from Nick?" he asked.

I didn't take my eyes off the road. "To keep you safe? I'd be sad but I'd do it. Same for Dara. But luckily, miraculously, it hasn't come to that."

"Johann said this show could crack things wide open and make a lot of trouble. Why do the kins hide?"

"There're a lot more humans than kin in this world. Most of the kins don't really want to be here. The place they come from was made for them. The ones who are here like the technology and toys humanity has come up with. They don't want to be a minority that people are frightened of. They've seen what happens to people in that position." I sucked in a deep breath and glanced at him again.

"Did Johann tell you what his solution to the problem will be if I can't stop it?"

"No. What does he plan to do? Talk it over with him, maybe bribe him?"

He had no idea. Good lord.

I worried about this friendship between them, especially because Johann seemed to be making an effort to get Jimmy to like him. Trying to manipulate Jimmy into being a willing servant? Maybe. Though, Johann was the one who'd made enslavement of mages in his realm punishable by death. He was a compli-cated man, though most of his complexities involved variations on being an ass to people.

"Hopefully, we won't find out. Just keep in mind that while Johann is nice to you right now, he's a ruth-less person. He has to be. Just like the others, he's used torture to back up his laws. He's killed people. He's tolerated terrible things in his time."

"Do you think he's a bad person?" Jimmy's voice was low.

Pausing, I considered. Jimmy wanted an honest answer. "No. He's a hard man who's capable of doing what he thinks needs to be done, no matter what that is, but I haven't seen him do anything that wasn't provoked. Sometimes, though, what he does to retaliate isn't proportional either. Just be careful, Jimmy."

I made the turn off of the county highway to the private road leading to the hill where the blind we'd built with Nick lay, several miles away. I hoped he was there already.

The hill overlooked the clearing where the show was shooting. The show, for its main segment, was to take place near where the ghost had manifested to the hikers.

Down the road, a half-mile away on the opposite side of the clearing, stood another house that Johann owned. Its upper floor windows gave a clear view of the shooting area.

The plan was for Nick to use his magic on the

metal parts of the cameras to screw up the filming. Which they might put down to the ghost, but they would also lose time and have nothing to show for it.

The road was slick. I slowed, took a curve, then had to jam on the brakes hard to avoid hitting a group of people in heavy snow gear who were standing in the middle of the freaking road.

Deja vu struck as we skidded, but this time the car went into a tree on the side of the road. Slammed back in the seat by the airbags deploying, I coughed, nearly choking on the dusty residue.

The people ran toward the car. Short, they were all thick bodied, their faces muffled by scarves and goggles. The dim light from the headlight sparked on sidearms.

Ambush. Darn it! I thought I was okay this close to Johann's.

The world snapped into focus, despite my throbbing face and ribs. Even as they wrenched at the doors, I used ribbons of magic to wrap around them and force them away. One clung to my door, and I shoved him harder. Plastic cracked, and part of the door splintered off.

I struggled to get free of the airbag and face them. "Run, Jimmy!"

Jimmy's face had lost all color. He'd frozen, his eyes wide and frightened.

I flung fire at the nearest trio to his door. A pop,

like a shot, near me. The electrical pulse that followed locked my muscles as pain grayed my surroundings.

Stabbing pain radiated from my ribs. I glanced down. Blood trickled from where darts had cut through my shirt. I grabbed for the wire, and another dart hit my arm.

The world stopped again as I shook, unable to control my movement or focus my will. When I could see, Jimmy was struggling in the grip of three of them. A thick black hood had already been pulled over his head. It muffled his shouts as they forced his elbows to meet behind him.

Stress positions were also a favored way to keep mages distracted.

Noir streaked into the sky, and gunshots followed him. I hoped he managed to escape since it was looking unlikely that we would.

Groggy, I clamped down on the pain, gathered my magic, and threw lightning at Jimmy's captors, trying to buy him a chance to run. One dropped, and the others staggered.

Another dart hit me.

When the pain stopped, hard strong fingers were pressed against the side of my throat. The world went black.

My shoulders ached. I was slumped forward, my arms pulled back and restrained, wrist to wrist and elbow to elbow. My shoulders screamed from the position. My legs were tied to something hard, probably chair legs. Cords wrapped around my stomach, securing me to the chairback. I didn't open my eyes or move my head. Dim light flickered against my lids. The air smelled of damp and dirt.

Likely a cellar. A faint hissing, probably a camp lantern, though why weren't they using the LED version? A creak, and the smell of snow. A chill breeze puffed against my cheek.

Muzzy, I tried to gather my will. The familiar dizziness of a sedative made my thoughts slow and difficult.

Defeated, I slitted my eyes open.

Three men, wearing modern body armor, Kevlar vests with ceramic plates as well as helmets, stood within the faint glow of an old camp lantern. All were perhaps five feet tall, though two were of strong builds while the third was even more skinny than Jimmy.

Their ashen skin appeared sickly in the faint light. All wore helmets. Their noses were snubbed and their mouths lipless. They spoke in a hissing language, the teeth revealed as they spoke were closer to fangs than teeth. For all the heavy boots they wore, they had made no sound when they entered the cellar.

Goblins. They wore helmets, but I'd wager the two

thicker ones had hair, while the slender one would not. I'd never seen them. They weren't normally let out on their own. Used as mercenaries and enforcers, the stories about their cruelty and efficiency all came running into my head.

I had to get Jimmy away from them.

The thin goblin turned toward me. I didn't shut my eyes.

"Ms. Gault. It's good to see you're awake. Be aware your son is being held hostage for your behavior. If you use your magic, we will tell the troop currently with him to kill him. If we don't answer our phones at prearranged times, they'll kill him. Do you understand?"

"Yes." My voice cracked. My throat was as dry as the hope of rain in a desert.

Three more came in, all of the stronger build, bringing more cold air. Fresh flakes of snow dotted their dark nylon armor.

"Darius died." The one who spoke stared at me, his red eyes reflecting the lantern light.

"May fortune's favor go with him," the skinny one said.

"The war chief said this woman is to be treated as a danger. May I beat her unconscious to protect us?" The words were overlaid with a kind of tranquil anger.

The restraints holding me kept my jerk at the suggestion to a minimum. They saw it, and the one who'd spoken approached me with a slow measured tread, fist clenched. The thin one paced him and blocked the blow with all the neatness I'd tried to instill in years of choreographing action for plays.

"She is a worthy opponent. She fought well and hasn't surrendered. We treat her with honor, otherwise our own honor is tarnished." The thin goblin's words bore a weight of authority granted and used.

The other hissed at me, giving an excellent view of his fangs. Goblins weren't complete carnivores, but they came close. Then he spun away and walked back to the others.

"We need to leave if we're going to be on time for the operation. We can't leave her alone and awake. Give her another shot?" A different one spoke.

"No. I'll stay with her while you go. I'm the eldest and most used to dealing with tricky mages."

"What are you going to do?" My voice came out higher than I wanted, but at least it didn't crack. I was fuzzy enough that I couldn't shove the terror into the emotional box where it belonged.

"Now that we have you, the assignment is to terminate Wheeler and the Wraith Stalking crew, making it obvious, so that Johann Schmidt has to expend more resources making it look like an accident. The crew have served their purpose, pulling you out into the open, and our lady has no desire to be exposed either."

The thin goblin smiled at me, a movement of his mouth that didn't expose his teeth. "This troop has been responsible for many—though not all—of the sightings that brought the TV show here. The dog, the ghost. Johann Schmidt will cover the deaths up, too, but our lady wants to rub his nose in the fact she took someone from his territory and killed others. With the Reckoning coming, she's spoiling for a fight."

"Why are you telling her all this?" asked the goblin who'd wanted to beat me.

"She's captured, right? That makes her a servant of Ariana's, by extension one of the chief of chiefs. Like us. Therefore, we can talk to her freely. It's not like she can escape. No mage could do will-work through the drugs we have her on, much less the pain."

I swallowed at the name. Morgan, chief of chiefs of the daoine sidhe. A woman renowned for her power and her absolute ruthlessness. Getting away with Jimmy was going to be difficult at best.

No one ever said I didn't do difficult. I taught hormone-addled teenagers English literature and grammar.

He tapped my shoulder at a nerve plexus. A strangled shriek escaped me.

The other goblins laughed. The sound was an odd cough, similar to lions I'd heard on nature documentaries.

"If you want to stay here, rather than go on the op, fine. We'll miss you." The angry goblin nudged the leader with a friendly fist to the shoulder.

"You're more than competent to run the operation,

Xerxes. It's time you worked without supervision." The thin goblin punched him back on the arm.

The goblin flushed, his skin turning an odd greenish hue as two others slapped his back. He staggered under the blows, then straightened, standing tall. "Thank you, Crixus."

When they walked, it was like they marched, matching steps without thinking as they exited. The door clunked behind them.

Crixus, if that was a name rather than a title or rank, settled in a chair across from me.

He regarded me with a level eye. "Well, this is a fine mess, Ms. Gault."

"WHAT DO YOU MEAN BY THAT?" I stared at the goblin. All my efforts couldn't keep my voice from trembling. With my limited options, a little wobble was the least of my worries.

"All the clean up that's going to need to be done to take care of your family, for instance. From what I understand you've got a daughter who's gone into hiding. We'll need to dig her out of wherever she's hiding to obey the Lady's command." His tone was clinical, his eyes sympathetic as he gazed back.

My breath hitched as I saw red, the anger burning through the drugs.

He got up, poured water into a small plastic cup, and held it to my lips.

Mind scrambling furiously, I drank. Sweet and clear, it soothed my throat a fraction.

Goblins were rumored to be literal minded. Perhaps I could trip him up in his orders and possible interpretations of them? "What command did she give you?"

"Find all the mages in Johann Schmidt's territory. Capture them, without permanent physical injury, and then bring them back to Morgan, our Lady, for training and assignment." He returned to his chair.

That made the threat to kill Jimmy a little less pressing. Goblins could bluff, then. Rumor had it they didn't. Rumor was incorrect.

"Why do you obey her? Why do the goblins serve the daoine sidhe?" If we had to talk, I was going to try to get an answer to a question that had bothered me since I heard about the situation. Daoine sidhe could be charming, but the goblins were well known to be slaves and not servants.

He leaned back in his chair, interlacing his thin fingers. Each digit had an extra joint, and the nails resembled claws, hooking over the tip of his fingers and thumb. I glanced up and met his eyes. A shade of reddish yellow, like amber I'd seen, they were weary in a way that I had only witnessed for a moment with Johann.

"A very long time ago, when we goblins were free and fearsome, a few of us served as mercenaries. Mostly to bring money and goods back to the community and our families. It was a different time, when luxuries were hard to come by. But we goblins have always acted to strengthen our community."

Leaning forward, he poured more water into the

cup. "I don't want to give you too much too fast, since I can't untie you to relieve yourself. Anyway, one of the troops had been hired to serve Morgan. She wasn't the leader of the daoine sidhe then, just a war chief like any other. Even more than most, she was ambitious. Some daoine sidhe have the power to geas, did you know? To bind people to a certain action or even to complete obedience to their commands?"

That was unfortunate. "I've heard of it. I've never seen it done. I believe it's very rare?"

"They've made it so. The ones who can create geasa tend to kill new ones who pop up with the talent, to keep the ability rare. To keep it from being used on them, too." He offered me another drink. I swallowed slowly. The thought I wouldn't be untied if I needed to go hadn't occurred to me. The thought made me cringe, memories of the past crowding me.

"Morgan hid her power to geas. She waited, and when she had the chance, she sacrificed an old and powerful dragon, a daughter of the NightQueen herself, and harvested the energies that poured forth at the dragon's death. Morgan wielded it, used it to shape a new geas, more powerful than any made before. Where a geas normally affects only a single person, she laid it on all of the troop."

So they were slaves. He gave me a long look. "Do you know what sympathy and contagion are in magic?"

I nodded. "Sympathy is like produces like. You stick a doll with a pin, the person it resembles is caused pain. Contagion is that you never wholly separate from something you've touched. You always influence each other after that."

"She made the geas contagious. Then she ordered us to go home." His face set in harsh lines, gazing at the past. The powerful jaw muscles rippled as he gritted his teeth. He closed his eyes and I watched as he relaxed muscle by muscle before he began speaking again.

"We couldn't disobey, or warn our kin, even though we knew exactly what was going to happen. Once everyone had been touched by the geas, we found the babes born later were also held under the geas. They suckled it with their mother's milk and blood. Morgan is an elegant woman, and it was an elegant way to acquire our kin." While his voice was calm, his eyes held a depth of loathing and hate that made me shiver.

I averted my eyes, drawing in a breath of my own. Gaze unfocused, I surveyed him with the inner eye. He was hazy to that perception, wrapped like a mummy in strands of magic, a gauzy veil that covered him from the top of his head to the bottom of his feet. The magic that concealed him was not unlike what I had seen wriggling through Johann and Drake's ward. It had the same dark silky opalescent quality to it. Which was strange, for everything I understood daoine sidhe magic was hard and bright as the sun or ice. Perhaps the geas was comprised more of the magic that Morgan had stolen?

There was so much of it. Lines extended from it, probably to the other goblins, binding them in a web of a single person's will. I fought the effects of the sedative and managed to focus my will enough to reach out to touch a strand of the magic. I wanted a better impression of its texture, what might cut it.

Hard fingers dug into the nerve plexus in my elbow, shocking me back to normal sight. Pain shot-gunned through my arm, and I screamed through the agony.

"I'm sorry, part of the general orders in dealing with mages are not to allow you to do any magic." The fingers loosened.

I panted, still shaking from the sudden jolt of pain. "You want to be free."

"More than anything." The sincerity in his voice could be felt in the air. "But please believe that Morgan has had a long time to lay a series of orders to make sure that I cannot actively seek that freedom."

"How did you know I was doing magic?" I tried to control my panting as best I could.

His brow furrowed. "All mages get a certain distant expression when they're working magic. Even in the middle of a fight, when a fireball or lightning bolt is blazing, they're not quite there."

I made a mental note to try to not look distant.

"Since you are physically much more capable than me, is there a way I can persuade you to at least loosen my elbows? I'm old and this position is going to cause me permanent damage."

Crixus laughed. "Clever. Why do you say it would cause permanent damage?"

"I had a rotator cuff tear, a shoulder injury in the past. Further strains on it will cause damage and lead to an inability to use that arm properly." It had the advantage of being true.

He considered, then nodded. "Fair enough." A knife flicked in his hand faster than I could see. In a blink, he was behind me. The strands popped as he severed them. The lessening of the strain on my shoulders was wonderful.

The door clanged open. A gust and swirl of cold air hit my face, and Noir whipped up to the ceiling, hissing. He breathed a cloud of vapor that seared into the concrete floor where Crixus had stood.

The goblin blurred out of it but with his gray skin flushed an ugly yellow in places.

I yelped, unable to move.

Nick ran in without the illusion he normally wore. His face was as dark as teak, contrasting with the silver armor he wore. The armor moved fluidly, composed of something like fish or snake scales. A hood of the armor covered his head and neck. His knife was clenched in his hand, shining silver and black, a faint trail of smoke wisping off the blade.

Crixus had his gun up. It clicked when he pulled the trigger.

"Did you really think I would come in here without disabling the firing mechanism first?" Nick's voice was derisive.

"I honor you, old enemy. By the hand then." Crixus leaped forward as he spoke.

I didn't know much about fighting techniques, but I could tell that Nick was trying not to engage in hand-to-hand and Crixus was trying just as hard to close. The dragon flitted about them until Crixus grabbed him and flung him into a wall.

I've never seen a living being bounce like rubber before Noir hit that wall, then he shot across the room.

The distraction let Nick score a strike across Crixus's arm.

Partners in a deadly dance, both of them inhumanly fast. Blood welled through a slice in the heavy armor the goblin wore. Crixus responded with a swipe across Nick's belly. The noise was like fingernails on a chalkboard, shrill and grating.

Fear for Nick and Jimmy splashed through me like ice water. Desperate, I closed my eyes, striving for the clarity to use the magic. Sweat poured down my back despite the chill as I found it. I wouldn't be able to hold it for long.

Using the inner eye, I stared at Crixus, willing all the magic in the air to wrap itself around him, joining the geas binding him, only this working created to stop his physical movement. He let out a startled shout and toppled, arrested in mid movement.

"Don't kill him!" I shouted.

Nick reversed his knife and brought the pommel down on Crixus's head. "You're going to have to do something fast. Goblins don't stay down, and you can't really keep them bound either. Too strong, too sturdy."

"Well there's not a whole lot I can do if I'm tied to the chair." The dragon stirred and flapped over to me, landing on my shoulder.

Nick gave a breath of a laugh, searching Crixus with brutal efficiency. He pulled plastic restraints off the goblin's belt and double-fastened them on Crixus's arms and legs.

"How did you find me?" The goblins had taken my coat. My phone had been in the pocket.

Nick fashioned Crixus's belt of combat webbing into a noose. "I can always find my work, if I want to."

I stared at him, then down at the bracelet.

The skin of his cheekbones seemed flushed. "I don't know where it is unless I work at it, though. I don't track your movements. Plus, your dragon helped lead the way."

Balanced between appalled and amused, I had no words.

During the pause, Nick wrapped the noose around the goblin's neck, then grabbed his clothing and dragged him over next to me, holding tension on the noose the entire time.

"Why are you doing that?"

"It'll keep him from moving too much and getting

loose too fast." The dragon fluttered to the pitted concrete next to me from his perch on my shoulder as Nick started cutting the cords and plastic. I slumped forward. My arms and legs had fallen asleep. Returning circulation was not going to be fun.

"I want to take the geasa off him," I declared. "Did anyone see you come in here?"

He shook his head. "Okay. Do you have any idea how you're going to do that?"

"Not yet. But I'm going to try."

The solution was elusive and fighting the haze that obscured it was exhausting. The fear and anger and resulting magical rush had burned off enough of the sedative I could focus the inner eye, though not well.

Shifting his weight, Noir leaned forward and nipped a fleck of chaos from the air.

Glancing from it to the wrappings, I had an idea. I flicked loose a bit of the chaos-tinged magic that wrapped Crixus. Cupped in my palm, it rippled, trying to wrap around my hand. Then I offered it to the dragon.

He nibbled at it, nuzzling my palm. A long tongue snaked out, wrapping around his muzzle. I set him on Crixus's chest. His wings mantled as he sniffed at the geas. With sudden energy, he nipped and tore at the gauzy magic, swallowing bits of it like a bird does fish.

Crixus struggled under the little dragon, writhing and trying to kick. The restraints groaned. Nick tightened the noose. Choking him unconscious seemed to be the only way to keep him down. Nick did it with grim efficiency.

Luckily the dragon's appetite seemed boundless. It didn't really take all that long, though with the pressure on us, it felt like ages.

The dragon's belly was round and swollen. He didn't try to fly, merely crawled up my legs and into my arms, claws catching on the fabric of my trousers and shirt. I petted his head. "Good boy," I murmured. He lay his head down with a soft thump on my chest.

A moment later, when Crixus opened his eyes, moisture gathered in them, streaking the ashy skin of his temples. "Free." He sighed happily.

"You'll understand if we still keep you restrained." Nick said, voice dry.

"I do. If you want to stop the others on the operation, you're going to have to move fast. I ask as a personal favor that you try to avoid killing as many of them as possible. They are as bound as I was."

"If we can," I said, leaning forward. "Where's Jimmy been taken? Where's your base of operations?"

CHAPTER 14

CRIXUS MET MY GAZE. His eyes held a mix of emotions familiar to me, dawning hope at his freedom and niggling fear of being recaptured. "In Columbus. He was taken to our base of operations there."

Thinking was easier when I moved. I paced away from him to the door. My coat lay there, discarded over what appeared to be camping supplies.

"Where is it located?" I grabbed my jacket, checking the pockets. No phone. My purse was gone as well.

Nick dragged Crixus to the pipes by the wall and knotted the rigid leather of the noose wrapped around Crixus's neck to a thick pipe. "It's ok, Ceri. Schmidt knows where Jimmy is. He and Pryce were headed there when I started searching for you."

Words failed me in my relief. My hands were shaking with reaction. I stared at Crixus. We needed protection if fear of Johann's reprisal wasn't enough. This had been a terribly close call.

"Well played with the bracelet, enemy mine. We dropped the mage's phones by the car." Crixus shifted to ease the pressure on his throat.

I stared at them. "Do you two know each other? That's a very thorough job of tying someone up, Nick."

"We've met," Nick said wryly. "I'll show you the scars to prove it whenever you want to see them. I know just how good Crixus is, and while you say he's free, I'd feel much better buying us some time before he's loose again, just in case. Ariana can be devious. And Crixus is one of the oldest goblins still alive, and not by leading from behind."

Nick helped Crixus shift position to ease the tightness of the noose, but his stance remained wary as he did so, ready to strike. "Apparently, there's some discussion ongoing about Jimmy's future between Schmidt and Pryce. They were in a physical meeting when the alert came through. When he hired Jimmy in October, Schmidt gave him a panic button."

Nick gave Crixus a lopsided smile. "It was in his shoe. Jimmy set it off. Schmidt promised to call me when they got Jimmy loose, but right now we still have the Wheeler situation to deal with."

I'd forgotten about them in my worry for Jimmy. Schmidt and Pryce were not on my favored list, but in a fight between them and a team of goblins, they had the advantage. Fear tightened my gut, and I lightened my thoughts. If nothing else, Schmidt could bargain them to death while Pryce made them fall in love with his shining hair.

Welcome familiar irritation welled within me, spurring me forward. We needed to move. "It's been how long since your troop left to kill Wheeler?"

"Twenty-four minutes," Crixus said as he watched us. His mouth had curved in a faint smile. "My brethren were setting up early for the operation. I believe the filming is not supposed to start until eight."

Something in his voice...the hint of hope. He fixed his gaze to me.

I dropped to crouch by him. "You were a slave. But you and they tried to take me. If I free your comrades, will you all protect me and my family?"

"Yes." Crixus's stare didn't waver.

"If I find a way to free your people, will you lead them to protect mine?"

"Yes."

Nick exhaled. "If that happens, it has the potential to change so many power dynamics it frightens me."

"And three times. If you and yours are freed, you'll keep me and mine free."

"Yes. Spare as many as you can. This is their first mission."

The air thickened, coiled with power as he spoke. I'd heard of oath bindings before but never experienced one. It resonated in the place where my magic lived.

"You need to go." Crixus grinned at me. "I'll be out of this in minutes, but they'll be killing the cast and crew soon. If you want to stop it, you need to be quick."

Unspoken, that he would avoid other goblins since the geas was contagious.

I let Nick precede me since I didn't know where we were. Up a concrete flight of stairs, we stepped through the ruins of a house.

"There's a path through here that is solid." He stepped carefully.

I followed his steps exactly.

It had stopped snowing, and the temperature had dropped. The half-moon shed enough light to make the new snow sparkle. Nick had pulled to the side of a road that ran right past the abandoned house. His truck gleamed in the darkness, familiar and safe. I climbed in, shivering. I hadn't brought a heavy enough coat, not expecting to be outside for very long. It would've been easy to heat the inside of the blind with a tiny bit of will working. And it had been chilly in the basement.

The dragon joined me, coiling in my lap. I put on the seat belt, and he sniffed at me, disturbed by the motion.

"Was he exaggerating about being able to get free?" With Crixus as an ally, I didn't want him hurt. Even an enemy dying of thirst didn't sit well with me.

Nick turned on the heat. "He'll be on the road in ten minutes or so. Less, probably. That just bought time to get out of here without him if he'd still been a hostile."

The heat brought even more aches to strained muscles. I leaned my head back in the headrest, taking a quick moment of relaxation.

"You've got a nice black eye going there. Did you manage to tag any of them?" While his tone was calm, his expression was hard.

"No, it's probably from the air bags."

"You crashed again?"

I shot him a sharp glare because of the chuckle in his voice. "It seems to be the order of the week, losing control on ice. Are we headed for the blind?"

"Yes. We'll be parking the truck soon. We have to walk to the spot cross country to limit the light and noise. Try and step where I step so you keep your noise down and not give our position away. All goblins have great hearing, but we don't have to worry about our scent. The blind's downwind from the shooting site. From what Crixus was wearing, they're in heavy kit."

"Crixus mentioned this is their first mission."

"One of the reasons I've lived to meet you is that I don't trust goblin commanders, they tend to lie. I'm assuming they're veterans. If they really are boots it'll be a pleasant surprise. We'll have a much better chance of surviving." Nick glanced at me. "Ceri, if they're veterans, the cast and crew are already dead."

I flinched.

"If they're boots, then they're likely to do it by the

daoine sidhe protocol, line them up and shoot them twice in the head, one at a time. That takes a little while, which is good for us. Bad for us is that the film people will see the goblins for what they are."

"I can shield the humans from being shot if we get there in time. As long as I can see them." I hoped I would have the chance. I didn't want them to all be dead.

"That's a thought. Keep in mind we don't have a good fallback position. If I tell you to run, you need to listen. The traps I set between the clearing and the blind should delay them. Pass the goggles in the glove compartment to me."

I opened it and pulled out goggles. There was also a heavy aluminum flashlight, almost a club. I clenched my hand on it. If this went downhill, I was doomed in a hand-to-hand fight with goblins, but I'd at least try to land a hit before they got me.

"These are night vision goggles. I'm going to be driving without lights."

I'd never seen Nick drive like this. Face intent, he seemed to ignore the snow, the dark and all the other conditions that would slow us down. We bore through the darkness and never skidded, the countryside speeding by even faster.

I liked the plan. If we could catch them, the dragon and I could dispose of the geasa on the goblins and rescue those who wanted to be free. I stroked the dragon's belly. It was as flat as ever now as he snuggled in my lap. Johann lived close by and had staff to help us with whatever fakery would be needed for the filming crew. I just needed to come up with an idea.

A field flashed by.

Crop circles? Alien abduction? Goblins did have gray skin...

Nick slowed and we glided to a stop. "Close the door as quietly as you can." I was out as fast as he was. He walked slightly in front of me, keeping a brisk pace, silent as a shadow.

"How are you going to snipe with no rifle?" I whispered.

"It's up at the blind. Leaving the rifle and the optic outside in cold weather keeps the optic from fogging up." His murmur barely reached my ears. "When we get up there and see them, my plan is for you to set off a flare of the brightest light you can make in the middle of where they're gathered. It doesn't matter if you blind the hostages too. I'll pick off whoever the selected executioner is, maybe one or two others. Then we run for the house and see what happens."

"Understood." I tried to match his quiet movements, but the snow crunched underfoot, and his longer legs outpaced me up the hill.

When I puffed to the blind, Nick was pulling off a white cover with a green lining from an enormous black rifle. He put the folded cover on the snow and laid three magazines on it, close to hand. The heavy barrel of the gun had a huge attachment to the front, with holes on its side. A bipod braced the front of what looked like a smooth handguard.

"That's legal?" I couldn't help the squeak.

Nick breathed a laugh. "This is a Barrett M107 50 caliber semiautomatic."

I must have looked as blank as I felt. He laughed again, a thread of sound.

"It has a lot of stopping power and shoots fast. We'll need it to take out fully equipped goblins. Some of them can take a hit from one of these and still keep fighting. Put these on."

He handed me ear protection. "This will enhance the noise we want to hear and soften the loud report of the rifle."

"What is the attachment on the rifle?" I'd never seen anything like it.

"A thermal optic. Best for night use. Luckily it's a still night." Nick knelt on the ground and began putting huge black-tipped bullets into the rifle. "These are custom load goblin killers."

With a tinge of asperity, I asked, "What does custom load mean?"

"I made them myself." Nick passed me a pair of binoculars. "Use these. I've upgraded them to be thermals. We're about a thousand meters away. Watch what's happening."

I took off the goggles and gazed through the binoculars. The binoculars showed a brighter white color in the outlines of people. The humans wore coats and hats. They stood out against the snow like flares of heat. Body armor covered the goblins, their faces a cooler shade than the humans. The background was dark, patterned with shades of gray.

My breath hissed between my teeth. "The goblins have them lined up."

Nick's soft even voice carried an undernote of relief. "Crixus told the truth. Blind them on my mark."

There were perhaps twenty humans kneeling in the snow, and eight upright goblins. Each goblin had a pistol on hand, except for the two who had rifles.

One of them moved toward the first kneeling human. Another shoved a figure that tried to rise down into the snow.

"Ready." Nick shifted.

The goblin took another step, pistol rising. I grasped all the magic I could handle, compressing it, ready to loose it like a small star. My headache exploded, and I wiped the blood beneath my nose, focused on the point where the magic would manifest —right in front of the executioner goblin.

"Mark."

The light I created blossomed in front of the goblin, my headache squeezing my temples. The force of the magic beat at me, even though the goggles didn't register the light. Goblins and humans alike recoiled from it.

A loud report rang out, even through the ear

protection. Bright splatter, like white lava, erupted from a goblin's mid-sections as he fell to the snow.

The humans had dropped down hard to the ground, but the blinded goblins still stood.

Two more shots. A spurt of white exploded from the goblin, and he fell in two parts while the one standing beside him fell, his neck and arm were blown off. I could see some of the white splatters hit the humans on the ground. The rest of the goblins ran for cover. One hit a tree at full speed and fell back in the snow, stunned.

The dragon flew up, away from us. I swallowed. The rest were under cover now.

My ears rang. Ear protection was a good thing.

An ungentle hand grasped my wrist, but he was right to do so. Pistol in one hand, my wrist in the other, Nick ran for the path we'd marked earlier. I tried to keep up, but his longer legs meant I was being half dragged down the hill and up another. Brush slapped my face and crashing noises accompanied me, while Nick ran silent as a ghost.

A huge weight slammed me into the ground. I crumpled, face first in the snow, a branch cutting my cheek. My shoulder spasmed with pain from the impact.

Nick swore.

I lifted my head, shaking it to clear it of snow, while a few feet away, a goblin grappled with Nick. The rifle lay in the snow, feet away. In a sudden vicious movement the goblin swept Nick's legs and they dropped to the floor with a crash. While he was shorter, the goblin had the advantage of strength. They were the strongest of the kins for their size. They could arm wrestle trolls.

A knife sparked in the goblin's hand, close to his body and Nick's belly.

I jerked to my feet, scooping up the flashlight.

Nick snarled as the goblin stabbed. Blood sprayed like a fan on the white snow.

Rage lit my veins. The moment crystallized into hyper focus. The sharp bite of cold air in my nose, the aches in my shoulders and back, the sound of Nick's hoarse breathing, the thick blood blending into the snow, shading it to pink. Power rushed through me, cool and light, from the cage where I kept my anger chained.

The magic flowed like water down my arm, strengthening it, then flared on the flashlight. Blazing light flashed as I brought it down on the goblin's head with all my strength, both natural and magical.

The flashlight sank into his skull with a horrible cracking noise. Blood and gray matter leaked around the improvised club. I dropped it, panting, trying to contain the magic that threatened to spill out of me. Small sparks danced around me. This was dangerous, but I couldn't figure out what to do with all the stored emotional energy.

Nick pushed the goblin off. His hand pressed

against his right side where blood poured between his fingers. I dropped to my knees beside him.

"It's ok, Ceri." The tone of his voice gave the lie to his words. He tried to get up then fell back gasping.

"No, it isn't." The flare of rage hadn't ended, hooking into all the emotions I'd suppressed from the time I was taken. So much anger. I gathered up the sparks, focusing on repair, on healing. Nick's body became a nebula, all its interconnected functions moving mists. Sections darkened and shredded, centered on the wound. The area spread.

He was losing too much blood. Nick was dying.

It took so much energy to fill the spaces that darkened. The magic twisted into the nebula. Svartalfar healed almost as well as trolls. If I could give him energy so his body could sustain itself while he healed, he'd live. The trick was that my gift wasn't for healing. All I could do was pour all the energy into him and let his body convert it into what it needed.

Like energy, it took a lot of magic to make a little matter.

His skin heated under my hand, and he hissed a breath between his teeth. "Don't drain yourself, Ceri."

I ignored him, the boundless anger transmuting to magic and pouring into him. I'd finally found a way to let it free, and he would heal. I forbade him to die.

Bit by bit, the ravaged nebula rebuilt itself. I panted, letting years of anger flow out of me.

Even when his aura of energy lost the dark blemish

of the wound, some anger remained. I sat back on my heels, feeling lighter. Magic still surged in me, wanting its outlet as the last of the anger drained out of the box that had encased it.

Slow and steady, he shifted to all fours then stood, letting me support him. He moved guardedly and with care. After a deep breath, he tilted his head, listening. "They're coming this way. Can you get me the rifle?

My head pounded as the remaining magic sang in my blood. "Let me try another way. You have to promise not to yell at me afterwards."

He shot me a grim look. "No promises."

I reached up with both arms, calling, "Noir."

A thunderbolt from the sky landed in the snow in front of me. The dragon, now the size of a German shepherd, leaned against my leg.

"Are you hungry? More to eat soon..."

Goblins toiled up the hill, low to the ground, the shifting of their heads indicating they were navigating by hearing. Five of them.

Even blinded, they were a threat. But I hoped if they were free, they'd be a greater protection. I simply needed to render them unable to hurt my dragon. Revenge for being tasered only motivated me a little.

Boy, was I good at lying to myself.

Magically manipulating electricity was easy. The potential always lay in the air. The filigree of energy lanced out in front of me—not enough to kill, but enough to knock them all down. Maybe a little extra on top of that.

They fell into the snow with choked cries. The goblins lay scattered in brush and drift, twitching. More jolts would follow, until the dragon was done.

"Now, Noir."

The dragon ambled over to the nearest goblin, long supple neck stretching. Delicate as a cat batting a toy, he worried a strand of geas on the goblin loose and sucked the magic into his mouth.

It reminded me of old movies and spaghetti.

The goblin writhed, and I jolted him again with the others, careful not to hit the dragon.

Much more quickly than it had taken for Crixus, the dragon finished. He waddled to the next.

I didn't jolt the goblin, instead calling, "Crixus is waiting for you."

"Indeed, I am," Crixus said in a low voice from my side. "Well done."

I jumped. "How do you guys do that?"

"Long practice," Nick replied. "He just came up out of the earth. The really old goblins can do that. Makes them even harder to kill."

Crixus bowed to me and strode forward. The two goblins clasped hands and Crixus pulled the other goblin to his feet. They moved away from the other goblins, trying to stay away from the contagion.

"I'm free..." The goblin whispered it as slurping noises came from the dragon.

"And we need to make sure we stay that way." Crixus inclined his head toward me and Nick. "They are friendly. Defend them after you bury our dead."

"We still need to do something about the humans. They saw you. They knew you were going to kill them. Suggestions?" Nick said, voice weary.

I should have one more will working in me to go with the idea I'd come up with. When the dregs of the power boost ran out, I was going to crash so hard it wasn't funny. "I have an idea, but we have to wait until the dragon finishes. The electricity is independent of me now, and I have to stop it as each one is freed." A shiver chased through me, then another. The cold had crept into my bones.

"Does this idea involve more magic? Your eyes are bloodshot and you're too pale. Your freckles look like ink dots. I think rest is a better idea." Nick frowned at me, his silver eyes concerned.

"One final use of magic. Then I'm done, possibly for weeks." I tried to smile back at him. He didn't appear convinced. "Can it wait until Jimmy gets here?"

"I don't know how long it will take for him to get here, and I don't want the cast and crew to freeze to death. Or recover enough to run away." Once I recovered from the strain, I'd be teaching him everything I knew. And trying to get Dara to come home for a visit so she could be taught, too.

Nick made the call as the dragon freed the last of the goblins. They formed around us, and Crixus walked next to me, hovering as if he wanted to carry me.

I was six inches taller than him. While tempting, it would've been ridiculous. Nick walked on my other side, wincing at the exercise.

"How are you?" I asked.

"Peace." He raised a hand. "I'm fine, just not in shape to run any marathons today."

It was slow going up the remainder of the hill. The house at the top, a two-story box, had a wraparound porch. The back windows directly overlooked the haunting site. The key had been in my purse, on loan from Lotus, but we could break in.

Nick touched the lock. A tiny click, and then he turned the knob and let us in.

"Convenient, that." I hurried inside. It was warmer than outside, though chilly.

I took the stairs two at a time, grabbing the banister when my head swam at the top. The shaking had started again, I needed to finish this.

"Ceri." Nick put his arm around my waist. "Lean on me. You've earned it."

"You're still wounded." I hadn't believed him when he said he was fine earlier.

"Not anymore. I heal fast, and what you did hurt, but it made it even faster.

He lifted his mail, and I saw smooth dark skin, unmarked by even a scar. Relief washed through me.

We wobbled down the hall. I said, "Can you call an

illusion, so you don't look like you're on the way to a Ren fair to cosplay an elf?"

"You are a cruel woman. Yes." As he opened the door to the overlooking room he blurred, and the Nick I was familiar with appeared, wearing a flannel shirt and jeans.

"What are you going to do?" Nick set the rifle on the floor in easy reach.

"I'm going to send them to sleep. When Johann's people arrive, we're going to get them somewhere warm to wait until Johann gets here. Probably downstairs."

My head throbbed as I looked out the window and curled magic around the frightened crew, still blind, some stumbling, looking for safety. Like so many little bubbles, set to lull them into sleep. I tied it to the quiet life of the earth, in case something happened to distract me.

Like collapsing.

One by one they lay down in the snow, loose and limp.

Noise downstairs distracted me, the low rumbling voices of Johann's trolls. The hissing voices of the goblins answered, but I couldn't make out words.

"What's the rest of your plan?" Gentle but insistent, Nick's voice focused me.

"Presumably the goblins set up something to jam what little cell phone reception there is here. So no uploads would be from their cameras." I touched beneath my nose. My fingertips came away red. "Have them make a snowy crop circle pattern and dump the humans in it with their equipment, away from here. It was all an alien abduction. If anyone's good at hacking, have them put pictures on the cameras for evidence."

Shaking with fatigue, I leaned against the wall and then slid down it to the floor. Warm arms wrapped around me, and I leaned against Nick as exhaustion mugged me.

I didn't quite go to sleep, but rested, content to listen as Lotus and the trolls came into the room. Crixus and another goblin entered before them and stood between us as Nick pitched the idea.

"Creative. Rusalka can manipulate the snow. I'll call Vasily." Lotus moved next to Crixus, a whiff of pleasant floral scent breaking over me. "Do you want to take her to the main house to rest?"

"She wants to be here. We can wait. Just make sure Jimmy comes here first." Nick's hand stroked my hair.

CHAPTER 15

I STIRRED as Nick's phone pinged.

He shifted position, checking the screen. "They have Jimmy with them. They're headed out."

Even tired, the tension in my chest unclenched a bit. Jimmy was as safe as he could be. "Then we should go downstairs, shouldn't we?"

"There's no furniture, and they're stacking all of the people in there, but if you want to be down there, I can walk with you."

There really wasn't much room for twenty sleeping people, and the trolls had left a clear path from the door to the steps. Lotus leaned against the wall, a tablet in her hands. She regarded me as I came down.

"They might be more comfortable if they took them to Johann's." A movement of her chin indicated the people.

"Did you ask Johann?" I called down, taking another step.

"Yes. He said to leave them here. I just wanted someone to support my opinion. Also, congratulations on your new goblin guard." She winked at me.

Nick and I had only just managed to reach the bottom of the stairs when the door flew open. Jimmy pelted through it. I didn't get a good look at him as he ran to me and wrapped his arms around me. I squeezed him back. He was shaking. I didn't say anything, just held on to my son.

An overwhelming wave of emotion hit me, and I gasped, looking for a lilim. It felt like their emotional manipulation, but it simply echoed how I felt, love and worry and the desire to protect Jimmy. It could be his lilim heritage manifesting, though from everything I knew heritages didn't blend. Unless he was using magic to do it...I didn't care to check. I just wanted to hold him and protect him from the world.

Three of the goblins moved to interpose themselves between me and the door as Johann and Pryce entered the room.

Johann looked around, a twinkle coming to his deep-set eyes. "And I didn't get you anything."

"That's fine, I've always been a gift giving person." I sneered at him.

He sneered back. "Your plan is to have them believe they've been abducted by aliens? It seems strange."

"No, my plan is to make it look as if they had been abducted by aliens and let them do with that as they will. If goblins become the new aliens, fine. This way we're all covered."

He inclined his head. "You have a point. How on earth did you free the goblins, Ceri?"

"Magic." I smiled at him. I wasn't going to go into details. I'd watched as the dragon ate, following what it did. I didn't quite have a way to duplicate it yet, but I was working on it.

Johann rolled his eyes. "And where do you plan for them to live? Are you going to buy them illusions?"

Crixus, who appeared at my side again, and how did he keep doing that, spoke. "We have the money and would be grateful for you to craft them as quickly as you may, so that we do not cause more strife between you and the daoine sidhe."

Johann laughed softly. "The strife is here to stay, Crixus. Morgan violated my laws. There's going to be a payment in blood for that."

Jimmy shivered against me.

"These goblins are our friends now," I whispered it to him. "They were slaves. And we're going to free more of them, and they'll keep the rest from taking us."

"I'm scared." He squeezed the words out softly.

Johann's gaze held compassion as he glanced at Jimmy's back. "Vasily called. The snow circle is finished. All we need is some way to put them into the circle without leaving tracks. I suggest Drake and that he take a shortcut through your dominion." Lotus spoke up, tactfully averting her eyes.

"He'll love that." Johann's answering glance was dry. Dominions were dimensions adjacent to ours, the true homes of the kins. I'd never been in one, they were dangerous places.

Jimmy's arms loosened. I let him step back. His hair was mussed and his eyes wild and still spooked. His face was white, and he stared at me. "You've been bleeding. Did they hurt you too?"

My heart clenched. "Only when they tasered me. Remember, they're on our side now. They won't hurt you again."

"So promised." Crixus bowed. "Chain Breaker."

"A title. How nice." Johann's voice was mild. "Pryce, you said you needed a moment to speak with Ceridwen privately?"

"If Ms. Gault will permit it, yes."

I eyed him, and he met my gaze with quiet determination. All the beings here had excellent hearing, and we all knew it. We'd have to go upstairs and shut the door.

I didn't trust him. As tired as I was, I couldn't fend him off. But I had Nick here, and Schmidt's presence would keep anything direct from happening.

"Jimmy, can you hold on for five minutes while I do this?" I asked.

He nodded, moving closer to Schmidt. He had welts on his face and wrists. They'd hurt him. My heart ached.

I could get angry even after all that. I used the

energy of it to get me up the stairs, followed by Pryce, and turned as he shut the door with a quiet click.

"What do you need to tell me?"

Pryce stuck his hands in his pockets, more emotional that I'd ever seen, even if it only communicated discomfort. "The lilim who fathered Jimmy was from a family who'd been altered by a mage in the lilim queen's employ to permit lilim abilities to manifest as well as mage abilities in any offspring he fathered on a mage. Jimmy needs to be taught how to control those abilities—the trauma tonight has made them manifest. I've been damping them down as much as I can, but he's strong, and I don't want to hurt him."

The words punched me. "How do you know this?"

"I know his father. Your son is my nephew."

UNBOWED

MIDLIFE MAGE

STARS ABOVE. Pryce's words brought back a tide of memories. Touch and sound. Scenes ran through my mind at lightning speed. Sweat broke out all over as I relived it for an endless moment, but hard-won discipline fought back. I gritted my teeth and beat back the memories with a mental baseball bat. It wasn't easy, but I managed. I'd found my way through these flashbacks often when I'd first escaped. I'd learned ways of coping to keep me from slipping into a dark place. A very, very dark place.

The sound of Pryce's sharp inhalation helped ground me. I focused on the sound and used it to drag myself back to the surface, the here and now. As a lilim, he had to feel all the emotions running through me. I hoped it hurt him even half as much as it did me. Vindictive? Yes, but I couldn't find it in me to be kind. Not at this moment.

Taking a long deep breath of my own, I focused on

the moment. No memories right now. I couldn't go there. I loved my son with everything in me, but that didn't mean that I was eager to find out who his father was or, somehow worse, that his father had a family. If he had a family who wanted to be in our lives... I wasn't sure I could live with that, even if they didn't approve of what he'd done to me that ended up giving me my son, who I could never be sorry for.

Now, at least, I would have a name to direct rage at when I woke up panting in the middle of the night from twisted dreams. That would be nice. Maybe I could even think about killing him. That would be even better.

On some level, I must have noticed how much seventeen-year-old Jimmy looked like Pryce and tried not to realize it consciously. Now, all I could see were the long lashes, the striking eyes, the high cheekbones. I'd put it down to shared lilim heritage, even though that kin had as much variety in skin and eye color as humanity... and as Jimmy grew to manhood, I bet he'd look even more like Pryce. That didn't mean, necessarily, that Pryce was his father. Lots of people looked like lots of other people, whether human, lilim, or yaksha. Heck, even the goblins and trolls.

A shiver worked its way through my body. I had long ago buried those memories. At least, as much as I could. Sometimes it was better not to think about the past, not to process it, not to deal with it. My time in the reconditioning compound had been just that, *past,* over, and done. I wouldn't let it dominate the woman I was now. It would not define my life. I would've snapped my fingers for emphasis if I hadn't been where I was.

Trying to control my maelstrom of emotions, I straightened my back and opened my eyes. The last thing I wanted was for Jimmy to sense my upset and think that it was somehow his fault, which couldn't have been further from the truth. Meeting Pryce's concerned and—even more horrible—compassionate gaze made self-control that much more necessary. I was about two Mississippi's away from losing my mind and shrieking like a banshee.

"Do you want me to help?" he asked softly. My emotions were probably hammering him, and he had the ability to lessen or heighten that emotion if he wanted.

I didn't want that. My emotions were my own, even if they hurt. Shaking my head no, I took a deep breath, trying to focus on each feeling one at a time so that I could work through them and let them pass through me so I could focus on the here and now and not on my panic.

Feeling number one: anger. Not anger specifically, because the word anger called up a feeling more like when someone used the last of the milk after you had already poured your cereal. What boiled in me was closer to white-hot, out-of-control rage, and unfortunately, I was pretty sure that it wasn't going anywhere unless I siphoned it back into a containment as I used to do, and maybe not even then. But that wasn't much of an option. It had been unhealthy and had created more problems than it had solved.

On the other hand, I very much wanted to punch Pryce on the general principle that it might help. Never knew until I tried. I was supposed to take the high road, sure, but action was much more satisfying. As would be the crunch of Pryce's nose.

From his half-smile and spread hands, he knew what I was thinking, and the warning gleam in his eye told me he'd make every attempt to dodge me. The picture of me chasing him with hands outstretched flickered through my mind, bringing with it a moment of amusement. That helped beat back the other emotions, so I kept picturing us running around and around the room, me screaming in delight, him in terror.

Pryce pursed his lips at me before speaking. "I'm shielding this area to keep Jimmy from experiencing this turmoil. You have privacy. This means, however, the goblins are feeling his fear and loathing of them. Feel free to expedite your coping with the situation." A surge of a different emotion rampaged through me at the sound of Pryce's calm tone.

Embarrassment. I didn't want Pryce's pity, and I certainly didn't want him to think that I was weak, because I wasn't. Not by a long shot. My time in that compound was the reason that I didn't trust anyone but my children and had only barely started trusting Nick.

Fear followed hot on the heels of embarrassment, but I shook my head and tried to focus on the problem at hand. I did need to get myself under control and now.

I focused on Pryce. I might have appreciated the information, because knowledge was power. I was willing to bet he'd figured it out the minute he'd seen Jimmy, about a month ago. And then he'd sat on it, though it could be argued he'd wanted to confirm it before he spoke.

What *did* he want?

"What is your brother's name?" I asked. It was a simple enough question, which was the easiest way I could think of to slide into the information that I still wasn't sure I really wanted to know. And if he wasn't willing to answer that simple question, then this whole exchange was pointless.

Pryce turned his eyes from my gaze, instead staring through the window as if appreciating the winter view, cold as his normal expression. When he spoke, his voice came out cool and void of any passion or emotion. "His name is Robert. Same surname."

Okay, then. It wasn't like I wanted to be his bestie.

"Why? I mean, why tell me this now? Why at all?" I recognized that I was in shock, completely overwhelmed.

I wanted his motives. Maybe it was a plan to blend

kin's powers, but that didn't make sense. Unfortunately with magic, and magic users, that was sometimes just how it was. Not everything made sense.

Pryce hesitated for a moment, selecting his words with even more care than usual. "Among the lilim-kin, the most potent rules."

I didn't interrupt him with a smart-ass comment, because he was being forthcoming, and I had no doubt interrupting would stop the flow of information. He wasn't the biggest sharer.

"The strongest of all lilim, Queen Zarah, is powerful and, forgive me if I misuse the term, but inhuman is close. I hesitate to say insane because her actions are rational when perceived from *her* point of view, her world's framework, namely that she was once a victim and never will be again."

My responding flinch couldn't be hidden. That was precisely how I felt day in and day out.

He ignored my recoil. "The only thing Queen Zarah fears are mages. Her only threat. Even though your kin, if it can be fully called a kin, is thought to be easily tamed and generally well trained by my peers, she and I have both seen what a fully trained mage, strong in their power, can do."

"And what is that?" I asked guardedly. His voice calmed me a fraction, even though he wasn't projecting the emotion or intentionally trying.

"Anything. A fully trained mage is almost limitless. Queen Zarah conceived the idea of a family of lilim who, instead of losing power by crossing with mages, would instead gain a measure of the ability while retaining the lilim-kin's strengths—and weaknesses." Pryce's dry smile almost struck sparks in the air. "Like anyone else, there are mages whose services can be bought. One of them altered the Pryce... I'll call it line, the family. He made *improvements* as well."

The air quotes contained even more irony than his voice. "Pryces only make male children. Robert and I are the last of the family, since the *improvements* made our ruler perceive us as competition, a threat. I was sent to this world when I was quite young, and Robert remained the focus of her attention."

Unable to stand any longer, I staggered over to a folding chair and collapsed into it. The storage room we'd gone into to talk was full of boxes and bags, and they probably helped muffle our voices against the many people downstairs who no doubt would've liked to listen. "Don't try to make me feel sorry for him." The words ripped out of me. How had Robert survived? Everyone in that building had burned when I left. It didn't seem possible he was alive.

Holding up one hand, Pryce shook his head. "I'm not. I'm giving you facts. Given his presence, my best guess is he was sent there when it became known a woman was being, ah, kept there." Pryce paused as my heart raced. Kept indeed. His nostrils flared, the only admission of his discomfort at what happened to me there, then he continued. "I would not be surprised if your contract had already been purchased by Queen Zarah since you were young and apparently fertile. He'd gone back to our dominion to report on your progress when you burned down the facility, by the way. You were admirably thorough in dealing with your captors."

I stared at him, my heart pounding. Adrenaline flooded me, making it hard to think. One of my rapists, the one who fathered my son, was still alive. Despite my best effort, my voice trembled. "How do you know this? Why aren't you angry?"

He scoffed. "Slavers are scum, no matter their kin. What you did to them has become a cautionary story. It is now common knowledge."

Swallowing, I fought the urge to scream. The last thing I wanted was for everyone and their damn brother to know what had happened to me. "So everyone in Columbus knows now that Johann introduced me."

A flicker of sympathy crossed his face. "Everyone knows a mage burned the facility down and no one escaped. Further details are pure speculation on their parts. Robert's methods were specific to the situation. The others will assume emotional manipulation and forms of torture, not necessarily the rest of it."

'The rest of it.' Way to avoid the discomfort the word *rape* brought. I drew in a deep breath and let it out steadily. "If they wanted a child, why didn't they buy the contract of a woman from one of the captive houses? Like the one in Texas, with Morgan of the daoine sidhe?"

"They aren't for sale. Your kin is rare enough that they don't get resold. You would have been the first, and thus far only, opportunity."

My stomach lurched, despite his soft, clinical tone. Suspicion, second nature to me, reared its head. "Then why haven't you tried to take us?" He could have at any point. If we were such a rare and amazing commodity, why had we lived so long in peace?

He raised an elegant brow. "Because I loathe Queen Zarah, and what she's done to my kin. We can't die of old age, so she's ruled for a *long* time, molding our kin to ease her fears. Like you, I object to being regarded as breeding stock."

Taken at face value, that made perfect sense. Yet... "What *do* you want, Pryce?" The edge in my voice could've cut a rock.

"An alliance. I don't want Jimmy in her hands any more than you do. You're in the process of acquiring powerful allies, and when she comes—because he *will* be discovered eventually—I want your aid in killing her and freeing the lilim from her rule."

The puzzle pieces clicked together, the picture now clear to me. It was a power play, and protecting Jimmy was a beneficial side effect. The world made sense again.

Something dark moved through Pryce's eyes. "You need to be sure of the silence of everyone here. If she becomes aware of Jimmy, a successful breeding, too soon, all bets are off, and she will do whatever it takes to acquire him. The hope would be that the trait would carry through to any children he fathered with a lilim." He sniffed and looked uncomfortable. "And you are still of an age to have children. I don't say that to threaten. You need to be cautious."

Another shudder worked through me. I didn't need any pictures drawn of what would happen to Jimmy then. And I'd already proven I could produce a half lilim child.

My magic surged to the surface in response to the stress, or it would have, if there was any magic to come up. Pain stabbed in my head. I cried out as ribbons of magic slid from me. Doubling over, I clutched my head between my hands to keep my brain in my head, which was the best that I could hope for at this point. My body had resorted to a very aggressive reminder that I had burned myself out.

I fell to my knees as the door burst open, slamming against the wall with a crack like a log exploding in an intense fire. Warm hands steadied me with Nick's familiar scent close by. I rested my head against his chest, trying to hide from the screaming, gnawing pain. I dug my fingers under his shirt, looking for comfort in the feeling of his arms around me, even while said arms were rigid with tension.

More footsteps sounded as others ran up the stairs. I tried to push away from him but failed. Everyone here could see I'd collapsed, and the additional stress and fear sent another stab of pain through my head.

"What happened?" Nick's tone was smooth and as cold as black ice, and even more dangerous.

I couldn't answer but sighed as Noir pressed against me, hissing. He must have gotten bored with the goblins and decided to fly up with Nick.

"Facts." Pryce's voice sounded weary. "Something no one can protect her from, Mr. Damarian."

Accurate, and yet he was still a bastard.

"Mom? Are you ok?" Jimmy sounded nearly frantic.

Concern flooded through me, along with worry and love and fear, a wild cascade of emotion that dizzied me as Jimmy crowded in beside me, putting his arms around me. The double hug felt good, but the emotions stole my words for the moment.

"Excuse me." The flood of comfort cut off as soon as I heard Pryce's voice. I opened my eyes to see Pryce standing near Jimmy, and Nick's unwelcome expression fixed on him. Crixus, one of the goblins, stood by the door, coiled for action. Lotus, Johann's assistant, waited beside him.

Noir flapped once and hop-skipped onto my shoulder. I grunted under his weight. Geez. He'd gained a lot of weight from eating the magic. He ruffled his wings again and then waddled off of me and onto Jimmy, getting lighter and smaller with each step. His actions were carefully controlled to break the tension in the air. It worked. I had to struggle not to laugh.

"I'm fine," I spoke quickly to keep any remaining potential for violence low. "No need to worry, Jimmy."

The sight of Crixus reminded me that Jimmy and I needed to come up with our own way to remove the geas that bound goblins to slavery. We couldn't always depend on the little dragon to eat the magic. If Jimmy encountered one when Noir was with me, I wanted him to be able to handle it.

Fortunately for them and unfortunately for our practice, there were no living goblins still geased in the area, and they'd be incredibly hard to catch. Seasoned warriors, goblins never traveled alone and rarely even in teams of two. It was normally four or more.

We needed to move. The rest of the goblins might come checking for us. I didn't know if that was the entire troop in the Columbus area. "Crixus, are there other goblins in the area besides your crew and those who were holding Jimmy?

He nodded once. "Yes. Rhys has his own platoon."

Nick steadied me unobtrusively as I wobbled to my feet. I hated appearing so vulnerable. The pain had receded enough I could think again, but it left me a weakened mess.

Speaking as steadily as I could, I directed my words to Pryce. "Thank you. I see the merit of your sugges-tion, and I'll consider it."

He bowed slightly in my direction.

Lotus flowed through the crowd with all the exquisite grace of her apsara heritage, ending at Jimmy's side. "Ceri. Is there anything to be done to help you or Jimmy?"

Not having everyone in the building crowded into the room with us would've been a starting point.

Even with the headache receding, I was beyond exhausted and had so many loose ends to clean up. This situation was like two balls of yarn after a cat was done playing with it—all tangled and snarled.

Jimmy remained crowded close to me like he had as a little boy. His eyes were still wide and haunted as he stroked Noir, who had looped around his shoulders like a scarf.

Torn, I glanced at Pryce. I'd heard lilim could heal emotional trauma as well as inflict it. At this point, Jimmy needed a shortcut. We'd been taken by goblins, and he'd seen me tasered unconscious before he'd been taken and beaten in another location. I didn't want to speculate how Pryce and Johann had dealt with the goblins.

I needed to find a way for him to get therapy. I didn't want him to deal with the PTSD as I had—and still did.

"If Johann is willing, I could reduce his debt for my services if he'll give me and Jimmy a place to stay tonight. I'd also like a further conversation with you, Mr. Pryce." I needed to take care of Jimmy first, and yeah, maybe I was avoiding dealing with my trauma a little.

Johann appeared at the door as I spoke, completing the gathering. "Of course, Ceridwen."

Jimmy jumped. As bad as it sounded, I was glad for it, because at least it meant that he was still reacting to the outside world, not withdrawing into himself. I could say from experience that withdrawing helped not at all. I'd dealt with it by walling my emotions into a magical space, and the years of rage had been almost uncontrollable when it had finally broken out.

Magic was a seductively easy way to deal with pain, rage, and fear, and Jimmy would be thinking of using it soon. If Pryce could help him and prevent it, I'd ally with him in his other fight. Me and my army of six.

If Johann noticed the undercurrents in the room, he didn't react to them. "Why don't we go downstairs again? We can all retreat to our corners and regroup. Or better yet, go home." What a novel idea.

Lotus was the first one out of the room. I followed at a slower pace, leaning heavily on Nick for support with Jimmy on my other side. Quiet Nick was something I was used to, but his eyes traveling from Jimmy to Pryce indicated he'd put pieces together himself. Hopefully, not incorrectly.

"We have a new guest here and more excitement." Johann's voice was airy, drifting back to us, as if this was a day out in the gardens, not the aftermath of a

battle. "A daoine sidhe has come to visit, offering information in exchange for my protection. And the goblins
listened to me and left her alone, judging by the
absence of screams. The day is looking up!"

My jaw wanted to drop at his audacity, and I felt
the breath of a grim laugh shake Nick's arm. Both at
Johann testing the goblins by leaving a daoine sidhe
with them, and the absurdity of one finding us here, in
an allegedly abandoned house.

I wasn't against the idea of getting information, but
I was still raw from recent events and not overly keen
to trust someone new. I hadn't changed *that* much.
Plus, my magic was kaput.

On the stairs now, I could just see the daoine sidhe,
a slim woman, fair skinned and golden haired,
surrounded by goblins.

They were keeping six feet away from her. Their
stance was aggressive and hers frightened, which made
me narrow my eyes. She had to be exaggerating, and it
made me trust her less. Only a very young daoine sidhe
would abandon their pride and cringe like that. As in, a
child younger than Jimmy. Their pride, justified or not,
was as much a part of them as their skeleton. And she
should've been certain the charm of her kin would be
able to ensure her safety.

"Tara O'Brien, thank you for coming here. Crixus,
please order your troop to give her space and let her
talk to us." Johann paused at the foot of the steps, his
hands on his hips.

Crixus spoke, the words crisp and clear in a hissing clicking language. Quickly, the goblins moved back three steps, as coordinated as if they'd practiced a dance. Then, in a blurring motion that put my heart in my mouth, they scattered, and in moments a small folding table and several chairs were set up in the room. They retreated to Crixus's side when they were done, gaze on me and Jimmy.

Hope burned in their red eyes, and with it, more weight dropped onto my shoulders. I gave them a nod regardless. They'd helped me and deserved the recognition. What had Crixus called me? Chainbreaker?

Pfft. Right now I couldn't unravel knitting, much less break chains.

"Sit," said Johann to the daoine sidhe, as polite and pleasant as ever. She dropped into a folding chair, baby blue eyes open wide.

"Stay with Lotus and Pryce, Jimmy," I said. When I met Pryce's eyes, he nodded, a tiny gesture.

This was a chance to calm Jimmy, even in the goblin's presence. I didn't blame him for his fear, but I couldn't let it cripple him the way it had me. "Johann, maybe Crixus and his troop could start moving the film people to the field?"

"Good idea." Johann nodded. "Since the crop circle is set up. I'll have someone call the police to make sure the crew don't freeze."

Another loose end taken care of. Good. As the goblins moved toward one of the sleeping bodies, a few quick if somewhat unsteady steps brought me to the table, and I sat down on one of the other chairs in front of Tara, leaning my elbows on the table as I met her frightened gaze.

It wasn't exactly the politest gesture and not a good example for Jimmy, but at this point, if poor table manners was the only bad thing he learned from me today, then I would consider myself lucky. It occurred to me that I was thinking about him as if he were seven, rather than seventeen. I needed to stop doing that when I was stressed. Or ever. He was basically grown.

"How did you know we were here?" I asked. This location was supposed to be at least somewhat secret, and it was concerning, at least, to me that she had managed to show up here. The coming was awfully suspect.

Nick stood behind me, his hand on my shoulder.

I felt the same way about this new girl, Tara, as I had about Pryce. I was *done* with not having my questions answered. If she was willing to tell me how she had gotten here, then that was a good sign that she might tell us some other things that we wanted to know. And if she wasn't going to tell us something, well, less time wasted.

"I knew where you were because one of the goblin troop called and gave me a status update —I'm Ariana's assistant—just as you guys attacked. The house is pretty obvious once you get to the location." The corner of her mouth curled up, and I could tell that she was impressed we had managed to take care of the goblins—as well she should have been. It certainly hadn't been easy, and it was also the reason my magic was bone freaking dry. Scraping the bottom of the well, as it were. "I'm ahead of the clean-up team," She continued. "I left a note, and Ariana's sure to have found it by now."

"Did she try?" I glanced at Johann. I was asking if she'd tried to order the goblins, who didn't now have to obey any daoine sidhe. I didn't say it out loud, in case that secret was still secret.

"No." His eyes were on her, considering. Johann had a heart, sure. But he kept it in a box somewhere in his house in case someone made a good offer for it. No sane person would come to him begging for protection without something to trade. It was all about money and power for Johann.

She gazed back with dewy, innocent eyes. Her face was as pretty and fresh as a newly bloomed flower, pleading in every line of her body.

Geez. She was laying it on thick, which suggested she needed help and was very young. Most daoine sidhe were smart and all too aware of their kin's reputation. Or, she could've been relying on that reaction. Daoine sidhe webs could trip up the spiders. They were consummate liars.

"Tara O'Brien. What do you want and what do you offer?" Nick's voice, from over my head. I twisted to look at him, surprised.

He'd reassumed the human illusion, and the hard silver eyes contrasted with the quiet, inoffensive face he presented to the world. A narrow-faced, middle-aged man with laugh lines and thinning grey-brown hair, someone who would live in a lab or a library.

She blinked. Wavering? Maybe. "I want protection," Tara said. "I can tell you why Morgan ordered her captured." She inclined her head toward me. "And why Ariana ordered the goblins rather than Rhys, who should have."

It would've been nice to know why she wanted me, if there were reasons beyond the fact of my existence. Which, from what I knew, was more than enough. And the fact that Ariana had usurped Rhys's privilege was alarming. Daoine sidhe followed a strict hierarchy, and their leadership turnover was bloody and often involved other kins as proxies. I waited for Johann's answer, since he was who she was asking.

"Ceridwen," Johann said in a quiet voice.

I glanced at him while he regarded me with an expressionless face. His narrow, greenish hazel eyes were deep-set in a round pockmarked face, with an oft broken nose for contrast. I was willing to bet none of it was real, but the illusion was perfect.

"Yes?" Bit too much attitude in that one word. Oh, well. I was worn out.

Johann's eyes sparkled at my snark. He thought this was all a lark. "I think it's time for all to retire. Would you feel safe with her in my home?"

"Yes." Otherwise, he wouldn't take her in, and I wanted her information close to hand. Since I was his guest, my safety took priority. He acted so like a fé, so concerned with his contracts, but I didn't buy it.

Johann continued. "Santo and Vittorio will drive her and any wounded goblins. They've found one who survived your shot, Nick."

"They're tough," Nick responded.

Hope surged in me. This was a chance to perfect removing the geas and give Jimmy and me more potential bodyguards. A living goblin still under geas but disabled. Jimmy could practice removing it with my directions. Score one for the mages.

LOTUS AND JOHANN made short work of herding everyone into vehicles. The troll, Santo, carried the two wounded goblins through the snow back to Johann's house, and his partner, Vittorio, escorted Tara. Johann was taking no chances.

Jimmy and Nick herded me into Johann's SUV. Lotus hopped in shotgun.

"Do you believe her?" I asked. Nick was squished on my left with Jimmy on my right.

Before Nick could answer, Johann laughed. "A fifty-fifty shot. But it's interesting, and I'll see what she says. That's why she's with the trolls. A chilly walk won't hurt her and gives us a little time to get settled. And I want a lead—even a false one—on who's violating my rules. Even if it's false, I could act on it in all innocence."

He flashed a grin at me in the rearview mirror.

Innocence and Johann were words that didn't belong in the same sentence.

Jimmy blinked at me sleepily. "Mom, it's safe at Johann's. Maybe I can sleep there."

Whatever Pryce had done to remove some of the trauma had left Jimmy calmer and a little sleepy. I leaned over, offering a hug, and he accepted it. I couldn't fault him for his fear. I'd lived with it all of his life, and Dara's.

His sister... Pryce's words about young female mages came back like a stone in my heart, but I couldn't talk about it in front of Jimmy. I'd hire Johann's people later, once he'd gone to bed. After we'd worked on removing the geas on the goblins by ourselves.

Panic for my Dara bubbled up my throat. I was desperate to hear from her.

We arrived at the compound and headed into the converted farmhouse that Johann had made his home. Nick helped me out of the SUV and walked me inside with his arm around me. I was glad. I really still needed the support.

"It'll take them at least an hour to get here. I'd suggest using the time to shower, at the very least." Johann's nose twitched as he said it and glanced at me.

It was hard not to tell him to bite me. Especially when he had a point. He just always had to put it in the worst possible way.

"This way," Lotus murmured, stepping close so

Nick let me go. "Mr. Damarian, I'll show you to your room once Ceri and Jimmy are settled."

The corner of Nick's mouth curled in a slight smile. "Of course, Lotus. Thank you for your consideration."

The rooms she led Jimmy and me to were next to each other in a short hall on the second floor. At Lotus's welcoming gesture, Jimmy opened one of the doors first. The interior, simple and restful, contained a bed covered by an old-fashioned quilt, a dresser, a nightstand, and a small desk with a tablet on it. Another door led to what I guessed was a bathroom shared with the next room over.

"The Wi-Fi password is taped inside the top drawer of the dresser. 1-2-3-4 unlocks the tablet." Lotus gazed at him. "Do you feel safe here?"

"You're right next door, Mom?" Jimmy asked as he looked around.

"Yes." I patted his shoulder.

"And it's true Johann has hellhounds patrol the grounds at night?" He met Lotus's gaze.

She laughed. "No. Drake often walks the grounds. He's worse than any hellhound pack."

He nodded with his eyebrows raised, then pointed at the door. "Then I'm good. That leads to the shower?"

Lotus inclined her head. "Yes. I'll be dropping off a change of clothing after your mother is in her room."

Jimmy nodded and headed for the door; the sound

of water running started almost immediately after he shut the door behind him.

We left and headed for the next bedroom down. "I bet getting all the bathrooms installed in no time at all cost a pretty penny," I said in a conversational tone.

After an attack in the fall, Johann had moved abruptly out here. It had only been two months and I'd never seen a single sign of renovations, but I highly doubted this old farmhouse had come this way, built to house this many people.

Lotus laughed again, the sound bright and infectious. "Yes. Johann had some favors owed, and so the plumbing was able to go in, and a few extra rooms."

Looking at the short halls, I cocked my head. "How?"

"Some of the rooms are located in a pocket between dominions, mostly the ones where long-term residents and staff stay. Guest rooms are still solidly here. The water comes from another dominion, the rusalki set that up. The plan's more defensible, too, with a smaller area here."

I opened the door to the next room. "Lotus, could I talk to you for a moment?"

"Of course." She walked in behind me, head tilted, her brown eyes curious.

I shut the door and lowered my voice, though I was unsure how much good that would do in Johann's house. "Can you give me advice on how to deal with your boss in a way that makes him *not* charge me huge amounts for any favor or service I need?"

She gazed at me with something like pity replacing her curiosity. "Did the lilim never feed you any gossip about Johann?"

Well now that I knew there was gossip to be heard, I wanted to know it. "Only that he's a fé, that he rules the area with an iron fist, has tentacles everywhere, and can provide you with just about anything for the right price... why?" I let an edge creep into my voice. "Oh, and that he jacks his prices up for me, let's not forget that."

"The reason he does that is that he wants very much for you to dislike him and avoid him." Lotus avoided my eyes, pacing across the room to look out the window. "Johann, until very recently, was married to a human mage. By the time you arrived here, she was old. She died just before the attack, saving a child. You're not like her at all in appearance, but you're not dissimilar in personality. And you're so very young, compared to her. Johann has taken every opportunity to drive you away because he could easily"—she waved her hand as if searching for the right word—"find you fair to look upon."

Her accent had crept in as she spoke, and her tone was sad. "Nor would he make an attempt on you now, it's well known that you and Nick Damarian are fond of each other. But it's his way. Once he finds a course, he doesn't consider wrongs or rights."

When her meaning sank in, I wanted to bang my head about the wall. "He's an asshole to me because he doesn't want to be attracted to me?"

She bowed her head. "Essentially. What is it you need? I can handle small contracts. Leave Johann out of the loop."

Hope soared in my heart. Could she help me? "I want my daughter, Dara, found. She left for Europe, but she's only left a few short messages and it's not like her at all. With everything happening, I'm worried."

"Unless something major happens, that's something I can agree to. I can actually just debit it against the credit you have for reinforcing the ward. Is that acceptable?"

More than. "Yes, thank you."

She left. When the water stopped running, I gave Jimmy a few moments to vacate the bathroom then scuttled for the shower.

Oh, this was nice. Whoever had stocked the room shared my fondness for herbal and floral soaps. I used the lavender liberally.

When I got out, I sighed in relief. I could get used to this treatment. Someone had obviously been in and out and left another outfit in my size on the bed and removed the dirty clothes. There was also a new phone. When I turned it on, it had already been set to my number. Speedy work.

Clean clothes were nice, though orange bell

bottoms with a purple and white paisley hippy shirt would not have been my first choice. No matter. Having a working phone made it all better. I used it to call off work for Thursday and let them know Jimmy wouldn't be in either. I said, truthfully, we'd been in an accident. I was not going to be loved as they tried to find a substitute. Subs were hard to come by these days. I'd need to be back to work at least by Friday morning.

The mattress swallowed me in a sigh of squishy softness. Feeling relatively safe, I dropped off to sleep almost immediately and then woke with the dawn.

Not eager to waste any time, I woke Jimmy, who would've slept until noon if I'd let him, and the pair of us headed for the outbuilding where the goblins were housed. Crixus and Nick met us at the door to that building.

"Stay outside, Jimmy." Nick nodded at my glance toward him. He'd stay with Jimmy for reassurance.

Noir rode on my shoulder, tiny again, as I stepped into the tool shed, now cleared of its usual contents. My breath puffed a cloud of vapor as I examined the goblins, both wrapped in bandages. One had lost an arm and the other was swathed in gauze around his abdomen. Both appeared to be asleep, and both had every limb manacled.

The smell of sickness almost took my breath away, even though the interior was surprisingly clean. Both goblins' ashen skin had darkened and mottled, and I had no idea what that meant. On a human I'd say it looked bad. Who could tell with a goblin?

I glanced at Crixus through the open door, since he hadn't entered the building. "Are the cuffs necessary? Are they likely to survive?"

He nodded curtly and cleared his throat. "Yes, and maybe. If you can remove the geas, they can get better treatment."

No pressure, considering I *couldn't* remove the geas.

"Jimmy, come in if you feel you can. If you can't, just tell me." I hoped he could, so we could try to figure this out. But if he couldn't, Noir could possibly repeat his earlier meals.

At the thought, the dragon in question rubbed his head against my cheek and then flapped away to perch above the door. His face wasn't terribly expressive, but I still got the impression he was laughing at me. Just a feeling I got from the little devil.

Jimmy walked in, rigid, much like he'd have looked for any photography session. He hated having his picture taken with a burning passion. And of course, he hated stepping in here. He was less than ecstatic to be around the creatures, not that I could blame him. People of that kin had beaten and hurt him yesterday, and he didn't have my practice at compartmentalizing. He was still a passionate teenager, too.

He swallowed, paling further as he took in the injuries. Had they been human, they would've been dying, especially considering the less-than-basic first aid they'd been given. "What happened to them?" Jimmy whispered.

"I shot them." Nick stood just behind him at the door. His force didn't betray his feelings about injuring the goblins. They were under compulsion, yes, but this had been kill or be killed.

Jimmy jumped and took a step further inside next to me. For a moment, I thought he was going to grab my hand, but he shoved his into his pockets at the last second.

If there was one skill that I had learned in this life, it was how to solve problems. Right now, the priority was freeing these two from the geas, or if we absolutely had to, from the burden of existence.

"Jimmy, look at them with your magical sight. Do you see them wrapped up like mummies? How do you see them?"

He squinted then sighed. "I don't *see* anything, Mom. I hear it, like a symphony, hundreds of instruments all playing, the same song coming off of both of them."

It was unfortunate that we didn't observe the magic similarly. Mages perceived magic based on one of the senses, and whereas mine was sight, for him, it might have been touch, taste, smell, or hearing. I was happy that it wasn't taste, to be honest. Partly for the fact that I didn't think I could deal with my son having to lick goblins to see if they had a geas placed upon them.

Then again, part of being a mom was embarrassing my son, and that would have been prime real estate.

But hearing was doable. "How do you manipulate it?"

His shy smile warmed my heart. "I hear the notes in my mind. Or I hum... like a melody, maybe?"

No wonder he'd hated music class and had refused to learn to play an instrument. He could've inadvertently created mass chaos at school.

"With the goblins before, I tried to pull off the strands. It obviously didn't work. Noir ate them, partly because there was no time and partly to save my strength." I shrugged.

"And you're not doing it now because you've just about burned yourself out." Jimmy took a step closer and gave me a brief hug. "I get it. No pressure, right? Let me try."

I couldn't help but want to fuss over him. "What do you plan to do?" I asked.

He frowned. "I'm going to try to change the melody then diminuendo it away."

"Diminuendo?" I hadn't the foggiest idea what that meant.

He waved his hands, rolling them down as if that explained it. "Make it softer and softer. I'm going to concentrate now, Mom. If you guys could step away and be quiet?" His brow furrowed, and without waiting to make sure we obeyed, he closed his eyes.

I tried to see what he was doing, but the immediate ache in my temples and dampness under my nose persuaded me to not even attempt to follow along. I had to trust Jimmy to be strong in his own right.

Nick passed me a handkerchief, frowning and shaking his head no. He didn't want me to attempt any magic.

While he was not the boss of me, I'd take his suggestion and his hankie. I wiped the blood away and grimaced. What I wouldn't give to be able to help Jimmy now. Or at least watch.

From the door, Crixus gestured us outside. Jimmy was in no danger from the injured goblins, so we followed him out and pushed the door mostly shut.

"Why not use the dragon?" His hissing voice blended with the wind, so soft I had to strain to hear it. Snow skittered on the grounds, swirling around our feet, reminding me of the cold wind.

I tried to match his pitch. Not being musical in the slightest, the form Jimmy's magic had taken had genuinely surprised me. "We can't count on Noir always being here to save our bacon. Jimmy's going to use his magic to drag it down to the studs then figure out how to strip it."

Crixus's lipless mouth curled. "We're a home improvement analogy? Ceridwen Chainbreaker, you're no poet."

The snort I gave started my nose bleeding again. "Ugh," I muttered and raised Nick's hankie again.

While I tended to my blood faucet, Crixus stared at me, and Nick stared at him.

"You've burned yourself out." Nick's tone was flat and contained a dictionary's worth of unspoken words.

"I noticed..." I kept my voice neutral, even if my words were dry. I knew what I'd done. He didn't have to point it out.

It was going to be fine. We did have Noir here if we needed him. He would eat the magic if Jimmy couldn't remove it.

I had no idea when I'd get my power back. At this point, I was so burned out that I was as crispy as bacon that shattered when dropped on a plate. On the inside, at least. I had no comparison to go by, but then I remembered Nick's previous comments about having known mages. And the goblin was old, maybe he'd know.

"How long does burnout last? Do either of you know?" After I spoke, the question hung in the air. Neither of them jumped to respond, which really made me feel great.

Nick sighed. "I hate to say this, but it depends."

His vague answer annoyed me. I folded my arms and stared at them. "Spill it."

Crixus laughed. "He speaks true... a day, a month, a year... I've seen all three. The strong injure themselves most deeply, and you're strong, Ceridwen Chainbreaker."

Oh crap. I was pretty strong.

A warm hand caught my cold one. "I'm here," Nick said. "And I don't want to leave you until your power's back, Ceri." His eyes crinkled as he smiled down at me.

I cupped his cheek but chuckled. "That might make going to work difficult for both of us, Nick. And saying something like that guarantees we're going to end up separated soon." I kept my tone light as worry flooded me. I couldn't even *see* magic right now, how was I going to defend myself and my family? Jimmy was still so green. I couldn't depend on him. Besides, I didn't want to. It wasn't his responsibility.

"If it makes you feel better, generally, the older you are, the faster mages recover. Kind of the opposite of physical injuries." Nick didn't let go of my hand until I tugged it gently away.

The magic right now was the issue, and not my age, thank you very much. Except it was. Kind of a grim joke.

"I hate to break up this lovefest..." Jimmy's voice was low and tired, but with a streak of triumph. "I've got them cleared, and I want a hamburger and fries and a large sugary drink with lots of caffeine."

"Do you mind if I double-check?" Nick asked Jimmy directly. He met my son's gaze with more than a little respect in his eyes.

"Nope. Not at all." Jimmy shuffled to the side, and I followed Nick.

Nick pulled a fog grey cloudy stone from his jeans

pocket and laid it on the bare skin of the gut-shot goblin. Nothing happened.

"Good," Nick murmured and repeated the process on the one-armed goblin. "Both are clear. Magnificent, Jimmy."

A flush of warm pride rushed through me, joining my own. It was an uncontrolled projection of emotion, Jimmy's lilim heritage coming to the fore.

Jimmy blushed and announced, "I'm heading for the house and some food."

I pulled him close for a hug, so happy he'd found a way almost completely on his own. "You're strong. And obviously talented."

He hugged me back. "I still want to learn how to stop people, Mom. I saw you do it, and I want to learn self-defense. Even if there's electricity and fire involved."

Just the thought of doing all that made me more exhausted right now. "When I can, I'll show you." I looked over at Nick. "Could you teach him in the meantime?"

With a smile, he nodded. "I could. I'd be happy to. You could ask Johann who he recommends. You might find me to be a bit of an old-fashioned teacher." Nick's smile held a world of wry amusement. "I believe in conditioning and strength training as part of my curriculum. I think you'll find that whomever you learn with as similar requirements."

Jimmy's sigh was a masterpiece of put-uponness. "I

guess, but I still want my hamburger and drink. And to go back to bed."

Nick accompanied him and they headed into the house. I watched as they passed goblins rushing out the door with stretchers. How they knew to come was a mystery. Some unheard signal of Crixus's.

They rushed toward us, then into the shed, loaded the injured goblins on them, and headed back for the main house as I shivered a bit in the cold.

"Are the chances of them living better, now?" I asked Crixus, who watched their progression from beside me.

"Yes. Both from better care and from no longer being under the geas. Your son did well, for all his fear."

"You could tell?" I gave him an appraising look.

His stony face barely moved, but I was fairly sure he smiled, just a little in the corners. "Of course. I could smell it. You've raised a brave child."

He was brave. And he'd been through too much the last couple of days. "Do you know what happened to the goblins who captured him?"

Crixus shrugged. "Against Schmidt and Pryce? Schmidt once killed a dragon, almost by himself. Pryce is a powerful lilim. And while you've been harmed by them, I don't think you've met them in a real fight."

I set my jaw. "Not one involving guns," I said darkly.

He blinked before saying, "Correction taken. All

kinds of emotions can be projected—terror, nausea, grief—it all depends on what the lilim has experienced in their life. So the pair of them? Against a troop of boots, probably surprised... My best guess is they're all dead. Schmidt isn't the merciful type."

Crixus paced beside me as I started the trek back to the house. "Do you know if there's a way to block the geas from reinfecting us?" he asked.

I considered. "It's possible. I'll think on it, but..."

"I know. May the return of your power be swift." Crixus saw me through the door then headed for the rooms where the goblins were being housed.

"Ceridwen?" Johann called. I turned and walked into the conference room. Johann, Lotus, Nick, and Jimmy were gathered around a table, tablets and laptops open, looking like some sort of fortune 500 supernatural corporation board meeting.

"Yes?" I replied in a guarded tone.

Johann raised his eyebrows and looked at me with his head at an angle that put me in mind of him peering over spectacles... though he wasn't wearing any. "Your suggestions on dealing with the daoine sidhe in the area after this aggression?"

I snorted and couldn't find it in me to be actually helpful. "Gas explosions where they live? A suitable amount of C-4 or other high impact explosives?"

"Subtle," Lotus murmured.

"Not in the least." I was tired of risking my neck, and the necks of my children. I fixed them all with glares, one by one. Even Jimmy. "Someone needs to make the hard choices. Blow them up. Poison them. Curse them. Send them a nice note with a fruit basket requesting they vacate the city immediately. And when I say requesting, I mean demanding. I don't care how, just get them far away from here and from the goblins that Jimmy and I have freed. When Morgan finds out her geas over the goblins are broken, she'll meet you on the field, Johann. Can you win and still be subtle?"

Jimmy took in a sharp breath and looked behind me. I whirled.

Even louder than him, though, was Tara. She stood behind me at the door I'd just entered, tears shining in her eyes. Simultaneous pangs of guilt and suspicion hit my gut. Her appearance at *just* that moment was mightily pat.

Apparently, I wasn't the only one with that opinion. "Tara. I'm glad to see you've had a chance to freshen up and come down to see us. Please, have a seat," Schmidt said in a dangerously mild tone.

Tara did so with slow care as if afraid the cushioned chair would bite. Too bad it couldn't. If I had my magic, I'd have been sorely tempted to make it.

"When does Ariana plan to take power from Rhys? Does she have Morgan's support?" Johann asked, fixing his stare on Tara.

"She *had* Morgan's support. The bliss failure has put Rhys on very thin ice, and him obsessing about getting his sister back from you is making him look weak. She plans to move soon. Ariana has her own goblins." She twined her fingers in her lap. "There's another attack coming, but I don't know on whom or using what resources."

Interesting. If she was telling the truth, then we were in serious trouble here. What reason did she have to lie, other than disinformation? It really depended on if Tara was Ariana's or Rhys's plant. She had to know what Schmidt would do—unless she was confident she could get clear and be defended afterward. Or unless he was killed.

While I wasn't exactly happy that I had basically threatened her entire race, maybe that would make it clear that I was not someone that she wanted to cross. Or someone easily trifled with.

Could it work out after all? Not with the structure as it stood, but maybe without the goblins acting as their army, the daoine sidhe would back off.

"Why do you care? Why are you here?" I asked.

I expected a shrug and a noncommittal answer, but she met my eyes firmly. My respect for her inched up a notch, although it wasn't as if that was an accomplishment. Slightly up from nothing was still pretty close to nothing.

She steeled her spine visibly before replying. "Because I want Ariana's place as second when you all kill her or make her look the fool."

All right then. Some ambition. That was a reasonable motive. It wasn't necessarily a bad thing, and it made it more likely that she was telling the truth. She had even less reason to lie now, and as sad as it sounded, I wasn't against helping her to achieve her goal. At least this way, it would be a devil we knew, and Ariana had already proven to be too treacherous to deal with. If Tara was in her place, then the daoine sidhe in the city were weaker.

"Fair enough. Lotus, would you be so kind as to see Tara back to her room to prevent her from running into anyone unfriendly?" The unspoken threat in Johann's tone was silken and cold.

Lotus smiled and motioned for Tara to walk with her. "Of course. We can stop by the kitchen for a snack to hold you over until breakfast. I've heard daoine sidhe have fast metabolisms..." Lotus's chatty voice faded a moment after they left the room.

"Where do we house the freed goblins now? It's too public here, Ceridwen." Johann regarded us.

I paused and considered the people in the room and our resources. "Nick, could they camp in your pole barn for the next couple of days? Just until we find a place for them?" There, at least they would be out of the way, not to mention they would be far away from anyone that they could hurt, although without the geas maybe we wouldn't have to worry about that anymore. At least, that was the hope.

"Yes, they can stay there. We'll have to schedule

showers, though." Nick shrugged. "But that's manageable."

From what I'd seen, that wouldn't be a problem for them. Their lives seemed organized in a military fashion. They'd figure it out and police themselves.

My phone rang, so I pulled it out of my pocket. Oh, ack. The school was calling. I moved away from them and answered. "Hey, Boss Lady," I said cheerily and totally fake.

"Ceri, how are you and Jimmy? How bad was the accident?" Amy Griswold asked, her tone alive with both concern and concealed avid interest.

I kept my voice hushed and walked farther away from the murmuring group. "We're both pretty bruised up. Jimmy had the worst of it. He'll probably stay home through the weekend."

She sighed. "I hate to ask. Odette Keller wanted to reschedule for Friday and we're having a terrible time finding a sub, do you think you're up for teaching tomorrow?"

I groaned internally. Saving the city and holding down a job was a pain in the tuchus. "Yes, I'll be there. Could you let attendance know Jimmy won't?"

This time her sigh was full of relief. And once she knew I was coming, she didn't bother trying to prolong the conversation. I was grateful for that. "Of course," she chirped. "See you tomorrow. Hope you both feel better!" She hung up. I turned back to the conversation.

When I returned to the group and sat at the table, Schmidt set his fingertips together and narrowed his eyes thoughtfully on Nick. "Do you have a place there where you can keep Tara as well? Her phone can be removed. I don't trust her, and at least this way she'll be out of the way."

I wasn't sure that was going to be enough to keep her from being a problem, but it was a temporary solution. I hadn't thought that far ahead, anyway.

Nick considered for a second, then nodded slowly, but looked reluctant. I could tell that he wasn't happy at the thought of taking multiple people, multiple kins, all potential enemies to the farm where he lived when he wasn't actively running experiments, but it really was the safest place for all of them to be right now.

Johann's home had a constant stream of people, and was pretty much gossip central. If we wanted the goblin's freedom kept quiet, they couldn't stay here very long. My home wasn't large and sat in a suburban cul-de-sac, not exactly isolated. Nick owned over a hundred acres, and the area surrounding his little farm was heavily wooded. Safer for them.

Safer for all of us, too.

"I will. But if she steps wrong, I *will* kill her." It was an uncomplicated statement of fact, and it was almost chilling how simply he said it. This was someone's life that he was talking about, and yet he discussed killing her as nonchalantly as he would've talked about taking out the trash or doing the dishes.

"I've never liked dealing with daoine sidhe, but I don't believe that she's a turncoat. However, if she puts Ceri or Jimmy at risk, she doesn't get a second chance."

Jimmy flinched, and I touched his shoulder gently with my fingers. It must have been hard for him to be around Nick when he was like this because it was hard to reconcile the man that had cared for us both so much with this brutally practical man in front of us. I knew that he was only doing what he had to do, but to Jimmy, it was no doubt a sobering reminder of what Nick was actually capable of.

"So we're going home?" Jimmy asked. He'd settled close to me after I sat down. I didn't mind the plaintive tone. Everything was happening so quickly, like a riptide in the ocean, ready to sweep our feet out from under us and drown us any second.

"I am at least," I said with a yawn. "I have to work tomorrow."

Johann grimaced. "I don't think that's a good idea."

Annoyance flared, and long habit made me strongly consider the contrary path. I couldn't do a lot at the moment, but I could make sure that my son at least *felt* safe. My wards at home were independent of my power and fully charged.

Lotus cleared her throat as Johann and I stared at each other like gunfighters, neither willing to give in. "Johann, she needs to work, since you don't employ her. Ceri, you're in danger. Will your wards protect you enough for the current situation?" Her eyes met mine calmly, clearly trying to make me understand what she was saying.

"Yes." My wards would keep out hostiles for more than long enough to call for help. I'd set plenty at the school as well. I was covered. I glanced at Jimmy.

He caught my eye. "You aren't going home alone, Mom."

Nick rose, grabbed my hand, and kissed it. "I'm off, then. As often turns out, you were right, Ceri. Johann, if you could arrange transport for the goblins and Tara once I confirm my home is secure?"

"Of course," Johann answered genially. "Ceri, if you need a rental car, I have several available for reasonable rates."

"Let me see them before I sign anything." I folded my arms as Johann's eyes twinkled. I wasn't about to pay him for some jalopy.

After making sure we were done with the discussion, Jimmy disappeared with Lotus. She was a soothing influence, I knew, and Jimmy genuinely liked her. He'd be safe.

Johann and I remained in the conference room, although I was careful to make sure that we kept our voices low so that Jimmy didn't hear us.

"I'm considering calling Ariana." Johann sounded less than eager, which was basically exactly how I felt about it. Speaking to her started a dangerous game, and yet it would have to happen if we wanted to reduce the bloodshed. And I really wanted to reduce the bloodshed. As long as we were dealing with this here, we weren't searching for Dara. And that was a worry-turning-into-blind-panic in the back of my mind.

There was no way to tell if Tara was ready to take over even if we did manage to take Ariana out of the equation, and a power vacuum was the last thing that we wanted right now.

Our thoughtful silence was interrupted by a tinkling chime from Johann's cell phone. He pulled it out of his pocket with a sigh, and I raised my eyebrows. Whatever it was, it was clearly important, because he stood up almost immediately and walked to the other side of the room.

My phone chimed seconds later, the message from Lotus informing me that Mary's fake ID packet was ready and in my room. Good. Another needed item off my list. Mary was the fetch who now looked just like Jimmy's girlfriend and always would. But it wasn't her fault she'd been used in an attempt to force me to help someone, so I was helping her as best I could, which included a set of fake papers.

While Johann was still occupied with his phone, I slipped away from the table to double-check everything in the packet was correct and then call Mary to let her know the ID had been set up for her. Even better, she didn't answer so I could leave a message.

Then I settled down to meditate and clear my mind. I hoped that would help me recover more quickly. It couldn't hurt anyway. Breathing deeply and slowly, repeating nonsense phrases over and over until my mind cleared. I sat there for a long time, but it felt like seconds later that my phone rang.

I opened my eyes to find Nick's smiling face beckoning me from the screen. With the way everything had been going lately, I wouldn't have been surprised if he had been calling to tell me that his barn had burned down and we were going to have to keep all of the goblins in my shower, which was going to put a serious cramp on my style.

"Everything is fine," he said without preamble. Bless him. "The goblins are settled in the barn and Tara in the guest room." How long had I been meditating? "I'm getting some work done. Rest, get yourself in fighting trim."

I looked at the time on the phone. Holy crow! I'd stayed in trance for almost eight hours. That had never happened before. I tucked it away to worry about if it happened again and followed my grumbling stomach downstairs.

He hung up, and I narrowed my eyes suspiciously at the ceiling. It wasn't that I didn't trust Nick, because I did. It was more that I didn't trust the universe, and this seemed to be just too easy. I didn't believe it. I was just hoping that it would be another shoe to fall, and not a guillotine.

When I went down for supper, Jimmy and Johann were already there.

"I kept him from eating all the pork chops, Mom."

Jimmy looked amused, and the shadows in his eyes were less noticeable.

If it was Johann's influence, I'd play along. "Thanks, I hope it wasn't too desperate a struggle."

"Not at all." Johann leaned toward me. "Ceridwen, would you be willing to help me get some information from Ariana?"

Ugh. I didn't look forward to this, but having Johann owe me either money or a favor was a good thing. "Possibly, what would it entail?"

"You would pose as my helpless prisoner. I would twirl my mustache, make vague promises, and be stupefied by her beauty. Then we'd listen to her brag and possibly reveal bits of her plans I haven't figured out yet."

"So long as I'm only posing, Johann." I tried for a light tone, but it came out flat. I didn't like the idea of being his little stooge, even pretend.

"Mom, Johann's ok, really." Jimmy looked up from his food.

Johann smiled at my son indulgently. "Your mother has reasons for not being a fan of mine, Jimmy. But she knows my word is good. And I give it to you that I'll not keep you in this house against your will on this occasion."

On *this* occasion. Um. "That's... not reassuring."

His answering grin showed me a row of pointy teeth. "That wasn't the intent."

I sighed and waved my hand vaguely at him. "Yes, I'll help."

We set up in Johann's office after Jimmy went upstairs to play video games. Better he distract himself while he waited for us to leave. And of course Johann had every imaginable gaming system.

"Please, sit here." He indicated a chair visible from the laptop's camera. "If you would, let that expressive face of yours shout all the things you won't be saying. Ariana likes to win."

He handed me a set of cuffs and the key. Then he pulled a square of tape out of his desk.

I looked from it to him with my lips pursed.

He motioned the tape toward me again. "Handcuff yourself however you want. This is kinesiology tape. It comes right off and has duct tape glued to its back. It'll look like a gag but will fall right off if you move too much, so don't. I have Jimmy in my dungeon, by the way, to make you obedient. Got it?"

"I'm not happy about this," I grumbled. But still, happy or not, I put the key in my pocket after testing to make sure it opened the cuffs. Then I put them on. Johann patted the tape in place.

"That'll make this more realistic." He grinned then cleared his throat and furrowed his brow. Returning to his desk, Johann placed the call then leaned back, a faint smile curving on his lips. "This should be hilarious but do try not to laugh."

The screen flickered, and then Ariana regarded us,

her thin brows raised. "Johann. To what do I owe the dubious pleasure?"

"It seems I'm running a lost and found now. Your goblins lost Ms. Gault, and I've picked her and her son up. I thought you might be interested in knowing I have an extra."

My right eye twitched. Ariana's gaze fell on me. It took no effort to glare back. She'd had Jimmy kidnapped and beaten.

A sweet smile brightened her face. "Why thank you, Johann! I'm more than happy to pay a finder's fee."

"We can discuss that in a moment, *after* you share why you've broken my rule against forcible recruitment?" Johann's face and tone had become even blander. That was more dangerous than if he'd gotten fiercer.

"It was only going to be temporary. Once our beloved leader"—I could've cut the sarcasm in her voice with a dull butter knife and spread it on toast— "Rhys has left the area, I would've released her back into the wild. You know how hard it is to get the undivided services of a mage, Johann, sometimes desperate steps need to be taken to maintain the advantage. Wouldn't you rather deal with me than Rhys? What with your feud and all? And I can offer certain advantages to you that Rhys can't." She leaned back, her thin silk blouse stretched over small but obviously bra-less breasts.

"It's true Rhys and I have a less than happy history," Johann murmured, an appreciative glint in his eye. Weird. I'd never seen him react to women in the slightest, not even Lotus, who was as close to physically perfect as flesh and blood could get. Was it acting?

"I'll make you a deal about Rhys, Johann." Her voice softened. "I'd love to spend an afternoon discussing it with you."

The sheer weight of innuendo hit me like a brick, and I wasn't even the target. Ew. I let my disgust show in my eyes.

Johann leered at her then glanced over at me. "As tempted as I am by your offer, I do have previous agreements with Rhys and a few others in town that I must keep. I would have to take a look at the, ah, *specifics* to see how I would be able to aid you." He nodded back at me. "Don't worry about her. She'll do whatever she's told as long as I have her son."

Ariana's eyes narrowed as she looked at me. I'd seen friendlier expressions on vipers ready to strike. No doubt my expression matched.

"Things would be so much easier if I had access to mages. You'll be useful in consolidating this area," she said.

I glared back, resisting the urge to throw something at the screen. It was a pretty emphatic no.

She continued as if she hadn't gotten my not-so-subtle hint of rejection. "Johann, what if I had the recipe for a version of Bliss that doesn't require a sacrifice of innocence? Would that help you consider faster? After all, there is already a readymade market for that. It would make us all very rich."

Johann nodded. "Money is a good thing," he agreed. "But I'm afraid Ceridwen's services are already contracted. I'll have to check with her protectors. I'm sure they'll be willing to cut a deal."

Her smile made me want to hit something. She murmured a soft assent, then there was a gentle chime as the video chat ended.

I glared at Johann, which didn't seem to bother him. As a matter of fact, he seemed to think it was hilarious because he threw his head back and laughed. Not a chortle, but an oddly infectious full belly laugh that made me want to join in.

I tapped my fingers on the arm of the chair I remained handcuffed to.

"Your face, Ceridwen." He pulled the tape off. "Of course, I'm not going to ask. We both know that you don't want anything to do with her, and to be frank, neither do I. Daoine sidhe are good lovers only when you enjoy pulling knives out of your back on a regular basis. But any good businessman knows you let them assume what they want to hear, especially with someone like Ariana. And if she does have a new recipe, I'll have another upsurge of Bliss to stomp." He tapped his chin and narrowed his eyes. "I don't think she actually does, though."

"I smell smoke…"

He gave me an alarmed glance.

"Liar, liar, pants on fire," I chanted. "And how *does* a fé lie?"

He spread his hands. "By omission, of course. Do you need help getting the cuffs off?" I shook my head, so he continued, "Are you going home tonight or tomorrow? You're welcome to stay."

"It depends on Jimmy, but I'd prefer to go home tonight. School is tomorrow."

I wriggled and got the key in hand and fumbled at the lock until I got it open. The other wrist was faster. I rolled my eyes as I stood up, leaving him to his quiet snickers as I went to find my son.

I didn't get far. "A moment, Ceridwen." Johann brought up several images on his laptop and turned it around for me to look.

Three daoine sidhe stared back at me. I recognized Rhys, the leader of the area's kin, but the woman and man with him weren't familiar.

"This is Una, Rhys's sister. This is Eoin. Their triad ran the bliss ring that operated here until recently. The mass grave you found was how they disposed of the bodies after they used the innocents up. Primarily human children, though they snagged a few from other kins." His voice was conversational, but his eyes were colder than I'd ever seen them. He hadn't cared for them using children.

I gagged as I remembered the spoiled magic in that

grave, poisoning the yaksha's home. "What did you do?"

"I broke it up. Una and Eoin went to punishments. Rhys has thus far eluded me. Be careful. Rhys has a new triad, but he wants his old one back and might try to use you as a leverage to get it."

I sighed. It never ended. Now that I was found, it wouldn't be peaceful ever again. "So, Tara really could be a trap from either side."

He blinked at me. "Yes. Be safe, Ceridwen."

I didn't answer. I just let myself out.

The events of the last few days must have finally caught up with Jimmy because the poor thing looked exhausted. He was lying spread out on the bed in his borrowed room, his lanky body sprawled out so that his head was almost hanging off the edge of the bed. It was a rather precarious position for him to be in, but I couldn't help but smile when I saw how relaxed his expression was.

My fingers gently stroked his thick hair out of his face before I slipped my hand under his head and carefully slid a pillow under his cheek, going so slowly that I might as well have been disarming a bomb. I didn't want to disturb him, but he was going to regret it if he slept like that for very long. Crick in the neck? More like constant head tilt for the next two days.

His breathing hitched, and I froze, but other than shifting his arms to a more comfortable position, he didn't move, so I breathed a fervent sigh of relief. It was good to see him so relaxed. It made me think of when he had been younger, and he had curled up in front of our fish tank and fallen asleep "watching the fishies dance." He'd loved those fish, and this was the closest that I'd seen him to being anywhere near that peaceful in a long time. If sleeping on Johann's couch was where he felt safe, then so be it. I was just glad that he was finally able to get some rest.

With one of my children taken care of and neither of us in any imminent danger, it was time to start worrying about the other child. I still hadn't heard anything recently from Dara. I took one last look at Jimmy and slipped into the next room, pulling my phone out of my pocket to call my daughter again. I had been texting her every chance that I had, which I was well aware was probably a panic reaction, because I knew as well as anyone else that sending a ton of texts did not guarantee they were going to get answered any more quickly. But I couldn't help it.

As much as I had hoped that something would be different, of course, it wasn't. Dara didn't answer my call. It rang for what felt like forever before it finally went through to her voicemail, her chipper tone from better times ringing in my ear. I tapped the button on my screen to hang up, fighting the urge to throw it against the wall. That wasn't going to help any. And even if it did make me feel better, that meant that there would be no way for Dara to get hold of me when she was ready, so the new phone got to live another day.

An unfamiliar footfall in the hall caught my attention. It wasn't the brisk tread of Johann or Lotus. I rushed toward the doorway, placing my body between Jimmy and whoever was in the hall. Adrenaline, never far away, rushed through me.

A shy smile and earnest stare met my panic. My shoulders relaxed as I recognized Katie. She was a strange girl, the source of the chaos magic that drifted in the air. I couldn't see it right now, for which I was grateful. It would be unnerving to be constantly surrounded by it.

The erebite born into Katie's body *was* Katie, but at the same time an aspect of primal chaos meant never to awaken. Human bodies were too frail to contain that power.

In only a few days, she'd gotten thinner. Even with the necklace helping move her power back inside her, her body was eroding. When I could do work again, I needed to find a better solution.

It was strange to know that this skinny teenager looked like a stiff wind could blow her over, yet she wielded immense power, more than I could ever comprehend. The worried crease between her eyebrows made me wonder what she needed to be worried about. She could destroy the entire city with a thought.

Or possibly that was why she worried.

"Hi, Katie. Sorry for rushing at you, Jimmy's in here asleep." I didn't want her to think that I was over-protective, so I didn't say anything more. Yes, a woman as old as me shouldn't have been worried about what a teenager thought of me, but in this case, I definitely was.

"How are you doing?" Katie asked, her soft voice somehow echoing despite her obvious effort to mute it. I stepped farther into the hall so that she didn't wake Jimmy. Katie's expression was the same as someone doing their best not to wake a sleeping baby that had just been put down for a nap, and although Jimmy was plenty old enough to deal with people waking him up from a nap, I still appreciated the sentiment.

Biting my lower lip, I paused, wanting to answer that at this point I felt like I had one foot in the grave and one foot on a banana peel. Though watching her erode almost before my eyes, I was pretty sure I was being dramatic.

"I'm okay," was the best that I could come up with. It was a lackluster answer, but she seemed to understand.

"May I help?" Her hands had started to glow, even to my blinded eyes, and she reached out, holding her hands out flat to give me a choice on whether or not to take them.

I had heard that magic could be loaned or outright given, though I had no idea how it was done. And I couldn't even really see how she was doing it, so I could try at a later date to copy... timing always sucked.

At this point, what could it hurt? My magic was

currently on hiatus, and if holding hands with Katie was going to help me until my own magic came back, then I was all for it. The worst case scenario was that nothing happened, in which case I would get a little bit of human contact to fulfill my people quota for a while and not hurt a young woman who'd been hurt too much.

Smiling in appreciation, I reached out and took Katie's hands, trying not to throw my head back and groan as her magic flooded into my body with a rush like... I couldn't think what it was like, only that it was awesome. Pull it together, me. This was darn near euphoric.

"It's going to feel a little strange at first," Katie warned. "And it'll want out so it can come back to me."

"So, magic does think?" I breathed.

She shrugged. "Maybe? But this is more like something falling when you drop it rather than it thinking. Gravity pulls the falling object to earth, I pull the magic back to me."

"Understood. So use it only in emergencies."

"Yes. But this gives you some power, at least. I don't like the thought of you being powerless with everything going on. And you're going to leave. Everyone expects you to go by day's end since you have to teach." Katie opened her hands. The magic within had sensitized me, and I could now see all the chaos magic in the air, like swimming through a forest of sea anemones.

I touched the magic coiled in me, like yolk within an egg, and nursed a scrap out, making a tiny ball of light. Her magic instead of mine flowing through my body. It felt like there was a live wire in my veins, but strangely enough, it didn't actually hurt. Instead, it felt like I had more energy than ever before, and I could do anything I set my mind to.

Overconfidence was the last thing I needed, and I noted that care was needed when wielding this power. I let the light play around my hands, drawing swirling designs in the air with my fingertips as I got used to it.

It felt good. Before, I'd always felt my magic, and I'd had to brutally suppress the nibbles of panic at being blinded and helpless. Though, if I'd had my magic a few minutes ago, I might have chosen to give Johann athlete's foot or warts. Which would have been a very bad idea, true, but the man could be so annoying.

I smiled at Katie. She held out her hands again, clearly offering more magic to me. I wasn't sure how much I could safely take from her without hurting myself. So much power in her fragile body... something needed to be done to reinforce her. I made a mental note to ask if anyone here was doing anything. The locket I'd made to help her keep her magic seemed to be working, but at what cost to her body?

Though I was almost jealous of her. What I wouldn't give for that much power so that I would never feel as helpless and powerless as I had at so many points in my life. With those moments in mind, I took her hands again, letting her top off the power. After all, if she were willing to give it, then I was willing to take it.

"Thank you," I mumbled to Katie, suddenly shy. Her power within me made me feel like we had a connection of some kind, like having her magic inside me would help me to understand her better. Like a friendship bracelet on steroids.

"It will only be enough for one or two uses," Katie warned. "But it should be enough to protect you if something happens, at least until your own power comes back. Then you can just blow off some steam and purge my magic from your system. Simple."

I took a second to think about the logistics of this. For a moment, it was hard for me to understand why I would be able to use her magic and not my own, but it was a different sort of magic. I couldn't reach for my ribbons because that was outside magic, and I didn't have the magical energy to pull it inside me and manipulate it. But Katie's magic was different. Her magic was ready, willing, and able, like ribbons coiled inside me that I could use for whatever I needed.

Katie's eyes went to the silver bracelet I wore. "I can fill that, too. He's enchanted it to store power."

Nick had made it for me, a wide bracelet set with lapis. I wondered what other helpful little enchantments he'd placed on it, and more, how he'd done it. He was a svartalfar, not a mage.

"Good idea." I held out my arm, and Katie rested her hands on it, one above, one below. Her long fingers flexed as her magic flowed into it, going until the bracelet had started to shake and grow warm against my wrist. I almost stepped back in surprise, but instead ended up grimacing as she shrugged apologetically. Not the most dignified approach for either of us.

The bracelet had clearly taken in more magic than I had and began cooling when she took her hands away. Of course, it was receptive to the magic. Nick knew what I was.

"Thank you again. Now we can go home with a whole card." My words were full of the gratitude I felt, and I resolved to do what I could for this poor woman.

ONCE JIMMY WOKE, later that evening, we headed home. As I put the key in the lock, I contemplated a nap of my own, but it was a bit too late in the day for that. I'd just end up staying asleep all night. The sight of an uninvited visitor in my house sent that thought winging into the mist.

Holy crap. A fetch. On my couch. It appeared to be a fully grown adult with a lean build, although whether male or female was hard to tell without the benefit of features. Features of any kind, really. No eyes, a slit for a mouth, a bumpy nose that looked like a kid had dropped an unfinished clay model on its face. Creepy AF. Under my gaze, it put hands on its thighs and bowed in our direction, a faint cinnamon scent permeating the room.

Jimmy gasped, having just seen it. His face went a bit slack with shock.

"What do you want?" I asked, forcing my tone to an even coolness as I stepped slightly in front of Jimmy.

Mary had given me the impression that fetches rarely permitted themselves to be seen and didn't seek out company, so this must have been a pressing matter. And boy, I was getting freaking tired of everyone's *pressing matters* landing on my figurative desk. I also didn't want to drive someone in genuine need away. So, I did my best to curb my irritation and waited for it to answer my question. The wards had allowed it to pass, so that meant no hostile intent.

However, I would toss it out on its vaguely formed rear if this was trivial.

Its mouth barely moved as a deep and raspy voice came out. "My name is Brandon Sauer. I am a fetch."

After a short moment's struggle, I bit back the urge to say yes, thank you, I had already noticed that. But sarcasm wouldn't help anything at this point. Without their shapeshifting, fetches were never going to be able to pass for a humanoid kin, and certainly not as a normal human. The closest parallel that came to mind was maybe a golem from old myths, since they did look like they were formed of clay rather than flesh and bone.

"Yes," I said finally. "But why are you in my house?" Waiting to enter until we had gotten home would have been a nice change and knocking on the front door would have been amazing. Instead, he had been waiting motionless in the dark on my couch like some new kind of horror movie monster. In retrospect, it probably shouldn't have waited on the front porch in the middle of the early evening. Maybe a good call, coming inside without permission.

Being a fetch in its natural form, I wasn't sure what senses it did or didn't have. I wasn't sure how their thought process worked either, but I highly doubted that they had seen enough horror movies to realize that sitting in the dark on someone else's couch was probably not the friendliest way to start a meeting. With that in mind, I tried to keep my smart mouth from running away with me and give him the benefit of the doubt. Depending on what he said, I was more than happy to show him the way to the door and boot him out of it if needed. Or, potentially help him.

"I am here to ask for your help." A sharp, almost vinegary smell accompanied the dreaded words. They always wanted my help.

It was strange having a conversation with it, not just because of the lack of features or movement, but also because his tone of voice never changed. Whereas a normal conversation with a person would have inflections and changes in tone, as well as shifting around and making eye contact, talking to a fetch had none of that. Its voice was deep and raspy, yes, but also flat and calm like a computer was reading from a script. I squinted briefly, seeing if there was any change that I could make out in this spot where his eyes should have been, but nope. Absolutely nothing.

"And what do you need my help with? And would you let me know what pronoun you prefer?" I asked cautiously. I couldn't keep calling it an it, even if I had no other alternative.

Jimmy slid past me, and I almost had a coronary. He went into the kitchen, grabbing a bag of puffcorn and two bowls, and poured the puffcorn in. Brandon and I watched silently as Jimmy offered a bowl to Brandon, then retreated to the big armchair in the corner.

While still a bit tense, he'd lost the edge of fear and had his phone out. I bit my cheek. He was surreptitiously taking pictures.

Ah, the resilience of youth. I, on the other hand, still stood here in the doorway and fought the urge to fight or flight. It was a natural reaction, because most people didn't have to deal with faceless creatures popping up in their house, but that was just one of the joys of my life, I guessed.

Super.

Silence from Brandon as he stood in front of the couch holding a bowl of puffcorn, though the smell in the air had shifted to a strange blend of pine and roses. What was with the smell? I really didn't know enough about fetches. I should've been quizzing Mary all this time.

Jimmy's move prompted me to move. I had to choose between sitting on the couch next to Brandon or go across the living room. Not a difficult decision. I hung up my coat and walked all the way across the living room to sit in the other armchair, still keeping an eye on Brandon. I was sitting at the edge of my seat, so I made a conscious effort to scoot back and make eye contact with its face. I could probably relax. Probably.

"I prefer to be male, so he." Okay, he worked. He continued. "We, my gang, our clan, want the same help as was given to the yaksha. We need to protect our children and our kin in Columbus. We know of your actions, and now we ask for that help."

I wasn't sure who had gossiped with so many potential candidates. Terror and pride rose in my heart at the same time. I'd hidden for so long, but now people knew me and asked for my help, even if I wasn't sure I could deliver it. I was already burned out. Now this?

Hard hearted I might be, but I was also a mother. Mary was a fetch, and I had her ID papers in my bag, ready to deliver. I had the ability to help these people. Didn't that morally obligate me?

She'd had her life stolen away, and she was only four by our reckoning. Older, with all the experience of Liz's seventeen-year-old mind, but beneath it a four-year-old fetch. It worked out to her being a rather immature teenager.

My weakness. I would do what was needed to protect children, whether they were my own or not, human or not. Children were children as far as I was concerned.

Brandon continued to speak. "We are being pressured to offer another child to the daoine sidhe. We do not want to, but that is not an acceptable answer to the daoine sidhe."

I winced. Yeah, I knew that better than anyone. None of the powerful liked taking no for an answer, and usually, the results were less than pleasant for whoever had decided to stand up to them. I could only imagine the terror that the fetches felt when a powerful kin came to buy their children within a few months of the last.

Their ability to shapeshift and take on memory and personality didn't make them outstanding fighters or rich. They had a long-standing tradition of yielding when the pressure grew too harsh, the life of one gone to save the collective. It was a horrible situation to be put in.

Coming to me meant that they had decided to fight harder. I had to admire that.

The situation they lived in was so unfair. And by doing nothing, I became part of those who destroyed their children's lives. Darn it. "Yes, I'll help you. How many people?"

"Forty," he said in his robotic voice.

I winced. "I just have to make a few calls and see what I can do first. Stay here." I glanced at Jimmy, who munched on puffcorn balls and texted back every time his phone pinged. I was fairly sure he was too discreet to send the pictures, but I was still going to ask later.

Clearly, he wasn't overly worried about Brandon. I retreated to the kitchen, to pretend to myself I had some privacy while I called Crixus. I had no idea how sharp fetch hearing was. I'd have to ask Mary, if she remembered, when this was done.

Of course, he answered on the second ring. It was only the professional thing to do, but it didn't exactly give me much time to think through what I was going to say to him.

"Chainbreaker." His clipped voice had a hissing undernote like a snapped salute.

Internally, I cringed. It was a lot of title to be saddled with. "Crixus, hello. From what Nick said about goblins, I think you might have a safe place the daoine sidhe don't know about."

"Correct." Again with the salute sound. How a voice could sound military was beyond me. "It is unknown to Johann or Schmidt as well as the daoine sidhe. I'd appreciate it if it stayed unknown to them."

"I can agree to that for myself. The fetches in the area are approaching me. They're being asked to tithe another child. Do you know of a place where they can hide until everything blows over? There are forty of them. I'm worried the fetch is intended to replace me or Jimmy, so you don't notice we're gone until they have a good head start."

"I do. A guide will be sent. I will call you back with further details'"

He hung up. No fuss, no muss.

The next ten minutes dragged like Jimmy getting out of bed at six am on a cold day. Trusting the goblins would seem like a no-brainer, but trust *really* wasn't something I was good at.

"Someone is on their way," I said, trying to sound reassuring. I wasn't sure I succeeded. I spent the time pacing. Jimmy played on his phone, and Brandon sat silently.

I'd called because Crixus had access to resources I didn't. It'd been a bit hard to do. Supposedly, a good leader knew when to delegate or ask for help, and although I might not have been a leader for long, I could only try.

Even though it felt like forever by the time Crixus called back, it really wasn't more than about twelve minutes, something that I only knew because I was obsessively checking the time on my phone in the hopes that maybe I would be holding my phone when he called me back, and I would be able to answer it more quickly. Yeah, yeah, a watched pot never boils and all that jazz, but a phone in a stranglehold would still ring, although I just about tossed it across the room in startlement when it rang. That would have been just my luck.

"Yes?" I asked the second that my phone was next to my ear. No, not a polite way to answer the phone.

Crixus didn't seem to be bothered by my abrupt greeting, if it could even be called that. "Is it Brandon or Annalise with you?"

"Brandon."

"Find out what they can offer you in exchange for

your protection. Your safety is paramount, as is Jimmy's."

"Thanks."

Crixus was not one to beat around the bush. The word was barely out of my mouth when the call ended. I shoved the phone into my back pocket. All the better if I didn't have to go through more of the niceties with him.

Now the fun part, which was going to be coming to an agreement with Brandon we could all live with.

"I've got Mary ready to call Brandon, Mom." Jimmy looked up from his phone.

"Thanks! Brandon. I've made an arrangement for a safe house for you and your people. To keep the exchange balanced, what do you offer in payment?" Ugh. I sounded like a fé. Yuck.

"I can offer my services."

And didn't that sound like a hook for a certain type of romance novel, I didn't know what did.

But it was an intriguing prospect. "I actually could use two of me right now." I flopped down on the far chair again. I was happy to have found a way to help, but it was another straw on an overburdened donkey. To be clear, I was the donkey.

But I was going to be hellishly busy for the foreseeable future. "The play's opening night is next Friday, and there are rehearsals tonight and all next week. I can't miss rehearsals. The show will fall apart without a director." I spread my hands in the air.

"I can stand in for you. Since I'm an adult, I can gain your skills and training, for some days, perhaps a week."

Fetch adults lost the skills and memories they copied over a period of days. Only their children had plastic enough identities; the impression of another's mind was permanent. Which is why their children were demanded. They weren't powerful in combat, so they tried to play factions off of each other to keep their young from being taken.

I stared at him, my eyes wide. If I could get help from the fetches with stuff like this in the future, things would be so much easier for all of us. That would free me up to help with lesson plans and other, more immediate magical issues.

"I will not let the community know that you are helping us so that your students are in less danger." Brandon added after a moment.

"I appreciate that," I said dryly. I was resisting the urge to point out that they never should have been in danger in the first place, because that was not actually going to solve anything. This was making progress. Brandon wasn't my enemy and I needed to chill out and not start a fight.

"It can only be a short-term agreement," I warned. "This is the best that I can do."

Jimmy's phone rang. He put it on speaker.

"Hi." Mary's shy voice. "Um, if everyone is in the same place, I can do online teaching for all the little ones, so they all have their own skill sets without having to borrow them."

"Good point," I murmured. There was no way that fetch children would be able to go to school, not looking the way that they did. They would never be able to pass as human, and it made me sad that they would miss out on some of the experiences of human schools. Sure, bullying wasn't exactly the best thing to look forward to, but meeting new friends and learning about math, science, literature... those were things that could help any kid, no matter what kin they were.

It made me sad and angry that the fetches couldn't experience those things because of the way they looked, but that was just the way it was. Mary's thirst for learning had not come from Liz's personality. It was all her own.

Being taught at home was the only feasible alternative, since there was no way that they were going to be able to afford the expensive illusions that would allow the children to look human enough to be accepted at schools.

Brandon nodded. "Mary has been a great help. She's been sharing what she has learned with us. With your skills, I could help her even more."

I raised my eyebrows, startled by what Brandon meant. I had thought that since Mary was officially dead to these people, that they would just ignore her entirely. Apparently, I was wrong.

"I didn't think that Mary was associated with your

kin anymore." I flushed, not quite sure how to explain what I meant. "I thought she was dead to you, so you didn't talk to her anymore."

Jimmy's phone gave a strangled squeak, Mary's reaction.

The air filled with the smell of honey. Brandon made a soft sound, and it took me entirely too long to realize that it was his version of a laugh. It was a strange rasping sound, but it made him seem more human, something that I was glad of.

"The elders who must keep the tradition may not speak to her. Likewise, she can no longer speak to them. Others of us do not keep the traditions yet. Though she can no longer speak or hear true, she's still dear to us. Some of us contributed to the mixing that made her and will not give her up so quickly."

I bowed my head in understanding. I guessed the scents were a form of communication, but I didn't want to ask. Sometimes asking for clarification was rude and intrusive. I'd ask Mary as soon as I could.

If nothing else, I was glad that Mary hadn't been abandoned. With all of the problems going on, this, at least, was a sign of kindness and love. It heartened me.

"Mary, can you switch with Liz and attend school for her tomorrow, and take Brandon to school? Let him in through the gym before you go to first period class?"

"Since it's Liz, I don't expect her to object," was Mary's mild reply. She was Jimmy's girlfriend Liz's fetch, who'd been kidnapped earlier this year when she was mistaken for a mage. It had ended well, something for me to be proud of.

Liz hated school with a passion and tried to get Mary to take her place at every possible chance. For Liz, this would be a treat, skipping school with my permission.

"Let's do this, then," I agreed. Brandon followed me as I stepped into the kitchen, digging under the table to grab my work bag for the next day. I would have liked to have said that I was one of those organized people who had everything neatly arranged in a binder for their lesson plans, but that was not the case at all. To be fair, I did also have a lot going on in my life right now, but even before I had been meeting faceless men in my living room, I hadn't been the most organized person in the world. It wasn't all in a binder. At this point, I was just happy that my school stuff was all in the same bag. At least this way I could find something, although when I had everything spread out on the table to do my best to organize it, it didn't look like it was organized at all.

"I need to learn you," Brandon said.

I leaned back a bit in my chair, worried about what that meant, but he just sat quietly next to me while I organized my lesson plans for the next day. Other than watching me, he wasn't really doing anything, and it was a strange feeling. But other than the initial weirdness, I wasn't really that uncomfortable, and I was able to focus more on the work that I was doing instead of trying to figure out why he was staring at me. Whatever he needed to do to help me get through the next week at school, so be it.

Brandon sat back, humming softly. It was another weirdly human gesture, and I tilted my head at him.

"I am a theater fan now," he mused. "I think that I will quite like helping the students with their production. It will give me a chance to learn more."

I fought down the urge to smile. He sounded almost surprised about liking theater, which was something that I could identify with. It was almost funny, how different live theater was from movies and television.

Starting the drama club when I'd first gotten the job had been the first time, I could express my love for anything other than my kids. Yeah, it was work but that didn't matter to me most of the time. I loved the expressions and fun that the kids were able to bring to words on a piece of paper.

Without them, it was just a script, just pieces of paper and a poor-quality binding holding it all together. With them, it was a genuine good time as they learned to play their roles, colorful highlights on their script helping them to learn more about their characters and how they wanted to bring them to life. And all the silly and sometimes not so silly ways creative kids interacted.

"We'll switch places in the morning, after my parent-teacher conference with Odette Keller." I would have loved for him to be able to do that as well. Who could blame me? But that wouldn't have been fair to him. That dance required experience rather than knowledge, and I didn't want to deal with the fallout if something went off. This way, I would complete the only thing that I needed to do myself, and he would get to enjoy his newfound love of theater while I tried to deal with current events and not get kidnapped.

It seemed that Brandon had the same idea because he nodded. "Knowledge like that, deep knowledge, is something that only children can do, a type of fusion. For adults, it is temporary only, small things that we learn from your most recent memories, or things you've learned almost to reflex. But it will be enough for now."

All right. Next step: more mundane things. I shot Nick a quick text, making sure that he could pick me up tomorrow so that Brandon could use my car to get home. After all, he would look and act like me, but someone was bound to notice if he didn't drive my car. The people at the school were entirely too nosy to miss something like that. I almost felt bad for letting Brandon deal with the things that I should have been doing myself, but I justified that it was like I was taking a sick day and using a substitute. Actually, it was even better than that because I was doing something that would help more than just one person. This wasn't a sick day, this was a mission.

Brandon had retreated into the living room with

Jimmy, and I pulled up my email and sent a message to Lotus, asking about Dara. I checked the news. A story about the television crew showing up in a snowy crop circle had hit the national headlines. All was going according to plan.

I left another voicemail on Dara's phone, as well. At this point, I would have sent smoke signals if I thought it would get through to her.

When it seemed like Brandon was done doing whatever it was he was doing, I smiled at him. "Brandon, you can use the guest room, you'll be driving in with me, and Jimmy tomorrow morning and Jimmy will let you in the back way when I leave out front at 9. Got it?"

"Of course." Brandon gave me another of those bows and retreated to the room I indicated, poking his head out the door. "Have I permission to raid the fridge this evening?"

I tried not to laugh. He'd mimicked my voice so exactly. "Yes. I'm going to bed."

THE NEXT MORNING, I called Jimmy in sick to school and left him with Noir, under directions that if anything happened, he was to hide and group text me, Nick, and Johann.

I arrived early for the conference but still I barely had time to grab coffee before Odette arrived and we headed for the conference room.

Sitting opposite Odette Keller, I wished I was less ethical. I would have loved to make Brandon take care of this parent teacher conference in particular, but I couldn't get it past my conscience to make him deal with the rich, rude mother of a student who could have been one of my best, if not for the fact that he was a goofball who had raised laziness in academics to a fine art.

Normally, I didn't bother with parent teacher conferences, since at high school age it made more sense to me to work with the students directly. And hand out detentions for too much missed work. Unfortunately, in this case the mother was part of the problem. Her attitude explained a lot about Evan, and the way he tried to float past inconvenient obstacles.

Having a bulldozer for a mother would foster that.

I gritted my teeth, doing my best not to lose what little patience I had left. Mrs. Keller was not stupid, in fact, she was incisive and perceptive, which made it difficult to deal with her when you were saying no. She wasn't wrong in her conviction that money could solve every problem.

Especially at a private school dependent on the generosity of parents. The discreet sparkle of diamond earrings for an eight in the morning meeting—though to be fair she was likely heading to work after—added a surreal feel to the meeting.

I still wasn't going to let her walk all over me. It was in Evan's best interests to learn other lessons than privilege. Like getting his work done on time.

"Let me make this clear," Odette said. I preferred to call her Odette in my head, because calling her Mrs. Keller put the onus of respect on my side of the table. "My son's grades are not going to be ruined by your inflexibility. Make his grades reflect his potential, or I will have your job."

I so wished I was recording this.

She'd have my job? The job was complicating my life, but it was my link with normality, and I wasn't giving it up or compromising my standards.

The rush of words that rose to my lips safely swallowed, I took a deep breath, refusing to get sucked into the riptide of her drama. If she wanted to act like a cut-rate Mafioso, then she was more than welcome to, but I wasn't going to stoop to her level.

"Actually, that is the problem. Your son's grades reflect his work ethic. When he starts putting in the work like the rest of my students do, then I will change his grades. Until then, they stay as they are."

Her eyes narrowed, and I knew that she was going to lose her temper here in a minute. I prepared myself for the fall out.

"Maybe I should have a chat with Anne and Jack Holmes."

Liz's parents? She was not going there...

"After all, they only want the best for their daughter, and I don't think her current boyfriend offers much," Odette finished in a firm, quiet voice coated in malice. "They contract with my husband quite often, so they value my opinion."

She went there. My shoulders went rigid. She had made a serious mistake bringing my son into this, and my hands dug into the edge of my desk so that I didn't come across it and wring her neck. I wasn't normally a violent person, but one of my children was not answering my calls and the other had been in danger multiple times over the last few days, so my mother bear instincts were in warp speed overdrive. But then again, my son was an obvious pressure point. I shouldn't have been surprised. Clearly, she couldn't read my "I'm about to throttle someone" body language, because she rose with a smug smile. "Let me know if you change your mind on Evan's grade," she murmured.

I will not slap someone today. I will not slap someone today. I repeated it over and over in my head like a mantra, trying to focus on containing my temper so that I could deal with actual life or death issues. •

At this point, the only thing I could do if I wanted to respect myself was to stick to my guns. I had told her the absolute truth when I had said that Evan needed to put forth the effort and then he would get the grades that he deserved.

The grades he deserved at the moment were failing ones because he refused to do any of the work that I assigned, even the easiest work there was. I pushed down a flicker of pity for him... if this was a form of him rebelling against his family, he was going about it all wrong. He was going to have to learn that good grades couldn't always be bullied or bought.

Jimmy had mentioned to me offhand Evan's parents wanted him to go east for college, the same his father had attended, but all Evan wanted to do was play football and basketball. Evan loved sports and had mentioned his dream of playing in college. Gossip had it he'd met with recruiters though his parents were apparently unaware of his ambition.

"As I said, he is getting the grades that he deserves.

When he does the work that has been assigned, then I will change his grades. Not before. He has the brains, but no college out there is going to put up with this kind of behavior from a student." And I returned to my thought that they weren't rich enough to buy good grades for that kind of pass, although I kept that part to myself.

Odette's icicle laden smile was one that a daoine sidhe would have been envious of. She snatched her Versace leather purse (the huge medusa head made the designer hard to miss) from the chair next to her and stalked out. Her low heels clicked an angry staccato as she walked out.

To say that I was relieved was an understatement. With a minute to spare, I could switch places with Brandon, who should be ready at the back entrance for Jimmy to let him in.

I made sure that no one was around, and then grabbed my own bag (a tote bought at the ren faire) and headed out to my car, relieved that I was finally able to get this show on the road.

I walked out the side door near the staff parking lot.

Fate was laughing at me somewhere. I headed out to my car, only to see Odette and her son sitting in their very silver luxury SUV, parked in the staff lot.

Why? Of all days and all places, why here and now? I fought the urge to throw my head back and groan. A soft chime pinged as I unlocked my car with my remote, sliding into the driver's seat and pretending that I was looking for something. I glanced at my phone. 8:55. Nick was never late, but he was rarely early either.

They sat there for another few minutes, and I was running out of places to rummage to make it look like I had lost something. At this point Odette was probably hoping that I was smoking pot in my car so that she had another excuse to get me fired; that was the only reason that I could think of that she would still be sitting there after so long, and no matter how many times I looked up, she was still watching me. Get out of here, stalkers!

She must've claimed he had an appointment, so shouldn't they be leaving already?

Heh. Nope. My luck couldn't be that good, as recent days had proven. A moment later, Odette climbed out of the car and headed for my car. I growled under my breath. Another glance. 8:58

I needed to be gone. Brandon, looking exactly like me, was going to enter using my swipe card by the door in the gym in two minutes.

"I just want to talk to you. Get through this like adults." That would be nice. Given she had ended up storming out after she didn't get her way, like a toddler that was upset about not getting to eat all the cookies in kindergarten class, I had my doubts that she could be any more mature than she had managed thus. I didn't have time to deal with more of her crap today, but oh well.

Oh well turned into oh shit when an unbodied

manifested between us. Odette's screams filled my ears as it lunged toward me. The same one who'd attacked me on the road, frock coat, Victorian clothing and all. Rage in his eyes, and hunger that could eat the world and want seconds.

How on earth had he gotten here? I was just outside the inner ward, true, but I hadn't felt my outer ward fail.

The unbodied lashed out at me with long bony fingers, mouth gaping wide. I backed away from the school, away from the inner ward. The unbodied might be here for me, but that didn't mean that it wouldn't go after anyone else that happened to be in its way. That was what monsters did, after all. I had to do everything that I could to protect those that were around, even if it meant trapping myself out here with this creepy creature.

I needed to hide us before the custodians and teachers on this side of the building came rushing out.

Odette screamed, and Evan jumped out of the SUV and ran for me. He was fast, getting between me and the unbodied in a heart-stopping rush.

Stars, no, this was the last place he should be!

Hidden unwilling by his bulk, I drew on Katie's magic, grabbing the broad shoulders in front of me and yanking back. He didn't move an inch, hunkering down.

Apparently, chivalry wasn't dead, and I was as

appreciative of that fact as anyone else at any other time, but not now.

I flung up a shield between him and the unbodied, aborting the illusion to hide us from the school so that no one could see us out here.

The unbodied's fingers raked the shield, piercing it, and just brushed Evan's upraised arm.

I couldn't draw on the external wards because I had no magic of my own to use. I was suddenly very glad that I had practiced with Katie, because even that short amount of time, standing there making flames with the new magic, was probably the only reason that I was still alive at this point. Unfortunately, shields tend to steal magic very quickly, and it wasn't long before I had totally run out of magic.

The doors slammed open on the school, both custodians, the principal and the dean running towards us.

I groped for words foul enough as the unbodied grinned at me.

Who do you choose? All but hung in the air in letters of fire.

Odette shrieked again. Evan fell to his knees, shaking, his arm withering as I watched.

The car, I could use it to batter it if I reinforced the ward with what magic remained in me...

"Get in the car," I snapped. "Move!" The words were a strangled scream as the unbodied swiped me again, the shield flaring under the touch of its hands. Apparently not enough, because my arm grew completely numb at the impact. It felt as though my arm was freezing, as if a shard of ice had impaled it and frozen all of my nerve endings.

All I needed them to do was get their booties in the car so that I didn't have to worry about trying to keep myself between them and the unbodied, who didn't seem to care who it got a piece of. Of course, I wasn't overly happy that it was probably going to be me, but the Kellers, as irritating as they were, also didn't deserve to die a painful death at the claws of a magical creature.

Nor did my coworkers who were now shouting and perilously close.

If there was one miracle for today, it was that they actually listened to me. Which might be the first and only time that that had happened. They scrambled into the car, both of them yelling as they fumbled with the door handles. Really, dudes? It shouldn't have been that difficult, but I was more focused on the unbodied.

They were in, thank the blessed stars. I danced to the side and threw myself in the driver's side, I scraped the bottom of the barrel of the figurative magic well, drawing out whatever drags of what Katie had given me to maintain a shield. I slammed the door and jammed the car into gear, my foot shoving down the gas pedal as far as it would go; the tires squealed and then a solid thunk as I ran him over.

He rose and waved at the rearview mirror. Blast it.

I swerved, staying on the unwarded side by a hair. My coworkers jumped back, away from the line.

A pickup truck turned into the parking lot. Relief flooded my chest, 9 am precisely, and there was Nick. I didn't know if he was going to be able to help me with this particular situation, but I had to at least hope.

Nick skidded to a halt and got out.

What was he doing?

He pointed at a spot in the air in front of my car as magic started to gather around his fingertips. As I watched, a portal opened in front of the car, and he beckoned me. He was close enough I could see sweat gleaming on his forehead.

"Ceri, what's going on?" Amy Griswold shouted, heading for the border she couldn't see. The unbodied swirled, waiting.

I was the target. He'd follow me. Nick's logic was cruel and inescapable. I drove through the portal, the unbodied followed, and a bunch of people didn't get slaughtered.

And we could act, away from so many watching eyes. I would have liked to have a little bit more time to plan what was sure to be an expedition into a hellscape —other dominions being what they were—or at least enough time to kick the Kellers out of my car. No time for that. I slammed my foot on the gas and drove through as the unbodied spun and pursued us, raking its claws along the back end of the car. There was a slight shimmer in the air behind me as the portal closed, Nick's figure in the rearview mirror as he jumped through after us.

All external light snuffed as the portal closed. Blessed silence reigned in the car, lit only by the lights on the dash. Good news and bad news. Bad news: Nick, my car, two unwanted passengers and I were now who knew where with at least one unbodied and who knew what else.

What were the chances that Nick knew what lay on this side of the portal? Pretty high, actually, he wasn't an off the cuff man. Good news: the unbodied was now safely away from the school. Neutral news: both of the Kellers had totally frozen in the back seat, which was a fairly normal reaction to the situation at hand.

Evan cupped his bad arm, face white, eyes glassy. Odette had her arms around him, eyes closed. I felt bad for dragging them into this, but it wasn't like I'd had a choice. I'd had to protect them, but there wasn't much to work with in the parking lot of the school.

I pulled the small flashlight from the glove compartment, flicked it on, and got out to separate myself, the target, from them. The door of my car scraped stone as I opened it and I winced, but at this point, I wasn't overly worried about the paint job.

"Welcome to Svartalfheim," Nick said, I flicked up the flashlight and there he was, illusion gone. His silver eyes caught the light, reflecting it back at me. "We have incoming, Ceri. Follow my lead, it's important. Promise me that you won't use any magic while we're here, not even magic from someone else. Unless it's an absolute last resort. Promise me." His eyes were fierce on mine as he searched my face, waiting for an answer. I didn't understand why he wanted me to make this promise, but clearly it meant something to him, so I nodded slowly. That wasn't good enough for him. "Promise me."

"I promise." Our eyes met and held. "The unbodied?"

"Here." He tugged me forward several steps and nudged the light direction up.

"Well that's a hell of a trick," I mused, staring in front of me at the unbodied, mouth set in a howl as it thrashed against the bars of a complex metal cage in the center of another cage of stone. It wasn't like anything that I had ever seen before, which I supposed made sense, considering the fact that this was an alternate world and we had been brought here by magic. It looked as if the cage had just sprung up from the ground, which made no sense whatsoever. Unless, of course, magic.

Boots thudded in the distance.

I wasn't feeling any effects from my fight with the unbodied other than the dull ache in my arm, probably because I hadn't actually used any of my magic. It had all been Katie's magic, since my own was still dormant, and I opened my palm to check if I had any more of her magic left after drawing everything I could into the shield. It was unlikely, but I wanted to know.

Frighteningly fast, Nick's hand lashed out, gripping my wrist as if to stop me from reaching for the magic Katie had gifted me with. He breathed his words in my ear, his face next to mine. "Don't. Seriously, only if your life's on the line."

I nodded slowly, my eyebrows raised. I wasn't entirely sure why it mattered to him, but clearly, it was, so I was willing to make that promise, even if I was puzzled about it. I could trust him that much. Then I leaned forward slightly, ready to break the tension between us and kiss him, then a high-pitched shriek started behind us.

"Always the moment breakers," Nick murmured, turning to face the ever louder boots. He gestured negligently and the room lit with a soft, bluish glow.

I glanced around, startled by what I was seeing. I wasn't entirely sure what I had expected from what was either another world or another dimension, maybe a grassy plain or something like that, but that was the last thing that was going on here. Instead, it looked like we were stuck in a giant cave, my car wedged in the opening that was barely big enough for it. Which was quite a trick, considering that it really wasn't that big of a car.

The noise came from another, larger opening Nick and I now faced. The car was to our right, and from the corner of my eye, I could see the Kellers.

Odette was still yelling. I couldn't make out exactly what she was saying since she was still in the car, but she was apparently throwing a hissy fit of epic proportions if her body language was anything to go by. Nick ignored it so completely that I was awed.

Wish I could do that.

And of course, bad luck came in threes, so Odette's meltdown wasn't even the worst thing that we had to deal with.

I slowly raised my hands as twenty some figures approached, weapons raised.

Male and female, though it wasn't very easy to tell; all were tall and muscular, wearing armor, their long hair tied up and back. They shared a skin tone with Nick, a black like spilled ink, or as if they were carved from onyx though their hair color varied from as pale as his to jet black. The light made it hard for me to really make out facial features at this distance.

A few wore armor like I'd seen Nick wear, form fitting silver, though how they got metal to do that I had no idea. One of them was definitely female though.

No guns or anything like that in their hands, just spears and swords, but I was under no illusion that they couldn't kill me with them just the same. None of the figures said anything to us; me raising my hands was purely an instinct to not get shot at, because they didn't seem like the type of people that would do a quick attack, like the unbodied. They seemed like maybe they could be convinced to not hurt anyone, and if that was the case, I was more than happy to give that a shot.

Nick folded his arms. "Here we go." He sounded... tired.

I rolled my eyes, even though it scared me to take my eyes off them. But I couldn't help it. What did Nick have up his sleeve other than his arm? Because he needed to produce it.

"Thanks, Nick. I figured that out myself." I raised my hands even higher, making sure they could see that I wasn't armed and really, really didn't want to start a fight. I'd had enough fighting for the day, thank you very much.

Why was he just standing there?

.

CHAPTER 5

MY EARS BUZZED, then popped, as if adjusting to pressure.

"Adalric! Welcome." The lips of the speaker didn't match her words. Nick's warning rang in my ears, I didn't try to guess what language the magic translated.

"Signy. Interesting welcome... have you all gone blind since I last visited?" Nick's words were directed at an armored figure I'd taken for one of the men. The leader of the band and uncanny as the rest. I didn't like being in the room with this much physical menace. I'd had enough of that when captured by goblins.

"Not blind, but you were so noisy... and someone is still screaming! Have you gone cruel in your old age, cousin?"

The rest approached Nick, their attention on him like adoring fans, which made the situation even more surreal. I slipped back toward the car and eyes tracked me, hands ready on weapons, but at Nick's gesture, they didn't impede me.

Nick reached out, embracing the woman, then several others in full strength hugs. Not at all like the contact he'd had with men back home, where he'd perfected the art of the manly pat on the back that men seemed to do, where they weren't quite committed to touching each other but they also knew that they had to do something to greet one another.

"I'm glad you've come back so soon, rather than waiting. Even gladder to see you've brought new thralls! And of childbearing age to boot! Shall we remove them from the odd shelter?" The words took a moment to sink in, combined with the happy tone in her voice.

"No, that's not necessary. They're just slow about moving." Nick said it hastily.

Continuing to the car, my teeth clenched. Excuse me? I knew what a thrall meant, a servant or slave, and I was not about to let that assumption on their part pass without a fight. Second of all, the part about the child-bearing age was definitely up for debate. I loved my kids dearly, but I was not feeling the whole pregnancy and raising children vibe, especially in that context. What the hell was it with the kins and 'breeding' humans? Straight out of any number of current dystopian miniseries, but apparently, they'd been doing it here for a while.

Why not just hire teenagers for minimum wage and take advantage of humanity that way? That was the modern version.

I got to the car, leaned in, and whispered, "Out, both of you. Nick's got this under control." Visions of people with weapons dragging them out danced in my mind if they didn't cooperate.

I knew how sensitive Nick's hearing was, and several of his people had even pointier ears swiveled in our direction. I had no expectation of privacy.

Odette's glare focused on me. "My son needs a doctor, you bitch!"

Couldn't blame her for the rage, looking at Evan. He was pale and sweaty, with the teeth-gritting that an athlete who'd learned to deal with pain could do. His arm had curled inward, the muscle was visibly withering.

And not a damn thing I could do, if I kept my promise. Maybe once we were private, I could sneak something... or, since their trap held the unbodied, maybe they had some kind of medicine they could apply.

I hadn't caught any more conversation, but they'd moved closer by the time Odette, and I got Evan out of the car.

"Easy to mistake, Agi. Those two thralls are her attendants. This one? She is my concubine."

Luckily, the jaws dropping on all his people meant

they didn't catch my stunned expression. It had to be an act. Even repeating that to myself, it took effort not to yank away from Nick when he gripped my wrist and held it up. "This is Ceri, called the Fierce, who defended her son from four goblins and won!"

"Look at the bracelet." The words came from Signy. Instead of jealousy, a beaming smile lit up her face.

The others were all smiles and nods in a matter of seconds, and I decided to play along. Unfortunately, Odette wasn't in the mood.

"I am no one's servant," she spat. "Where's a doctor for my son?"

There was a resounding crack as the back of Nick's hand struck her face, and she staggered back. Evan supported her, his face even paler. In contrast, Nick turned to gaze at me, his expression going from frigid to lustful.

He must have been a better actor than I thought. Even knowing—hoping—he was playing the crowd, sweat broke out on my skin and shivers tried to fight their way free. I opened my mouth to say something, but his foot stepped on mine, not grinding his heel into my foot but definitely enough to make me stop for a second.

His expression became triumphant as he looked back at the elves, as if he'd forgotten he had just struck someone who didn't deserve it. At least not right now. I might have wanted to slap the crap out of Odette earlier, but things were different now. She had been attacked by an unbodied, driven through a portal, and had even less of an idea of what was going on than I did. Everything about this situation was off.

Odette started crying, and Evan moved to support her, letting out a yelp when he moved his arm.

Nick sighed, every line of him impatient and weary. "Agi, this one's damaged. Send a healer to my home, so I can get what I paid out of him."

I had made the mistake of trusting the wrong people before in the past. With no magic, there was nothing I could do but hope he really was acting. I'd never seen him do something like this. I held on to the tap on my foot like a lifejacket.

Nick sighed, looking at the female svartalf with what I could only describe as an apologetic look. "Signy, could you spare someone to help the boy and the women, since they're not acclimating well? You know how it is with the untrained."

She nodded. "He looks young, even though he's well grown. Gunther, accompany them. Carry the old woman, if needed."

Well, childbearing had been revised in Odette's case, apparently.

I had a sinking feeling in my chest about the situation. At this point, Nick was the devil we knew, and it would be best if we stayed with him until we figured out what else was actually going on.

I slipped under Odette's other arm, catching Evan's

eye over her shoulder as he helped his mother as well. She was still standing, which was a surprise. I fully expected that she would shove me away since she had already proven that she didn't like me very much and the feeling was mutual, but she didn't even react as I took part of her weight on my shoulders.

A firm tap came on my other shoulder. The svartalf, Gunther, shook his head. "Not appropriate for you, fierce one. Nor for the boy. I'll carry her. You stay by the Adalric."

Evan and I stood away as he hoisted her into a wedding carry with no apparent effort. Evan remained beside him as I joined Nick, not talking to him, taking in the sight of this place before we had privacy and I could find out whether this was all an act, or my worst nightmares come true.

The entire settlement appeared to be either underground or built out of a mountain in a place with no sun or moon. I couldn't see far, the dim blue glow surrounding us didn't go up very high, but the street we walked on was bordered by natural rock. The homes on the other side were also carved from rock; firelight or something very like it, gleamed in some windows, and everywhere eyes, some silver, some golden, some red, catching the light and watching us as we passed. I caught 'Adalric' spoken many times, but whatever had been translating wasn't working at the moment. What they said sounded Germanic to me.

It was creepy as anything.

We reached a large house, carved from pale stone, and the doors opened immediately, with two men and a woman, all humans like myself, waiting. Gunther handed Odette over, and we stepped in.

"Sit, please." The woman, elderly with salt and pepper hair, wearing a long green dress over a white shift, spoke briskly to Evan. "Adalric, he needs that healed now."

"Ms. G, are we safe yet?" Evan spoke very quietly.

"Are we, Nick? What's going on?" I couldn't keep worry, confusion, and a trace of fear-fuelled anger from seeping into my voice.

The... staff?... looked surprised. Both men had carried Odette to a stone couch, softened by cushions. She stared off into the distance.

"You're safe.'"

Evan lunged forward, lashing out at Nick, stifling a gasp of pain. "How dare you hit my mother!" He hissed the words through clenched teeth as he swung his good arm, hand clenched in a fist.

Nick sidestepped, grasping Evan's bad arm. I started forward as the boy screamed, then noticed the wasting vanished as Nick let him go. Evan curled around his arm, making gasping noises, obviously trying not to weep. The woman knelt by him.

"It's all right, it won't hurt in a moment, but he had to do that, otherwise you would have died."

My eyes flew to Nick's, and he gave a tiny nod. "There was no time for discussion."

How had he done that? I'd ask later.

"There's time now. Have you done something to Odette to keep her quiet?"

"Yes."

He waited as I fumed, one of his least attractive habits. Also, I kind of envied the ability to shut her up, which didn't help matters. "When are you going to remove it?"

"When you're done shouting at me. Can you stand, Evan?"

"Yeah." Evan flexed his hand and arm. "That hurt, but thanks. I'm still mad at you for slapping my mom. Where are we and who are these people? Why do you look like you should be in a fantasy book? Was that a ghost attacking us?" His eyes were bright with mixed fear and curiosity, glancing from me to Nick. "You're Ms. G's boyfriend—I saw you with her at the grocery store. What you looked like before we got here, I mean. How do you do that? Wait, is this like *Every Heart a Doorway* and we'll get powers?"

Once. I'd shopped with Nick once. I'd run into the Kellers and another teacher, bad luck. I hadn't known Nick had morphed from friend to boyfriend in the gossip mill. Also, Evan had read a book of his own volition?

A quick smile lit Nick's face. "Magic. All of it. You're on another world now, and all of this is a secret. This is what I look like, and what attacked was one of the angry dead. I don't know if you'll get powers."

"When are we going home?" Evan asked, glancing at his mother, probably not used to being able to talk in her presence.

"When people are recovered." Nick glanced at me. "The... ghost hurt her, and she needs time to get better. And time here is much faster than on your world, so it won't be long there."

"Oh-kay." Evan rubbed his arm. In a smaller voice, he asked, "Can you let Mom be Mom, please? She was right to be upset that you hit her, and whatever you're doing makes her feel wrong."

"Fair." While Nick didn't move, Odette's eyes focused, and she got up and pulled Evan to her, away from us. Nick continued, "In my defense, I didn't have a lot of options. Those who stay in here like the old ways. Short of individually beating them into agreeing with me, small change to an incredibly conservative society is what I can do. With long breaks, because, frankly, most svartalfar are jerks."

"You're a svartalfar?" Odette's voice was remarkably subdued.

"Yes. And I'm a jerk." Nick's quick smile settled my stomach. It seemed to help Odette too... the flicker of jealousy on my part felt strange.

"Speaking of jerk, how exactly is telling people that we're your slaves going to help keep us safe?" I asked, trying not to snap. Technically, he had said that I was his concubine, which did not make the situation better.

The situation was stomping on some of my tender

spots. If it turned out that I had trusted him and he had betrayed me, I was never going to forgive him. Once was enough for that mistake.

Nick rolled his eyes, and I tensed. He was a smart guy. He definitely knew better; this was him being provocative. The only thing worse he could do was tell me to calm down. I might stab him with a rock if he tried that with me right now. Even if I knew he was only needling me.

I was already regretting my promise not to use magic here, even though I had very little to use; I wanted the comfort of it and to be able to retaliate for what I'd just been put through. My logical mind warned me that I should just calm down and give him a minute to talk before I freaked out about what he had to say.

"My people don't allow intruders in our halls. Only svartalfar or thralls live here. Why do you think I prefer to live among humanity?" His tone had gone dry and was heading toward desiccation. His servants listened with interest, apparently not feeling threatened by all this.

That fact made the tenseness in my shoulders relax a little. They weren't cringing or adoring.

The explanation seemed plausible, although it didn't exactly make me feel any better. Actually, it made me feel worse. The niggling fear manifested as pissiness. Yes, it made me a bitch; but Nick also knew about some of my issues and didn't get a pass for being cavalier about them.

"If the bracelet is proof that I'm your concubine, why did you never tell me?"

The woman made a stifled noise of protest.

Again, Nick rolled his eyes, and again, I resisted the urge to throttle him. "You can take the bracelet off, which means that you're not a taken concubine. It was a gift."

Fine. Satisfied that he was telling the truth, I turned to the servants. "Is there a place where Odette and Evan can rest?"

Odette's cheek was still red and swollen where Nick had slapped her, darkening into a bruise. I might not have liked her, but I still felt bad for how miserable she looked, although there was literally nothing that I could do to help her. There wasn't even any ice for me to give her to put on it.

"Can you heal her eye, Nick?"

She didn't flinch as he approached her, but the muscles in her neck were rigid as he touched the side of her face. Under the brave front there was fear.

The swelling eased, though some bruising remained. "I used most of what I had stored on Evan," Nick said.

Well, that answered that.

"Giselle and Tristan can take all of you to rooms. And after the excitement, you might all want to clean up."

Ah, his sensitive nose again. At the moment, annoying him trumped wanting to get fear sweat off my skin. "And we're safe here from random slaps and swords and so on?"

A small smile tugged at his mouth. "Yes. My word on it. Nothing will attack you here, on pain of their existence. I'd like to talk with you for a moment, privately, Ceri."

I turned to Odette. "I'm sorry I got you guys into this, but we're going to get through it. I promise. We just all have to cooperate for a little bit, and we'll get home. I'll be right back." That was the best I could tell them, because I knew just as little about this whole situation as they did. At this point, my goal was to make sure that they didn't get killed. And all of us got home. Wait—

"We need to get back! As soon as possible!" I spun back to Nick. "How long have we been here?"

"A second back on earth. Maybe two. Time runs much faster here right now. I thought that getting away from the unbodied and giving you a quiet place to heal might be best, since you weren't getting that at your home."

He had a point, minus the jerks who lived in this dominion. But he seemed to have some status here.

Giselle murmured, "Adalric, you're right that pleas have accumulated, and need your rulings. A blood feud has been called, too, in the week you were gone."

Nick sighed. "I'll explain everything, but I need to

get this taken care of; once I'm here, they want results quickly. Please. You're all safe. Giselle, would you stay with them a moment? Ceri, are you coming?"

Nick turned and went to a door, opened it, and gestured me forward. The door shut behind us with a quiet but final thump. The room had a large metal desk and table, both overflowing with papers.

"Ceri." He caught my hands. "Why are you freaking out about a show rather than an unbodied trying to kill you?"

"I..." It was hard to explain. "You... they assumed I was a possession. A thing. I know you were just playing along, but I'm helpless to stop it if it were really going to happen, and that makes me crazy. I don't like being helpless."

"Ceri." He let go of my hands when I tugged them. "We've been friends for years. Why would you think I might do that?"

I wrapped my arms around myself. "I knew Dara's father for four years, we were married for two, and he sold her and me to the lilim. I didn't see it coming. I'm sorry if I know I have terrible taste in men and I worry."

Nick bit his lip, looking like he was fighting laughter for a moment. "Flattering. Try not to judge me by other's actions, ok?"

"I'll try. Honestly. But it just... sometimes it's really easy to start thinking really suspicious things about you. About everyone."

"I know. You're safe here. Take care of them, I'll see all of you as soon as I get the most urgent work done."

I nodded and slipped out of the room.

"There she is!" Giselle smiled. "Are you ready?"

"Yes."

"If we can't go back soon, what can we do safely?" Evan, of all people, asked Giselle.

"Stay in the house. Listen to me and the others who tend the house. Other than that, do as you will."

"What is going on?" Odette finally spoke, her voice overcontrolled. She winced as she talked, evidence her face still hurt.

"Do you have ice?" I asked Tristan. He looked to be in his thirties, with dark hair and blue eyes, wearing a loose smock and trousers secured with strips of leather crisscrossing up his legs.

"Yes. I'll bring it to the resting rooms with some tea," Tristan said.

I nodded once. "Please come with me to a place where you can rest. I know it's strange here."

Odette didn't move. She repeated, "What is going on?"

"We're in another dimension to keep a ghost from eating us." I decided to be blunt.

Evan shivered. "We're safe now, right? Do you know that guy? Even though he punched my mom?"

I paused. "Yes. He was acting in the way the

people who live here expect, not as he would have chosen."

Giselle beckoned us forward. "He slapped your friend?"

"Hi, Giselle. I'm Ceri. This is Evan and Odette. And yes, why did they expect him to hit her?"

"Was she acting inappropriately in front of witnesses?"

Go for it. "Sure."

"Then if he didn't punish her, they would. And the punishment for a human being disrespectful of the Adalric is death."

"What?" Evan squeaked.

"The svartalfar are a strict people, and they can be cruel. Adalric is not, but everyone must abide by the Law."

I took Odette's arm, suddenly wanting us all in a room with a door that would keep interactions down to a minimum. "Witnesses would be other svartalfar, right? Do any of his people live in this house other than him?"

"No. The Adalric prefers to maintain his distance from other svartalfar; partly because it's his preference, partly because it keeps his staff and secrets safe." She stopped by a door, opened it, and warm moist air rolled out. I peeked in. A series of pools, some steaming, presented the opportunity for a bath and the question of how to manage it, since Evan glanced at me then his shoes, his face reddening.

"Do you have screens?"

Giselle nodded, a flicker of amusement in her eyes.

Later, cleaned up and each of us in a separate room, with all of us in new ren faire style clothing similar to Giselle and Tristan's, I paced the length of the room. The heavy skirt and shift swished around my ankles, and I'd kept my regular shoes.

Tristan brought tea and ice for Odette's still swollen face while we changed. Given Nick had reduced the injury, I hated to think of what it would look like if he hadn't. Odette and Evan drank thirstily, and she went to sleep in short order, stretched out on one of the stony benches. The cushions that padded them were thick and soft, making the furniture comfortable. Evan fell asleep shortly after her.

Despite being thirsty, I hadn't drunk yet, waiting for it to cool. Giving my tea a dubious glance, I smelled it and took a tiny sip. Peppermint, no taste or smell of anything else. Either Evan and Odette were tired, or the staff had spiked their tea with a sedative... probably not a malicious act, given the situation. Though they should have asked, or if Nick had given orders, he should have.

I thought best when I moved. I needed to solve problems, even though I hadn't technically solved the last one. Or any of the ones before this, actually. But whatever.

The current issue was that I had to make sure that

we got home, and once home, ensure neither Odette nor Evan told anyone anything.

It could be argued that this was my fault, even though I hadn't started this whole situation. The unbodied had been after me, and I had told the Kellers to get in the car, so yeah, that was on me. The fact that it saved their lives probably didn't even enter into the equation. Nor that someone had sent it after me.

But that was not the point. The point was that I needed to come up with a way to keep them from telling anyone what they had seen. Their lives, and to a lesser extent mine and Nick's, depended on it.

Once I was healed, I could try to blur their memories, which I preferred not to do. Nick had done . I'd have to ask what, once I could see magic again, because I might be able to alter it and instead of complete silence, create silence on a single topic. And also *how* he'd done it since that wasn't a thing a svartalf should be able to do. At all.

Nick and his secrets...

Speaking of whom, the door opened softly, and Nick poked his head in and motioned for me to follow him, barely sparing a glance at Evan and Odette, who were still curled up on the couches.

I followed him. I very much wanted to talk to him, but he set a quick pace and we left the house almost immediately. He offered his arm, and I took it, curious as to what we were doing, or rather where we were going. I didn't feel safe here, and I probably never would. It would be better for all of us if we could just pack up and go home, but apparently that wasn't in the cards right now. So I kept a wary eye out for svartalfar and accompanied him through the maze of tunnels set in the mountainside (or cave wall) behind his home.

We were still going to have that conversation, but it could wait until we were indoors, and private.

The tunnels were wide and smooth and opened out into what looked like rooms, many of the entrances covered by curtains. Other humans lived here, and none of them flinched at Nick's presence. The silence —proof he wasn't the total asshole he'd played in front of his people—made me feel a little better.

After some time we arrived in a small area set back from the rest of the dwellings, and Nick tapped on the side of the opening like he was knocking on a door. There was a man alone inside, sitting on a stool, running twisted wire through his hands. A small bed, a chest, and a variety of what looked like wire sculptures filled the rest of the cave.

I squinted. The stranger had turned to face us, his long brown hair falling forward. A bushy beard concealed his jaw and chin, and savage scars ran down the right side of his face. His eyes were clouded and white, possibly with cataracts?

Nick stepped to the side, motioning to the man and making sure that he and I could see each other. His clothes were simple, like those the other human men wore, though his seemed more worn... and possibly more comfortable.

"Hjalmar, this is Ceri. Ceri, this is Hjalmar." It was a strange name, pronounced Yall-mar.

I just nodded, stepping into the room, and stopped quickly when he flinched.

"Ceri," Hjalmar said as if he had never heard anything like my name before. His thin, soft voice made him hard to understand.

Nick took my arm and gently pulled me to the floor, seating himself cross legged. I regretted my lack of yoga classes as both my knees popped.

"Hjalmar, Ceri is a mage too."

The other man's light eyes didn't seem to quite focus on me. "It's good to meet you, sister. You've injured yourself. Do you want my help?"

"Maybe later?" Innate caution made me pause until I knew what 'help' meant. Especially since Nick had been so emphatic about caution with magic.

Hjalmar nodded. "Is she yours?"

I stiffened.

"She's not marked by any svartalfar clan, so she is being careful. She's just come here from your lands, Hjalmar. With your permission, I'd like to tell her about your journey here."

"Always, Adalric. You need never ask me, who saved me."

This was getting a little too high fantasy for my

tastes. I'd have written cranky notes in any story that crossed my desk with dialogue like this.

"Hjalmar came from your world and was the property of the whole of svartalfar, before the clans decided to hoard their resources when mages became very rare. Steps were taken to ensure he couldn't leave, like the smiths of old, who were lamed so that they could never leave their village." Nick's tone was quiet and reflective.

I swallowed hard, thinking of the stories I had read about cooks who were chained to their stoves and worse abuses, horrified that it was still happening here. We weren't in the human world, where it was illegal, even if people still did it in the shadows. Things were different here.

Suddenly it made sense why Nick had told me not to use my magic here unless I had to.

"As he grew older, Hjalmar cared less about living and defied requests again and again. He was to be put to death, as an example, but the Adalric had just changed, and the new Adalric said that the lives of mages were all his to give or take, though he didn't take them all as his own. That would have started an instant war. Instead, he took Hjalmar and hid him within his staff, so the old man would find time to rest and heal."

The 'old man' looked younger than me under all that hair.

I was grateful that Nick had warned me about using my magic, but to be truthful, it hurt me that it was necessary. It should have been safe for my kind everywhere, but we were safe nowhere. This was just another reason why I needed to help free the goblins. Everyone deserved to be free and freeing the goblins would help make sure that mages like me were safe as well.

Clearly, this was why Nick had brought me here to speak with Hjalmar, and now that we had done that, he was ready to move on to the next problem. It was a sobering reminder of how quickly things changed here, especially when it came to Nick. But now what did he want to talk about?

"Hjalmar, Ceri is being pursued by an unbodied, part of why she's injured. Would you show her how you deal with them when you find them?"

Hjalmar nodded, reached for a crutch tucked behind him, and followed us as Nick led us back into the tunnels.

Our slow pace gave me plenty of time to think since neither of them appeared to be the kind for light chitchat.

I was so tired of being an object in other's eyes. I would like to go back to being perceived as just another thin blood, a no one that wasn't a threat to anyone, please and thank you, and not get attacked outside of my parent-teacher conference. But unfortunately, nobody cared what I wanted. I needed to fix that.

The tunnel led to the remains of my car, mostly gone. I swallowed a protest; I still had payments left on it! The silliness of the protesting thought made me stifle a laugh.

Hjalmar followed us to the cage where the unbodied was trapped. It flung itself against the bars, arms scrabbling at us. Again and again, he threw himself against the side of the cage, unable to pass through the bars.

I stared in horror as the door of the cage gave, the metal twisting as it worked itself free.

Why now of all times?

"Blast," I snarled, grabbing Nick's arm as I tried to put as much distance between it and us as possible. I snagged a rock from the floor and straightened my arm, fully prepared to start bashing it in the head with a rock if it came down to it. The only other thing that I could have done was to use what little remained of Katie's magic, which wasn't enough to do anything but make a little light. Nick might be able to help, but if I had to guess, I would have said that the most powerful one here was Hjalmar.

He was staring at the unbodied in mild interest which startled me.

"Hjalmar!" I snapped. "Do something. Can you retrap it?"

We'd come here; I'd assumed they had a plan. This didn't feel like a plan at all. the unbodied charged me. Hjalmar held his hand up. I couldn't see what he did, but suddenly the unbodied keeled over, spasming. Wisps of mist curled up off it, as it lost cohesion, dispersing evenly in all directions. I took a step back to avoid contacting the mist.

I had no idea what Hjalmar had done, but whatever it was, it had been enough to stop the unbodied cold. I needed to see it; I needed to learn.

CHAPTER 6

I STARED AT HJALMAR. "What did you do?"

"You couldn't see?" His bushy brows met over his nose. "Your burn is that bad?"

"Yes."

"I can't help you until you can see the magic. We can hide deep in the living rock, maybe, Adalric knows places. That will conceal what we're doing from the svartalfar who will come hunting you. And who taught you to wield the magic? They did a terrible job, they should be whipped. They didn't teach you not to burn yourself out to this point. You're helpless now, and terrible things can happen to you."

As opposed to being enslaved? I paused. He'd said it like he meant it. A chill crawled down my spine.

Nick nudged my arm then gently grasped my wrist and motioned for Hjalmar to follow us. I had no idea where we were going, but I was still more curious about how Hjalmar had managed to kill the unbodied and wondering if he had more to teach. The long narrow route led to yet another small cave.

The area brightened with a pale yellow light, more like the sun and easier on the eyes. Elderly cushions lay scattered on the floor, covered in leather. Hjalmar, guided by Nick, moved to one and sat. I prodded one to make sure nothing had made it into a nest. When nothing ran out, I lowered myself gingerly to sit. It was almost as stiff and unyielding as the rock under it.

"Is there something you want to ask before I show you how to make the angry dead rest?"

Nick was motioning for me to say something. I stared at him, not quite sure what he wanted from me, and he rolled his eyes again.

"Tell Hjalmar about what you think you can do with the geas on the rest of the goblins. The ones with the geas still on them."

"Hjalmar, how do you see magic?" I asked.

"I feel it on my skin, like the wind, or a touch."

"Have you seen the magic that wraps goblins up?"

He paused, eyes staring blankly over my shoulder. "Once. Long ago... like oil and dung, coating them and reaching out to spread on others. Thick and difficult to clean off once it touched you."

"...yes." I really didn't want to know how he'd come up with that precise description. "There's a way to clean it off. But I'm trying to find a way to keep it from coating them again once they're cleaned."

"Humph." His long fingers twined together restlessly as he considered. The knuckles were swollen on his right hand. "You'd need to keep it from touching the target, I think. Once it touches, it's too late."

"Even if it can be cleaned?"

"A little wet, a lot wet, you're still wet. That's how control magic works. Once it's on, they're done." Hjalmar pulled out wires from a pocket and began braiding them, humming under his breath. He did not have a musical voice.

"I feel the bits of other's magic in you, girl. Show me the geas, let me see what I can do to ward it off."

At Nick's warning stare, I didn't comment on Hjalmar's use of 'girl.' Pulling on what remained of Katie's magic, I carefully constructed the geas, giving it almost no power while retaining its basic structure.

"Ahhh, you have talent, Ceri. Good. Can you hold it?"

"Yes, but not forever."

He nodded, still twisting the wires.

I maintained the magic as he poked and prodded at it. It was resistant to what he did; only the wholesale destruction had worked for me and Jimmy.

Nick asked, "Can you make something else feel like a Goblin to the magic, the geas, so it strikes that in preference to a real goblin?"

Hjalmar hummed more. He twisted the wires in a circle, and I watched as he threaded magic through them, illusion of life, of the earthy tang of goblin, sinking it into the metal. How was he *doing* that?

It answered how Nick had stored magic; he always had metal on him. For all I knew, all the change in his pocket was actually enchanted by Hjalmar. Which explained why he would have changed, come to think of it.

Hjalmar held it up. "See if the geas strikes."

I let the magic go. It flowed into the wire circle, sinking into it.

"What happened?" Nick asked.

"We did it. We just need to figure a way to flush it out."

"Tomorrow." Hjalmar slumped forward slightly, clearly weary. Using magic was exhausting. I was tired too, for different reasons. And another day was soon enough to ask how he'd killed the unbodied, or simply torn it apart again.

The journey back to his cave took even longer; he shuffled slowly but refused Nick's or my help. Pride.

Once he was settled in his bed, we headed back to Nick's home. I remained quiet for the time we were on the streets, but once we were inside, I glanced over at Nick. "Why can't you free him?"

It wasn't an accusation, although it wanted to be. No one deserved to be trapped in another world, held captive by creatures that likely didn't care anything about him. It hurt, to see someone like me held against their will here. But I was unsure how Nick would react since he had clearly spent a significant amount of time in this dominion. So I asked rather than accused.

Nick bit back his immediate answer, mouth tight. After a moment, his eyes softened. "He's from the eighth century, born in a forest that is long gone, in what's now Germany. He doesn't speak a modern language, he's almost blind, and he's lame. How kind will your world be to him if I don't keep him there, the same as I do here? Do you think he'd enjoy being institutionalized and medicated more than living here? Or being taken by the predators of your world?"

I winced. The world tended not to be overly kind to anyone, but particularly not people who were different, especially mages. I hadn't truly noticed any problems with him once I got used to the pace we had to set. Eye surgery could help his eyes, but as for the rest... Nick had a point.

Giselle appeared, followed by a girl in a shorter dress that hung only to her upper calf. "Good, you're back. It's time for the afternoon meal, your other guests have awoken and are asking for your lady. Please hurry so the food doesn't get cold."

She continued briskly on her way, her shadow trotting on her heels. How many people lived in this house? Humans didn't just show up here; they had to be brought here, like we had. Or had she been born here? The childbearing age comment came back to mind.

"How many people live here with you?" I asked Nick, trying not to sound rude. He'd increased his pace.

"A dozen. Maybe twenty. It fluctuates. And you need to herd the Kellers down. I'll use a separate stair to keep from agitating them. They should be rested and healed by now."

I headed for the room where they'd gone to sleep, surprised at navigating the maze-like 'halls of this house.

"Where were you?" Odette pounced as I crossed the threshold. "Where are we? What's going on?"

"We're in a different dimension with a bunch of slaveholding elves stuck in the Middle Ages." It summed it up, right? "Also, we're expected to show up for lunch in a few minutes."

"Like in TV, that show where there's all those alternate worlds?" Evan asked.

"Essentially."

"You said slaveholding. How do we escape?" Odette cut right to the chase, sparing a glance at Evan.

We weren't besties, but I could respect her grit.

"Our host is going to take us home. He's a friend of mine."

She arched her brows. "With someone who owns slaves?"

"It's complicated. Lunch. Now." I walked out. They could follow or not; her observation stung with its tinge of truth.

I ran into the girl in the hall, obviously sent to fetch us. Her open friendly smile soothed raw nerves.

"Lady. Would you please come with me? The meal is waiting. Are your attendants hungry?"

"Yes, let's go." I ignored the choking sounds behind me, trusting to the good sense I'd just seen a flash of.

The room she led me to had a series of tables and benches set up, like cafeterias worldwide, and another table on a platform. Nick sat there, and she led me there before taking Odette's hand and leading her and Evan to the nearest table with Giselle and Tristan, a table for higher status servants.

That was going to be an interesting conversation.

The dishes were glazed pottery in vivid blues and reds, with mugs of the same material. Spoons and knives were produced for me, and I saw out of the corner of my eye for Odette and Evan as well.

The food turned out to be a heavy flat bread with a thick meat laden gravy served over it. No vegetables in sight, which made sense, given the absence of sunlight.

I chewed. "Is it safe to talk here?"

"Reasonably." He nodded to the girl who'd just dropped a large pitcher of water onto the table. "Thank you, Solveig. Go eat!"

I watched as she ran to Giselle's side and leaned against the older woman for a moment. "Her grandmother?"

"Yes."

"What happened to her mother?"

"An accident. She fell while hunting, cut herself, and bled out before anyone could reach her."

The bite I'd just swallowed went down hard. "Why are you willing to keep them here? Why not take them back to Earth? At least the ones who work in your house?"

"I've tried. They don't want to go. They'd be leaving all their families here. Most of them have inter-married and going to an alien place, then concealing everything about themselves, changing themselves? Mary was born in your world, Ceri. How easy has it been for her to become a person in the eyes of the government?"

"You could pay for their papers."

"And get them jobs and homes? Or would they end up working for Johann or someone like that? And I've suggested it, especially for babies, but for some strange reason, parents don't like their children being taken from them for 'their own good.' " His tone was mild and ironic.

I grimaced. "Point. But thralls?"

He sighed. "There are svartalfar who distrust the newfangled invention of fire. Better to use the lightning and magic, as our forefathers did."

He wasn't joking. The mind boggled.

"When should I ask about Adalric? Or explore the fascinating comment 'Time runs much faster here right now' which implies sometimes it doesn't?" I'd remembered the old stories of fairy circles and things of that nature, about how people would disappear into Faerie for what to them felt like only a few days, only to return and find out that centuries had passed and that everyone they knew was dead. Since I knew for a fact Nick had an upcoming deadline, I wasn't too worried, but confirmation would be nice.

"Too smart for your own good," he murmured.

"Is time variable here?"

"Not while you're here. It can be adjusted when exiting or leaving by those with the knowledge and power. Normally time here runs much more slowly... Our time, it's been fifty years since I was last here. For them, about five weeks. I flipped the ratio when we came through."

I tried to do the math in my head. Nick snickered.

"It works out to an hour equaling twenty days. You've been here maybe six hours. One minute on earth is five hundred minutes here right now."

My head hurt.

"About forty-five seconds have passed on earth in the time you've been here. A day here is three minutes there. Which means you have time to recover from your burnout and we can deal with the fallout once you're better."

He had his mulish expression on, rarely seen and almost impossible to overcome. The thought of not being helpless when I went back, after my brush with death at the hands of the unbodied, had its attractions, too.

Odette and Evan were talking with Giselle and Tristan, Evan chowing down on the food as if he hadn't eaten in days. They were adapting well. I couldn't imagine how terrifying it was for them, to be attacked by a strange creature, driven through a portal to another world, and then trapped in a place where humans were inferior beings.

"Is that how Hjalmar is still alive?" I asked, thinking back to what Nick had said about the eighth century. That would be two and a half years here?

Nick gave me an assessing look, tilting his head to the side.

"Time ran closer to earth's for a long time, until the new leader here decided there would be no more raids on humanity for thralls."

"When was that?"

"About the time Ivan Vasilyevich drove the Mongols out. That was the most noteworthy event of that year."

I gritted my teeth. He knew damn well I had no idea what he was talking about, but when we got home, I'd have a date out of him. Even if he hadn't said it was, he who made the decision.

Nick's sidelong silver glance held a definite twinkle. "Before then, Hjalmar sustained his life with magic, like any other mage." He clearly didn't understand my confused look, because his jaw dropped as he looked at me. "You don't know how to do that? You didn't choose to age?"

Choose to age? I wasn't aware that aging was optional. "No."

Nick drew an audible breath. "That's another thing you can learn from him, then. Tomorrow, maybe, he did too much today."

I made an indeterminate sound, mulling the concept over. The search for the fountain of youth showed people would do terrible things for the dream of living forever, much less the reality. Knowing that there was magic out there that could do just that... maybe there was a reason my family had forgotten it. The learning I had came from my grandfather and his books, and the few I'd managed to get over the years. It would only take a single decision for our family to forget it.

How long had some mages been held in their servitude to the kins?

I wasn't sure that the knowledge of stopping aging was something that I wanted to take back to my own world. But I was human, of course I wanted to learn it and anything else Hjalmar could teach, just because knowledge was power, and it was never a bad thing to learn something new.

If nothing else, I could at least teach it to Jimmy and Dara and let them decide what they would do. One day, they would have to make their own decision about what to do with it.

. . .

"**B**ack to work. Feel free to interrupt me." Nick smiled at me then left.

In moments, Solveig collected his dish and mine. I watched as people dispersed then followed Giselle and Solveig to the kitchens. I wanted gossip.

Odette followed. Evan left with Tristan; I'd overheard Tristan offering to give him some lessons in basic fighting. It might not end well, but better the boy be tired and covered in liniment than frightened. Especially if we were going to be here for days.

"No, Lady!" Solveig looked scandalized. "You can't do dishes!"

"Can I?" asked Odette.

The girl paused, and Giselle nodded.

"Well then." Odette took off her wedding ring. "Would you hold this, 'Lady?'"

The air quotes were loud enough to rattle my teeth. I accepted the ring and retreated to a bench across the room.

Odette shuttled back and forth with the dishes as Giselle dipped water from a large pot over a low fire into a long shallow tub next to the stacked dishes.

Solveig took up a position next to another tub filled with water and handed Odette a towel. Giselle scrubbed, Solveig rinsed, and Odette dried, and once Odette got used to their rhythm, the work went surprisingly quickly.

I just sat there awkwardly, offering help intermittently and listening to them chat as they got more comfortable.

"So who is this Adalric? Is that a name or a title?" Odette asked.

"A title," Giselle replied. "Solveig, rinse them and check to be sure it's clean, don't just hand them over."

"Is he elected?"

Solveig giggled. However, the thought of elections translated to a concept that was apparently hilarious, since Giselle joined her.

"No, the old one dies and the new one is selected by the world spirit." Giselle pointed back to the gently steaming rinse water.

I could see Odette consider and discard questions. I kept quiet because they were talking to her.

"Does that mean he's in charge here? Everywhere? Or are there Adalrics all over?"

"Only one," Solveig piped up. "I wish he'd stay longer! His deputy isn't as kind."

"Does his deputy live in this house, too?"

"Oh, no. In another city. He only visits when he has to—since the Adalric visits regularly."

"Does the Adalric have a name he uses when he's not being formal?" Odette cast me a glance.

My ears perked hopefully.

"His name before he became Adalric was Sigiward."

Well, that was nothing like Nicolas.

Giselle inspected a dish, not looking at me. "What he's called informally is more a matter for the Lady."

Meaning me. At this point I would have taken any information that I could get from them. I cared for Nick very much, but this whole series of incidents had made me question whether or not I actually knew him. I knew nothing about his life here, but clearly, he had responsibilities that he attended to here. I could see why he hadn't told me, but it bothered me. I concealed things from him, true, but it was because I didn't want to share trauma, not conceal a hidden kingdom.

"We're so glad that you came." Solveig smiled at me. "I heard Tristan and the others talking about how he hasn't been with a woman in years…"

She hushed when her grandmother patted her head but seemed unrepentant.

"Rinse," said Giselle firmly.

Should I focus on the part that he hadn't been with a woman, because there were a few ways that I could take that. Or did I focus on why Giselle had hushed her, beyond the obvious.

"What happened?" I asked curiously.

Odette began stacking dishes industriously.

Giselle bit her lip. No doubt she was loyal to Nick, and she didn't want to tell me his secrets, though I got the impression she cared more about his happiness, and this was somehow tied to that. Still, Solveig had brought it up, and now my curiosity was killing me.

They couldn't just bring something like that up and then not tell me about it.

"The Adalric's fated mate chose someone else. They found each other after she had wed another. It's good to finally see him with a woman that he clearly cares about," Giselle finally said, stacking the last of the dishes.

That confirmed Nick being the one to stop the slaving expeditions. I wished I knew my history better.

"The Adalric had every right to annul her union with her husband, even though they had loved one another long. He said he would not steal her happiness by sundering a long-standing union. He has been alone ever since."

The concept of fated mates made no sense to me. I'd heard of it from those in the kins, but the idea that Fate was a person who chose a perfect lover for everyone made my head hurt.

And if such a thing existed, and that woman *had* been his fated mate, then by letting her go, he had been dooming himself to being alone, in this world or the human one. Did it show that he had cared about her so much, that he had been willing to put her happiness above his own?

I wanted to know why. I wanted to hear it from him... and find out if I was the shadow of a love that could never be matched.

"Excuse me," I murmured and headed for his office.

I knocked then entered. I'd never been in the room, but no details registered, my attention on Nick, seated at a desk that wouldn't have been out of place at a government surplus, large and metal and an ugly green.

Nick looked up at me, eyebrows raised at my expression.

"Why did you leave your fated mate after you found her?" I asked.

NICK FROWNED AT ME, annoyance sparking in his tone. "Because she was in love with another man and had been for decades? I don't remember asking you for your dating history. And that is something that we need to talk about someday. Or you should discuss it with a qualified therapist, given your issues."

I stared at him. The shudder that rippled through me was filled with so many mixed emotions I didn't know how to process them. I glanced away, taking in the room now, giving myself a moment to calm down.

It was a big room. Ugly desk notwithstanding, the wall behind Nick was made of carved stone, an eye-catching geometric pattern. The stone had flecks of quartz that caught the blue light, making it almost seem to move. The other walls had paper maps and notes hung on them.

Several of the familiar stone couches and chairs

were beside me in front of the desk, a table, completely covered in books and papers, occupied the space to my right. The globes of blue light hovered near the ceiling, equally spaced.

Very little decoration other than the cushions and wall, but somehow the room managed to feel cozy and efficient.

Nick cleared his throat, and I glanced at him. His face softened as he met my eyes, and he got up from the desk and came over and put his hands on my shoulders. "That was unkind. I apologize."

"No," I answered, my voice thick. Staring at the narrow line of embroidery trimming the neck of his tunic made for an easy out. "I just... When I heard that... Why do you want me?"

The question took me as much by surprise as it took Nick.

"Because I look at you and I see a valiant woman. I see someone who doesn't give up. I see someone devoted to the people she loves, and I want to be found deserving of that love. Also, you have a really nice ass." He blinked again, the smile that I had a hard time resisting breaking free of the solemn lines that had been in his face a moment before.

I didn't rise to the bait. "No, really. That's a general kind of statement. You've been there for me for years, wanted to date for at least three years I noticed before you even knew my true kin. Why do you want me as me? Why do you want me as a woman? I don't look like the women here. All flawless skin and cheekbones and long legs and pointy ears and swords and..."

"And growing up with them would not make them at all standard to me." Nick's response was dry enough to dehumidify the air. "You're fierce. You care about just about everyone you come into contact with. There's something at the core of you... that I want at my side. Other than your body. Which I also want. Just to be sure we have that clear between us, because sometimes it seems to me that you like to ignore that fact."

"Why me? Even back home you could have been with any number of women. I heard about the couple of lilim who tried to bag you." The words popped out. I winced.

Nick laughed. "They talked about it after and admitted they lost?"

At least he was laughing. "And speculated you cheat really well at poker or have the luck of the gods." What kind of lunatic would play strip poker with lilim?

More laughter. My kind, apparently. "Made them buy the clothes back too... and I kept a sock from each of them. Their expressions..."

"My point being you could have been with them."

He shrugged. "I have a type? There's just the one person I want?"

"Did your fated mate look like me?"

"Not in the least." His answer still held amusement rather than hurt. "She's a pretty typical svartalfar. And I don't really buy the fated mate ideal either. She and I were obviously physically very compatible, had similar interests, could hold a conversation, and she remained blindly in love with the husband she'd been with for centuries. What kind of asshole would break something like that up? Just because," he made air quotes with his fingers, "she was my fated mate?"

"And what if her husband dies? Or she changes her mind?" I snapped.

"Ceri. I know who I want." Nick's pointed stare made me want to squirm.

A mixture of emotion that I now recognized as being more than a bit of panic and jealousy had started to recede. I started feeling embarrassed, looking for a graceful way to retreat. "Okay, well then, okay. I'll just be off..."

"No, Ceri." His voice was gentle, but as yielding as a rock. The warm weight of his hands didn't move from my shoulders. "We do need to talk. And this is actually the safest place I can think of in two dominions for us to do it. Anyone who wants to interrupt us here has to get through the defenses on this dominion, the defenses on my home, and the defenses on this room."

He let go of me, walked across the room, then dropped the bar across the door. "And that will keep the staff out."

I stared at him helplessly. I could see the Nick whom I'd known for years in his face, he hadn't really changed that much. It was mostly skin color and a general sharpening in his features. I... cared for him. I had for years, and I'd been afraid for years. And given everything happening at home, this might be the only chance that we'd had to... talk. Or anything.

Finding my voice was harder than ever. "I do... I care... Nick, I don't know what to say."

He came back to me, holding his hands out. "That was all you needed to say. You know I care for you. I take it the kitchen gossip upset you?"

Mute, I nodded. Nick sighed. Taking my face gently between his hands, he kissed me on the mouth. My lips parted under his, and a moment later he nipped my lower lip and drew back. "I want you. Both physically and with the heart. I'm also a patient man and willing to wait for you. But the way you're acting... Do *you* know what you want, Ceri? Are you willing to tell me what you want, so I'm not speculating?"

He had a point. I knew I wanted him, and I had been too frightened to say it for a very long time. So many bad memories, from one huge betrayal.

"I want you too." The words came out in a rush.

"Well, I'm yours. That makes it simple." He tipped my chin up, smiling.

After I paused, I said, "Now what?"

Brilliant. You can take charge of any situation, Ceri.

"Do you want to do anything about it?" Nick stroked my arm, which tingled pleasantly.

"Yes." The word came out small but firm. A little unexpected to me in how firm it was.

"Well, luckily for us, when I'm having to sort through a stack of pleas and judgments I don't like being interrupted. And I'm not a fan of being the object of an assassination attempt, so I don't sleep in my official room. However, here..." He reached out and touched one of the decorative carvings on the wall, then pushed on another panel. A section pivoted inward, revealing a small bedroom.

"You've got to be kidding me." I glanced up at him.

"Nope, not a bit. I just change the linens and Giselle pretends there's not a secret room located somewhere off the study. Safe, secure, private." He walked into the room, stripping his tunic over his head. The muscles of his arms and back moved, emphasizing his wiry fit build. I'd watched him for years—and the body he had here was pretty much the same as the one I've been watching.

I swallowed, mouth dry.

He slanted a glance at me. "Going to join me?"

I walked in, moving until I stood close enough to feel the heat radiating from his body. He brushed a wisp of hair back from my face. Then he sat down on the bed, kicked off his shoes, and stripped off his trousers, leaving him naked.

I felt my eyes get wide. "Oh my."

The corners of his mouth quivered. "You did not just say that."

It felt good to giggle, even as I admired him. I'd only seen him with his shirt off a few times, and never in swim trunks or anything revealing. This... he was hot. And it was arousing to me to be still fully clothed, too.

I sat down on the edge of the bed next to him and put a tentative hand on his arm. The warm firm muscle under my hand felt so good... as did the fact that I was choosing to touch him. He touched my knee, still covered by my skirt.

"Does it help you to be the one in control?" he asked gently.

The thought made my heart beat a bit faster. "I think so."

I reached for the long braid confining his hair. "Why does it look short in your illusion?"

"Because middle aged men with butt length hair stick out."

"Longer than that..." I undid the twist of leather that secured his braid, and combed my finger through it, letting the heavy softness of it fall on my hands when it was all free. It felt thick and smooth between my fingers, without a hint of wave or curl, even though he habitually wore it braided.

Words tangled up in my throat. So many important

things to tell him, but at this moment I didn't want to say anything. I leaned against him, and he steadied me with his hands on my waist.

The touch sent shivers up my spine, even through two layers of cloth. The room was warm. His touch soothed lingering traces of anxiety. Knowing Nick, he was trying to make this easy for me.

With my enormous amount of experience... I let the thought and protective sarcasm go. This was time for me and Nick, no room for my ghosts at this party.

I tilted my face up and kissed him, nipping at his lower lip. He returned the gesture, hands pressing on my back as he pulled me even closer. I let go of his hair. My hands slid over his chest, down over his side, drifting in a lingering caress. I nuzzled his ear, amused by its definite point, then I stroked my hand down his thigh.

He smelled so good.

I drew back and let my eyes sweep down the line of his powerful chest and flat stomach and I couldn't help the smile that curved my mouth. I glanced at him through my lashes; his face held a mixture of desire, affection, and something close to laughter.

"Do you want me to touch you?"

"No, not yet."

I slid slowly down, off the bed, letting my mouth skim over his skin as I went. I took my time, enjoying the journey. His muscles shifted under my mouth as he drew a long deep breath.

"Ah," he said. "Are you sure?"

I laughed against his belly. It flexed as I nestled my cheek against him for a moment before I relaxed my knees, drifting further down.

He murmured something I couldn't catch. Then, "Ceri..."

Kneeling, I cradled his erection, enjoying the velvet heat. Thankfully, he'd thought to have a carpet in his literal man cave, thick and well padded.

I stroked him. The mattress creaked as he dug his fingers into it.

"You're certain?" The words were strangled.

I traced the length of him with my tongue then drew back. "Yes. Can't you tell?" Laughter bubbled in my tone. "Well, you can touch my hair, I guess..." I let my voice trail off before I took him into my mouth.

His thighs flexed as his hands clenched in my hair. The change in his breathing as he tiptoed towards losing control, the scent of him, the texture of his skin, all made me shiver with desire. I did want his hands on me, but I wanted to enjoy this feeling of power more.

His hips flexed as he shifted his grip. A steady rhythm, that I encouraged, using my hands as well as my mouth. I enjoyed his taste, that he relaxed his guard enough to do this, that he let me be in the driver's seat, as it were.

Nick pulled back. "Ceri, let me."

I laughed up at him. "I guess, since you asked so nicely..."

He was still holding on to my hair. I made a protesting squeak as he tugged up. I stood, and the kiss that met me was ravenous as his hand skimmed under my skirt. Underwear hadn't come with the outfit and his hand went between my legs unimpeded, stroking slick flesh.

I moaned, my mild protest forgotten in the sensation. I helped him whisk dress and tunic over my head, then flushed as his eyes ran down my body.

"You're beautiful. I want our first time to be for both of us," he whispered as he pulled me into the bed.

I arched against him, but he didn't enter me, instead finding my nipple with his mouth as he continued stroking. I was more than ready, digging my nails into his shoulders.

He rolled us and pressed me down into the mattress, his mouth moving down my ribcage to my belly.

"I want you inside me," I said.

"Soon enough. It's been a while, I have needs too," he answered, gazing up my body with a slow smile.

Laughter bubbled out of me, and I tugged his hair. He ignored me as he slid between my legs. Settling into place, kissing my inner thigh, teasing.

I rocked against him as he licked, unable to control the motion as the coiling tension reached its boiling point. Thought fragmented under his caress, wicked and knowing, skillful and hot.

Just before I tipped over, he shifted up my body. I

tasted myself as he kissed me hard, entering me with a single hard thrust. Ecstasy cascaded through me too fast, slamming my head back.

"A little early, but I'll make do," he murmured against my throat, nipping gently. He didn't stop moving, the continuing friction awakening new spasms of pleasure.

His hands twined in mine, our bodies still joined, moving hard and fast. A new orgasm built in the quivers of the just ended climax. I gave myself up to it, wrapping my legs around his waist, as he crushed me close.

My cry mixed with his growl as he followed me into ecstasy. I curled into him as he shifted to the side a moment later, waited until he opened his eyes. "Back to the paperwork?"

"No, I think a break is indicated for a while. They'll find me kinder than I normally am if I went back to it right now. You?"

"I think I like you right here, yes." I rested my head on his shoulder, the omnipresent faint headache of burnout gone for the moment. Relaxing further, I could see the ribbons of magic in the air.

Sex helped with burnout? I had no idea, but I did have a willing subject...

Speaking of which, one of his hands had moved to my breast, a gentle caress, and he kissed me again. "Are you up for seconds, given we're taking this break?"

I kissed him back.

While Nick had a bedroom off his office, he didn't keep food there. And his staff were relentless about feeding him; I could empathize. He had a bad habit of skipping meals when he was focused. My stomach was growling loud and clear when we decided to emerge.

Knocking came from the barred door. Nick shook his head and opened it, accepting the tray thrust toward him. Solveig peeked in under his arm and a pleased smile beamed from her face as she took in my bed hair and Nick's loose hair.

"Solveig, please bring Hjalmar here." Nick delivered the request in a firm tone. She trotted away like she was on a mission, though whether to fetch Hjalmar or to gossip was a question.

Nick handed me a comb and I tidied myself as he broke his flatbread in two and set a hunk of cheese next to the half. Hair back in a semblance of order, I ate.

Oh, the looks I was going to get...

Solveig returned in a short time with Hjalmar.

"How may I serve, Adalric?" he asked Nick, sinking into one of the chairs. Even with a limp and his silver-streaked hair, I would never have thought that he was more than a hard-lived thirty or forty years old.

"I want you to teach Ceri how you keep from aging." Nick took a bite of cheese.

Hjalmar tilted his head, and I thought I saw a very faint smile hovering on the corner of his mouth. Hard to tell under the wild beard though.

"Can you call enough magic to see yet?" he asked.

I blushed. Nick chuckled, damn him.

"Yes."

"I thought you might," Hjalmar said blandly. "Look at me, see the magic within me."

I settled, gazing at Hjalmar. Despite the slightly porn-ish sounding invitation, he did have an intricate web of magic within him, connected to what seemed to be every cell.

A rustle of paper told me Nick had moved back to his desk and started work again.

"Do you see?" Hjalmar asked.

"I do... how did you do it? There's so much..."

"It's like washing... you move the magic over the area and will it to connect. You don't concentrate on each individual touch; you focus on the mass."

"Can you take it away after you do it?"

"Yes."

"Can you do it to another person?"

The pause stretched. "It's not easy, and a mistake will kill them. Those I know who know how don't try."

"I will it to connect to me?"

"And sustain you, like the sun sustains a plant. The energy flowing into you, but just the slightest trickle."

I focused, wrapping myself in strands of magic. When it was so thick, I couldn't see out, encasing me head to toe, I pictured it sinking into me, a web of silk flowing through me, like a ghost of a veil.

"Very good. You got it first try. A little too much

energy, though, you're going to have to bleed a little off. It'll help with what remains of the burn, too."

I could see Hjalmar again, and Nick. Did Nick seem... relieved?

He must have been thinking about our different lifespans. Or the fact I was no longer helpless.

"Is there a mirror?"

"On the table."

I picked up the intricate silver mirror. I still looked like me, which was a relief. I'd worried it would you then me. I'd teach this to Jimmy and Dara when I got home. Of course, both were way too young to stop their aging, but was there ever really a good time to stop aging?

Legends of the fountain of youth showed the terrible things people would do if they thought it might let them live forever. I wasn't sure if I wanted to keep this connection once I got back to my world, though the thought of growing old let alone dying while Nick remained young hurt my heart. Still, knowledge was power, and it was never a bad thing to learn something new. I'd let Dara and Jimmy make their own judgment about it.

The strange and not altogether pleasant sensation of magic reinforcing my life energies would take some getting used to.

Hjalmar smiled a little. "It's good to find a talented student."

He bowed in the direction of Nick's desk and shuffled away.

"Will you keep using this knowledge?" Nick asked.

I folded my arms around myself, the burden of decision heavy on my shoulders. "I'll try. If I can maintain it without anyone getting hurt, I will."

I GASPED as I surged awake, the remnants of my dream sliding away from me like the sweat currently running down my forehead. In the week since we'd arrived here, the magic burn had healed enough that I felt comfortable drawing magic again, rather than nervous.

Nick had wanted me to share his bed openly, but I'd decided against it. While Giselle and the others hadn't teased me at all, the sheer happiness in them that Nick was getting laid made me nervous, especially when none of them would explain why.

Evan and Tristan had bonded well, and Evan spent most of the day training with Tristan and the couple of others who were trained in using weapons and wearing armor; he actually looked impressive in the leather armor they'd put together for him.

Odette had been less than pleased when Tristan

told her Evan was a natural; that he had a talent for swordplay.

"Even less useful than a literature degree," was how she'd put it, giving me the side eye. I hadn't taken offense, since it was true. That was why my degree was in education.

Still, more than twenty minutes had passed in my world, long enough for something terrible to happen. Or long enough for Lotus to have found out what had happened to Dara.

While I really enjoyed the time with Nick— in and out of bed—I had responsibilities back home, even as Nick did here.

I couldn't remember exactly what the dream had been about, other than a nightmare. A jaw cracking yawn caught me off guard as I looked for the clock; they used a variation of a night candle, a pillar that gently smoldered and told you the hour by the line on its side it had burned down to. Five in the morning. It was time to get up anyway.

The door to Odette's room was open when I emerged into the hall, as was Evan's. Odd. Normally she didn't leave her room until later, and Evan was up at six as regular as... heh... clockwork.

I was concerned about the fact that Odette and Evan weren't around. This dominion wasn't the kind of place where they could wander around without repercussions, and I didn't want them to get themselves in trouble.

I'd learned Odette was stronger and smarter than I'd thought, but this place was dangerous outside Nick's direct control. And she seemed to chafe at perceived confinement.

The irony of me judging her for that was not lost on me.

I dressed in one of the shifts and kirtles draped on the clothes chest and went down to the kitchens. There was almost always someone there.

Muffled voices came from the kitchen, and I walked in. A strange svartalf stood near the door, faced by Evan and Tristan. Odette stood near the large wood stove; a poker clenched in her fist.

"What's happening?" I asked, keeping my tone calm.

"This person wishes to visit the Adalric and is being persistent despite the request that he not be disturbed in the time he's here." Tristan's voice was cool and measured, and as I came into the room, I could see he and Evan had live blades.

Why on earth was he trying to come in through the kitchen rather than the front door?

"The law is clear. The Adalric has no right to take any but a svartalf to his bed before he's begotten an heir. The line must continue."

"The people we met didn't seem to care," I said, retreating toward Odette and her poker. The cast-iron cookware could serve as a weapon as well.

Nick had said his home was well defended, how had a strange person shown up here?

Odette's eyes were wild as she clenched the poker in both hands. "There's a dead man on the step, by the way. Just FYI."

"It's not wise to try to force your way into the Adalric's home. This one lives only because he's of the blood." Tristan's voice was still eerily calm.

"Yes. And I want more to be born to the blood, so someone else can inherit! I don't care about his 'happiness,' I care about the law!" Silver eyes sought me out over Tristan's shoulder. "You have to go back to your dominion. You can't stay here." His voice was almost pleading, if you could plead and snarl at the same time.

And it compelled me. I found myself considering exactly how to comply before I wrenched myself free of it. As if he had sensed that I needed him, Nick appeared in the door. It was nice to have him here, not just because he presumably knew what was going on but also because I felt safer with him next to me, more secure. It was a strange feeling, balancing my learned paranoia with the desperate desire to be near him. It was also frustrating beyond belief, and not something I needed to unpack right now.

"You have to kill her or send her back to her home. Or sell her to someone else," the svartalf said. He sounded sad about it. I felt sad about needing to die, too.

The poker clattered to the floor as Odette clutched her temples. "I won't," she whispered.

"Cease, Ulrich," Nick said softly.

His words reverberated through me, almost rattling my teeth. What was happening? Squinting, I could perceive energy flexing all around us, but it didn't seem to come from any single source. It was like the world was doing the magic, a pervasive wave beating down on all of us. Wrapped in the energy, I started trying to figure out a counter, but it was like drowning; I couldn't focus enough to manipulate the magic I could access to stop the influence.

"I will do as I see fit." I coughed as the sheer authority in Nick's words clenched around my chest like a fist. Odette's eyes widened.

"No! You don't get to call on that authority if you don't follow the Law!" The other svartalf screamed the words, like knives being driven into my skull.

"It seems I do." Relentless, the force of Nick's words drove Odette to her knees, me joining her a moment later.

Struggling not to simply yield to their words and will, fall to my knees and wait for their commands, I wanted to scream. I would not be reduced to this again.

"Go, Ulrich. Now. Know that I will not forgive."

I of all people knew what it was like, to be manipulated by mind magic. Even though Nick hadn't directed it at me, I couldn't handle the fact I'd been overwhelmed... and knowing that he could do it again.

368 DAPHNE MOORE & L.A. BORUFF

The other svartalf backed away from the door, rapid footsteps receding.

"Ceri..." Nick's hand on my shoulder.

I flinched. "Don't touch me. What happened just now?"

I felt cold when he removed his hand, but I stood up anyway, keeping my spine straight with an effort of will. Gazing at the wall over his shoulder helped, too.

"You got caught in the overflow of him trying to force me to do something, and me telling him no. He'd already tried to nudge you but hadn't had the effect he wanted."

"There's more to it than that."

"Yes, but I've already been tried and convicted, so I see no reason to offer a defense," he snapped. It was so uncharacteristic it pulled my eyes to his face. He appeared frustrated, angry, and sad.

"I think we should go home."

"Very well. You aren't a prisoner."

A slash of his arm pierced the barrier between dominions, and Odette bolted for it. Evan followed, though he cast a wistful glance at Tristan. I marched toward it as well, aware Nick followed close behind me.

I was grateful when we landed on the hard pavement on the sidewalk outside my house. My neighbors weren't home. At this point, I didn't care. I'd had enough. Yesterday, I might have bent down and kissed the pavement as ardently as I had Nick the other night.

Right now, I felt empty. With all my responsibilities still weighing me down.

And no way to apologize. Feeling safer now, the realization of just how terrible I'd been crashed down on me.

I waited. Odette looked like she wanted to make a break for it, not that I blamed her. I wanted to bolt to a place where I felt safe too. Evan looked sad and confused.

Regardless of my feelings, I needed them to understand that matters could get very out of hand if they tried to tell anyone about what had happened. While I regretted that they had been pulled into this situation in the first place, I also didn't want them to end up dead. The kins and magic had been secrets for a very long time, and there were a lot of people who were invested in the status quo.

As if she could hear what I was thinking, Odette shook her head. "We won't tell anyone," she said, looking over at Evan.

He nodded.

I sighed, tired beyond bearing. They could have simply been telling me what I was wanting to hear, but I didn't think so. And I hated removing their memories when both clearly didn't want me to.

What good would it do for them to lie to me? No one would believe them if they told about what had happened. I glanced sidelong at Nick, and he gazed at the shrubbery with profound interest. Maybe take a little longer to make the decision.

The wind was chilly, and we were none of us dressed for it. My keys and phone were still in Nick's dominion, and I didn't want to ask... Luckily, I kept a key hidden outside for emergencies.

"Let's go inside and decide." I got the key, disarmed the security system and walked in, not really caring if they followed.

Of course, they cooperated. I only wanted to be alone.

"Mom?" I'd also forgotten Jimmy had stayed home from school today.

Now what?

"Cool armor, Evan. Did you end up in a weird land?"

"Yeah... you know about all this?"

"Yeah. Want to play a game for a bit? I've got an extra controller."

"Sure."

The resilience of youth. My son was awesome.

Should I try to make sure that they got home safely? How was I going to look Evan in the eyes after this? It was going to be strange, teaching him in class when I knew that he knew.

I checked the microwave clock. It was nine thirty; Nick hadn't exaggerated. It was almost impossible to believe everything that had happened, but we had only been gone for half an hour.

I could use my magic, though at least for now, I didn't want to push it. The longer that I gave myself to rest, the easier that it was going to be for me to heal, and the more powerful that my magic was going to be when I actually needed it.

"I'll be right back." As I changed, I realized I also had no car—it was still in svartalfheim and destroyed. And Nick's truck was still at the school, likely being taken into evidence by the police.

I came out with a T-shirt and sweatpants. "Do you want to change? I know it's not your usual..."

Odette gave me a funny little half smile as she took the clothes and headed for the half bath. "Neither is my current outfit. Thanks."

Nick's phone rang in the pouch he had on his belt. He pulled it out, snorted, and answered it.

At least he thought to carry it in a land with no signal. That was so... Nick.

What was I going to do? I couldn't be with someone who could control me, I couldn't. Even though he'd never done it, never tried, the fact that he could stuck in my throat. And I didn't want to tell him to leave, either... Not knowing what to do was new to me. Usually the decision was just to run and hide.

"Hi, Johann. Yes. I know. Why, thank you. I'll cover her bill, thanks. You too, asshole." He hung up. "There'll be a car here you can use soon."

He wore the comforting Nick illusion, but his silver eyes were angry and sad.

I bit my lip, then hurried to the kitchen to compose myself. So much for that iron self-control and fierce spine. Making coffee steadied me.

When I came back out carrying a creamer and sugar, I saw Odette had settled in the recliner and Nick on the couch. I glanced out the window, motion catching my eye. A red sports car had just pulled up in my driveway.

"Oh no," I said.

Nick was up and staring, then started to laugh. An unfamiliar daoine sidhe got out of the car, the only one I'd ever seen with black hair and deeply tanned skin. She wore jeans and a gorgeous thigh length leather coat.

"Well, that's odd. I didn't know she was working with Johann."

"You know her? She's safe?"

"Safe for you, yes, Ceri." Nick didn't smile. "Trouble follows her."

I put my chin up, grabbed my spare coat and headed out, Nick a few paces behind me.

The daoine sidhe stopped halfway up my driveway and waved. "Hi, Ceridwen Alarie?"

"Ceri Gault, please," I said. "You are?"

"I'm Nia. That's your second loaner car, but I don't know its name." She grinned, then her eyes narrowed, looking to my left. It was my only warning, and I whirled around, instinctively sinking lower so that I could face the threat better.

Male, with a lean human body, but a tiger's head and claws. His swipe followed me down, cutting across my shoulder. I couldn't help but scream.

They'd blended in and been waiting... rakshasa, masters of illusion. And not just one; there were six more, closing in on me from all sides across my neighbors' front lawns. If any of my neighbors looked out their window right now, they were going to get a horrible surprise. Rakshasas were mercenaries and assassins, gifted with natural weapons and enhanced speed and strength. I had heard that they were also able to fully shift into a tiger, although if one of them did that, then I was pretty sure that we were totally screwed. Magic or no magic, they wanted a piece of us, and I didn't think Nick and I alone would be able to take them all on. I had no idea what this Nia person could do.

She let out a whoop and flashed by me, producing two blades from somewhere on her... I had no idea where she could have hidden them. Her long black braid whipped over her shoulder as she spun, putting herself between two rakshasas. Nick charged forward, between me and the rest, knife in hand.

With a moment to think, I threw an illusion of peace and calm around us to keep the neighbors from panicking and then wrapped one of the rakshasas in strands of magic, grabbing and holding him. He struggled. This I could do, and it might give us someone to talk to at the end of the fight—Nick seemed to do permanent solutions.

My shoulder bled, and the pain made me feel sick.

An attacking rakshasa fell over, and Nick twisted to gut the other.

Blood sprayed my porch. Nia had apparently attended the same solution school as Nick.

The final two rakshasas must have seen the writing on the wall, because they hustled out at speed, blurring and fading from sight.

Nia pulled a handkerchief from her pocket and wiped her blades. She looked at the remaining bound rakshasa, raising her eyebrows. "What are we going to do with this one?"

She didn't seem the slightest bit bothered by the fact that she and Nick had redecorated my house in gore. And why should she? She didn't have to clean it up. To be fair, the chances of me cleaning it up were low at the moment and getting lower by the second also.

My shoulder screamed at me. "Do either of you know how to tie someone up?"

"I can question him." Nia smiled at me. "Just get him in the garage."

"Yes, Johann sent you because of your winning personality?" Nick asked.

I expected her to be offended, but she just shook her head and shrugged. "I'm surprised it wasn't a milk run, to be honest. And it'll be fun having a conversation with this fellow."

I opened the garage door as she dragged him in, saying, "I don't want to get blood everywhere. Can you let him go after?"

"I can. I even might, if he's a good boy and answers all my questions quickly." Nia's smiles were making me more and more uneasy, like she often played bad cop/psycho cop with a friend.

"Why are you in the city?" Nick asked.

"My triad just moved into the area, and Johann has been wooing us. I don't normally bother with stuff like this, but it was supposed to be a milk run. And better than yet another three-hour meeting." She glanced back at the bodies. "Unfortunately for them, I don't like rakshasas. Even though there wasn't a bodyguard clause in the delivery job."

I wobbled. These clothes were ruined, and the kids were going to freak out when they saw me.

"Ceri. You should get that bandaged." Nick steadied me.

"Ok." I'd mislaid my objections to pushy people somewhere back in the fight. I should try to supervise Nia, who I didn't know, but Nick seemed ok with her, and I didn't feel good.

Maybe she'd get some useful information, there was no doubt she knew more about interrogation than I did. Rakshasas didn't just kill people for no reason. Someone had hired them.

Nick got me to the couch. Odette stood up and gasped. I must've put together a better illusion than I'd thought because she seemed to have no idea we'd been fighting.

"First aid kit is under the bathroom sink, if you'll get it for me," Nick told her, settling me on the couch.

She was back in a flash with the kit. Nick cut my t-shirt off and began using saline to clean the wound, not caring about getting blood on my couch.

"We need to get you and them somewhere safe," Nick said softly.

"Your house for the day? Then decide?" I was so tired.

Nick's place was the only place that I could think of that wouldn't freak them out even more, even with the goblins.

He nodded. "We need better transport. The sports car won't hold everyone."

I felt so dizzy and tired. "Call Johann?"

I couldn't understand his answer, sleep dragging me under like a riptide.

I WOKE up in an unfamiliar bed, my shoulder bandaged, and wearing a loose cotton t-shirt. The dragging exhaustion was gone. Sighing, I raised myself on my elbows.

"Mom!" Jimmy jumped up from the chair next to the bed. "You're awake!"

Disturbed from sitting in Jimmy's lap, Noir hopped on the bed and stroked his head along my arm.

"Where are we?" I patted the little dragon.

"Nick's house. After you passed out, Nick got on the phone and shouted at Johann, and a van showed up in, like, five minutes! And we all drove out here. You were poisoned, but it was to make you sleep, and Nia said it was best to just let you rest."

"How long?"

"It's supper time."

So about twelve hours. I shifted. I wasn't wearing pajama bottoms. "Did they bring clothes?"

"Nick said to ask for them if you felt well enough to ask for them, and said he'd come up to talk to you. Are you ok to be alone for a second?" He scooped Noir up and put the dragon on his shoulder. "He keeps trying to eat things so I'm keeping him away from temptation."

Noir nibbled on Jimmy's shoulder-length hair.

"Ow!"

"Yes, dear. I'm ok alone." I closed my eyes as he scuttled out of the room.

The thump as the door opened again made me jump. Nick pulled a chair over and sat next to me.

"Did Nia get any information? Did you let him go?"

"We found out the venom used on you. He didn't know who hired him; we killed their contact person. He thought it might be Johann, but he was grasping at straws. And we let him go after breaking his dominant arm, to slow down any reruns of today." He touched my hand gently, watching for my reaction.

I turned my hand up so I could hold his. Broken arm was better than dead, which would have been their default. I'd take it. Especially if he'd been stressed I was out.

"I'm sorry about what happened at my home. It's a side effect of the world heart, the way the dominion expresses itself through my people—I don't control the effects, and he was invoking it to mess with you. The alternative was to kill him, and he's the only heir I've got." Nick squeezed my hand.

"He doesn't seem to want to be... he wants you to have a svartalfar baby." Not that I was really wanting to become a mother again at this age, but...

Nick snorted. "He can want to his heart's delight. I only just persuaded you to give me a chance; I don't *want* a svartalf."

"Why doesn't he want your position?"

A shrug answered me. "It's a pain in the ass, a huge responsibility. The world heart doesn't choose people who want power."

"Can I have some sweats so I can get up?"

He gave me a dangerous smile. "Do you promise not to get attacked on your way to the bathroom?"

I considered. "I'll try."

He dropped them on the bed. I detoured to the window after taking care of the necessary.

Crixus and the goblins were drilling in the yard.

"Do you have anything we can use to ground the magic to protect them?"

"Yes, but you can do that in the morning."

"Nick, I just slept for twelve hours. I'm fine. I promise I'll sit in the workroom."

He rolled his eyes. "Fine. Hang on to my arm, what they used can give you dizzy spells."

Clutching his arm and the banister on the way down was my best bet during a wave of dizziness. At my glare, he didn't say anything. It was a long trip to his workroom.

The space was ruthlessly organized and cluttered, Nick never met a gadget he didn't want. I settled in a rolling chair and scooted toward where he kept his jewelry supplies.

"Silver, I agree," he said dryly as I reached for a bar.

"How do you want to do it?"

"Virgin metal rather than recycled, to make sure it holds your magic tight. I think I'll just twist wire; it's fast, means I work it less. Since you're pouring your magic in, I don't want the metal contaminated with mine." He gave me a lopsided grin. "Would you care to supervise?"

"Sure."

"I think they'll need to be discarded once they're used... they might be effective more than once, but it's risky."

Nick went to the minifridge and pulled out a nutrition shake and gave it to me. I made a face.

"I hate these things."

"We could spend time making food if you don't want to drink it."

I glared at him then chugged it. And stuck my nasty strawberry flavored tongue out at him.

"Promises..." he murmured as he pulled wire out of its drawer.

An hour later, we had six circles of braided wire.

Nick was both strong and deft, and watching him was pleasant after the day I'd almost had.

"Let's try this," I said, blowing out a puff of air.

It took a dozen tries and adding more wire and weight of silver before I could get the magic to stick.

Nick held it up. I could feel the magic sticking to it beautifully, but then I noticed the size and unfortunate shape. I winced.

"It looks like a collar," Nick admitted, which was pretty much exactly what I had been thinking but hadn't wanted to say aloud. It was a little too ironic. We were making them to make sure that contact with a goblin who was still enslaved couldn't put the free goblins back under the geas, and it looked like a dog collar.

A throat cleared at the door of the workshop. I jumped.

"Ceri, Crixus has been watching us for the past half hour." Nick shook his head. "Crixus, what do you think?

The goblin shrugged.

"Lose your head, you're done. Hand or leg, not so much. Shaped like a collar is fine. We'll call it a torc." He didn't seem the slightest bit concerned about it.

Now that Nick and I knew what we were aiming for, the rest were made quickly. I was glad to be sitting at the end. Crixus gathered them up and left.

Nick brushed his lips against mine. "Want to see if it helps with recharging as well as burnout?"

I laughed, and his phone buzzed.

Nick pulled his phone out of his back pocket. I could tell by his expression that he was less than happy about the news he was getting, although he mostly just snapped curt responses to whoever was on the other end of the phone. As soon as he was finished, he hung up without a goodbye and turned back toward me.

"There's a threat at Johann's. We need to go. Now." I stood up immediately, already planning on what we needed to do next.

Jimmy joined us in the living room, phone in hand and mutinous expression on his face as I opened my mouth. "I work for him, Mom, and they need me."

Noir landed on my shoulder.

Outside, Crixus and the goblins already had the van running.

I couldn't help but laugh a little at Nick's expression. "Feeling unneeded?"

"And old, given how eager they all are. I'm going to leave the Kellers here, since we're going into an active firefight."

The attack might only have been just starting at the time Nick got the call, but by the time we got to Johann's, it was in full swing. Nick's foot slammed harder on the gas rather than the brake as bullets rattled against the van, and we all instinctively ducked for cover.

Apparently, Johann had sent an armored van. How thoughtful of him.

Even with occasional glimpses, I could tell that the lead attackers were rakshasas. Worse, they had goblins as backup, and the whole lot of them were having the time of their life spraying the van with bullets.

We were all as far down on the floor as we could get, Jimmy and I with the goblins crouching over the top of it. If I got any closer to the floor, I was going to melt into it. Although at this point, that might have been for the best.

The van lurched as Nick slammed on the brakes, and he yanked a knife from his belt before he twisted around to look at me. "Get up to the house."

"Help them, Noir," I whispered.

After being the sole decision maker for myself and my family for so long, it was hard for me to be told what to do, but right now was as good a time to shut up and listen as any. Nick and Crixus jumped out on the driver's side, Noir flapping behind them. I yanked open the back door nearest to me, focusing on getting Jimmy and me to the house. There was a mass of debris in front of us that Nick couldn't get around in the van that Jimmy and I needed to climb up as fast as we could.

Thank the stars for heavy winter gloves.

The two goblins escorting me, and Jimmy hung back, providing covering fire, as Jimmy and I scrambled up.

Jimmy made it up first. Even bent close to the apex,

his lanky frame was silhouetted against the dark sky. I followed. A bullet hit him, and he screamed.

Adrenaline and magic flooded me, and I grabbed him, pulling him into a fireman's carry as I jumped off the pile and ran for the porch.

I blazed with light, drawing fire, but my terrified rage also fueled the protective ward around me. The automatic weapons fire sprayed away from me in a universe of ricochets, some of which hit the unfriendlies.

I didn't care. Jimmy was bleeding. Why, oh why, hadn't I taught him how to ward himself against bullets yet?

Magic poured through me, providing the strength my body needed to move like this, carry his dead weight. I reached the porch, almost running over Johann, standing on his front porch and raging that his new house was being attacked.

I passed him by, into the house, tumbling both of us to the floor so I could see his wound.

A firm hand yanked me back. Nia said, "No, I'll handle this. You shoot out."

Nia knelt next to Jimmy, with Lotus singing on his other side, a soft murmur of sound that washed over me like a calming wave. Nia had a first aid kit, one of the biggest I'd ever seen. She opened it and quickly put on plastic gloves, then opened a pack of bandages.

"Do you know what you're doing with a human?" I snapped.

"I'm certified as an EMT in this world," Nia said calmly, pressing on Jimmy's wound. He groaned.

His eyes flickered open, focusing on me. "I'm okay, Mom. It just hurts."

More blood leaked from the wound.

"Go," Nia said. "You're worth more in a fight shooting out."

Everything in me wanted to stay with my son, but he wouldn't be safe as long as there were rakshasas and goblins out here.

I moved to a window. It was hard to tell the difference between the "good" and the "bad" goblins, so instead I focused on Nick and the rakshasas that he fought. Noir breathed and they dodged away nimbly. A body on the ground showed the little dragon had connected with it at least once.

Something dark moved in me as I stared at them, bleak and lightless as the ocean's deeps. They'd helped hurt my son. My Jimmy might die for their games. "Die." I whispered the word.

The rakshasas surrounding Nick convulsed and fell as the magic rolled out of me, and I gripped the windowsill, staggering.

That took the fight out of them, though I wasn't certain why. Within moments, the enemy goblins had retreated.

Nia crouched by me. "He's going to be fine. He needs surgery to get the bullet out; Johann is calling someone in. He's not bleeding out. I gave him something to make him more comfortable, so he's going to nap for a bit."

"You're an EMT. How can you give him drugs?"

"Who said it was a drug?" Her smile had edges. "I have a pain dulling amulet. I'm loaning it to him. Brave boy."

Cold comfort. I sat, my back braced against the wall, Jimmy next to me. He dozed as people moved around us. Noir arrived and settled in my lap, nuzzling Jimmy from time to time.

A hand pressed my shoulder, and I looked up, ready to tell someone off but paused when I saw that it was Nick. I glanced down at Jimmy again.

"They're going to take him off for surgery. The room's been set up, and Johann needs to talk with us."

"Is there a reason he couldn't just text?"

"I assume so," Nick answered mildly.

As much as I hated to leave Jimmy, I had to, and Nick wouldn't have gotten my attention if it wasn't important, so I accepted his hand up.

A gurney, pushed by an unfamiliar person, stopped by Jimmy. Noir hopped on the rail. I watched as my son was loaded onto it and hurried away from the main room.

Noir would guard him.

"Tara disappeared while we were fighting," Nick said grimly. I huffed, running my fingers through my hair. On top of everything else, now we had a rogue daoine sidhe to worry about. Just great. I hated it when the world confirmed my low opinion of people's motives. Enough of this. I was tired of chasing my tail, and it seemed like lately, everything that could go wrong had, and I was sick of it.

When we reached the library, Johann tapped his phone to put it on speaker.

"It's Rhys," he said quietly. The chief of the daoine sidhe in the area, the man Ariana was trying to oust.

The leader of the daoine sidhe of this area, Ariana's machinations notwithstanding. Which of them had sent the goblins to attack?

"Let me be clear," Rhys said on the other end of the phone. Crisp and clear, each word enunciated as if he was biting them off in chunks. Not at all how I would have expected him to speak. Most daoine sidhe sounded wonderful until you figured out what they were saying.

Why was he calling?

"I have the upper hand here, and I want my sister back. For that to happen, I need the services of a mage. I don't care how that happens."

Nick's eyes narrowed, and he shook his head.

Johann hadn't lost his cool. He was, after all, a fé, and to him this was just another transaction. At least, that was what I thought until I saw his eyes, which were all but setting the curtains on fire, and I instinctively leaned back on my heels a little. It was always scary to see someone that never got mad become angry, because that meant that a line had been crossed that nobody could come back from.

Nick might punch someone and then work with them at a later date if that was what was required, but I'd heard stories about Johann. He was all business until that one thing pushed him over the edge.

"Una deserves her punishment. Allowing her to return to you renders the deaths of those she killed meaningless. It also threatens my position. Do you want war, Rhys? Because I can bring that to you."

Clearly, Rhys had expected some resistance because he didn't seem bothered by Johann's refusal. Perhaps he was like Johann, a businessman. After all, wasn't that how all negotiations started? An offer was made, the other person said no, and then they continued until an agreement was reached. Then again, I wasn't entirely sure that was going to be the case this time.

"How about a compromise?" Rhys offered. "Una, Eoin, and I will leave this area and never come back, as soon as I get my sister back."

None of us said anything.

A sigh came clearly through the phone, followed almost immediately by the chime of a message received. Johann pulled up the image, and his mouth set even harder. I leaned forward, not waiting for his permission, and my heart felt like it dropped through my shoes.

"No," I whispered in horror, staring at the image of

Dara on the screen, held firmly in place by several rakshasas. She was pale as a ghost but also stared fiercely at the camera like she didn't want Rhys to know how scared she was. That was my girl.

"Bring me my sister, and the girl will be returned unharmed. You have an hour to answer." Rhys hung up.

Drake leaned forward to speak, and I almost jumped into Nick's arms; I hadn't even noticed that Drake was now in the room with us.

"I like the idea of just killing them all," he suggested.

"It wouldn't mean anything," Crixus pointed out from the door, and my head swiveled toward him with an irritated sigh. So much for discreet meetings. "Are we willing to risk the losses that it will take? The rest of the daoine sidhe would have to take direct action."

"I don't care," I burst out. I wasn't asking anyone else to risk their life, but I wasn't going to leave my daughter in that position for one second longer than I had to. "I'll do whatever it takes. Point the way and tell me what I need to do." I would have walked into a volcano if that was what it took to save my daughter.

"Where is Una?" Crixus, of all people, asked. "I'm good at fetching people unnoticed. You can always put her back there after we get the girl back."

"Wait!" I straightened. "A fetch, have them imper-sonate Una?"

Johann drummed his fingers. "She's in the House of Mists, in the tender care of their leader."

Drake's jaw dropped. "You're kidding, right? You know where they're located?

"Yes." Johann paced the room. "Ceridwen, did anyone in your family ever tell you the name of your house?"

Mage lineages were called houses. I swallowed, then gave up one of my family's great secrets. "Sisitu."

"That gives me an out, then. We're in-laws. I can do this at a reasonable fee for family, rather than a random kidnap victim, even if she's related to an employee."

"What are you talking about?" My head ached. I needed him to tell me where the House of Mists was, but he seemed to be persuading himself. Another minute of silence might save me hours of searching.

"Esther was from that house?" Drake asked, voice gentle.

"Yes." Johann's answer was curt. "I can help pull the daoine sidhe bitch out, then kill Rhys for putting me in this position if they don't all run and hide very, very fast."

"So, where is it?" I asked, keeping my voice quiet and tone unhostile.

Nick shook his head. "The House of Mists has a foul reputation. Their leader is worse. Ceri shouldn't go empty handed or alone."

That sounded even more ominous than Drake's

reaction. I didn't say it, my eyes on Johann, but I knew I'd gone rigid. "Johann, I want to know about the house of Mists, its location and its leader."

Nick spun out of his chair and strode to the window.

"What price do you offer for this knowledge?" Johann spoke slowly.

"Don't ask for my freedom or my children."

He nodded. "A kiss, freely given."

I swallowed. That... was hard. I wished he'd named a dollar price. "Yes. I will give you that."

A pause, then Johann gave Drake and Crixus a sardonic grin. "I'll tell her with her lover in the room, but you two aren't included in the bargain."

Drake laughed and strode out. Crixus followed, closing the door behind him.

"Can I take a fetch there, bring them back?" I asked. I felt bad; I'd be asking them to take a huge risk, but Una's crimes were sickening.

Johann shook his head. "No. I doubt they'd live beyond the first step past the gate."

Damn.

"I'll lead you to a gate to the House of Mists. It can't be accessed through normal means; it isn't adjacent to this dominion."

Nick turned back. "You've just challenged the cosmology we all know. This world is where all the dominions intersect, even Godhome."

"No, just stating facts. I know a gate there. It's

hostile; the very dominion will attack anyone who doesn't belong there. And you won't belong there Ceri; you'll have to use your magic every moment to keep from dying. Get in and out as fast as you can."

Johann paused. "The smith is right; you should take a bribe to trade for Una. One of his weapons should be enough, Una's been there long enough Raphael is probably bored with tormenting her."

I bit my lip. "Is Raphael the leader?"

Johann stared at me. "You found the mass grave of the children she used to make Bliss. I don't do mercy. I do justice. And justice is that she suffers for it."

Couldn't argue with that, even if I wasn't focused on getting the information.

"Yes, Raphael is the leader of the House. He's an enkimmu."

"They've been rumored to be extinct for millennia." Nick said in a helpful tone.

I'd never heard of them.

"Enkimmu are a cousin kin to lilim, emotion manipulators and eater... but," Johann raised his hand as I relaxed a little. "They also drink blood. And once they've bitten someone, they can control them. Utterly."

A shudder ripped through me. My worst nightmare...

"Don't let Raphael bite you, Ceri. Die to the dominion's magic before you allow it. Given the situation, hospitality should protect you from it, but be wary. He likes new toys, and he likes breaking them even better."

"I agree with Drake. Let's just go and kill all the daoine sidhe. Don't do this, Ceri." Nick had produced three knives already and pulled out a fourth and laid it on the table next to the others.

"Rhys could kill Dara the moment we attacked," I said quietly.

Both men nodded.

"Then I'll go to the House of Mists. Done. I need to check on Jimmy, then we'll go. Can Nick come to the gate, too?" I didn't want to be alone, even if it was selfish.

"I considered you as a unit when I made the bargain," Johann replied. "Smith, let me look at the weapons to see which is best to trade."

It didn't take me long to find where Jimmy slept. Nia's long braid was flipped over her shoulder as she leaned in the doorway, keeping an eye on those sleeping within. She looked at me, then back at Jimmy.

"He'll be fine." She grinned briefly; her smile bright against her warm skin.

I kissed Jimmy gently on the cheek, smoothed his unruly hair back. Noir nuzzled my hand.

"Stay with him, Noir." So pale and still but safe here. My baby boy. Noir would help keep him safe. My girl needed me now, needed me to be strong. My heart ached, I didn't want to abandon my boy when he was injured, either. I straightened, squaring my shoulders. My chest felt like I was ripping in two.

If I started crying, I'd never stop.

Johann waited in the hall. As if he could sense what I'd thought, Johann's gaze met mine.

"No matter what happens, he'll be safe here. I promise. I have to lead you to the gate, but Drake and Lotus will protect him as they would their own children."

I nodded. Presumably, Johann meant they liked their children. I could believe it of Lotus, anyway, she'd always been kind.

We walked to where Nick was talking with a goblin. I did a quick headcount and noticed that there were only two. Surely, we hadn't lost that many in the attack, had we? Heart sinking, I looked over at Nick, raising my eyebrows as a silent question.

"They went to get their own back. They'll be back soon. It might be best to wait, to be sure all the defenses are in place, since Johann is leaving with us."

It was sound advice, even if I didn't want to take it. I knew that goblins were fast and dangerously capable, but I didn't like another delay. On the heels of that thought, brakes squealed outside.

Four goblins exited, three carrying a fifth who struggled madly. The silver around the necks of the four had gained tarnish.

They had been successful in their mission.

Nick turned toward Crixus. "Time for the trial.

They're being protected, but they'll need new ones after this."

Crixus held another collar. "We will owe you, too, Nick Damarian, if this works."

He strode out, collar in hand. We watched from the door.

The magic in the collar flared as Crixus put it on the struggling goblin. The geas leaped to it, the silver blackening in real-time. The goblin stopped struggling.

"I'm free," he breathed. "The geas is gone."

Now to deal with the fact that my daughter was currently being held captive by a ruthless daoine sidhe in exchange for his mass-murdering sister.

JOHANN LED us into the woods. While he and Nick made no sound and almost no tracks as we moved through snow and underbrush, I more than made up for both of them.

"This should be far enough." Johann stopped by a fallen tree. "Fair warning, the transition to the dominion we need to visit to get to the gate will be unpleasant for you. Are you sure you want to go with her?"

Nick snorted and said nothing.

Johann's crooked grin appeared. "I thought not."

He cupped his hands. Darkness dripped from his fingers, thick as oil. It hit the ground and slithered, running toward me and Nick. I desperately wanted to get away from it and clenched my muscles to stay still. The blot of shadow twined over my feet, slithering up my legs.

The chill of it struck right through my clothes. I held my breath as it engulfed my face, shuddering as it enveloped me in a void without sensation or sound.

A scream built in my chest, and I swallowed it grimly. I started counting in my head. I'd reached my twenties and really wanted air when the pressure and blackness crawled off my face.

I sucked in a great breath of air and winced as it stung my nose and throat. I hacked a cough, eyes watering. I could hear Nick doing the same, but I could see nothing, it was pitch black.

A tiny light clicked on... Nick had brought a penlight. I could have kissed him. My breath puffed the air in white bursts where the flashlight illuminated. Outside the tiny circle of light lay utter blackness—no stars, no moon—though cold-killed grass crunched under my shoes.

The darkness devoured the light from the flashlight, keeping it a small circle.

"Follow me." Johann's voice. Nick swung the penlight and caught Johann's shoes in the light. Nick chose to keep it on the ground we needed to walk on, a decision I applauded.

A few minutes later, keeping pace behind Johann on the frozen and level ground, a breeze sprang up, making it even colder. I gagged at the rank smell that it carried.

"What is that?"

"Don't worry. It won't bother us." Johann didn't slow down. "We're close."

A clicking noise scrabbled nearby, loud enough to make me jump.

"Are the sounds real?" I asked.

"Yes." Johann's laugh drifted back. "It's a creature like a giant insect, but it won't bother us. Come on."

You need to work on that sense of humor, bucko.

The grass field ended by a hedge. It wasn't green or welcoming; made of spiky branches with several inch-long spines hooked like claws. Withered vines twined through the branches.

"Lovely gardening." I couldn't help the comment.

"Isn't it though?" Johann hadn't lost the amused note in his voice.

We walked along the edge of the hedge, the dark-ness now a physical weight pressing down on us. It felt horrible. Cold and angry and huge.

"Is there something watching us?"

"Yes." Johann didn't elaborate.

Nick sighed. "We get it, Johann, this is not a good place."

Johann stopped. Nick's little light showed a door set into the hedge, made of a heavily tarnished metal, mostly green and flaky. Maybe brass? In a few places, I could see the remnants of reliefs- maybe a hunting scene.

Johann pushed the door open. "Go through; I have to be last, so I can close it."

I stepped through. Dizziness whipped through me, and I staggered, closing my eyes for a moment. When I opened them, we stood in a hallway set at regular intervals with twisted metal sconces bearing faceted gems that gleamed with a low, dull, red light. Nick stood by me, and a stranger faced us.

"Johann?" I squinted at him.

The stranger nodded. "Yes."

Interesting. I wondered why he'd changed his appearance so radically unless this was what he actually looked like. Now, he was a warrior with long, pale hair twisted back from a face made of angles though his eyes were pools of darkness that shifted color, subtle gradations of blue and green and red. He stood taller than Nick, with an impressive build, one that had seen a great deal of labor to create that level of muscle.

He traded that for a shortish potbellied man with a crooked nose and pockmarks? I knew it was an illusion, but the contrast was still surprising.

I glanced away and swept a finger on the stones of the wall. While uneven, they contained a subtle smoothness that my finger slid over. The stone shone like an opal containing all the shades of darkness from reddish black to blue-black to charcoal grey. The hall stretched as far as the low light let me see, a waiting silence coating the walls and air as if the building held its breath.

"Let's go." While Johann set a brisk pace, our steps didn't echo. We passed doors at regular intervals that all gleamed with a dim red light, a different shade than that shed by the sconces.

"Is there anyone else here?" The silence brooded harder when I spoke, compressing my words to a whisper.

"None who can speak with you or me."

The place was creeping me out. Nick walked next to me, hand on his dagger, wariness telegraphed from every inch of him.

A metal gate came into sight at the end of the hall.

"Is this it?" I asked.

"Yes."

My heart beat faster, thudding in my chest. I quickened my pace to match Johann's. Now that I could finally see the gate, so close to what I needed to get my daughter back, there was very little that could stop me. If the only way that I was going to get my daughter back was to go into the House of Mists and break Una out, which meant that I was going into the House of Mists. I would do whatever I had to in order to save Dara.

Johann slanted me a wry smile as we covered the distance. "So brave. This place is not kind to those with shorter lifespans. Luckily, you've found a fix for that."

"True; if she didn't have that in place this place would have killed her. And then I'd have to do the same to you." Nick finally spoke.

"I wouldn't have brought her here without it." Johann shrugged.

We reached the gate set against a stone wall, made of a metal that looked like cast-iron. It gleamed with an odd glossy finish. Every inch of it was carved and patterned, a work of art.

Leaning close, I could see the picture of a grate woven through with thorny plants. Tiny faces decorated each joint of the grate. Each face was different, with expressions ranging from joy to rage to fear. All the kins I knew were represented.

This place had just managed to get creepier, no mean feat. I didn't know anything could be this beautiful and creepy other than a daoine sidhe.

I stepped back and bumped into Nick. Johann regarded me with a patient expression.

"You'll never see the likes of it again. I'm glad you admire the workmanship. It says it enjoyed your admiration, and it'll try to be gentle to you as you pass through even if your mortality burns it." Johann touched the metal with a gentle fingertip. "This is a gate to the House of Mists."

"Making an object conscious is dangerous and cruel." Nick's voice was sharp.

"Yes, it is. My people made this gate when the House came into being in the beginning, just in case." Johann's appearance shifted further as he spoke, the fair skin fading to a shade never touched by the sun, the hair lengthening and brightening to true silver. A warrior like Nick but shining like the moon.

"What kin are you?"

"You've called me a fé, Ceridwen. No reason to stop now." Johann's eyes narrowed with amusement like black opals in the colors that swirled within. They had no whites.

I sighed. "Why did we have to walk all this way to the gate?"

"This fortress has defenses. This gate is a weak point."

"How do I use it?"

"Blood. Ceridwen, Nick... only Ceridwen can go and live."

"What." Nick's voice was flat.

"She can hold off the dominion attacking her. I doubt she can do two people. You'll have to wait with me."

"Then stay here, Nick. I don't want to risk you." I met his eyes. "Gender reversal at its finest, right?"

Nick's jaw clenched as he fought his internal struggle. He nodded finally, eyes narrow, lips thin. My heart pounded. I didn't want to go alone.

He turned to stare at Johann, a dangerous expression crossing his face, then turned back to me. "Are you sure you want to do this?"

"Yes."

He pulled me into his arms and hugged me hard. "I don't like or want this, but it's your decision. Keep in mind you need to take care of your ass, since I'm very fond of it."

I snorted a laugh despite my nervousness and

hugged him back. Then I pulled back, holding Nick's hand, to face Johann.

Johann nodded. "I'll collect my fee then."

A kiss? Here? Now? He needed to work on his timing. Still, I'd agreed to that price.

I tilted my face up to his. He leaned forward, framing my face with his hands, and his lips touched mine. I'd expected them to be cold, but they burned against mine. He tasted of sun-warmed apples, like all of the summer.

He stepped back. "That should give you a little protection against Raphael, as well, Ceridwen. You're not of the blood that dominion demands, but your magery will protect you if you give the land what it wants. You need to fool it."

Nick handed me the knife, in its sheath, and I secured it on my belt.

"Here goes nothing." I pressed a finger lightly against one of the metal thorns.

Impossibly sharp, a mere brush of my fingertip pricked deep, blood welling and coating the thorns. A deep blush passed over the metal, and it heated, blazing up white and yellow.

The gate swung open. The passage was entirely obscured by fog, whorls and swirls of it that gleamed with shades of red and blue like sparks in the water.

I ran forward, holding the magic ready. A cold fog swallowed me, like clammy fingers caressing my entire body. I let the magic shape itself to fit what the fog sought, letting the intent of the defense be the lock and my magic the key.

The opalescent haze bloomed a warm pink, and pain flicked my skin. I held the magic and the two clicked together. Then I took another step and tripped, as if on a threshold.

The mist parted as if I had stepped through a barrier. A thin layer of blood coated me, head to toe.

Above, the sky blazed with stars, a bright half-moon giving more than enough light to see clearly. A few trees gathered around me, maybe ash, with smooth pale bark and thin leaves. I stood next to a worn archway made of light-colored stone, with streaks of a darker color. Next to it was a destroyed house, mostly stones choked by bushes and tall grass.

A wrinkled old man stared at me with yellow eyes. Thin wispy hair drifted around his face as he tilted his head. His skinny face and roman nose combined to make an intense whole.

"To what do we owe this pleasure, little mage?" His voice, resonant and slow, echoed in her head.

"I need to find the House of Mists and Raphael." I decided bluntness was my best option.

In the pause before he answered, the layer of blood dried. It felt disgusting. I rubbed my face, the flakes cascading to the ground. The grass stretched up and grabbed the dried blood.

I wanted steel-toe work boots on my feet instead of tennis shoes.

"Why?" The old man rose and walked over to stand by me.

"To save my child."

His stony face rearranged itself in an unexpectedly kind smile. "It's like that, then? You're very brave. My blessing on you finding him can join Lou's blessing shining out of you. You might even return in the same skin you wear now."

So many questions, with no time for any of them. Johann was Lou? Or was it Nick?

"You'll find it if you walk here."

Well, that made no sense, but I started walking anyway. With my shoulders back and my head high, I headed into what was potentially the most dangerous place I had ever been.

And my stomach somewhere in my shoes.

Maybe a hundred feet away, a path came into being under my feet. Following it, I walked through meadows and scattered trees. I passed several buildings, gathering mists rising and falling like the sea.

More buildings appeared as I walked. I stepped off the grassy path onto a stone road, heading for the largest dwelling I could see.

It was gaudy as anything. Golden bricks and marble flagstones created a patio that reminded me of a chessboard. The house—actually a mansion—stretched for hundreds of feet to either side of me. The mist surrounded it, concealing most of it. Where the fog thinned, the marble stones gleamed white with shining golden trim.

So. Tacky. It was hard to be scared with this much bad taste staring me in the face.

The steps that led up to two large brass doors were gold, too. I climbed up. They were ajar. Knocking would have been polite, but I barely offered a cursory tap of my knuckles before I slipped in.

They opened into a huge chamber, intersected by four halls. All around, furniture made of precious wood and metal stood, reflecting in flooring so polished I could have used it as a mirror.

Slip hazard, much?

Maybe I could find Una and get her out of here without encountering Raphael. That would be nice.

Tapping footsteps jerked my attention to the nearest hall.

Una, the daoine sidhe I'd come to ransom emerged from one of the halls. She wore a tight red halter top, ragged cut-offs that barely covered her upper thighs and strappy high heels.

Her neck, elbows, wrists, and ankles were crusted with dried blood. My own blood ran cold. I had expected to find her here, but not in this state. This went beyond any punishment I would have thought of. Perhaps I lacked imagination or thought Johann kinder than he was.

All righty then, grab her and run.

Una blurred, running toward me, the taps of her

shoes on marble like gunfire. She grabbed me by the arms, her wild eyes fixed on me. "Kill me!"

"I'd love to, but how about we leave instead?" I spoke fast, looking side to side.

A man was walking in our direction. Blast!

In the moment it took me to glance back to Una, the stranger reached us. He didn't stop at an acceptable distance, continuing to approach. I let go of Una and backed away until I hit a wall and had to tilt my face up to keep his face in view.

Young. Handsome. The perfection of his face hurt. His hair fell in a shining cloak over his shoulders, palest golden blond. Hungry eyes met mine. An icy blue but hot as the edge of a flame."

The sheer force of his presence beat against me. It was charisma wielded like a bludgeon, not permitting the others present to decide what their opinion of the possessor was, only that they should fall on their knees before him.

Screw that. All my instincts screamed be careful, but bold might be the better way to handle this.

"What do you want in exchange for setting Una free?"

He laughed. "What, no foreplay?"

Una's whimper affected me exactly like fingernails on a chalkboard.

"Nope. I'm a cut to the chase kind of gal."

"Well." His resonant voice caressed my ear as sweet as a daoine sidhe who wanted something. "I'm sure I can set a price... What are you willing to pay? And what should I call you while we negotiate?"

Calm and amused. This was a trivial decision for him, though lives hung in the balance. My daughter's. I had to play this well.

"I don't see anyone else standing here, so you can hardly get confused if you don't have my name, right?"

He chuckled.

"If you'll move back a bit, I can show you the trade I brought."

Raphael stepped back with a flourishing bow, his eyes never leaving my face. Una paced at the other end of the room, producing rapid-fire clicks. I knew better than most what captivity did to people, but I liked to think that I had dealt with it a tad better than she was. I would take trust issues over Una's feral actions any day.

"This," I said slowly. I feared a knife wasn't going to be enough for him, but it was also the only thing I had.

I pulled out the knife slowly. Raphael watched me, intent, his gaze moving from my face to my body. "The Adalric of the svartalfar made this. It's one of a kind, will never dull, as unique as Una is."

Raphael shook his head. "I have plenty of weapons, and do not need another, no matter its quality or rarity."

My heart dropped.

"I want you." Raphael stepped forward.

It would almost have been flattering, had I not

known what he was capable of. It didn't matter to him what I looked like or who I was, only that I was a new play toy for him to break and discard.

I held up a hand. "To alleviate the boredom, correct?"

"Yes."

"Then there will be rules."

"I'm listening."

"You do not bite me, ever. You do not touch me without my explicit verbal permission, ever. You do not use any powers to control or manipulate my emotions or body, ever." I wanted to say never touch me ever, but I could see myself hanging by one hand off a cliff with Raphael saying, 'Sorry, I can't touch you, do you want to revoke that condition?'

"And what do you offer me?" The delighted smile Raphael gave me did not reassure.

"Intelligent educated conversation. Someone to play cards or board games with or be nauseated when you torture rats."

He laughed again.

"Oh, we'll have a fine time together. I'm very persuasive." His voice stroked my skin like a rough purr.

I wondered whether throwing up on him would put him off.

"You will not mess with the time of this dominion, making it slower than my home's. And we'll deliver Una to the gate immediately; I'll see her through the gate and say goodbye to those waiting for me."

He held up a finger. "You will make yourself available for companionship whenever I call for you. You will not call for or accept aid to leave this place before I weary of you."

I shook my head. "A month."

He snorted. "A century—remember, Una doesn't age and still provides a little entertainment."

"And my lifespan isn't unlimited."

"It is if you want it to be... otherwise the mists would have eaten you and we wouldn't be having this conversation."

"Fine. My friends and family have limited lifespans."

"Fine. A decade." He mimicked my tone. His expression had gone intent... it was going to be hard to push the time down further.

"A year and a day." I held up my hand as he opened his mouth to deny me. "And I'll use my abilities at your request for reasonable actions. I won't help you torture rats, but I'd help repair buildings and that kind of thing. In exchange, no torture, no threats from you."

He considered, pale eyes intent on me. Something moved in them... like some huge predator surfacing from the deeps.

Nice assumption I wouldn't try to get out by myself. I could handle that. All I needed was to get Una back to the human world so Dara would be saved.

Johann had promised that Jimmy was safe no matter what happened to me, and I knew that would extend to my daughter as well. A year and a day I could handle, even if it left my life and career in ruins.

"Let us send Una through the gate, and I will stay here with you."

CHAPTER 11

RAPHAEL SPARED UNA A GLANCE. "FOLLOW."

She moved like a puppet.

I watched carefully as he spoke. The magic strands tangled around Una were very like the pattern that enveloped the goblins. Unlike the goblins, she wasn't wrapped in them so much as they interwove, plunging into the center of her being.

Time to reinforce that shield. Since it was already set to keep his dominion from eating me, I added a second layer as I walked out the door. It was difficult to craft a secondary ward to keep magic from penetrating me while I walked, but I also had incentive. The magic presumably took hold with his bite. Defending against that might be hard... but he'd said he wouldn't. That should give me a little time to figure it out before he broke his promise.

And if my shield didn't block it all, I'd feed all the

energy I had into it. Raphael would have a dead woman instead of a toy.

Once we stepped out of the house, and traveled down the street, I noticed that while I had walked for well over an hour, the tumbledown building and the gate seemed only maybe 50 feet away. It was like a land worked under Raphael's boots.

Nick could control time in his dominion... Who had that power in mine?

As we approached, the gatekeeper rose and put himself between Raphael and the gate. "No."

"I merely come to deliver someone to you to pass through the gate. I do not intend to pass it." Raphael's voice was silken smooth.

The gatekeeper glanced from me to Una and sighed. "Do you wish me to open the gate enough for you to make your farewells?"

My throat was tight. "Yes."

"Go, Una. Walk through the gate. Hurry!" Raphael's tone was sardonic.

Una ran forward and bounced off an invisible wall. She staggered back and turned to face us. Her nose bled freely, and she'd cut her lip, probably on her teeth.

The air in the gate behind her tore like a piece of foil, edges folding back. I could see Nick and Johann, waiting on the other side. Nick's fists were clenched, his face worried. Johann's arms were folded, and he looked vaguely bored. He hadn't yet reverted to the form I was more familiar with, still tall and impressive looking.

"Lou. Still sad and lonely?" Raphael's voice mocked, with enough of an undercoating of malice it raised goosebumps on me.

"Asmedaj. Still chained up like a junkyard dog?" Johan's voice, in contrast, sounded bored and a little amused. He turned his attention to the gatekeeper. "You go by Diego at the moment, don't you?

The gatekeeper nodded. I noted the names Lou and Asmedaj for later—if they were real names, it might solve some mysteries.

Nick said, "Ceri?" The quiet worry, verging on fear, in his voice, drove other thought out of my mind.

Una ran through, shouldered past them and ran down the hall.

"Shouldn't you catch her?" Raphael's voice came from behind me, now bored.

"No. Are you coming, Ceri?" Johann asked, unfolding his arms.

Not trusting my voice, I shook my head. Then I took a step forward. "Nick... I'm sorry. I know that you didn't mean it. I was bitchier than you deserved. I wasn't going to say he hadn't deserved none, even now.

Nick stretched his fingertips toward me but didn't quite touch the gate area. I echoed the gesture.

"I'll take care of Dara while you're gone. Make sure she actually gets her degree." Nick's calm voice was overcontrolled. "And keep an eye on Johann to keep him from overworking Jimmy."

"Hey! I resemble that remark, Damarian." Johann stared at Raphael as he spoke.

"How touching." Nice to know the peanut gallery, specifically Raphael, was watching. "Have you finished sorting out your affairs, Ceri?" The way he said my name made the goosebumps worse. I wanted a shower.

"I love you, Nick." The words tumbled out of me.

"And I, you." Nick said. He moved to take a step forward, and Johann caught his arm.

"No," Johan said.

"Oh, let him pass. He'll die, and I won't have to deal with all the pathetic gooey longing for next past lover. And Lou—don't think I didn't notice the protection you put on her. Rude." Raphael's voice had returned to a lighthearted pitch.

"If she had the wit to ask for it, why wouldn't I give it to her?" Johann replied.

I hadn't asked for it... and then I realized how Johann phrased it.

"Goodbye, Nick. I'll be back." I willed him to believe me.

Raphael moved and stood by my side. I glanced at him sideways. The smug, 'I've got you now, my pretty,' smile on his face made me want to slap him.

Better thinking about slapping than the gibbering terror looming in the back of my head.

"And thank you Johann. You know I like the feisty ones." And then he said to the gatekeeper, "Close the gate."

I continued staring as the rip mended, until all I could see was fog.

UNSAID

A YEAR away from Nick and my children, my job, everything. My whole life. I blinked rapidly and took a deep breath to compose myself, fighting back the terror. I missed it all already, not five seconds into my sentence.

And, frankly, this dominion was anything but a vacation spot. I couldn't even look forward to the amenities.

I stared at the spot where the gateway had faded away, turning back into the twining vines of an old, untended rose bush, taller than I was, with no flowers, only thorns and sharp-edged leaves.

There was probably a visual joke there if I could find my sense of humor. Too bad it was on the other side of the gateway with Nick.

Another swallow and I smoothed my work expression on, one that yielded no points and took no prisoners. It wouldn't do to show weakness to the monster at my back.

I needed to keep telling myself that, keep it on repeat, even though all I wanted to do was start screaming and never stop. Or start throwing punches, and ditto on the never stopping part.

Focusing on details helped me control those impulses. I grounded myself with the chilly embrace of the fog rolling in, the dark green of the uneven tufts of grass I stood on. The slate gray of the sky, evenly illuminated by some unknown light source, with no hint of an actual sun.

This dominion must have very different physical rules than Earth. I was in no mood to ask at the moment.

"And thus is the bargain sealed." Raphael's words came from behind me, but the intonation lacked all the creepy weirdness and malice I'd come to expect. A smooth baritone, his voice was pleasant on the ear, as much as I hated to admit it.

I didn't answer.

"Witnessed." The gatekeeper, Diego, answered him. *His* voice was completely flat, without inflection. Oddly similar to Raphael's, though, if I listened closely. And why should he care? Why should it matter to him that I'd just signed away my soul?

Well, not really, but certainly not far off. For a freaking year.

I'd just traded myself for a prisoner in this dominion. I'd done it to save my daughter. That was the important part.

The House of Mists had a foul reputation. That's what Nick had said.

My interactions with Raphael, the leader or owner or prisoner, whatever he was, whoever he was, hadn't changed that assessment. The enkimmu was creepy and lecherous and the embodiment of all negative characteristics associated with men, so far as I could tell. If the land that he controlled was anything like the man himself, then I'd just signed myself up for a year of hell here, but what choice had I had? He'd wanted payment for the prisoner.

Whom I'd found surprisingly easily... Now I was suspicious about that on top of everything else.

My daughter's life had been on the line, and I'd do anything I had to in order to make sure that she was safe. No matter the cost to myself or Nick or our relationship. We could afford to pay the price far better than she.

Arriving here, I'd discovered this dominion's mists tried to consume those who traveled to it... I still had a shield up to keep it from sucking all my blood out. Cross a vampire's lair with another dimension, and this dimension was born. All kinds of Outer Limits nastiness that really wanted a piece of me. And if I wasn't careful, it was going to get some, too. It wasn't going to be easy, keeping my guard up all the time.

One year. It was just one year. I could do it...I *could* do it!

Ugh, I didn't know if I could do it.

As if Raphael read my mind, and *oh*, I hoped he couldn't, a pulse of magic shivered through the air behind me. It swirled around me, all in ribbons of gray, ranging from silver to slate. They wrapped around me, brushing against my body gently, and I stiffened. Then the constant assault that had latched on to me when I arrived, trying to consume me, which I'd been repelling with my magic, stopped.

Whatever Raphael had done to make his realm stop trying to kill me, I breathed a sigh of relief. Being constantly vigilant to keep from being killed was not a state that I wanted to try to spend the next year in. Not being superhuman, there was no way that I could keep my magical guard up constantly.

On the other hand, should I trust it would *stay* stopped? What if I was deeply asleep and Raphael revoked this magical protection?

I couldn't risk that. Wherever I ended up sleeping, I needed to set up personal wards, just in case. Around my bed or bedroom, wherever it was. And I'd need to craft something to counter it unconsciously, for the times I left my wards. That would take time and concentration, even though I was well practiced at creating and maintaining them at my home and the school. I put it on the old mental to-do list, just below keeping myself alive and whole.

My forehead tingled warmly where Johann had kissed my brow earlier. I assumed he'd left some type of protective standing magic on me, but there was no way to examine that right now either.

The jury was out on whether I was annoyed at him for doing it without my permission, too. Being annoyed with Johann could wait a year, though.

I turned around and blinked. Viewing Raphael now was a strange experience. It was like looking at someone's twin where all of the body language you were expecting was completely different. His wasn't a friendly body language, but at the same time, it wasn't the full-on psycho creep that he'd been just moments before. Not a good sign that he could flip his switch so easily.

He gazed at me, brilliant blue eyes not unsympathetic, and said, "You're a fool, you know."

Rude, but not so much untrue. I lifted my chin. "Be that as it may. Do you have a hotel here? Or should I just find material to make a tent?" I was trying to keep my sarcasm to a minimum, even though what I wanted was to unleash the full force of my frustration on him.

A smile flickered on the gatekeeper's lined face. Nearby, one of the shrubs that covered the tumble-down building closest to the gate rustled out of time with the breeze. I twitched briefly, startled by the sudden movement. Not to mention confused by the fact that it hadn't rustled with the breeze, as physics said it should have, but this was not my world. For all I knew, it rained upside down and bushes and grass moved however the hell they wanted to, thank you very much.

Raphael shifted his attention in that direction, following my gaze, then sighed. "Out. Now."

The tone of weary command in his voice was different from how he'd spoken to me before, too. A man of many facets.

The bush went very still before rising a little less than a foot in height, but it grew on top of a tumbled wall from the nearby ruin. Its body was comprised of thickly intertwined branches and full foliage, dark green and red, contrasting with the fog.

"Now." The way Raphael spoke left no room for argument. But who was he talking to? The bush? It certainly wasn't me. I was standing right here.

Two people slithered out from behind the shrubbery. A boy and a girl, teenagers, best I could tell. The boy, with dark skin and pale hair, was obviously of svartalfar heritage. The girl... I couldn't tell. Her long, dark hair lay in twin braids, her eyes a strange shade of violet, with no other unusual characteristics that could make me surmise her kin. Or possibly she was human? Who knew? Especially in a place like this. They could've been bush spirits, and I wouldn't have been terribly surprised.

"Albrecht. Ilani. What did I warn you would happen the next time you eavesdropped on matters that were not your concern?" Raphael's voice was calm, the undercurrent of menace plain. But a different kind of menace than he'd directed at me earlier. It sounded more like a principal's 'I'm going to give you detention' speech rather than 'I'm going to flay you alive'. Maybe he liked them better than me, which wouldn't have surprised me in the slightest.

On the other hand, both teens attended to him closely, indicating that possibly flaying alive was still on the table. Clearly, they knew him better than I did, and the fact that they seemed to view him with the same caution and concern that I did only confirmed that I should still watch my back even if the land wasn't actively trying to eat me at the moment.

After a long pause, the boy glanced at the girl.

She stepped forward, smiling brightly. "You said that we would be punished appropriately. And I think that the very best punishment for us would be helping the new woman. The newest person in our land. It would be very inconvenient and difficult to acclimate someone who does not know this place to your magnificence and the wonders of the land you rule."

I caught the underlying sarcasm and didn't quite know how she could be that smartass to Raphael, who was in the top three most frightening people I'd ever met. Actually, he might be the worst, at least from what I'd seen so far. But if she was that much of a smartass and managed to get away with it, there was hope for me. I did have a hard time suppressing my attitude... pretty much all the time.

428   DAPHNE MOORE & L.A. BORUFF

The gatekeeper snorted. Oh, good. He had an attitude as well.

Raphael tilted his head, regarding them both. "Since you volunteered, Ilani, the task is yours. This woman's name is Ceri. She comes from... I have no idea, but presumably, she'll tell you. I've other business to attend to for the rest of the day, so make sure she doesn't get herself killed. Return her to the house this evening."

A dark smile crossed his face as he turned to me. Despite everything, he was terribly attractive, if I could manage to ignore the psychotically dangerous and cruel parts. "Enjoy. These two are among the best my *magnificent* land has to offer."

Nope, no sarcasm there either. And strange that he'd given me free rein to roam his dominion. What was he up to?

Raphael strode away, the thick silver-gray mist closing around him. Not even his outline could be seen after two steps.

When I looked back toward the gate, the gatekeeper had resumed his seat and was ignoring the three of us. Apparently, he only needed to pay attention to us when Raphael was present, which was fine by me.

Turning my attention to the pair standing near me, I might've over guessed their age. They could've been somewhere in their early teens, perhaps thirteen or fourteen. Perceiving them magically, the boy had a good measure of magic similar to Nick's, while the girl was wrapped in a never-ending flow of magic unlike any I'd ever seen. It enveloped her, and she seemed not to tap into it at all.

In the moment's pause it took me to perceive them, the boy eyed me warily and the girl smiled at me in the same sunny fashion that she had with Raphael. Given that that sweet expression had overlaid a great deal of sarcasm, I waited expectantly. A little snark would be refreshing after the day I'd had. Plus, I was more than used to teenage mockery.

"What do you want to see?" Ilani asked. Her voice was as bright as her smile.

"Other than the house where Raphael lives and a few ruins between here and there, I haven't seen anything here. Is there any pleasant place? Is there anywhere where the sun shines? Without the fog?" I waved my hand toward a patch lingering nearby.

Albrecht snorted. "No."

Ilani shrugged. "It all depends on what you mean by pleasant. This isn't a *bad* place. If you're going to be staying at the big house, that's where Albrecht and I live, and it has a lot of interesting stuff in it, but not many people. Albrecht and I can show you around, where people live, and also the mourning swamp, and the devouring forest, and..."

I raised my brows. "Great names. You must get a lot of tourists."

Her smile went wry and more real. "New people do come here. Not often, but they do. The mist brings them here. It brings a lot of humans, sometimes some of the other kins. Nobody knows if it's random or if the mists somehow pick people.

The only thing is, the mists can only bring people here, not take them away, as far as anyone says. We can show you where some of them live." She squinted at me. "Did you bring any of those little phone machines? I've been wanting to see another one while the energy thing was still running."

Phone-machines and energy-things. Okay. "I do. I might let you look at it. Especially if you answer a couple of questions." Hopefully, it would incentivize her to cooperate and not get up to any mischief.

She made a *get-on-with-it* gesture, foot tapping. A trade of information was welcome, which was good to know.

"If you live in that house, did you see much of Una before today?" I'd never met the woman in all the time I'd lived in Columbus. We moved in very different circles. She'd been one of the movers and shakers of kin society, which I'd avoided at all costs... until recently.

"Yes. She's crazy." Ilani's violet gaze was as direct as her words.

"But was she that way before she got here?" My real question was how long it'd taken for her to lose it. I would've heard if she'd been that erratic through the gossip mill at home.

Ilani shrugged. "I saw her back when Raphael's son brought her. Gaius said that she needed real punishment, not what she'd get from the Johann-man or her own kin. I felt a little bad for her at first because Raphael can be cruel, especially to people who've done bad stuff. But after she'd been here a while, I got to know her, and she was the mean kind of crazy."

Albrecht added, "That was before she just started begging people to kill her."

Even though I'd experienced Una doing that, my blood still chilled. I very much did not want to know what precisely had brought her to that state. "And how she looked didn't bother either of you?"

Ilani shrugged again. "Raphael's an Enkimmu. They bite, they drink blood. Raphael's bitten most of the people who live here at least once. It's like us eating soup, except he doesn't have to kill what he eats."

"But he controls those he bites." My tone had chilled, despite my best effort. Had he fed from these children?

She rolled her eyes. Her voice came out low, obviously mimicking someone. No doubt Raphael. "And now, do as you normally would in all things."

It took me a moment to figure it out. "Is that what he usually does?"

"Yeah. He once said that controlling thousands of people was the most stupefyingly boring thing he can think of." She regarded me. "*But* I wouldn't let him bite you if I were you, because he's interested in you."

I raised my brow in silent question.

She sighed like I was dense and not getting it. Maybe that was true, but... heck, I *didn't* get it.

"He's always bored. He didn't look bored with you. He put on a big act of being an evil pervert for you. And you still stayed here. So he knows you're smart and strong and tough and want something. And *he* really wants something that no one here has ever been able to give him. So if you're able to give it to him, it would be best if you didn't get bit."

My other eyebrow raised. The boy nudged her, his cheeks going pink. The two of them were opposites. He seemed embarrassed by the potential sexual implication, and Ilani hadn't realized it. I wasn't even sure if that was what she was referring to—if so, there were other troubles here.

Ilani sighed. "Not sex stuff. Why does everybody always think it's sex stuff? But I'm not going to get into trouble by telling you what I think he wants, because he'll tell you what he wants when he feels it's time. I don't cross him. Real punishment hurts." She shrank back slightly as if speaking from experience. One she never wanted to repeat.

I bit my lip on other questions and pulled out my phone. A deal was a deal. She accepted it eagerly, fingers dashing across the screen.

The tinny notes of Candy Crush filled the air. Absorbed, Ilani tapped on the screen. I'd give it a couple of moments before I started pushing to explore the area.

Albrecht moved to my side. "Have you noticed your new piece of jewelry?"

Erm, what?

He gave me a sidelong glance as he continued, "You weren't wearing it when you came up to the gate with Raphael, but when you turned away, it was there." He touched his forehead.

My fingers flew to my forehead. The warm spot remained, what I'd presumed was magic from Johann, but my fingers touched a cool bump. I tugged. It came off in my hand, the warmth on my skin cooling.

A luminous golden stone lay in my palm. It felt like Johann's magic, elusive and hard to see with the inner eye, even though I held something physical.

it'd been located where he kissed my forehead... should I put it back or simply carry it? Wisdom suggested I put it back and independence said to leave it behind.

I compromised, putting it into my trouser pocket. Carrying it but not wearing it like a brand. Albrecht watched the action without comment.

"I wish we could've computers. I wish we could've cars." Open longing tinged Ilani's voice. She hadn't yet looked up from the phone. She was a teen longing for the lifestyle of the human world's children.

Albrecht said, "We will. When we go to humanity's lands, we'll see them all."

Erm, when was that? I gave them another moment, gazing at the mists, and called up the ability to see magic again, remembering Ilani's words about the mist bringing people here.

It was entirely woven of magic, the mist appearing as a veil over the magical power that formed its being. Strands of magic, thin as hairs, radiated from it into the distance, possibly connecting it to other patches of fog. Was it an entity? Or a tremendously large spell that had possibly stood for years?

I wanted to probe deeper into it, but this was not the time or the place. Better to gain a basic familiarity before I started tampering with something that might be fundamental to the functioning of the dominion.

Though if it would give me an independent route back home...intriguing.

Shaking my head, I directed my attention back to the children. "Why don't you power it off, show me around, and then you can play on it more later?"

She gave it back to me with a wistful expression on her face. "Ok."

Ilani led us in the opposite direction from the route Raphael had taken. The grass shifted underfoot as it grew longer and thicker, almost grabbing at my calves. We passed a grove of trees where the branches reached for us, long and thin as a willow's.

The *terrain* was handsy? That was new.

"Don't go near those, their leaves are sharp," Ilani said as we passed.

"You never answered. Is there a sun here?" I eyed the groping pseudo-willow.

Albrecht sighed. "No. This is as light as it gets."

How did the plants grow? I mused on the thought as a tent, surrounded by stacked wood, scattered bones and hides, and what looked like trash, appeared as we curved around the grove. It stood far from the trees, which continued to move in a sinuous and disturbing manner.

"That's where Mac lives. He's a human, I think. He doesn't like people." Ilani pointed as we followed the edge of the clearing, not approaching the camp.

As if on cue, a long-haired, bearded man crawled out of the tent. His eyes were wild, his face gaunt, his movement jerky. "Go away, you stupid bitch! And take your friends with you!"

The breeze shifted, and I gagged. it'd been a long time since he'd washed. He stared at us, hands clenching and unclenching, and I kept a wary eye on him until we lost sight of him as we passed to the other side of the grove.

"The other camp is a ways away." Ilani glanced over her shoulder. "Why do you want to know where other people live? They don't like the people associated with Raphael much, so they probably won't be very friendly."

"It's good to know things about the place where I'm going to be staying for a little while. Besides, what else is there to do?" I answered. "What do you two do?"

"Spy on people," Albrecht murmured, tone dry.

Ilani shrugged. "It's good to know what's going on,

and nobody tells us anything. Hunting gets boring after a while... I can't travel the way some people do, and I can't use the tech things that have been changed to work off magic." She shrugged one shoulder and kicked a rock as we walked. "And I don't have good magic."

I blinked. Say what, now? She had huge amounts of magic, why was no one teaching her? She wasn't human, I could tell that, but I didn't know what her kin was. I'd hesitate to try to teach her to use her magic until I knew what she was. Improper training could stunt natural talent.

"What kin are you?" I asked, deciding to be blunt.

Ilani threw her hands wide. "Mixed? Nobody's ever told me. My parents left when I was born, and I lived with Albrecht's family until they left a couple of years ago."

How odd.

"If you show me the technical items that work on magic, I'll see if I can help you figure out how to activate them." That shouldn't hurt, since it was likely a binary on-off thing rather than actually using her magic.

"Really? That would be great! I'd love to learn how to use the television..." And she was off. Every item she knew of was named, and how she'd like to use it. I listened, but Albrecht remained silent. Possibly because he'd learned he couldn't get a word in edgewise without physically stopping her from speaking.

After walking long enough for my calves to start

aching, we paused for a meal. Albrecht pulled it out of his pack. Normal-looking plastic wrap, holding mundane-looking sliced white bread with fillings. Sandwiches.

I unwrapped mine and peeked inside. Ham and cheese. "Where did the food come from?"

Ilani said, "There are a couple of people that can come and go to your dominion. A lot of our supplies come from big places with food on all the shelves—they call them supermarkets. They have guardian machines that carry them there and need to be locked up in order to enter the supermarkets. I can hardly wait until I'm old enough to do that. Have you ever been to one?"

Was it worth it to correct her and explain? No. "A few times. Could I come and go?"

She shook her head vigorously. "No. It's something only people of the blood can do."

"The blood, meaning what?"

"Kin to Raphael." She took a big bite and chewed rapidly.

I nibbled on my sandwich, considering. "You're both related to him?"

"Yes, though I'm not sure exactly how he's related to me, I think he's maybe my great or great-great-grand-father? But we know he's Albrecht's grandfather on his father's side."

Ilani took another bite, allowing Albrecht to speak. "I have to go to apprentice with my father's family soon. Now that there's someone nice here to be with

Ilani, I feel better about it. Since you're not crazy like Una, I'm hoping that you'll be able to keep her company while you're here." He stared at me in a measuring fashion.

How did I manage to pick up strays wherever I went? I still needed to take care of the goblins and the fetches back home. What was I doing picking up another kid? "You just met me."

Albrecht shrugged. "Yes, and you're still a better candidate than anyone I know here. Except for Diego. And his duties mean he can't do it."

Diego—the gatekeeper, yes.

"I'll do what I can." I spread my hands. "However, I'm not quite sure what that is yet."

"Mostly trying to keep her from getting into trouble." Albrecht's side glance was full of fond exasperation, much like an older brother, though physically he appeared to be the younger of the two.

Ilani finished chewing. "I do not get in trouble. I have adventures."

A chill ran down my spine. "What kind of adventures?" I wasn't the adventurous type, despite the shenanigans I tended to get into.

She giggled. "Fun ones. I like exploring places."

Time to think of other fun activities that didn't involve danger. "Do you know how to read? Or write? Or how about math?"

Her eyes twinkled as she chewed. "Of course! But I'm old enough that I don't have schoolwork anymore.

There are not that many books here, just what's in Raphael's study, and most of them are boring. Philosophy and history and geography, that kind of stuff. Nothing fun to read."

I tapped my fingers on my leg. She was a tween or early teen and was out of school? "Are there many others like you?"

Albrecht shook his head no, a dry smile on his face. "She's one of a kind."

Ilani shot him a crabby glance. "There's a couple of babies. Nobody our age, though. The last human who came through was a couple of years ago and he was older. He's the one who yelled at you. Some of the family—Raphael's family—bring a husband or wife here, but they have to ask first so Raphael and Diego can do the thing that keeps the mists from eating you if you come through a gate."

"I see." Actually, I didn't. Why would anyone *choose* to come here? And how did I get an introduction to them as well? I needed to examine the mists later, too, to see if I could duplicate how they'd told it to stop trying to eat me.

Just in case I needed to be able to do that independently.

A thought occurred. "Do you know what this dominion is called? Does it have a name?"

"Ha'al," Ilani answered.

Really? Hell? A bit on the nose.

WE FINISHED EATING IN SILENCE. When we were done, Albrecht packed up the trash into his bag. Only the thinnest wisps of mist lay in strands, weaving through the clumps of grass. The sky remained a pale gray, shading to white directly above us. The air was warmer here, and a light breeze began to pull wisps of my hair away from my head.

The waist-high grass ahead of us was dotted with white, and I paused to examine the flowers when we got close enough. White, tall and spiky, with six-petaled blooms like little stars...close up, some of the silky petals darkened to a delicate pink.

Asphodel. Flower of the afterlife in Greek mythology. After the reveal of what this dominion was called, this place really couldn't get any more blatant, right? It made me wonder if the other Underworld motifs could be found here. Rivers of boiling blood? A three-headed dog and the boatman asking for his coins? On consideration, I decided not to pursue that train of thought, for fear that I'd find them.

"Do you have seasons? This is a spring flower," I asked. That wasn't technically very important, but I was curious about it. Any information was good.

"I'm not sure..." Ilani glanced back at me. She'd walked ahead as I paused.

The long grasses grew up to her chest, swaying gently in the breeze that had appeared out of nowhere. It felt good, even if I was a tad concerned about how it was created. Then again, at least it wasn't blowing us out of our shoes. It only made things more dramatic.

"It gets warmer and colder here," Ilani said. "And I've read about seasons in Raphael's books and scrolls, but the pomegranate and apple trees have fruit and flowers at the same time, which isn't how it works in your world, I think. The beehives are always awake. We don't have fields of food, but we used to. Once supermarkets and bakers were invented, we stopped growing wheat and grains."

Had she seen the change personally? Appearances could be deceptive. Though since she didn't act like she was thousands of years old, I rather doubted it. Then again, I'd been wrong in the past, and I wouldn't have been surprised if there was more to her than met the eye.

We skirted a stand of trees, and Albrecht held up his hand for us to pause. "Pigs here recently, Ilani."

I looked down as if I knew how to read tracks. The

ground was pretty torn up, and I'd read feral pigs were big and smart. I understood his caution.

She considered for a moment, tilting her head to the side as she thought. "We're headed for the town, though, the pigs don't like going there much. We should be fine."

Famous last words? She should have known better than to say something like that. It was tempting fate, but too late now. It was already out there in the world.

The ground rose, and we paused at a ridge.

A little more than a dozen small structures lay at its bottom, made of wood and stone, with thatch roofs. They sat in the middle of what was obviously a cultivated area. I recognized tomato plants and cucumbers even at this distance.

A gathering of people had gathered in what seemed to be a town square, that all the buildings faced. Trees and bushes hid most of the details from me. I wiped my suddenly damp hands on my shirt as we proceeded forward.

I distracted myself from nervousness at meeting people the mists had decided to take to Ha'al by musing more on how *did* things grow without the sun? Magic could do it, yes, but it still seemed very strange. It would take an insane amount of magic to grow everything here since there wasn't a single ray of sunshine that I could see. What was the light source here?

The rocks making up the ridge were redder than any sandstone I'd ever seen. They were also rough and jagged, and my hands were sore and dotted with pinpricks of blood by the time we climbed down. The same for Ilani and Albrecht, who treated it as normal. For them, it probably was.

I wasn't a fan.

As we walked closer to the little town, more details emerged of the gathering of people near the well in the middle of the town square. Roses and olive trees bordered the small common area. On neatly mowed grass, men and women, a variety of nationalities but all of them human, glanced up from various chores. In a small garden next to the well, a few people were weeding, while others sewed or did woodwork. A gaunt older man was stretching an unfamiliar animal skin, one with thick brown fur and a ruff or mane. It looked like a combination of a bear and a lion, and I shuddered to think what the actual animal looked like if the skin was that big.

Their clothing was an odd combination of styles and eras—many wore jeans, some tattered and patched, and a variety of shirts. T-shirts contrasted with obviously hand-woven smocks. For want of a better explanation, it was almost like they were shipwreck survivors. Some wore their own clothes, and some wore whatever they could find.

Three children played near one of the women, chasing a ball made of rags bound together with string. Two were young enough to cling to their mother's leg at the sight of a stranger, and the eldest appeared a little younger than Ilani. All three of them watched us warily, implying they were well aware of the dangers here, despite their age.

A dark-skinned man straightened from weeding and stepped forward. "You found someone new to live here, girl?"

His words were gilded with a trace of an accent... maybe Caribbean? He wore cut-offs and no shirt. His gaze assessed me, brows almost meeting in a frown. I wanted to frown back, purely because I'd done nothing to deserve that expression, but carefully schooled my features. I had enough enemies without making more over something stupid.

Ilani shook her head so vigorously that her braids smacked her in the face. "No. Raphael wants her."

Several sharp inhalations of breath followed her announcement. Just great.

The man nearest me, working on stacking wood, edged away, one careful shift at a time, creeping along the ground on his knees. Others stared, a mixture of horror and fear on their faces. It was as if they were afraid that they'd catch my misfortune like a plague if they stayed too near me.

Stranger things could've happened.

I'd never been regarded in quite this way before. The encounter was *not* helping my views on Raphael or this place. To be fair, I wasn't sure anything could help at this point, but still. These people did *not* react well to hearing I was meant to cure Raphael's boredom.

Ugh, they probably thought I was a sex slave or something.

"Hi!" I smiled at them all. It might've had edges. "I'm Ceri. I'm pleased to meet you all. I've been here an hour or so and would love to have some idea of what's going on. I, uh, hope we can help each other out."

"Good to meet you," responded the man I assumed was their leader. He directed his attention back to Ilani almost immediately, now that he had at least said hello to me. Polite to a fault, if you didn't count the fact that he switched to ignoring me and talking about me like I wasn't even there. "Why did you bring her here?"

He did not seem pleased.

"We were showing her around. She's not one of *those* people—she's not here for special punishment. Himself just wants to talk to her." Ilani folded her arms, frowning. I didn't miss the subtle emphasis on himself. "Do you think I'd bring a bad person here? And I always bring a way for more food when I bring people to you."

Horror and fear shifted to worry and pity on the faces of several people staring at me. I wasn't sure which was worse.

They might not have thought it, but there was definitely something more here than I'd expected. I tried not to be insulted. It wasn't their fault that they couldn't trust anyone that *Himself* wanted to see. If I was in their position, I would've felt the same way, as much as I hated to admit it.

"Well then. You see us." Impatience and exasperation edged the leader's words.

Ilani gave him an equally grumpy look in return. "Yes."

She moved to where the children clung to the woman I assumed was their mother. "Do you need anything?"

The woman stroked her hand over the youngest child's tangled hair. It was a simple, fond gesture, one that made my heart ache with memories of my own children, so far away. "Not right now."

She sounded wistful, as if she wanted something but didn't dare ask. Part of me wondered how she felt at this moment, what it was that she wanted that she didn't feel she could request.

"This woman, Ceri," Ilani pointed at me, "has said that we need more school. If she wins the argument with Himself, and we have to learn more, I'll come and get Henry."

A surprised smile curled the woman's lips. The children might not be pleased about the possibility of more schooling, but she was. "If there's a school, you do that. And take Allie too. They need it."

She had a New England accent, a little bit nasally. It was strange to hear it here, but almost comforting. Made me feel closer to home than since I got into this strange place, not just her nasal pronunciation, but everyone else, too. I'd only been here a few hours. Imagine how I'd feel in a month or two.

The thought of people trapped here through no fault of their own disturbed me greatly. Especially small children.

The air rippled around the gathering, somehow thickening, and mist curled up from the ground as I watched. The steady light from the sky darkened like a dimmer switch had been thrown.

In a moment, the area was clear of everyone but me, Albrecht, and Ilani.

"What's going on?" I asked.

Albrecht surveyed the area, eyes calm but narrowed. "It's later than I thought. That was the twilight signal. We need to get back home. Dangerous things roam at night, and you'll get in trouble if you get hurt. You get in more trouble if you hurt the monsters." What he didn't say was that *they* would get in trouble if something happened to me. It wasn't hard to figure that much out.

His magic flexed and shifted my senses to perceive what he was doing. Ilani was doing a similar flex, and both wrapped their magic around me, twining me in glittering strands.

They interacted with the power that underlay and interwove all aspects of this place—this dominion was so intensely bewitched it hurt my eyes when I focused and brought all the magic to the foreground.

The children gripped the strands of magic, using a

connection with it that I lacked, and pulled themselves through the fabric of the dominion, taking me with them with a slight yank that made my stomach drop, like I was on a roller coaster. It was as if the distance was a long sheet of fabric, and they were pulling ends of it together rather than crossing all the intervening space.

We stood by the handsy grove. Both of them had sweat on their faces, breathing heavily.

"Long jump," Ilani panted.

"Need to do one more," Albrecht gasped.

A terrible cracking noise erupted from the grove, and I spun. A humanoid figure, bigger than a troll, at least ten feet tall, with a boar's head on a man's body, strode out of the trees, a log clenched in one hand as a club. Oh, fantastic. Everything was proportionate, which was just a lovely sight.

Defense now, brain bleach later. Lots of brain bleach.

Albrecht swore, and I had to stifle an inappropriate snicker as I grabbed the nearby magic and slapped together a shield between us and the giant. Hopefully, that would buy us the needed time.

The giant made a loud snorting noise, his glittering pig eyes fixed on us. They glowed red in the dim light. He stepped forward, and his club and hand blazed with magic.

I fell back a step, grasping at more magic, heart accelerating. The safety of the magical shield suddenly felt much less in face of the power in his hand, and I grabbed everything I could field to create a second, stronger shield as the other evaporated under the force of the club's swing.

Running wasn't an option. With those legs, we'd never outrun him. I was probably slower than the kids, but I didn't particularly want to die by a pig-giant's club. Or anything else, if it came back to it.

"Almost ready to go!" Ilani chirped, voice a little breathless.

Famous last words. I braced the hastily put-together new shield with all the magic I could yank together.

The club slammed into it, and I gasped. Feedback ran through the shield, and I took the weight of the impact all over my body.

Before the next swing, I braced physically as well as mentally. This had never happened before, and while I'd no doubt spend time figuring it out later *if* we survived, for now, I needed to focus.

Mr. Naked-Pig-Giant raised the club and slammed it down again, and my arms creaked with strain as I braced.

"Any time now!" I croaked.

The pig giant snuffled, then looked over his shoulder. The trees behind him parted and two more of his kind stepped out. All three naked. One was female.

Super.

A line of cold sweat ran down my back.

A hand grabbed the waistband of my trousers and magic jerked me away. Relief cascaded through me, warring with nausea and dizziness as I caught my breath. I was going to have to figure out how to duplicate that.

When we stopped moving, we stood by Raphael's gaudy mansion. The building glowed a silky silverish light that enhanced its color scheme. Light from the glow illuminated the pair of teens clearly. Their faces were strained as if both had just run a marathon in very hot weather.

That magical movement technique would make getting around here much easier, and presumably safer when close to twilight. If I could do that back home as well, so much the better, even if it seemed to cost the user physically. We'd walked for a long time, and two steps took us back to the house. Worth a bit of breathlessness.

Ilani staggered, fair skin paler than I'd like to see.

Steadying her, I glanced at Albrecht with questions in my eyes. He seemed in a better state.

"Two jumps together is a big drain," he said, sitting down on the steps and tilting his head back. He was soaked in sweat. "Being eaten is a bigger one, though. Never seen them come out that fast after dark before."

"You're probably hungry?" I made the statement a question. I'd like to know what made the monsters want to come out. Was it me? I was the only new thing in the realm, presumably.

"Yes." Ilani shivered and leaned on my arm as I guided her down to sit on the steps as well. "Also, I want a nap. Night came much earlier than usual today."

The sight of the two of them huddled on the steps of gleaming marble and gold chilled me. They could easily have died under a gross monsters club, and I'd gotten the strong impression they roamed this place as they pleased. This shouldn't have caught them so off guard.

"Does that happen often?" I asked.

"Twilight came a little early, but that happens occasionally. The giants being that active was a big surprise. The really bad creatures don't wake up fast. I don't know what happened or why." Ilani gazed at me with big eyes.

I glanced at Albrecht. He looked better, a slight smile crossing his face.

He met my glance and laughed quietly. "Often enough to make it exciting. You well enough to get to your room, Ilani? Since that's where the food's going to be soon?"

She nodded and they both got up. Apparently, we were going to ignore the incident. I'd wait until tomorrow to ask them to teach me how to move like that, though. They both still looked too exhausted.

"My room?" I prodded them gently. They were tired, but so was I, and I did want to know where I was supposed to sleep so I could ward it. All the more so after the giant. And his giant... club. Ugh. Gross.

"Oh, yeah. This way." Ilani headed into the mansion, not seeming to notice all the glitz.

Albrecht and I followed, climbing the seven steps leading to the open doors. The, um—for lack of a better word, I was going to call it the reception area—was like a ballroom, all glitter and open space. Three halls extended from it.

"How do we access the second floor?"

I saw no stairs, but unless all the rooms had tremendous cathedral ceilings, there had to be a set. I was capable of a lot of things but jumping to another floor was not one. The whole setup was strange, and unlike anything I'd ever seen before. It felt ancient, like some long ago king had designed it for all of his godly guests.

Possibly that was the reaction that Raphael wanted, but I wasn't sure. He didn't seem the type to need to pose to show off his power.

"This way." Ilani pointed down the right exit.

The hall stretched endlessly. I'd seen buildings larger on the inside than they seemed, whether an architectural trick or plain old magical enhancements, but this was impressive, bordering on ridiculous. No carpet cushioned our steps, but small tables edged the walls between the wooden doors. Each bore a vase with roses, poppies and asphodel—both poppies and roses ranged from red to colors not found in nature.

The silver roses were gorgeous, sure, but certainly not natural.

Each door had a symbol burned into it, some of them looking very old. No lights shone under them, so far as I could see. I was with the only other people who lived here.

Twenty-five doors down, Ilani paused and pointed at a door that smoked faintly. "This one is your room."

"How can you tell?" I asked.

"The sigil on the door. It's new, you're new. Mine is straight across the hall, Albrecht's is down ten doors."

The character burned into the door was a mixture of curves and angles, unlike any symbol I'd ever seen. It bore the faintest resemblance to cuneiform, but that could've been my mind looking for patterns where none existed. It looked as if it'd been branded there, the faint smell of charred wood lingering in the air, competing with the smell of roses.

Taking a deep breath, I opened the door, but I was pleasantly surprised. The decently-sized room contained a double bed with a dark blue puffy comforter, a low wooden chest, and a small table and chair under the window. The curtains were drawn, made of pale silver velvet, and beaded with glittering blue stones. It looked fine until the curtains. So close.

The furniture's wood was all dark, and gleaming with polish. A China pitcher and basin decorated with realistic-looking violets sat on the table, with a small white towel beside them. It was all sparse, but still sang of the same wealth and luxury as the enormous halls outside. Overdone.

And no dust at all. Like *none*.

Who cleaned this place? Whoever it was, they'd done a remarkable job. I needed the name of the cleaning service, assuming that it wasn't some strange little gremlin hiding in the walls. Which, considering where I was, was more likely than not.

Across from the bed, a large mirror dominated the wall, framed in gleaming silver polished enough to nearly be a mirror itself. A stack of clothing lay folded on the chest. Thankfully it wasn't leather or bondage gear or anything outré. Mostly solid-colored T-shirts and jeans. Thank heavens. Or, thank ha'al would be more accurate.

Apparently casual was the order of the day for dress, which was a relief. The last thing I needed to be worrying about was figuring out how to put a harness on or something equally mind boggling.

Or a corset. Ew.

I turned around at the soft thump of a door closing. Ilani was gone, but Albrecht stood in the doorway. They were both so quiet, which was quite a trick considering the marble flooring, not to mention the acoustics. I fully expected every step to echo in this place, and yet they were both almost completely silent when they moved.

"Raphael will be in the kitchen." Albrecht gave me a solemn stare.

"And?" There had to be a point to this, or he wouldn't be here, but that didn't make it any easier to figure out what it was.

"He said that you'd associate with him. He'll be cooking supper tonight. In the kitchen. You should go there."

With a sigh, I nodded. It wasn't Albrecht's fault I was in this conundrum. I was starving, but I wasn't sure I wanted to set the precedent of being obedient either. Or of anticipating Raphael's wishes.

I could stay up here and totally ignore him, but I doubted that would go over very well, and I wasn't sure that I should push hard this early. Raising two children had taught me to pick my battles, and not eating when I was this hungry would be foolish.

Albrecht's stomach growled audibly.

"What about you?" I nodded toward his belly.

His pale stare grew more pointed. "Raphael will send up food to us. I know he probably wants to talk to you alone, so Ilani and I aren't going to make the effort of going down there, only to be told to go back to our rooms." A logical choice, even if it did make me sad. And a little nervous.

A small smile joined his stare, although the smile didn't reach his eyes. "You'll figure things out how things work after a while. And at least this time there won't be screaming, the way there was the night Una came here."

Another chill ran down my spine. There was no doubt Albrecht was warning me in a sideways manner. Not needed, but I appreciated the effort nonetheless.

He stepped out and shut the door. I shoved the nervousness down, poured water from the pitcher into the bowl and splashed it on my face. It was bitingly cool, more refreshing than I'd expected. Then I changed into clean clothing, a comfortable pair of jeans and a shirt that fit me perfectly. Like it'd been tailored for me. Either someone was very good at picking out clothes, or it was simply a part of the magic of this place. I was pretty sure that the latter was more likely.

I'd ask Ilani where the tub or shower was later. A soak would be my reward after getting through this meal with Raphael.

Squaring my shoulders, I went searching for the kitchens, and my new host.

I WALKED DOWN THE HALL, the small sound of my steps the only noise I could hear, and I was walking as lightly as I could to avoid making said sound. Suffice it to say I wasn't as successful as Ilani and Albrecht had been.

This place was huge, and as far as I knew, only four people lived in it. It made no sense...Why have something so big with so few people, when the people I'd seen earlier could certainly have benefited from having a stay here? It wasn't as if there wasn't any room.

On the other hand, judging from their reaction, it was possible they wouldn't live here if invited.

I stepped out of the hall into the reception area. In the time I'd been gone, three couches had appeared, and a patterned rug concealed the gleaming marble floor. A large widescreen tv—at least ten feet long!—now hung on the wall near one of the couches. I'd never seen anything that big before, except at an actual movie theater. It felt like overkill for a personal home, but then again, this whole place was total overkill, and it wasn't as if someone was going to tell Raphael that he was being weird. They wouldn't dare.

How could they even get a signal here? It made my head hurt. Maybe it was just there for decoration? Or a DVD player?

A click. My heart accelerated, and I pivoted toward the sound. In what had been a bare spot just moments ago, two chairs now sat, wood and velvet in the baroque style, all gold and curlicues, next to an end table in a similar style. One was occupied by a woman, who leaned back in the chair, crossing her ankles daintily. The teacup on the table next to her must have made the sound.

I stared at her in shock. What in the ever-loving eff?

She smiled back, all pearly white teeth. "I apologize for startling you."

Her inky black hair fell past her shoulders in a smooth cascade. Expertly applied makeup emphasized huge dark brown eyes and a plump mouth. She was dressed in an open-necked shirt, chinos, and flats that screamed money on a subconscious level, similarly to what the daoine sidhe wore. Not plastered with jewelry and labels, but it still had every appearance of money in a way only someone who had a lot of money could make it seem like they didn't. And did.

A dozen answers flitted through my mind, but I

chose carefully. I wasn't sure who exactly this was, and if she was anything like Raphael, then I needed to be careful. I ended up saying, "In a place like this, it's easy to do. Who are you?" It seemed calm enough, not to mention neutral. And I kept my tone lilting and curious, with no edge to it at all.

"I'm Therese. Please, have a seat, I only need a moment." She spread her dainty, well-manicured fingers.

Sit or stand? Maybe she knew the way to the kitchen, and she might tell me if I sat with her for a few minutes. I perched my butt gingerly on the second seat.

She poured a second cup of tea and handed it to me, then tasted her own. "I'm one of the jailors who keep Raphael in this dominion."

Holy sh—I didn't drop my cup. Nor did I take a sip, setting it down gently, quite proud of myself for my lack of reaction. Internally I was gaping at the woman. "Pleased to meet you. I'm here for the next year."

"Yes." She put her fingertips together and rested her chin on the point. "He wants to be free. You and the people of your dominion should not want him free. Whatever he offers, whatever torment he visits on you, keep that in mind." She sighed and sipped her tea again, then nodded at mine. "Please."

I picked it up but didn't sip.

She noticed but made no comment. "I cannot remove you because of the bargain you made with him, either by death or by ejecting you. Which creates quite the puzzle for me and Diego."

Diego. Okay. He was a jailer. Lifting the cup, I inhaled. The vivid red tea smelled of chamomile and hibiscus.

Her words sounded like a warning, not that I needed it. I knew I'd been a fool for making this bargain, but I hadn't had a very long list of choices. Needs must when the devil drives had not had such a personal meaning for me before. "I'd very much like to leave. But my promise was to stay a year, and I'll keep my word." Even if I super-duper didn't wanna.

She took another delicate sip of her tea. "A woman of sense. And you bear an old protection, as well, so you should survive this year with your mind intact. I caution you to be careful, human. He will destroy you if he can."

On that cheerful note, she set her cup down and stood, walking out of the front doors, with grace and surety. I sat staring after her, belatedly realizing I'd forgotten to ask where the kitchen was. I sighed, but at least I wasn't any worse off than I'd been before.

Two halls left. I walked to the first and inhaled deep, hoping onion or garlic was on the menu tonight. If it was, then I'd probably be able to smell it from here. No dice. Just more doors.

The whiff of cooking meat came from the second hall. Congratulating myself, I followed the scent.

For a wonder, it was only three doors down. I

surveyed the room from the hall. The door was a swinging half door and didn't obscure sight, so I peeked in without having to fully commit to stepping inside the room, not just yet.

The kitchen was a comfortably-sized room, but not overly large. Somehow, I'd expected it to be so big it'd be a pain to cook in. It had a butcher block island near the stove and a gleaming table with six chairs around it on the other end of the room.

Raphael stood by a large iron stove behind the island. Wood burning—the flicker of fire peeked through the oven door as he moved to nod at me. Whatever he was cooking smelled incredible, but Therese's words kept repeating in my head.

Not that I needed the reminder. I was already plenty worried about Raphael as it was, even without the warning.

The familiar smell of hamburger meat cooking was weird in this setting. But food was food, no matter where it came from. And I was famished. It'd been a while since my sandwich with the kids.

Raphael slid fully loaded burgers and fries onto two plates, which promptly vanished into thin air from the counter. "Have a seat, the food is almost ready. I just sent Albrecht's and Ilani's meal upstairs."

So they'd been right about him sending food up to them. I should've expected as much, but still, I raised my eyebrows as I stopped behind the chairs. So, he really didn't want anyone at all to be bothering us this evening. Good and bad. Their presence would've constrained my words and actions. I wasn't sure if it would've done the same to him.

"How did you do that?" I asked, seating myself. The answer was pretty obvious, but I still wanted to ask.

The table was already set, with a bowl of salad and another of fruit in the center.

"Magic." The smile that quirked his lips was dry as he turned back to the stove.

As I watched, he flipped two hamburgers onto a draining rack and scooped a pat of butter and added it to the skillet. He produced two buns and put them into the skillet. It all looked absolutely delicious, and I couldn't help how much my mouth watered as I watched him work.

As the ruler of a dominion, the last thing I would've expected was that he'd be the one cooking for us this evening, but maybe he was trying to impress me. If so, despite my best efforts, it was working. I was starving, and this all looked absolutely amazing.

"The salad dressing is on the butcher block, please bring it to the table."

Ooookey-dokey. I fetched the carafe as he fried the buns, then assembled the burgers with quick, deft movements before bringing them over to the table.

If he wanted to impress me with his fry cookery skills, he had a long way to go, even if the burgers did smell like heaven. The skills meant nothing to me. The food, on the other hand...

I took one off the platter, served myself a salad, and then took a bite of the hamburger. Unfair. It was delicious. Probably because I was starving.

"What is it you want to talk about?" I said after I finished chewing the first bite. His appraising stare almost turned the food to dust in my mouth, but I was too hungry to fuss.

"Straight to business. Good." Raphael regarded me with approval. He took a bite of his burger, then set it back down on his plate. "You know I was watching while you and Ilani and Albrecht were wandering, correct?"

I hadn't, but there was no way I was going to admit that. "Of course," I lied.

Raphael chuckled, a rich warm sound that would've suited a friend better than whatever he was. Manipulative, at best, although an enemy was probably a better term. "Liar. From that observation, even though you tried to be subtle about using your abilities until the end, it became obvious that you're a gifted mage. You offered your help. The help that I wish most from you is for you to set me free of this dominion."

"No, I offered to fix houses and such. Spruce the place up a bit. Jailbreak is a bit beyond the scope of my offer. In addition to that, I don't know if I *can* do that." I took another bite of the burger, taking refuge in the act of chewing. If nothing else, he did seem to have some manners, and therefore wouldn't expect me to answer while I had my mouth full. Maybe if I could keep my mouth stuffed this entire time then I wouldn't have to make any promises I might regret.

Oh, stop being foul-minded. A dirty mind is a terrible thing to waste.

"I'm also aware of your conversation with Therese. My sister is not herself an unbiased source. You'd do better to talk with Diego, or me, or just about anyone else. She's very vested in the current status quo, which I want to disrupt."

His sister, then? The woman who'd awaited me? No matter how hard I looked at him, I could see no resemblance between the two of them, but that didn't necessarily mean anything. Ironic, and worrying, that she was the one keeping him trapped here. That must make their version of Thanksgiving very tense.

I also wanted to know what her other name was then, given that Raphael was also called Asmodaj... Johann had called him that, at the gate. Given how close it was to names I'd heard at home, it'd stuck in my mind.

Raphael leaned forward, gesturing with the hand still holding his burger. A nicely calculated gesture to relax me, very homey, personable. A twinkle had appeared in his eyes that I trusted not at all. "You did say you'd help. I assumed you wanted to help the people who live here. What would help them more than me being gone?" He took a bite and chewed before gesturing again. "Go ahead, eat, I'm going to give you a bit of a history lesson from my perspective. Consider it an education, as I understand that you're a teacher."

I stared at him. He was playing to my strengths here, but it was also a perfect opportunity for me to point something out. "Yes, I am. I want answers to my questions, too. There are children here, innocents. Why? And if they must be here, I want to set up schooling for them. Even if they're trapped here, there's no reason to waste their minds."

He shrugged. "Fair enough. Let me know how you wish it to be done. My schooling was long ago in a different style than you're accustomed to." How nice, a personal revelation to make me like him better. And an agreement that cost him little to nothing in the scheme of things. Hmph.

He served himself a heaping mound of salad. "What do you know about the Reckoning?"

"Nothing." It actually was a topic I knew very little about. I'd heard the word used, and I'd figured from the context it was an important event, but I had my own business to attend to. When I'd tried to make inquiries, my few sources hadn't wanted to talk about it. That'd told me that it probably wasn't a very good thing, and it'd again fallen to the bottom of my list when I had my own problems to work on. It felt like I was being tested here, and I was going to fail this pop quiz.

Even here, the thought amused me.

"The Reckoning is when the DayKing and the NightQueen walk outside of the dominion where they live, Godhome. They usually choose to spend the time on your dominion. Before they go, they send visions to seers that show the location of the metaphysical keys that will release them. Once those keys are retrieved, the gate is unlocked, and they can pass through for a time. For the past few Reckonings, there's been political interference between the kins which resulted in the NightQueen not being freed."

Raphael regarded his forkful of greens. "When they walk together it's almost always accompanied by disaster and war among the kins. When only one walks, it's even worse. Have you heard of the Antonine plague?"

This was something I did know about. "That was in the second or third century? It traveled with Roman legions and the theory is it might've been a form of smallpox." I wasn't a historian, but I did have a general knowledge of major historical events. Generally, disasters, because they were easier to remember and had more information available about them. No one wrote pages upon pages about someone having a nice lovely picnic.

He regarded me with approval. "Correct. The DayKing's physical presence encourages the spread of disease. You can take a good guess how often the Reckoning has happened by how often a large portion of humanity is wiped out by plagues. The NightQueen is more associated with natural disasters and long-term climate effects." He ate a couple bites of salad with gentle crunches. "They were sent to the Godhome—by their own agreement—when they trimmed the population of humanity and several other kins back almost to extinction. Long, long ago. Before recorded history, well, before your recorded history. That Reckoning was... *difficult* on all the dominions. The two of them were making up for all the time that they hadn't been able to meddle with the kins or simply destroying what displeased them. When the time for the second Reckoning came, I and a few other leaders of powerful kins took the field against the two of them."

Brave of them.

He sighed and gave me big puppy-dog eyes. "We lost. Partially because at least one of our allies was late to the battle. My kin, the Enkimmu, were almost wiped out. I and two others survived, and I ended up in this dominion. This is a place of punishment, Ceri. The pig giants you encountered today are actually a minor hazard here."

He inhaled, steepling his fingers, his gaze sweeping over me. I fought the urge to cross my arms over my chest. "Your friend, Johann, is another of the first created, born to one of the first kins to arise from Tiamat and Marduk's loins and will. His people were late to the battle and his punishment was different. We were once almost friends, which is why I permit his... spell...on you in my home."

Well, that shone a small light on some topics. Johann was Lou, whoever that was, and I really wanted to know. He'd decided to offer his protection to me. I wasn't sure if his stated reason was completely true or not. *If* I were a distant relation to his wife, still, he'd expended some effort on my behalf that left the scales of debt unbalanced. Regardless, that protection had been enough to keep me safe thus far in Raphael's space. I wasn't sure how much of what Raphael said was a lie, how much of it was half-truth, and how much was truth. My guess was a mixture of all three, of course. As was the case when anyone told their version of events.

I'd need to research to find other views on what he'd just told me. And more on him, why people were so determined to keep him imprisoned, beyond the obvious. And on entities whose name sounded like Lou, to see what Johann really was in mythology. Not exactly a name that struck terror into the heart, but that was without adequate research.

An important question remained to be asked. It would help me decide how I should react going forward. I'd heard from everyone else that Raphael should be trapped here, but I wanted to make my own decisions about that. I wanted to hear his goal. "What would you do if you were let loose?"

"I'd finish the task I began before your people learned to write. I'd end the time of reckonings and have all of us kins freed of the weight of my mother and my father. If possible, I will destroy them."

To my credit, I didn't choke on my last bite of hamburger. He was talking about killing godlike beings of infinite power.

Raphael smiled at me benignly, taking my plate. "You're a scholarly sort. My study is two doors down and is open to any who wish to use it. Feel free to pass time there this evening or any other. If you get bored, I'm also more than happy to entertain you."

One of his fingers moved to tap my chin. The agreement said he couldn't actually touch me, but I'd seen children needling, 'I'm not touching you!' to know what he was doing. I glared, cold and hard, and he gave me back an innocent expression. The light of amusement in his blue eyes burned like the edge of a candle.

Not a reassuring expression. I took the opportunity to leave and decided to see the study.

I PUSHED the door down the hall open, crossing my fingers that Raphael had not lied. I wouldn't have put it past him, which was why I was being so cautious. For all I knew this room was like a giant dungeon or something.

Flames bloomed into existence in a series of glass lamps on the ceiling and walls, illuminating the room with a soft golden glow. My heart skipped a beat. Just for a second, I'd thought maybe I was right about the dungeon thing

Gaping, my eyes wide, I surveyed the huge room. I probably looked like an idiot, but I didn't care. I couldn't help it.

As with most of the other rooms in this building, this area was far larger than it should've been. It made no sense, but aesthetically, it was amazing. Lined floor to ceiling with shelves that were full of books, the ceiling a good three or four stories tall. Several ladders of varying heights leaned against the shelves so that all the books could be reached.

In the clear central space, a man wearing jeans, a dark t-shirt, and a short leather jacket sat in one of the overstuffed chairs. He turned his head to regard me.

Yet another person awaiting me, probably for another conversation, an echo of the one with Therese. Irritation welled up in me. I very much wanted to explore this room, but I'd have to deal with whoever this was first. Once that was done, then all bets were off. I was all over this library.

Nearby, a desk piled with books and a wooden chair looked as if yet another person had just left.

I raised my brows. "Are you going to warn me against letting Raphael loose too?"

He laughed, rose, and approached me. A few steps away, he was taller than me by about a foot, his dark clothing attenuated into nothingness at their edges, fraying into shadow. His face reminded me of someone, but who? It hit me in a second. He reminded me of Ilani. He could've been her father, his eyes the same deep violet color, with a similar facial structure, and long black hair pulled back in a ponytail. Was it possible, or was I just seeing things?

"Not at all. Raphael impacts this conversation only in the most marginal sense." I liked his voice. It reminded me of my grandfather's, cool and firm. Strange how the simple memory of tone relaxed my shoulders, brought a little serenity.

I stuck out my hand to shake. "Hi, I'm Ceri. Pleased to meet you. Is there going to be another ghost before morning comes to tell the future? And are you related to Ilani, the girl who lives here? You look like her." I was proud of the reference, since this was the second visitor I'd had. I didn't really feel like I fit with Scrooge's personality, though. At least hopefully not.

A smile flickered across the stranger's face. He didn't seem to be bothered by being compared to a ghost.

Leaning forward, he took my hand. His was cold, and I fought down a shiver.

"To answer the first last, I look like her because she's the person who's been most touched by me living here. A sweet girl. For the first, I don't think so, but these visits to you haven't been coordinated as far as I know either. I'm Death."

I stared at him. "As in you plan to kill me or as in you're the personification of a universal force?"

A little tremor worked itself into the carefully casual note in my voice despite my best effort. He felt like power, and if what he said was true, I didn't want to view him magically. If he was who he said he was, I was liable to be blinded by the amount of magic that he contained. Or worse.

"The universal force. I've not come for you now, don't worry." The soothing note in his voice awakened a semi-hysterical giggle in my throat, although I managed to strangle it with effort. "Though," he continued, "you've flirted with me for the past twenty years or so. I came to talk about what you carry."

My mind went immediately to the gem, my free hand pressing on that pocket.

He nodded with approval. "Yes. That. You have no idea what it is—"

"Feel free to tell me," I interrupted. Then I slapped my free hand over my mouth. This was Death I was talking to, Death with a capital D. He might've said that he hadn't come for me right now, but discretion was always the better part of valor.

If anything, he looked more amused by my interruption. "Certainly. It's the lives and essences of an entire kin. Concentrated in a form that affords you both a measure of safety and allows you to shield it from harm. It's a case of a very old being having chosen to pass on the responsibility—either temporarily or permanently—of carrying it and guarding it. I'm not sure if it's because he plans to die, or if he wishes it better hidden. My guess is he wishes to protect it, since it is safer here than it would be in your dominion."

"Why?" My mind whirred with possibilities and assumptions of why Johann would've left me such a gem.

"Because while his personal power is great, the sacrifice of all the energies of an entire kin is an even more powerful energy source for the person seeking to trigger their apotheosis. For your information, it's protective capabilities are greater if you actually wear it rather than just carry it. Given where you are, you're going to need as much protection as you can get, unless you'd like me to visit you sooner than later."

His violet eyes met mine. So deep, so much power...the connection burrowed directly into my soul. I had no idea why he was telling me all this, but there had to be a reason. Obviously, I didn't know Death very well, but I had a feeling that he didn't do anything without a reason. Beings as powerful as he was tended not to. "Do you?"

My heart thumped. "No. Not today, and not any time soon if that's at all possible."

"Well, then. It's been good to speak with you, after all the near brushes we've had through the years. It's hard to manifest like this in your world without harming the people around you. And I don't do harm where I can avoid it." He hadn't let go of my hand. Strangely, I hadn't thought to pull it back. Even as cool as his skin was, it was still weirdly comforting to hold it.

He raised my hand to his lips. "Until we meet again, Ceridwen Alarie."

He vanished from sight, and I half fell down into one of the chairs, shaking.

It took a little while to get the anxiety attack under control, but I did it. Then I looked at the vast store of books around me and swore in my head. Lots and lots of books, but no visible cataloging. It would take days to find what I needed, if not longer. I groaned deep in my throat, but I felt it in my soul.

Raphael was a bastard.

Calming deep breaths, and I started examining the nearby books, searching for ones in English, to see if there was any rhyme or reason to how they were shelved. I wanted to know about Johann on a priority, especially if what this visitor had said was true.

I paused, unlaced one of my shoes, and wrapped the shoelaces around the gem, making a pendant, then tucked it under my shirt in my bra. That should keep it safe.

T he next morning, the children and I arrived in the kitchen at almost the same time. I'd slept very little, after combing through the study. I'd found a section devoted to biographies, but many of them weren't in English, and I needed—in addition to everything else—to try to figure out a way to translate them using magic.

The siren scent of tea wafted from a brown ceramic teapot sitting on the butcher block, next to three mugs and a honey bear.

"You look tired. Are you not a morning person either, then? I'll cook." Albrecht pulled a cast iron skillet from the shelf. He made a shooing gesture toward me and Ilani, motioning for us to sit down. "If I let her cook, she'll burn everything because she saw a butterfly or something and forget about it." He inclined his head toward Ilani.

Maybe not the most tactful thing to say, but I couldn't deny that I preferred my food unburned.

"What languages do you know how to read, Albrecht?" I asked.

"Norse, Finnish, Swedish, English, enough German to get by, a little French. The language of my people, of course, and that of the daoine sidhe. Why?" Albrecht opened a normal looking cabinet and pulled out eggs, cheese and butter.

Ilani settled at the table. She surveyed both of us with a grumpy expression, but she didn't speak. She did glare at us pointedly.

Albrecht outright laughed. "Ilani's not functional until she's had her tea. Would you pour, Ceri?"

Wanting it too, I took the teapot and poured three mugs of tea. I grabbed the honey bear and headed to the table with two mugs. "Later, would you be willing to help me sort through books in the study?"

"Of course." He produced a bowl, plates, and a whisk from a different cabinet. They were not the same cabinets I'd glimpsed Raphael using last night.

"Thank you. How are you making the cabinets work?"

Albrecht didn't pretend to misunderstand me, which was refreshing. "I want items to be there. The one I got the food from I've always used like that, and so it's easier for me."

"Do the people who live outside have similar options?"

"No. It's more from magic and will than the actual container, and they don't have magic. Or if they do, it's so buried they can't use it."

Ilani volunteered, "In bad times, we deliver food."

"And Therese?" No segue for the conversation, but I was too sleepy to be tactful.

Albrecht winced. "Best if she doesn't intersect with breakable things. Like people. She gets impatient, quickly."

As he whisked the eggs hard enough to make it difficult to hear, I decided to pursue that topic later. I wasn't sure that he was intentionally trying to make it difficult to speak, but I also wasn't sure that he wasn't. At this point it could go either way, and I wouldn't have questioned it. He paused, and I jumped into the moment of quiet like a cat pouncing on a mouse.

"Do you know other languages too, Ilani?"

"A couple of Gaelic languages. A little Spanish. That's it, I'm not good at languages. I can help too, but I want to do things outside first."

Which brought me to another topic of interest. "How far have you traveled in this place?"

"All over." Albrecht expertly poured the egg mixture into the skillet. The scent of butter and egg wafted toward me. It smelled delicious. He added cheese, making it smell even better. My stomach grumbled, reminding me just how hungry I was.

"I'd like to go to the farthest places you know today. That smells delicious, by the way." A little flattery never hurt, and it was truth in this case. Strange to see two males preferring to cook in quick succession—it would be even stranger to see both clean up after themselves. Finding someone who could cook was rare, but finding one who actually preferred to, or offered to, was borderline strange in my life. Then again, this was another world. Literally.

Albrecht rinsed the bowl and whisk, eyeing me warily. "Okay, but you're going to need to agree to haul ass away from there when Ilani or I tell you to. Those places are dangerous. More dangerous things than piggiants. And I won't let us go on a trip to any of the places that we're not allowed to go."

Interesting. But I doubted that their orders to protect me had ended when they had brought me here, so I shouldn't have expected any less.

Ilani emerged from behind her now empty mug, looking a little less grumpy. I was impressed by the fact that she'd somehow managed to chug the entire thing, and I hadn't seen her breathe once. Did she have gills somewhere that I didn't know about? Tea gills? "We can go to the shore. We can show her the mountains."

"Where do the mists gather the thickest?" I wanted to examine it and its magic where it was most concentrated to try to puzzle out what exactly It was. Knowing how things worked was my best defense.

"By the sea." Albrecht served us each a portion of

the omelet he'd made. Ilani and I attacked it; it tasted as good as it smelled. He wiped out the skillet, settled at the table with us, and finally nodded. A miracle. He'd cleaned up after himself.

It was strange, learning the ropes from a pair of adolescents, but this wasn't my home. It was theirs, and if they said that it was dangerous, then I believed them.

All of us jumped as a rap sounded on the entryway to the kitchen. I nearly choked on my last bit of omelet as I turned to see who or what it was. I hadn't realized that there was someone else here, and certainly not so close.

A tall, well-built man wearing tan dockers and a light jacket walked into the room and leaned against the butcher block. Strikingly good looking, he could've been Raphael's older brother, similar in face and sharing eyes of the same blazing blue. "Hello. I'm Gaius."

How many people were here? Geez.

Both the children smiled, bounced over and put out their hands expectantly. He pulled chocolate bars from his jacket and dropped them in both their hands. "Eat them after you finish your breakfast."

Ilani snorted. "Where's my phone?"

"Available when you figure out how to charge it here," he answered mildly, then returned his attention to me.

"I'm Ceri." I did not rise. Clearly the children knew him, and he must have been to the human world recently to have brought them the candy. It made me both sad and jealous, to know that he could move freely back to my home while I was stuck here.

The children took their plates to the sink and rinsed and stacked them. They scampered in a hurry, probably to enjoy their candy bars in peace. I'd find them and go on the tour later. I wanted to see some of the other places here, perhaps the shore that Ilani had referred to.

Gaius took a seat at the table, not speaking until they'd left. Or possibly lingered near the door to eavesdrop, although if I was right about children from remembering the way that my own had responded to candy at that age, they had almost certainly slunk off to eat it somewhere in peace. Or perhaps squirrel it away. Though given Ilani's temperament, she might have far too much interest in our conversation.

"Johann requested I come here to check on you. As soon as I arrived, Raphael accosted me and demanded that I acquire schoolbooks and supplies and bring them here for you. Which was an admirable thought on your part. You appear to be not gibbering or crying, which is also a bonus. Is there a message you wish taken back to Nick Damarian or Johann or anyone else?" He spoke crisply, subdued curiosity on his face.

"Yes. Tell them all I'm fine, and I'll be home as soon as I can. Tell Nick to let my children know the general gist of what's happened. And...how is Dara? Jimmy?

Nick? Where is Dara, after Rhys set her free? He did set her free, right?"

"He did. I saw your son at Johann's home. He seems well, if argumentative. Nick has made an alliance with the goblins and is harassing the few daoine sidhe in the Columbus area. Dara has taken shelter with the lilim, specifically the leader, Pryce."

Oh, okay. That was odd. "She's not being coerced to shelter with him, is she?"

"Not to my knowledge, and I believe her brother and your lover would intervene if she were." Gaius's tone was brisk but not unkind. He produced a notepad and a pencil and pushed it across the table. "Make a list of the things you want for teaching. Be specific. I'll have no idea what you're talking about if you're not."

I wrote the list down, taking care to keep my hand-writing neat and clear. I'd never much had to worry about that before, but I'd also never been in a situation exactly like this before. I'd been a teacher for a very long time, but it was still difficult to come up with everything that we might need for a classroom for a variety of ages off the cuff and without the internet to aid me.

No matter how often I ran over things in my mind, I still couldn't shake the feeling that there was something I was forgetting. It was made even more difficult by the fact that there were so many differ-ences between this world and my own. Yes, Ilani might know what a phone was, but computers and other technology were not likely to work here, so it wouldn't make any sense to ask for those. As near as I could tell, we were somewhere between chalk and slate and pencils and paper, so I made my list accordingly.

"How's Nick?" I asked as I printed my neat words.

A long pause. I paused in writing to look up at him.

He regarded me gravely, his expression sympathetic, if distant. "Worried. He's not a demonstrative man, and I don't know him very well, but the worry was obvious."

I bit my lip, then went back to the list. I couldn't change anything and brooding on it wouldn't help. It would only make me more desperate to get out of here, and desperation bred mistakes. I had to keep my wits about me. "Will you carry a note to him and my kids?"

"Of course."

My note to Jimmy and Dara was mainly reassurance. The note to Nick was harder, and mostly composed of stiff phrases on how it wasn't terrible here, and I was still myself. I sighed, looking down at it, and added 'love, Ceri' at the end. If I tried to say how I felt, then I was going to start bawling, and that wasn't going to help anyone either.

"I'll let him know you're whole in mind and that you aren't feeling excessive emotional distress." Gaius took the note from me and tucked it into the same jacket pocket that he had pulled the chocolate bars from earlier.

"How are you and Raphael related?" I cocked my head up at the man.

"He's my father." The answer's tone was distant. It wasn't a secret, but he wasn't proud of it, either.

"What, exactly, do Enkimmu *do*? Is he really the founder of your people, or delusional?" Maybe a bit cheeky of me to ask, but he seemed fairly amiable.

It took a moment as he folded the paper, taking his time. "Yes, he's the first of our people. Enkimmu—we are empaths, like the lilim, and we can control people we bite. We gain the powers of those we bite for a period of time. We don't gain any training with those powers, so it's not a useful talent unless you feed from a particular type for a long period of time. The other legends about vampires don't apply."

I drew in a breath...even more obvious why I needed to never permit Raphael to touch me. It was part of our agreement anyway, but this had only strengthened my resolve to not ever give him permission.

When I couldn't think of more questions, Gaius departed with my list and the notes.

"Hello, Ilani," floated into the room as he left.

I couldn't help the amusement.

She came in, looking a little sulky.

"Could you bring Albrecht here? So we can travel?" I asked.

She nodded and hurried out.

They used the quick traveling method I'd seen the

night before to take us to the mountains. It only took one jump to get here.

I inhaled the cold air deeply. "Will you teach me how to do that?"

"Of course," Ilani said. "We can do that tonight, before supper."

In the pause that followed, I drank the scenery in. I'd seen the Rockies, once, and these mountains seemed to dwarf them, clouds drifting well below their peaks. The air where we stood carried the breath of winter on it. Every breath puffed in front of us in a small cloud.

Odd that they were bigger. In the human realm, the younger mountains were bigger. The Appalachian mountains, small by comparison to the Rockies, were many millions of years older.

Was this realm young?

"Do any people live nearby?" I shivered, wishing I'd worn a jacket.

There were plenty of clothes in the room that I'd been given, but I hadn't even thought about wearing even a sweater, despite knowing we were heading to the mountains. I was kicking myself, mostly because I had more goosebumps than skin right now.

"Sometimes. It depends," Albrecht answered. "When svartalfar come to visit, yes. The metals here take magic into them easily and well."

I clasped a hand over the bracelet I wore. It

comforted me, even if Nick wasn't here. The magic within it comforted as well.

It was the first he'd mentioned visitors. I chose not to press him on the topic. Unlike Ilani, Albrecht considered his words before he spoke them, and if they weren't freely forthcoming, then I wasn't getting any more.

"Do you want to go to the sea now? I've got enough energy to take us." Ilani smiled at me. "It's warmer there."

I nodded, and the world blurred around us again.

Wind gusted over us, warmer than the mountains but carrying the feel of rain. The smell of petrichor filled my nose, and I tilted my head back as I inhaled deeply. Lightning flashed further out. The water alternately flirted with the rocky shore and flung itself against it.

The mist swirled along the beach, thick and gray, the billows of it revealing and obscuring the water and sand. Once I learned their technique, I'd come back and study it without company, so I could concentrate.

"Do people live here too? Is there trade with other places?"

"You've seen the people you're allowed to see." Albrecht's tone was abrupt.

"That *we're* allowed to see," Ilani corrected. She smiled sunnily, probably because she'd gotten the chance to annoy her sibling. Bonus points.

Allow didn't sit well with me. I was a grown

woman, and I didn't appreciate anyone telling me what I could and couldn't do, no matter what realm I was in. I let it go for the moment. Soon enough I'd explore further when I learned the magic they used for rapid traveling.

By the time we returned to the house, Gaius had apparently had enough time to return with the various items I'd requested. That indicated someone was playing with time between my home dominion and here, since we hadn't been gone for more than a few hours and there was no way that he would've had time to gather everything in the human world, let alone travel back and forth between the two.

That was worrisome. How long had I actually been here? Our agreement had said Raphael wouldn't manipulate the dominions' time, but was there a quirk in how dominions interacted that I'd missed?

I DECIDED to dismiss the worry about the relative rate of time passing for the moment. I'd gotten a sworn promise from Raphael that he wouldn't tamper with the passage of time in this dominion, and magic bound people to their word. He couldn't break his word, not without something terrible happening, and I doubted he'd take that chance.

I'd also ask Gaius if I saw him again. Until then, one problem at a time. A bath, specifically, because I smelled like...it was indescribable, and not in a good way, either.

Standing beside my door, I glanced from Ilani to Albrecht. "How do I find the shower here? Is there a specific room that we share?"

Ilani smiled. "Your bathing area is behind the door next to your room." She pointed at it. "Depending on what you want it to do, either you need to visualize what you want, or it'll pull something from your mind and set it up."

This house was the weirdest combination of strange layout and overuse of magical power. Still, if it got me clean, I could overlook it.

Albrecht said quietly, "You just got a note on your door."

I turned back. A folded piece of paper had appeared, taped to the wood below the symbol for my name. I pulled it off, broke the wax seal with my fingernail, and opened it.

Ceri—I have other matters to occupy me this evening. Supper will be at the usual time. If you don't go to the kitchens, then it'll appear in your room. You can ask your guides for details. I look forward to our next meeting. Raphael.

"Well, I guess we get to eat together," I said.

"Yay!" Ilani's smile broadened to a grin. "Do you want to eat in the kitchen or up here? We can eat in my room!"

"Only if you clean it." Albrecht spoke drily.

I didn't want to touch that comment. I wasn't sure if he was implying that I was a messy eater or she was, but either way, it wasn't overly flattering for us. "We can decide that later. Is showing me how you travel something you can do indoors, or does it have to be outdoors?"

"We can do it indoors, that's not a problem." Ilani spread her hands as if we could get to it right here in the hallway.

"Then I'm going to clean up, which should take us about to suppertime, and we can eat in Ilani's room like she wants."

Ilani dove into her room, door slamming, presumably to straighten it. Righty then.

Albrecht shook his head. "You're a brave woman."

I went to the next door, ignoring the comment, and opened it. A palatial room confronted me, with a hot tub, showers, a dipping pool...floors and walls all done in shimmering blue-green tile. Little crystal flagons of presumably scents and salts gleamed on a wooden shelf on the wall next to the hot tub. Thick fluffy white towels lay folded on benches.

Ilani wasn't kidding when she said the magic would just pull what I wanted out of my head. I stepped forward with enthusiasm. This was the perfect bathroom, even if it was a little bit of overkill. For the next hour or so, I basked in the warm water, enjoying the bubbles floating on the surface and the heavenly scent of ylang-ylang. It'd been entirely too long since I'd had a bath, let alone a luxurious soak like this, and I was going to enjoy it for as long as I could.

When I finally climbed out, the towels were as soft as clouds and large enough to contain my mass of hair. It was good to finally feel clean.

Later, spotless, I waited for Albrecht to knock on Ilani's door. It opened and she gestured us in with a flourish, standing back with her arm flung wide as an invitation to enter.

Her room was like an explosion of color met a magpie's trove. It was larger than mine, with a canopied bed tucked against the wall. Glittering strands of stone and bright lengths of cloth decorated the bed, while metal objects were stacked against the walls. If it was shiny or colorful, then it was here, although there was no recognizable rhyme or reason to it that I could see. I recognized several old computers and laptops in the clutter, although we'd already proven that they didn't work here. Still, it explained why she'd been so fascinated with my phone, because there they were. A line of old phones marched across her desk, partly obscured by scarves with sequins sewn into them. Every surface was covered but one—she'd arranged a small table and three chairs in the middle of the room, which had nothing on them. It was strange, to see how bare they were compared to the rest of the room.

The room had a certain charm, but it was incredibly full of collected treasures—mostly bright and or shiny. She had a certain type of thing that she enjoyed, and what that was shone clear. Shiny and colorful.

When we sat, three covered dishes appeared. I blinked, and Ilani and Albrecht uncovered theirs with the speed of long practice. The vision of golden brown pastry crust with bubbling pale gravy peeking from under it met my gaze, and I hastily uncovered my own.

Potpie. It smelled and looked like chicken. It also smelled absolutely delicious.

Silence reigned as we ate, and I was more than happy to focus on the food in front of me. The crust was perfect, the sauce velvety, the chicken and vegetables meltingly tender. It was so unfair that someone that terrible could cook like this.

After devouring the last bite, I sighed. They'd already finished, but I didn't regret being the last one to finish. I'd savored every bite.

"You want the lessons on traveling now?" Albrecht asked.

"Yes, please." What I wanted was to curl up and watch a movie with Nick, but I had about a year before that was possible.

"Yeah, but you should go outside to practice when you want to go somewhere. The walls here can have a funny effect on it." I wasn't sure what exactly he meant by a funny effect, but I made a mental note to do what he said. Because I didn't really want to find out from the inside of a wall.

They both demonstrated grabbing and holding magic strands. I examined what they'd grasped and how they did it, since they didn't grab all the magic available, but instead specific strands. Those strands led to the earth, like cable lines, and they weren't pulling power from the magic, which explained why it tired them so much. It looked like using the strands prevented the user from pulling magic externally. Interesting.

"Do I have the right strands? Can you see them?" I asked after carefully mimicking their grasp.

Ilani looked sheepish, which gave me the only answer that I needed.

Albrecht gave me a more concrete answer when he shook his head. "I learned this when I was young, and so did Ilani—neither of us see the magic, it just *feels* right. What you have feels right, but everybody messes it up the first few times. It's hard."

"Then let's go out and practice." As we'd worked, the dishes had vanished, a nice touch. Another little magical luxury.

Outside, I grasped the magic strands again.

"See a picture in your head of where you want to go, it should be of something you've seen. Like maybe near the bush where we met," Ilani said. "We'll meet you there?"

I nodded, then built the picture in my head. The kids vanished, and then I pulled on the strands. I slid through the dimension, a strange and not pleasant sensation. There were odd bumps and curves along the way as if there were barriers. I decided that I'd rather walk if it were feasible, but this would be good for traveling quickly in a pinch.

They stood by the bush. I lay flat on my back, one arm partially buried in the soil. Not as bad as it could've been, but it definitely could've gone better.

Diego, the gatekeeper, laughed with a noise like a rusty gate as Albrecht and Ilani helped dig me out.

"That went well!" Albrecht said.

I could find no sarcasm in his face or voice, which made me wonder what had happened to him when he learned. If being partially buried was a good attempt, then what did he consider a bad one?

The process did drain a lot of energy, but I'd be able to improve that once I mastered it. For a first try, I didn't think this was too bad, and now I at least knew what I needed to work on. "Back home, since it's late?"

They nodded, and we popped back. This time I fell ten feet, having arrived at a point in the air. How had I accomplished that? I hadn't done anything differently, at least as far as I knew, so nothing should have changed. Of course, I only thought of that when I was midair and falling rapidly, so it wasn't like there was time for me to figure out what I'd done wrong.

"Ouch," I said, after landing rather harder than I would've liked. More practice could wait until tomorrow, and until my back stopped throbbing after falling onto the hard ground.

Now to secure time alone to practice. "Will the pair of you scout for a place for me to teach tomorrow? It should be close to where the people live, since I don't think they'll come here. And close enough for them to walk, but not in the village since their leader—who never gave me his name—seemed very uncomfortable with my presence."

Albrecht nodded. "It'll give us something to do. It should be pretty easy. It does rain here, so we need some type of shelter there as well."

I didn't ask. I'd wait to see what they came up with.

"In the afternoon, I was hoping that you'd be willing to go through the study with me. I'm looking for a specific piece of information, but I don't speak the languages that you do."

Ilani's eyes flickered with sardonic humor. Her tone didn't match her expression, light and lively. "It'll be like a treasure hunt!"

I paused, then decided to ignore the potential sarcasm. The task for the morning would keep them busy, leaving me the privacy to experiment with the traveling. Then go to the sea and see what I could find out about the mists without risking others. At least now I had a plan.

The trip to the sea took a fair amount of power. Enough remained that I was confident that I'd be able to study the mists and return to the house without too much worry, but it was truly draining.

I scuffed the toe of my shoe in the damp sand, watching the water surge and ebb to fill the space. Foam flew against the rocks, and out of the corner of my eye the fog slithered closer. Turning my attention to the swirls of fog, I watched the gentle drifts and sparkles of magic within. I carefully called the mage sight, since scrutinizing it on that level was key, and examined the interconnections in it.

Based on observation and what I'd been told, I was willing to bet that it was intelligent, or it had an incredibly sophisticated question-response system built into it. Either way, I should be able to communicate with it. I twisted together a rope of magic intended for communication, one I planned to tweak to see if it could work for translating books, and gently extended it to the flickers of magic. There were different ways to accomplish anything, but if this worked, I'd be overjoyed.

When the rope connected to the flickers, awareness flooded down it to my mind, huge and curious. I pushed back, heart pounding, establishing a barrier around my sense of self. I had no desire to be overwhelmed by it or anything else. I wasn't about to take that chance.

Given its nature, I was surprised at the strength of the personality I'd contacted.

The internal voice boomed through my head. *What do you want?*

"Simply to talk." I subvocalized, to help lessen the pressure pressing against my temples. I didn't want to actually speak for fear Raphael was listening. My phrasing was blunt, but the pressure in my head made it harder to think.

You're not Diego. You're not Therese.

I interrupted before it could iterate everyone in the

universe I was not. I was well aware of who I was and who I wasn't, and I didn't have time for this. Hopefully, sending the kids on the errand to find a place for me to practice would keep them occupied for a while, but I had no guarantees of how long, and I wasn't going to waste any time. "No, I'm Ceri."

What are you?

"A human. A mage. What are you?"

The guardian.

"Do you keep people from passing, or merely Himself?" I didn't need to say Raphael's name, because I had a feeling that we both knew who I was talking about. The voice seemed to approve of the choice.

Himself. And you're wise not to name him.

"Why do you bring other people here?"

Because he's lonely. I am supposed to keep him as happy as possible while he's imprisoned here.

"You can pass freely through the barrier?"

Yes.

"Would you take me if I asked? How do you decide who you're going to bring here?" Just in case. I liked having backups for when plans and contracts fell through.

I could if I desired to, for the first question. Though Himself can block people leaving if he's aware and he wants to. In reference to your second question, I seek interesting people, for people whose despair is so great that they no longer belong in the land where they live.

"Is there anything that I can offer you that you might enjoy?"

Company. Tell me things I don't know.

"Do they need to be true things?"

A long pause. *If they're not intended to deceive, I'd like to hear untruths as well.*

I had time. And I'd read enough magical academy series for teenagers as a part of my curriculum at school that I could retell at least one story without needing recourse to the books. "Let me tell you a story about a boy who was forced to live under the stairs by his cruel aunt and uncle..."

When I was finished with the first chapter, the creature wrapped around me. *You can tell me more of this story if you connect with the mists' anywhere. I want to hear more.*

"I'm fine with that. I do have to go back now. I have other tasks to do."

Where do you wish to be?

"Himself's house."

The mist darkened around me, then dissipated. I stood behind the house. No energy lost. Handy! I circled round in time to see Ilani and Albrecht running toward me, laughing.

"We found a place! It's an old building, but the roof and floor are still sound. It's not too far, and they said they'd be willing to go in if we all keep the ghosts away!" Ilani chirped.

502   DAPHNE MOORE & L.A. BORUFF

It sounded like a plan. "I'll look at it later, well done. Are you ready to help me research?"

"Yes." Albrecht strode past me into the mansion. For someone who looked twelve, he had a firm and decisive tread. He knew exactly where he was going, and he was going to get there rather quickly if he kept up like that. I could appreciate that, if nothing else.

"What are we looking for?" he asked as we walked into the study.

"References to a kin that was destroyed long ago, *or* a man named Lou—I don't know the correct spelling, or a man called Johann Schmidt." I threw the last in for thoroughness, even though he'd likely not used that name long enough for it to be found in this library.

I pulled books in English while Albrecht and Ilani browsed for tomes in languages they could read. Soon enough there was a substantial stack of books on the table, more than enough for the three of us to work on for hours and still get nowhere. I tried not to be disheartened just looking at them.

Searching through the books, I soon found Albrecht to be good at skimming books, while Ilani was someone who I would've asked her parents for a consult to see if she had ADHD.

Still, her darting back and forth became a soothing counterpoint to me finding almost nothing. It was frustrating, but research never went rapidly for me. I was slow, but at least that usually meant that I'd find something eventually.

"I found something," Ilani said excitedly.

"What?" Albrecht took her announcement in stride. She'd made it several times.

"Lugh Lámfada, Lugh of the long arm, also called Samildánach."

"What does that mean?" I asked.

"Equally skilled in many arts. He is one of the Tuatha de Danaan...the Tuatha that vanished a long time ago! After a battle with the NightQueen and DayKing, nobody has seen them since, and Lugh vanished at the same time. His powers were illusion, he was a mighty hero and warrior, a trickster. Sound like what you're looking for?"

"Yes." That sounded *exactly* like Johann.

"Nobody knows what happened to his people, but they were one of the first kins created and very powerful."

I resisted the urge to touch the gem. No sense in drawing attention to it. It wasn't that I didn't trust the two of them, but if they even offhandedly mentioned it to Raphael, things could go very poorly for me. "Is the book in English?"

"No, it's in Gaelic."

I sighed. "Please, continue, and thank you, Ilani. I appreciate this."

Her smile was blinding. She loved being useful.

Most of the rest she read was descriptions of the Tuatha, their battles, and their fall when they tried to fight Tiamat and Marduk, the NightQueen and DayK-

504 DAPHNE MOORE & L.A. BORUFF

ing. Given the secretiveness that Johann practiced, if he was hiding an entire kin, I could understand why. He had people to protect.

The twilight alarm went off.

"We should stop by the kitchen for leftovers," Albrecht said. "I told the humans the school would be tomorrow."

Yes, I'd forgotten that. I'd need to sort through the supplies tonight.

Learning about the people here was important too, especially if I was going to need to persuade the mists to let them go back to their homes. Being trapped here simply because Raphael wanted company seemed profoundly unfair to me. I'd find a way to help them.

THE NEXT DAY, the children and I arrived at the site they'd decided on. It was a shelter, with a roof but no walls. They'd moved chairs and small tables into it. It would do.

"Go get your friends, and we'll see how this goes."

This gave me a chance to talk to people who'd been in Ha'al. I was hoping to see what I could do to help them the next time I had a real conversation with Raphael.

I sorted books and papers and waited. It didn't take them long to return. Novelty and boredom worked in my favor here.

Ilani returned with the three children I'd seen earlier, and Albrecht returned with a young wolf, who cringed away from me.

I let him handle soothing the wolf while I sat down with the other children. Perhaps seeing me do this would help with her fear. She was so timid. It might take time to get them to trust me.

For right now, the kiddos were mostly curious about what they'd been missing out on, and that'd be enough to get them to show up. For a while. I wasn't sure exactly how long it would last, but I'd take their attention as long as I could get it.

Hopefully they'd help me pass the time as well. A welcome distraction.

By the end of the assessment, I found their skills woefully behind, but they weren't illiterate or innumerate. The oldest boy was bright, the other two also, but they'd obviously received much less in the way of schooling. Thankfully, Gaius has provided workbooks and many pencils, and I sent them home with them.

From what they'd said, none of them were born here, but only the eldest had any memories of a place other than this. They were all eager to spend the time with me and listened, a strange contrast to many of my days in my other classroom. While many kids in my world weren't fond of school, these kids had never had anything like this before and they were eager. Hungry, almost.

After they left, the wolf whined. Both Ilani and Albrecht looked sad.

"We were hoping you could teach her some magic, so she figures out how to go back to human shape," Ilani said as Albrecht ran a soothing hand over the wolf's head.

Ah. No pressure, then. I wasn't familiar with shapeshifting, either, so that was great.

"What about her parents?"

"They're dead."

My heart thumped painfully in my chest. I swallowed back the tears. Then I sat cross-legged and called up the sight to look at her while using it.

The observations I'd made in the past of the shifting kins, when I had the time and space to focus on them minutely, had shown me two forms, one dominant, one ghostly. The connections were subtle, but I'd been motivated. I'd had too many wolf-changers sent after me in the early days.

I'd learned to collapse them to human form, and how to kill them, too. Luckily that trick didn't apply here. No need to kill the pup.

The translucent form of a girl about Albrecht's age superimposed over the wolf, who squirmed under Albrecht's hold and my gaze. I focused on the image.

The two had become tenuous, ghostly, and one was twisted on itself, as if it'd been injured. This poor child. "I need to touch, is that allowed?"

The wolf whined louder and bellied down to the ground.

The gem pulsed on my chest, and a tiny flow of magic reached for the wolf, pausing first as if checking out Iliani, but then gliding along the magic the little shifter radiated, glowing at the connection points between girl and wolf. The gem radiated helpfulness, which was odd, but I'd take the hint and see if it might work.

Above her body, I traced the connections, starting with the twisted one. It responded to my touch, shifting as I used a fine stream of magic to manipulate it. Straightening the joining was possible, though it wouldn't be fun.

"I think I can repair what's wrong. It'll probably hurt. But if you attack me, I'll have to stop and leave. I want to help, but I can't if you hurt me. Do you understand?"

A whimper answered me. Ilani moved next to the wolf now too, grabbing her hindquarters. Since Ilani was a wisp of a girl, I didn't know if she was strong enough to try to hold the wolf down, but I appreciated the offer.

I pulled more magic and returned to work, starting with the tenuous connection, slipping magic into them, making sure they were well secured between the two forms. They glowed, responding like dehydrated plants being watered.

The wolf spasmed and gave a muffled howl, Albrecht and Ilani almost lying on top of her, Albrecht's hands clamped on her jaws. Poor child. I wasn't even to the difficult part.

Now for the twisted connection. I wished I could do it fast, but I didn't know precisely how to do it, so I proceeded in a steady fashion. Filling it with magic, then working it around, as if it were a tangled necklace chain, keeping in mind that the howling scrabbling wolf beneath me was *feeling* every moment.

Nudge, nudge—it twisted itself into its true shape finally, the magic flooding through the massage, and the howl morphed to a scream, which blessedly stopped as I leaned back.

Exhaustion punched me the moment I let go of the magic. My soaking shirt clung to me, and rivulets of moisture ran down my back, sides, and gathered in my bra between my breasts.

The girl looked at her hands, sobbing. Naked, though Albrecht had already produced a small bundle of clothing as he delicately looked away. Ilani covered her while trying to coax her into them.

"Thank you," she whispered, her voice rough and uncertain.

"You need to stay with us for a little while," Albrecht said. "It's safe here, and you need to get used to this again.

Fear slipped across her face, but she nodded.

"What's your name?" I asked.

"Tatiana." She rose, frowning at Ilani, who'd grabbed her arm and was trying to push a sleeve on it.

Albrecht, despite Ilani's help, managed to get the rest of a bathrobe on Tatiana without actually looking at her. "Let's go."

I needed to clean up again, and time had definitely passed. None of us wanted to be caught out when the warning sounded again.

In the reception area of Himself's mansion, Ilani paused and stared at the television. "Could you make that work for us?"

I eyed it. "I could try, but I'm not a technical person."

"That's fine, it's magical." Ilani laughed. "But if you *could* make it work, Tatiana can see it and maybe have something fun to look at later this evening?"

"I'll try." I made no promises, but I'd try anything to cheer the waif of a wolf up.

No note waited on my door, so I would have company for supper tonight—I'd let the children handle the guest arrangements. They knew more of what to do than I did.

When I headed down for supper, after spending more time in the luxurious bathroom, the aroma that greeted me in the hall made my mouth water: chili and cornbread. Raphael smiled at me, and I returned the expression warily.

While he had been nothing but polite, and an amazing cook, I knew his reputation—and I'd seen Una, regardless of whether or not she'd deserved it. She hadn't reached that state through a surfeit of kindness.

"Wine? This is an excellent red." He held out a bottle.

"No, thank you." Wine was not on my list of consumables while I stayed here. Nothing that could lower my defenses.

If he was acting, though, he was very good at it. I'd yet to see a smidgen of his evil since our bargain had been sealed.

"Ilani mentioned that she thought I was only allowed to see *some* of the people in this dominion?" I asked pointedly.

He took a sip of his wine. "Correct. There are dangerous, terrible people who exist here."

I stared at him. His eyes were full of humor as he gazed back, fully aware of his reputation and my opinion.

"While I appreciate your point, I am unwilling to give up my independence." I said the words flatly, then tried the chili.

Delicious. It wasn't completely to my preference —a hair too spicy, and he'd made it with pulled rather than ground meat, but it was still among the best I'd ever had. I'd discounted magic as his cooking ability, because it was off, not perfectly tailored to my preferences every time. If he'd used magic to cook, the meals would've been completely to the eater's preference.

"Your safety is important."

How nice of him. "Mm. I've met some of the people living here. They don't seem to live in safety."

"If they came to live here, they would be utterly safe, but unaccountably, they prefer not to." His smile deepened.

"What would it take for you to let them go?" This

was what I wanted. To free these people. Maybe I could convince him.

He sipped his wine before answering. "Similar to you. Have you found a way to open the dominion and let me out?"

"Not yet. That brings up another point, based on your son's visits. How much time has passed? How long is left in my stay?"

He took another sip of wine. "Difficult to calculate. This dominion isn't well moored to time, so when you leave can be variable."

"You bastard." I said the words with venom and punctuated each syllable.

"Consider it an incentive. And you might be able to help those poor people, too, if you work fast." A sheen of mockery glimmered on his words.

I contemplated flinging the chili at his head, then flattened my hand on the table. "I will not be forced."

"Was ever woman in this humor woo'd?" he quoted.

I smiled at him, showing teeth. "I know the quote and the context. Richard, wooing Anne after murdering her husband, in Richard III. Are you implying that you're an evil scheming ugly person who ends up dead at the end of the play?"

"Not ugly." His laughter wrapped around me like velvet. Not a point in his favor. I'd had experience in dealing with involuntary physical reactions to men I disliked or despised, and all these little tricks were winning him zero points.

Not that he'd started with any.

But damn if he couldn't be charming on occasion, like a beautiful and dangerous animal who'd gained the ability to talk and have witty conversation. I didn't want perfection, but that was what he was serving up to me. I wanted to go home to Nick so much...

Fuming, I headed for the reception area. At least puzzling the television out would be a distraction.

CHAPTER 7

ILANI AND TATIANA sat in the reception area, finishing their meals.

"This soup is pretty awful. Why does it have beans?" Tatiana said.

"It's chili, not soup that's why," Ilani said. "And the cornbread is pretty good."

"Yes." Tatiana nibbled on a yellow chunk. "Sweet is good."

It was sweet cornbread, which paired well with chili, but most southerners from the States would've revolted.

They were a world away.

Both of the girls smiled at me as I walked over to the television on the wall. The first oddity was the lack of a power cord.

I examined the TV, probing for magic and was immediately rewarded with the sight of strands of magic trailing off the sides and back. I'd never before seen anything quite like this—the machine looked normal, but an intricate braid of at least four strands of magic interfaced with it. On the other side, they connected to nothing, but held stable, floating, waiting. For someone to grasp them? Interface with their power? Energize them?

The base structure reminded me of the way they traveled. It looked as if you were supposed to grasp the strands of power.

I squinted, then focused on Ilani. "You know how you connect with the land? When you want to move fast?"

"Yes."

"I think you could connect with the TV the same way. Why don't you try to feel the magic trailing off it?"

Her brow furrowed with concentration.

The standing wave of magic around her bulged chaotically, spiking out into the air all around her. It was like a blind person's arms being extended, to check for barriers. Unlike that image, Ilani's flailed against the air.

It brushed Tatiana and she jumped, moving halfway across the room. Her hair stood half on end, as if with a static charge.

My hand fell from where I'd reached out to Ilani. I didn't want a nasty shock.

"Try moving closer to it," I suggested.

She took several steps forward, her expression frustrated but determined, magic stabbing and spiking around her like a sea urchin's spines. I held my breath as her magic brushed against one of the connections.

It stirred and plumped, siphoning magic away from her. The television screen flickered and then lit up, blurry figures appearing on the screen that wavered in and out of focus.

Ilani's face firmed into a triumphant glare, and she stared at the screen. Her magic solidified, spiking even more, reaching for the other connections, those strands latching on too.

Her brow furrowed, and the picture on the screen wavered, and then the familiar music from the introduction of Princess Mononoke came from the speakers.

An anime about the conflict of nature and industry? I dismissed the question of how she'd seen it.

Tatiana came closer, staring at the screen. They both settled in comfy chairs, enthralled.

I'd come back later to experiment on my own. Even with Ilani's impressive magical reserves, she'd probably be tired by the end of the movie. In the meantime, I'd enjoy a short nap to replenish my own energy, and then see if the TV had uses other than watching movies.

I was pretty sure it could be used to scry people or places. It would explain so much of Raphael's knowledge.

Later that evening, I shooed both girls to their rooms and reexamined the television. Without distraction, analyzing the various magical connections was a little easier, though the purpose of many of them escaped me without connecting to them.

While Ilani had energized several, and the extra energy she'd fed those was still visible in how thick they were compared to the others, I perceived dozens. They ranged in size from perhaps a half inch thick to thin, floating opaque strands that looked like spider silk.

I wondered what sense they fed, or where they reached to bring information. What sensory aspects the extras connections fulfilled. Perhaps some of them were tuned to senses I didn't even have.

Raphael hadn't mentioned his scrying mirror. Given it was situated in a public area, I was taking it as a passive invitation to use it, especially since Ilani had shown no hesitation.

It all boiled down to a chance to see my family. There was no way that I was going to not make use of that chance now that I had a moment of semi privacy. No way at all.

Focusing on Nick sprang first to mind, yearning, but I decided against it. If any problems sprang up, then it would only worry him about me more. Practicing with him would be a bad idea. Not to mention that it would hurt to see him—but then it made my heart ache to see my children too.

It was hard to put thoughts of them aside.

Before I tried to see any of them, practice seemed

called for. Somewhere that wouldn't make someone worry about me.

Focusing on the sea I'd watched yesterday, I selected one of the strands that Ilani had activated and tethered my magic to it, feeding it a slow pulse, not the torrent she had.

A sensation of resistance passed over me, as if walls or hedges kept me from seeing it. Interesting. I navigated my way around the barriers, and in a few moments, I was rewarded with a picture spreading across the screen, of waves rolling on a pebbly sandy shore near a distinct rock formation. Sight, okay. With a second thread of magic came the hissing of waves and the lonely cry of the wind.

What would the third and fourth be? Especially since Ilani'd tuned into a movie?

Tentatively, I engaged with the third. A strange sensation flooded me, a mixture of hunger, wariness, repletion, emanating from multiple points in the water. Emotion? Intriguing.

The realization made my connection to the fourth even more tentative.

A male voice thundered in my ears, familiar, faintly accented. *Stop that.*

The voice from yesterday. The one who liked stories. I disengaged in a hot second. I wasn't sure if these threads connected me to the real world, but I wasn't going to use them there without knowing exactly what it was, given the warning.

Perhaps with a very small amount of magic in the third and fourth, they might give impressions rather than explicit detail. I wanted so much to see my loved ones...

This was an ultimately invasive device. The magic that must have gone into making it was mind boggling. While I was thoroughly unnerved with how much information could be gathered, the amount of knowledge and craft that it'd taken to create something of this magnitude was beyond impressive.

Even with that worry, I chose to focus more on being glad to be able to see my family, rather than the implications. That would come later.

So many more connections. Exploring them would take a long time, and it certainly would happen because I wanted to use it to its fullest extent. But not right now. I knew enough to see and hear them.

I opted for Dara first. Focusing on the picture of her as I'd last seen her, defiant as she'd been held by the Daoine Sidhe. She'd be free now, though.

The image on the screen flickered then sharpened. Dara sat at a desk, with her laptop open. Even lightly connected to the third strand, the background drumbeat of her sadness tore at my heart. Thoughts ran into my mind, along the fourth connection. The surface was colored by the history of the lilim, the pdf she was reading.

Apparently, Pryce wanted her to know the story of his kin.

Under it, like a pulse other thoughts beat. *I shouldn't have let myself get trapped, so stupid. Where's Mom, is she ok? Why won't they tell me what happened? Jimmy and I can find her, I'll check out his latest idea tonight.*

Deeper thoughts crowded forward, and I disconnected the strand hastily. She deserved her privacy. I'd never even read her diaries. This went so far beyond the limit. These were her innermost thoughts, and I had no right to hear them.

Severing all the connections, I saw the rest of the room around me again. Raphael stood next to me, expression neutral.

I fought the urge to cringe, ingrained from long ago.

Enough. I wouldn't fall back into that time. I was stronger than that now, and I refused to revert to those habits.

I turned my back on him and walked down the hall to my room.

Inside my room, I calmed my heart and breathing. Despite my best efforts, the aura around Raphael terrified me, especially when I was caught off my guard. I fished the little gem out and stared at it.

Maybe it would help. Though I hoped the souls within it weren't too aware of the outer world.

I pressed it to my brow and took a cleansing breath as the fear subsided. It didn't go away entirely, but it became much more manageable. The gem radiated peace. I'd take whatever help I could get.

I bit my lip before I whispered thank you. If Johann heard it, even at this distance, a new bill would start.

That humorous thought steadied me too.

I'd try the TV again tomorrow, after being away from the house and steadying my nerves by teaching the children a little more. Tonight, my curiosity had been piqued by the sensation of barriers. It'd been similar to the resistance when we'd traveled. I could start tracing those as a bedtime exercise.

Knowing this dominion was in my best interest.

Settled in my room, I crossed my legs and breathed deeply, letting my senses expand so I could examine the underlying magical structure of the land.

Letting myself sweep upwards, then looking down, I watched the magic that filled the sky, sending the needed energy for plants and animals to thrive. Not a sun as I understood, but still a way for life to thrive. There really was no sun here.

The waters edged a barrier thick and vast. Behind it swirled a level of energy that would've made me gasp were I physical—tremendous waves, beating against the dam. Whatever dominion lay there was one of intense magic. And it seemed to desperately want in.

Turning my attention away from those two vast sources, I began examining the land, starting with the mansion where my body sat. Nothing appeared, and I focused harder, refining the sensitivity of my search.

Barriers appeared like smoke, boxed in areas. I couldn't perceive the interiors at all. Magic woven into those invisible walls directed people away from them on a subconscious level, erasing awareness also. This made me intensely curious.

Nothing like a *keep out* sign to make me want to see what was inside. More interesting was the fact that it wasn't even a visible keep out sign. If it had been, I might've been able to suppress my curiosity, but the secrecy of it made me *really* want to know what lay within those blocked off areas.

A hobby, something to pass the year, after I once again spoke with the mist and taught the children.

It was time to go back to the TV and try again, now that I'd calmed down.

No dice. Raphael sat there, reading a book, with a cup of tea at his side. He nodded at me. "You have so much talent. Have you made progress at piercing the dominion's wall?

"I'm looking into its fabric, yes." A guarded answer that didn't give away much.

It wasn't a lie. My beginning explorations of the internal barriers had found them tied into the fabric of the dominion itself.

He got up and smiled at me, its charm hitting me like a physical blow. "Sleep well."

I didn't glare after him. I refused to dignify his actions with a reaction.

Focus, Ceri. He's gone. Use it to see what you want.

I returned my attention to the screen and the strands, playing the unfamiliar ones between my mental fingers like sorting embroidery silk. Teasing them apart, seeing the nuances of difference in shade, even if I didn't know precisely what all of them did.... I wanted to experiment more with contacting people.

There was no way I'd talk about anything I cared about in front of him, and now was a perfect chance to experiment.

My heart still very much wanted to find Nick, see him, talk to him. My head knew that I needed more practice first. He was a deeply private man and while he'd be happy I had the comfort of seeing and talking to him, he'd want to keep his thoughts his own.

And I didn't know how interconnected the threads were, or if it was possible to accidentally tap thought even if I didn't want to.

Instead of Nick, I reached out for Jimmy's familiar face and personality. The connection latched on, a picture flowing onto the screen almost immediately. I engaged the threads for sound and sight, sorting through others, trying to see what they did. One showed patterns of magic in the area, and I marked that one as important.

Sun and shadow dappled Jimmy's face, leaves

dancing in the breeze. He was outside, walking with Drake, one of Johann's trusted lieutenants, along the edges of Johann's property. The snow was gone, the trees blushed with green from new leaves, a carpet of spring flowers and plants and mud under their feet. Birds chirped lustily, the sun bright and cheerful in the sky, shining on it all.

I missed the sun so much. A spasm of pain clenched my heart, missing my family. Heck, I even missed Johann.

But I'd made this deal, in full knowledge of the consequences. Time would pass, but not so much that it would ruin my life when I returned. No one I loved was a small child, where a year would make all the difference.

I'd done what I had to do.

On the screen Drake tilted his head and scanned the area around Jimmy. He was frowning, his expression quizzical. "Here."

"This is a section that needs to be reinforced?" Jimmy closed his eyes, expression becoming blank as he focused.

I could see the ward, using the magic detecting strand. It looked frayed and worn, though still plastered on the interior with chaos magic.

"Yes. Johann's expecting trouble, and this is a weak point." Drake leaned against a tree. Taller and broader than Jimmy, dressed in dark clothing. The aura of magic around him, ebony, extended wings and shifted.

The sight of him warmed my heart. With him around, Jimmy was well defended.

Even if he measured his words like gold.

Jimmy nodded, extending his arms. Working carefully, my son's magic connected with the wall, flowing into it and reinforcing it.

Drake's questing and restless eyes kept my attention. Black as his hair, piercing, he was searching for something. He hadn't started until after I'd been focused on them for several moments. An indication that some people could detect what I was doing right now.

interesting. Why were there some people who seemed to be able to sense my presence and some that couldn't? Did it have something to do with their magic, or was it something that I was doing differently on my end? If I made one like this at home, it would be important to know if it could be detected.

I'd ask him how he managed it when I got back. The thought of being spied on like this without knowing was nervous making. If I could figure out how he knew he was being watched, then I'd be able to learn how to do it as well.

A moment later, I withdrew, and went seeking Dara again.

She and Pryce, the leader of the lilim and Jimmy's uncle, stood in a lavishly furnished living room. Curtains were drawn back from floor to ceiling windows, the furniture was pale wood and light fabric, the few decorations perfect for the space. It oozed tranquility. Dara stood by one of the curved couches, one of her hands clenched in the fabric covering its back. She was dressed a bit more formally than usual, in a light spring dress. Pryce stood across the room, dressed casually.

I quelled the instant panic at the two of them alone together.

Dara yelled at Pryce, lips thin, eyes flashing. "You do not have any right to tell me what to do!"

"Correct. However, I do have the ability to assign bodyguards, and you need to stay unmolested and unkidnapped if at all humanly possible. I owe your mother a debt, to make up for my brother's actions, and I take my liabilities seriously." The quiet, cool, controlled tone was familiar.

I winced. He couldn't have chosen words or tone better to infuriate her more. Nothing he said was untrue, but that didn't mean she was going to take well to the way that he'd said it, or the particular phrasing that he'd chosen. If he was irritating people, it was because he wanted to. Why?

"Then go find my mother!"

"The question is not finding, the question is retrieving, and is being answered by Nick Damarian and his people. Keeping you safe is something that I know that I can do, Ms. Gault. Deal with the situation like an adult, not a petulant child. She went there to buy your freedom."

Dara stormed out of the room, and the focus followed her into an unfamiliar bedroom.

I wasn't quite sure how to take all this. Instinct suggested he was making sure a mage was kept secure so he could use her services later to strike at the lilim queen, his enemy. Jimmy working for Johann was not the safest profession. Since he wasn't influencing her magically or touching her, I decided to think of it as a good thing on the whole

Now to find Nick.

His familiar face, wrapped in a feeling of security and normalcy. I called it up in a surge of emotion. The connections were all still there, but all the screen showed was a picture of his house and the surrounding yard.

Nick obviously had protections. I was going to have to wait until he went outside to try to contact him and see if it was possible. Or if he had personal protections as well.

Even through the disappointment, the fact that his home was safe made me feel good, it also made me wonder why the protections for Pryce and Johann were lesser, or if they had to be activated and hadn't yet.

I'd never heard of a device like this. Maybe they hadn't either. I'd warn them when I got home again.

THE BARRIER intermittently occupied my attention in the evenings for several frustrating weeks. More often than not, Raphael would ask for my company after the meal, usually in the reception area.

The first time, I'd followed him warily. He'd gone to one of the tables and pulled out a chess set.

Internally, I sighed. I *hated* playing chess. With a passion.

Raphael cocked his head, as if he'd heard something. "Do you prefer board games or cards?"

"Either. Both." Anything but chess.

He set the case aside and pulled out a backgammon set. Much better.

"Do you want to bet anything?" A raised brown indicated what he'd prefer to bet.

"Do I look insane? No, let's just play for points." I settled in a chair opposite him.

He lost with good grace. Other evenings, other

games, proved he won most of the time, but he was graceful with that, too.

On evenings when I was alone, trying to pierce the barrier made for a problem that distracted me a little bit from the longing coming from watching Jimmy and Dara daily. I couldn't catch Nick on the screen, and I reluctantly concluded he must have had personal protection as well.

Tatiana, Albrecht and Ilani made for an amusing trio to watch, though Tatiana was often tentative around me. She flat out ran and hid when Raphael appeared.

School proved a wellspring of information and gossip; I learned from the kids attending that there was a small settlement of lilim some distance away; they'd chosen to live in isolation rather than feed on the emotions of the humans in the village. There'd been violence in the past against them, Albrecht had said softly, enough that Raphael had intervened.

Tatiana's people, a changing kin, shifters, lived in the wilds near the mountains, in caves that the monsters couldn't get into.

Other groups of unknown kins avoided each other and humans, scratching out a lifestyle near the swamps, which were apparently fertile and full of fish.

One morning, coming out of my room, I found a dejected Ilani and worried Tatiana in the hall, rather than finding them in the reception room, waiting to go to school.

"What's wrong?"

Ilani shook her head. "Albrecht's people came and got him a little while ago, and I'd like to see him. But I can't concentrate. You could maybe turn it on?"

"Let's see." We walked down the hall, Tatiana hovering. I wanted to put my arm around her, but Ilani had her arms wrapped around herself, clearly signaling she wanted space.

I glanced at Ilani. "Do you think this will help?"

"Yes."

"I'll try then."

I concentrated. The television flickered and wavered, blurry figures appearing on the screen that wavering in and out of focus. Again, probably protections, but I'd learned ways to weasel around them, though I'd never been able to get through Nick's. Focus.

Three figures: Albrecht and two adult svartalfar. They stood in a darkness relieved by the light of stars, the outlines of the trees around them disturbingly off. It was confusing, and for a moment I thought that it was just the scrying mirror, but that didn't make any sense either. The images were too clear to be false. So why was it like this?

Albrecht stood, his mouth moving with no sound, his expression intent, almost angry. One of the svartalfar glowered down at him, arms folded, and spoke a few words.

I adjusted the sound strand. No sound came

through. Argh. I understood why people banged on electronics, but I hadn't known this kind of thing could happen with magic too.

Gaze angry, Albrecht answered. It was clear they were arguing, although without sound, there was no way for me to tell what they were arguing about.

The other adult svartalf's expression wavered from stoic as he spoke, and Albrecht glowered at him. Were they in Nick's home, or was this yet another place where they'd worked and settled?

Silent movies without dialogue placards. Annoying, especially given I wanted to know what was going on. It was frustrating beyond belief to be able to see them and nothing more. All I knew was that the situation was tense, but there wasn't a single thing that we could do about it from here.

Ilani breathed a heavy sigh of relief. "Good. Raphael wasn't lying when he said they'd come for Albrecht. His family, I mean."

"Does he lie often?"

"Raphael will lie if he thinks it's better for you. And generally, he thinks lies are better for people."

Not a far stretch, though I would've argued the *good for you* part.

"So Albrecht isn't in this dominion anymore."

Ilani shook her head no, eyes sad. "They wouldn't stay long. Nobody stays here that doesn't have to, except for those who are trapped and the people who come because they love them."

"I see." I didn't ask which she was.

She stared at the image for a bit longer. I let it fade slowly, Albrecht's face the last thing to disappear.

Her lips trembled. "I can check on him. And if I ever get to leave, I can find him." She held out an awkward hand to me. I took it and shook. Handshakes might be something that were from my world, but she was giving it her best shot, and I appreciated it. Part of me wondered who had taught her that particular gesture. "Thank you."

Head averted, she ran outside, Tatiana following. But it was too late. I'd already seen the tears.

Neither of them came to school that day, and I hurried back when the lesson was done. They'd vanished somewhere, and I didn't use the scrying TV.

Privacy was a good thing.

I missed Nick so much. I'd finally had a chance to enjoy physical closeness, and now I was separated from the man I'd chosen.

No way was Raphael worming his way into my bed, despite all the means he kept using to make himself seem more likable—good food and good company. I'd never, and would never be, that desperate. Not to mention I'd never betray Nick like that. There were bad sexual decisions, and then there was catastrophically stupid, Stockholm Syndrome decisions. Not. Happening.

No call to supper tonight, so I went back to working on a way to penetrate the barrier. The internal blockades were very similar to the one between the dominion and the outside world, so I chose a corner that they shared to experiment on.

I created a twist of magic, much like a corkscrew. The new plan was to pop it into the barrier and remove a tiny portion of the block so I could see what was on the other side. If it worked, then I'd try it on the dominion barrier as a possible passage out.

I'd given my word to stay, but it never hurt to have a backup plan. I had no intention of letting Raphael out either.

Caution was the rule of the day for this experiment —I didn't want to bring the barrier down and create mass havoc. Also I wanted to see if Raphael noticed or not.

He'd definitely pay attention if I accidentally brought the whole thing crashing down around my ears.

My magic corkscrew sank into the barrier. I sat in the chair, conserving my energy—this was *hard*!

The resistance lessened, and I tugged it back, triumph shooting through me. I'd done it. The small gap opened as I finished pulling the magic back.

A blast of heat flooded my room, carrying the smell of sulfur and rot. I gagged, nearly bringing my dinner back up before I could make myself extend my awareness through the gap. What in the world was behind there?

Screams ripped my ears before darkness swallowed

me. There was only the faintest gleam of magic here, not enough to show me anything. The overpowering coppery odor of blood filled my nostrils, sweet with rot.

I set my will and expanded my magic, trying to use it as a lamp to see.

A knife glittered, held by a skeleton frame of magic, approaching me. The hint of life force, of many creatures, all ebbing low.

I reeled back as the knife swiped at me, pulling myself back through the little hole in the barrier and returning to my body.

Blood poured into my room, from a tiny rift that connected to the opening in the barrier. The carpet had soaked up a little, but as I watched, it expanded to a gush, and I scrambled backwards.

The bit of the magic of the barrier remained on my corkscrew of power. I grabbed it.

Long clawed fingers and hands with jagged broken nails ripped the small opening wider. More screams, like the howls of the damned.

Using my magic and the piece of the barrier, I tried to press it shut again, but it resisted. There was flesh in the way.

I'd only created the corkscrew to manipulate energy. The hole was larger than the bit of energy I had from the barrier. I patterned some of my own after it and tried again and a long tentacle dropped from the ceiling and groped toward me.

My door slammed open, and Raphael strode in. He

swept his hand up. The screams intensified as the severed arms, hands and tentacle fell to the floor and the hole closed. He turned to me, brilliant eyes blazing with anger. "I'll talk to you at supper."

Then he walked out without another word.

My stomach heaved, and I barely made it to the facilities before I vomited.

When the spasms passed, I felt Ilani's and Tatiana's quiet presence. Normally I would've been embarrassed to have an audience when I was puking my guts out, but right now I was more concerned about the fact that there were dismembered limbs in my room, not to mention I could smell the rusty tang of blood even from here.

It helped that she didn't seem to be judging me. Ilani crouched next to me, holding a cup of water in one hand and a toothbrush in the other. Tatiana shifted to wolf form, bristling, and faced the door, obviously guarding.

It wasn't the toothbrush I'd been using, but it looked clean. At this point, as long as it was cleaner than my mouth, I'd take what I could get.

"I'm sorry." She offered the cup of water awkwardly. "That was your first time?"

I straightened up on my knees, my hands shaking slightly as I accepted the cup from her. "Yes. You've seen that before?"

Tatiana whined.

"That's what took her family and hurt her," Ilani

said quietly. "I've seen it too. Sometimes they get loose near the edges, but I've never seen them come in here."

She sounded shaken. Guilt added onto the other emotions stewing in my gut.

The sheer rage in Raphael's expression and demeanor had set off this anxiety attack. The bits of fear in my stomach still fluttered, but I had it more under control. I needed to sort out what I'd learned before our confrontation this evening.

"Would you like your toothbrush?"

"Thank you, Ilani." I stood shakily, taking it from her. "But I don't think you should go into that room."

"It's ok. Those messes are awful to clean up. I've done it before, but I don't think Tatiana should. You could show her nature movies in the reception room while I clean it up?"

The words sank into me like a stone. Her voice spoke of experience, so matter of fact. I had to get them both out of here.

"Have you cleaned up those kinds of messes often?"

She shrugged. "Yeah. But those were after an attack, not after an accident. Near the human village. Yours is a lot bigger."

I would've thought the opposite, but okay. Mischief gone, Ilani's eyes looked a lot older than I'd ever want to see.

She painted on a smile and wiggled her fingers. "Though since you have the human magic thing, you could use that to clean it up without me having to get a mop and trash bags and so on? Tatiana could wait for us down the hall, and we could get it done fast?"

Good point. This was a major biohazard—I had no idea if that blood or flesh was toxic or not. It could've been poisonous for all I knew. I considered her question.

Her head tilted to the side. Eying my expression, Ilani said, "If you make it really hot you could burn it down—and then I could help you sweep up the ashes. Lots easier than cleaning up a big wet mess. Svartalfar do it, and I've seen Albrecht do it. You should be able to, as well."

I blinked at her. I *definitely* needed to get her out of here. Still, some small part of me was flattered by her confidence. I was glad that we had a little bit of time together before she'd watched me heaving into the toilet in the next room, because that definitely wouldn't have been a very good first impression. Not exactly the badass warrior mage I sometimes wished I could project.

On the other hand, what she suggested made sense. I just needed to figure out where to vent the smoke. Because it would smell awful, and possibly be toxic. Besides, if I thought it smelled terrible now, there was no way to tell how much worse it was going to be over time cleaning it up. I honestly didn't know if I could sleep there at all, given the memories it now contained.

Time would tell.

I brushed my teeth thoroughly, leaving the toothbrush propped up on the sink, and then turned to face the mess in the next room. I'd manipulated wards enough that I could probably form a bubble of force that would contain the smoke and then I could just move all of it outside. If I was lucky, I'd be able to just shoo it out one of the windows. It would be a challenge to control it long enough to walk it out the hallways of this strange maze.

Time enough to deal with it when I knew.

I steeled myself and walked to the door of my room. Blood pooled everywhere. The thinner areas were already drying rusty red. The rug in that area was a loss, too—I had no idea how to burn the blood without burning the rug, given how saturated it was. And the bedding. Curiosity killed the cat and all that, or in this case made a serious mess of my bedroom.

I pulled out a nub of chalk from my pocket and set a visual reminder of the boundary, to make it easier to do, since much of it was a new exercise. I'd never done anything exactly like this before, but the mess was a good motivator. Beyond that, it wasn't that complicated.

All I needed to do was envision what I wanted to happen, and then use my magic to make it so. I sketched the rest of the hemisphere in my head, creating the ward, a glowing half circle shining to my inner eyes.

It was hard to focus with my stomach shifting uneasily at the smell of blood and worse. I did my best to ignore all of it, to distance myself, as difficult as it was. The last thing that I needed was to get sick again right here and now, because my legs were shaking from crouching on the floor in the bathroom, and I really didn't think that I'd be able to make another run for it if I had to throw up again.

Ilani watched me, bright eyed, with Tatiana sitting at her side. The wolf gave me a polite tail wag, to make the moment more surreal. She must have refused to go down the hall.

No questions were asked, which was a small mercy that I hadn't expected from Ilani. It wasn't that I thought she asked her questions to be rude or cruel. It was more that she didn't seem to have a filter, nor any control over what she said, and anything that popped into her head also came out of her mouth almost immediately. I was just glad that she hadn't started asking me any questions about what precisely had happened here, because I didn't have any answers for her.

Once the ward held steady in my mind, no matter how much I poked and prodded it, I called fire. The blood and tentacles and other bits of flesh ignited with a soft hiss, like meat on a grill. My stomach lurched.

Oh, ew. It smelled like meat on a grill too. I'd never look at a steak the same way again.

I kept the fire on it long enough to reduce all of it to ashes. It was actually more difficult than I thought because I originally hadn't thought to reinforce the ward against the heat spreading out. That hasty magical ward patch happened in the first backwash of heat, and thankfully it was a simple fix.

Ashes and smoke contained, I carefully held the ward together as we walked down the hall, toward the outdoors. The windows didn't open, which we found out once the floor was clear enough to cross. Oops?

It was fine. We made it outside.

"I need a little time alone, I think." The words came out in a burst once the remains were disposed of.

A paw tapped my foot. Tatiana leaned briefly against them, then ran towards the trees.

"Be as safe as you can. It'll be twilight soon." Ilani followed Tatiana.

THE SEA ROLLED UP. I stood close enough to let the spray hit my face and clothing, trying to soothe my jangled emotions.

Growing up, my grandfather had lived near the Pacific, though in a state too cold to swim most of the time. It was one of the reasons why I'd decided to move into the center of the country, to be as far away from familiar surroundings as possible. Because the people sent to look for me would have expected me to go to a soothing environment, something I was used to. As much as I'd have loved to be near the sea, I'd chosen safety over comfort. Here, I had just left behind the one person that I knew might want to hurt me, and if he wanted to find me, there was nothing I could do about it. If I wanted to see the ocean, then I could.

I considered the traveling technique, distancing myself from emotions. It'd become easier with use, relatively simple to do in this magic infused land. Whether it could be used on earth was another matter—but I was going to try soon after I got home.

I was in Hell. My mind shied away from the thought, even as the gem pulsed against my skin. I placed a hand over it.

Johann had known what this place was, and he'd still entrusted me with it. To shield me or for me to protect them? At moments like this I could almost feel their presence. They calmed me.

The nearby mists had drifted close to me, and I smiled a little. Establishing communication, I asked, "Do you want the next chapter?"

I'd gotten about halfway through the first book in the time I'd been here.

Yes!

That soothed as well, sponging away at the memories of blood and pain, softening the knowledge that I'd have to interact with Raphael.

When the story ended, the mist lingered. *Are you well?*

"Yes, just worried, Would you answer a question?"

I can try.

"If Himself escaped, could you bring him back here the way you bring people here?"

A pause, the magical lights flickering and flashing. *If the way he exited was closed behind him on his return, yes. But I could not close the passage on my own.*

A thought to keep in mind.

"Could I call you from another dominion, if I wanted to finish stories after I leave?"

Yes. I will listen for your voice, but you might have to be very loud. Call for the Guardian, reach with your magic for my essence, and I will hear you.

The mist enveloped me from a moment, then drifted away, coiling through the rocks.

The heaving water, gray and green and glimmering under the gray skies, eased the knot in my gut. I missed the sun, but I could pretend this was a cloudy day, with a warm breeze full of salt spray blowing on my face. There were no seagulls here either, nor dolphins leaping in the water. Other than the waves themselves, the water was still, or at least not filled with the sounds of creatures. Although knowing this land, there were probably plenty of creatures, just not any that I'd be able to recognize from my world.

The rhythmic sound and movement of the waves embraced me, and the scent of rotting seaweed and fish mixed with the salt to match a familiar if not entirely pleasant sensory memory. The magic in this region was slightly different than the rest of the dominion, wilder and purer somehow. It was almost as if it arrived here from somewhere else, a more primal location.

Though I didn't know how it could get much more primal than this dominion and still remain cohesive. The place reeked of magic. It was as if the very air was tainted with it, as if it was in every breath, in every speck of dirt on the ground, every atom of water in the ocean.

The water stretched to the sky. The spray was chilly, no temptation to swim. Even had it been warm, I didn't want to experiment and end up possibly eaten by a sea monster. I had no proof that there actually were sea monsters here, but I had no proof that there weren't, either, and I was more willing to err on the side of caution.

Walking along the mixed pebble and sand beach, I found a rocky outcropping that shielded me from view on three sides. Three sides was the best that I could ask for, since I didn't want to totally box myself in, and at least this way it would protect me from view. A secluded nook in the rocks, with a shelf exactly the right height to sit and far enough back I wouldn't get soaked by a rogue wave. Settling my butt on the shelf, I stared out and continued thinking.

I'd yet to find a thread on the scrying TV that would allow for two-way communication. That would've been wonderful, and it was still entirely possible, since I hadn't yet been able to fully explore all the different strands. I'd be able to ease my mind about current events, and make arrangements for Ilani, Tatiana, and all the other poor souls trapped here.

I pondered the other events of the day, now isolated from them. The combination of the phrase 'place of punishment' and the horrors that I'd glimpsed hidden in the compartment of this dominion, my observations of Raphael's appearance and actions led to scary thoughts. Johann had called him Asmodaj.

I really didn't like the thought of Hell being a real place, especially not with the idea of innocents being trapped here.

Gazing over the water, breathing deeply to calm the heart that had started racing again when the thoughts came to mind, I jumped as the waves surged forward, bulging as something enormous reared out of the water. A sea monster.

I freaking knew it!

A terrible, primeval combination of sea monster and dragon loomed out of the surf. My mind skittered straight to Leviathan. I jumped to my feet and backed away, hitting the rocks behind me in my panic. The creature lumbered forward. I was trapped. My heart thundered, and I grabbed at all the magic around me. I might not know exactly how to use all the magic in this strange world just yet, but that didn't mean that I was going to just sit by and get eaten. I wasn't going down without a fight.

I directed the magic toward the creature, fire answering my panicked call. This was the second time in as many hours that I'd called fire to my command. It answered me quickly. Then again, it might also have something to do with the fact that I was panicking out of my mind and magic at least wasn't completely abandoning me.

Flames roared, then the surge of magic dissipated, letting me see clearly again.

A singed, Middle Eastern man with an irritated expression stood where the monster had been. Built like a bodybuilder, he had long black curly hair falling down his back, and tattoos on chest and arms.

I gaped.

The newcomer glared at me. "Was that an accident?"

I swallowed. "No. But if you weren't planning on eating me, I'm sorry, for what it's worth."

He considered me. "No hard feelings. I know what I look like in my true form."

I searched for words, but they had all run away as I kept my eyes square on his face. Focus was important, and as long as I kept my gaze in his northern hemisphere, I might be able to keep that focus.

"You're Raphael's newest acquisition?" The newcomer's eyes didn't stay on my face, as his gaze swept up and down in curiosity.

That was about enough of that. I was not property. I'd done him the courtesy of keeping my eyes on his face, and the least he could do was to do the same. To be fair, I was still clothed, an advantage I had over him, but I still didn't appreciate it. "Nope. First, I'm a person not an acquisition. Second, I'm here for a short time, and then I leave." I put my chin up.

The newcomer's eyebrows rose. "And you're damned brave. I am Nunamnir. You're called Ceri."

He cocked his head. "You bear Lugh's people too. Interesting. What do you plan to do with this favor? And how exactly do you plan to return?"

"What do you mean?" He has a lot of questions.

"You're human, and your people are human. This place is disconnected from time, so if you want to hit the right time period—say, close to when all you care for are alive—it can get tricky. Especially if Raphael doesn't cooperate with your aim. So you could be free a thousand years before your people have been born."

I swallowed. "I didn't know that."

He snorted. "I figured, so that's why I told you. He can be a sharp dealer with people who make bargains with him."

"And you're being kind why?"

"Lugh apparently likes you. And things have heated up on your dominion with the most recent Reckoning, and you might make a difference.

"Can I go into the future?"

"No, because it's not yet determined."

"Where did you just come from?"

"Godhome. The Reckoning's near enough that the barriers are thin. Too thin for comfort, actually, since a sneeze would break through. Even worse, close to your dominion." Nunamnir spread his arm, chest flexing, tattoos rippling.

The sneezes of his other form would be very large...

He continued, "It was no effort to come here. I'm

tempted to cross to humanity's dominion, since it's now full of forward women like you, but I've been waiting to see if the seers pick up both keys. I don't enjoy Marduk's unadulterated company. Ušumgallu and Lily seem determined not to cooperate this time."

Who were they? I needed a damned scorecard. Or an index of all these people, complete with spelling, because I couldn't keep them all straight. "And they are?"

"The seers who know where the keys are." Nunamnir grinned. "There were storms in Godhome the day the King and Queen found that out—that they want to prevent the Reckoning from happening."

"Can you help me?"

"No more than by telling you what I have. Good luck, Ceri. You'll need it."

"You're not going to warn me to keep Raphael here?"

"I don't think you're stupid. I hope you find a way to deal with all this mess, since all the principles are willing to destroy everything to get their way. You're mortal, so you have a different perspective." He laughed. "No pressure."

Then he walked back into the sea, changing to dragon form part way in the surf.

The *time* question was going to feature in this evening's conversation too. A plan had started evolving in my head.

Then the twilight alarm sounded. Blast.

AFTER MY LAST EXPERIENCE, I hurried back to the mansion. Since I wasn't pulling anyone along with me, I could make it in one jump.

I walked into the reception area to find Raphael standing there near the television, hands clasped behind his back.

Trying to ignore Raphael's presence, I settled one of the rococo style chairs, put my chin in my clenched fists and concentrated on the television as well.

So many, many strands of magic attenuated off the television. I'd already identified several. Now I wanted to find which would permit me to communicate. There were at least a dozen more visible now. Part of the question was whether Raphael's presence made them visible. He was connected to the television, though no picture showed on the screen. Did it function like a phone as well?

It would likely take me hours to figure out how

many of them there were, let alone what they were. On this examination, it appeared as if some of the strands could connect the flow of magic to me, rather than away. For what reason, I was unsure, and I hesitated to connect without knowing.

Old mages, bold mages, but very few old, bold mages. You didn't get to be old by doing stupid things. You got to be cursed or dead.

The texture of the first reminded me of hearing, the methods that could be used to enhance perception. I shifted to observe Raphael covertly. He was actively linking with some of the strands as I watched. The method he used to connect to it appeared very similar to mine. I'd always been taught that only humans had magic, but that appeared inaccurate now. Out of all the creatures in the world, why would Raphael also have true magic rather than his kin's talent?

It made me wonder. And worry. Was it possible that some of the kins had a portion of that talent and had hidden it all these years? Or was he a special case? It would make him even more terrifying.

The screen flickered suddenly, showing Raphael's son Gaius and a woman with the look of one of the changing kin, probably a tiger, judging from the colors intermingling in her hair. She was sitting in what looked like an ancient recliner, with a baby nursing at her breast. He looked down at her, a world of love in his reserved face.

"Charming picture." Raphael's dry comment raised

my interest. Mockery, yes, but also deep affection and perhaps a touch of envy. Not expected emotions from him. Nor was the invitation to comment expected.

"Actually, it is. Is one of the connections that you're interfaced with one that you could use to speak with them?"

"Yes. The tenuous one, the one that shifts and unravels, next to the one that transmits their thoughts."

With his description I could see the additional strands, translucent, more detectable through their motion than their color.

"Are you going to talk to them?" I prodded.

"No."

That was a very definitive no. "If I were to use that strand, would it be only in their mind, or actual physical sounds?"

"Physical sounds. The mental connection for two-way communication is done through another channel."

"Why are you showing me this?"

He faced me fully, an intent expression on his face. "It will become apparent. Matters are coming to a crisis point and permitting you to fully see what is going to happen—what is *likely* to happen," he amended himself, "will make you more willing to see reason."

Somebody didn't want to anger Fate by telling me exactly what had been predicted. Smart man. I'd heard she was nothing to trifle with.

I didn't touch any of the strands while the images Raphael had called were on the screen. I was barely acquainted with Gaius, and not at all with the person I assumed was his mate or wife, and I didn't particularly want to intrude in their privacy or startle them. Ancient members of the kins tended to take surprises badly, especially when there was a helpless infant involved. Not to mention that it was rude, and this was the closest that I'd been to domestic bliss since I'd come here. I wanted to enjoy it, if only for a few minutes.

"He's a handsome boy." Almost a note of affection in Raphael's voice, surprising me. Just a moment ago he'd been dry enough to desiccate the air, but his eyes were soft as he looked at them now. "I think he's going to take after his father."

Raphael watched the three of them for a while, a happy family group, with an air of contentment at odds with my every other encounter with him. I didn't trust this expression in the slightest and used the opportunity to also observe how he manipulated the strands.

The picture brought memories bubbling up for me —Dara, her damp hair coiled in tight curls, snuggled to my side while I read to her, and Jimmy nursed. We were sitting in the front seat of the car, where I'd pulled off in a metro park and put a little 'nothing to see here' magic around our vehicle.

Metroparks had working sinks and we'd settled in after washing up.

We'd been living out of my car to save money, right after I got to Columbus. Lotus had found us there and persuaded me to meet with Johann's...I'd often wondered how she'd seen us. Maybe it had been meant to be, or maybe there was something more. Given fate and death had become involved, probably something more, not to be revealed to us lowly mortals until the end.

The screen blanked. Raphael disengaged from the threads and settled into a recliner that hadn't been in the room the last time I looked.

That was annoying. This was his domain, so it made sense that he could change things as much as he wanted to with very little effort, but I hated the fact that I hadn't even noticed the magic required to summon the chair. I needed to stay on my toes if I was going to get through this without him getting the upper hand.

After a moment I gathered the strands. To practice, and possibly ask more questions, I visualized the human form of the dragon on the beach, Nunamnir. A neutral party, because I was damned if I was going to let Rafael see me interact with Nick, or my children, or anybody that I cared about. I'd given him enough in the way of tells already, just by living here. At least if I chose Nunamnir, then he wouldn't learn anything important from me, with the added bonus of the possibility of me learning something from him. And if I didn't, then I wasn't any worse off than I had been before.

The screen wavered, then showed not a man, but a spiky gigantic dragon moving through water. His toothy jaws gaped wide as he rushed forward in the dimness. A huge squid fled, but the dragon moved in a burst of speed, and I winced as he ripped a squid in half. Not perhaps the activity that I'd expected, but very much in keeping with what he was.

Even though it must be pitch black at the depth of the sea where that squid that large must live, I could still clearly perceive Nunamnir and his meal. Perhaps it is part of the scrying magic, some slight tug of magic that I was adding without even realizing it?

I avoided the thread that would let me hear his thoughts, reaching instead for the translucent ribbon Raphael had said permitted audible speech. I wasn't ready to reach inside his mind, especially when he was in his dragon form. There was no way to know what things would be like in there, and I didn't think that sitting in front of Raphael was the best time to start an experiment. If I'd been alone, then it would have been an entirely different situation.

"Hello. This is Ceri, the woman from the beach. Can we talk?"

The monster rolled smoothly in a circle and then shook his head and started a sharp ascension.

In a matter of moments, the monster had breached the surface of the water. He bellied up on the rocky beach of an island. Lush palm trees swayed on the edge of the television screen. He blurred for a moment, then stood in human form.

Once again naked as a jaybird. Why did so many

of these people lack any kind of body consciousness? I looked to a corner of the screen, although I doubted that he was able to see that I could see him. Actually, that was a great question. Could he see through it? Was he able to see me, or was he just staring off into space and hearing my voice, with a sort of "are you there, God?" situation?

It was an interesting question, although it was only one of many. I could almost see the breeze, see the ocean rippling behind him. You'd think he'd be cold, since he was still soaking wet, his mane of hair dripping.

Nuramnir cocked his head, flattened a hand in a questioning gesture, and said, "What?"

"I had a few things I hoped to ask you."

"Raphael's loitering about, isn't he? You're using the scrying toy? This feels like a device rather than organic magic."

He could sense things to that level? Interesting. "Yes, to both questions."

He shook his head, smiling. "Be wary of that old snake. Hello, brother, if you're listening."

I paused. I wanted to pursue the topic, but the image on the widescreen kept distracting me. He was well put together, safely far away, and I was human. It was only natural to be distracted. "Do you have any clothes?"

He laughed. Then he made a scooping motion with his hand and water and pebbles combined to make a kilt, clasped with a broad belt. "You're a shy one. Funny, I thought Raphael beat that out of his toys pretty rapidly."

"He can't lay a hand on me." A little smugness leaked into my voice despite my best effort.

Raphael cleared his throat behind me, and I swallowed hard. I shouldn't have said that. Raphael might not have been able to hurt me, but that didn't mean that he was warm and fuzzy. He couldn't be trusted. Tension gripped me, and I hurried to the topic I wanted to talk about.

"Where are you?"

"Godhome. I've too much magic to spend time in most other dominions."

"Can you show me what you meant by the barrier becoming thin between Godhome and my dominion?"

He tilted his head, the mass of wet dark hair slopping around, and then pointed in front of him. "Use your other sight. Perceive. The barrier is as thin as paper all through Godhome right now. Magic leaking everywhere."

It took time, and fatigue crept in as I sorted through a number of the threads, connecting and trying with each. Finally, colors and strands exploded around him on the screen. The thinnest of barriers curved around the edge of the screen, ragged and translucent.

I gasped at just how thin the barrier had become. He wasn't joking. The wall between dominions was tenuous there, and tremendous magic pushed against it and leaked through into adjacent dominions, like water through a colander.

Humanity's dominion was adjacent, as were many others. Grandfather's cosmology lesson sprang to mind —Godhome touched all dominions.

"Will it harm my dominion if it's any thinner?" The question burst out.

"Maybe. Probably not. But it's thin enough for the King and Queen to cut right through to your home if they have the keys presented to them." He settled cross legged on the beach, scooping up a handful of pebbles and letting them fall in a glittering stream.

Despite the room being cool, his casual mention of Tiamat and Marduk brought a light sweat to my back. I had no doubt that was intentional. Just like Raphael, he knew exactly which buttons to push.

"Do you have a dog in this fight?" I wanted at least a hint as to what motivated him. Even if he lied, it was an insight.

He shrugged. "I love the seas on your world. I want to swim in them again. But unlike my parents, I don't destroy what I love. I can enjoy the memories if my presence will destroy the reality, until I can swim in it once more."

It seemed a common problem with the oldest beings—too much power accumulating over time. Perhaps if a way could be made to drain off some of that power...and not with the purpose of collecting it for someone's use...some grievances could be fixed.

"Thank you. Do you have any words of wisdom for dealing with your brother?"

Again, the throat cleared behind me. Raphael was getting on my last nerve. I should have tried to come up with an excuse to scry on my own, that I could think better by myself, which wouldn't even have been a lie. Instead, I'd let him sit here this entire time.

Nunamnir shot me a wicked grin. "Trust him just as far as you can throw him."

"Is he too powerful to be in my world?"

"Not once he finishes the task he's been waiting to finish since he was imprisoned." Pain splintered through my head as the connection broke. I didn't know the person on the other side could do that. A warning would have been nice.

"Remember, we need to discuss dimensional barriers here as well. I'm looking forward to supper." Raphael's words sank into my back like a knife.

I stiffened. This was going to be a long evening.

When I turned around, he was gone. My clothing, part dry, was tacky and sticking to me. I headed down the hall.

Ilani popped out her room, like a gust of wind slamming a door open. "Hurry! It's almost supper time!"

"I take it you're invited?"

She nodded vigorously. "It's spaghetti! I love pasta. Tatiana is staying in her room though. You should shower real fast, your clothes are wet and you have a little time left. Better to be cleaned up."

Her voice spoke of prior not-cleaned-up experiences.

I headed into my bathroom. More than a dozen sample shampoos were lined up next to the shower. The tiny little bottles were a welcome sight, even if it did boggle my mind a little bit at the thought of having to choose one of them. There were too many options, so I grabbed some of the plainer options, rather than the more colorful ones that made me think of the warnings of toxic frogs.

I chose a neutral scent for soap and shampoo, I didn't want to inadvertently issue any kind of invitation. If I could've stood myself smelling like body odor or anything worse, I would've radiated that, but I wanted to feel clean at the very least. I was pretty sure that my expression would be deterrent enough, but if not, I was more than ready to back it up with words.

The hot water pounded on my body, soothing muscles knotted by the events of the day. I had to be at my best tonight, and the shower felt absolutely amazing after the stress of the past day.

While he planned to confront me or have a fit about what had happened, I planned now to confront him back. I wanted information—I was tired of flying blind. Instead of worrying, I focused on the sensation of carefully running my fingers through my hair to make sure that all of the shampoo was out.

I'd encourage him to brag about his power here, or his past. It seemed to work well on older creatures. People wanted to tell everyone about how awesome they'd been, so it was a trap that they tended to be more than willing to step into. It was also one that I was more than willing to take advantage of.

Rubbing another layer of shampoo through my hair to get the last of the grit and salt out, I collated what I did know.

Raphael had said repeatedly he wanted freedom. I had tested for weaknesses in the barrier between dimensions when I'd examined the partitions in this place. I'd had a difficult time drilling through one of the weak spots in the internal barrier, and that experience had proven that I did not want to do it again.

I hadn't perceived much difference between internal and external barriers, but I hadn't tried the external yet.

I wasn't sure if or when I would, considering what lay within this dominion. The process of passing between dominions wasn't something I'd ever particularly studied, since I hadn't actually planned to leave earth. Nor had I gotten much opportunity to do more than study books in the process.

The basics had been all I learned, partly from watching Nick and others when they punched gates between dominions. The process didn't seem overly difficult, but that had also been worlds that they already knew, ones that hadn't been shielded and weren't hidden away. Worlds that people wanted to visit. Not like this one.

Not the theory, the whys and hows. Sometimes I wished I could've had real training, especially now. I was kicking myself for not asking Nick about it when we were at his home. It was always better to know something and not need it than to need it and not know it.

The area—the gate—guarded by Diego must be a weak point in the dominion's fabric, though whether it was natural or artificial I didn't know. Not one Raphael could use, nor I before my year ended.

Nor did I plan to try to run, no matter how much I wanted to. I was wary of violating that agreement—your word and your power were often intertwined. Risking mine was out of the question. I had a family to go home to, and I wouldn't be able to protect them if I didn't have my power. I couldn't, and wouldn't, risk it.

Which left a direct assault on the secrecy—finding out what was going on outside this dominion, what his sea monster brother was talking about—and whether it meant danger for Nick or for my children. And what I needed to pay or do to get the innocents out of here.

From what I'd seen, admittedly little, many of the people I'd met here in no way deserved to be trapped in hell. If anything, the only people who deserved to be here was the one in charge, which was totally and entirely backwards. But wasn't that always the way of the world? Those who deserved to be punished were the ones who were doing the punishing, and those who were innocent were in the worst shape.

Raphael: who had condemned him and how?

And how was I going to get these answers?

Asking was probably a good start. I doubted he'd hide it from me, because hiding implied that he was ashamed of his actions, and that wasn't the case.

Rapping on the door made me jump as I dried off. I sighed, mentally preparing myself for everything that was about to happen.

"It's time!" Ilani's voice.

"Coming!" I answered, hurrying into my clothes

Off to the meal and confrontation.

ILANI'S PACE quickened as we turned down the hall. She radiated energy with an undertone of nervousness, and I wished Albrecht were here—his calm usually tempered her.

The rich smell of pasta and sauce made my mouth water as we walked into the kitchen. It was also unfair that the man was an excellent cook. If there were a personification of Justice, like Fate and Death, Raphael should have been absolutely atrocious to look at, had terrible manners, and completely unable to cook. Instead, it was the total opposite. It wasn't fair, and if I hadn't already been attached, this year might've gone very differently.

Instead, I wanted to push him away with a broom handle and hiss.

"Ceri. Ilani." He plated the pasta. Sauce was already on the table. I appreciated that. I had a certain amount I liked, and just pouring sauce over pasta made it too saucy for me. I didn't like my noodles looking like they were drowning.

Ilani rushed to the table. I followed at a more sedate pace, braced for anything. Once seated, I picked up my fork.

Ilani had already commenced inhaling her food by the time Raphael sat down with us.

I met his eyes and went straight to the point of what I wanted to know. "Do you know what Nunamnir was talking about? Is there trouble at my home?"

"Possibly, but not for the reasons you think." Raphael gazed at me, eyes lingering on my face long enough to make me uncomfortable. He was playing the silky sexual menace card again, and the muscles in my jaw flexed as I gritted my teeth.

"Excuse me," Ilani said in a muffled voice, reaching for the garlic sticks. Interrupting was brave of her.

"Do explain, Raphael" I said with immense fake affability, then stuffed pasta in my mouth. Measuring my words seemed safest. If he was expansive, I'd learn what I wanted to know. Patience until he proved he wouldn't tell me.

He scooped sauce out over his pasta as if he had no cares in this world. "Morgan will do everything within her power to open the gate for Marduk, now that her scheme has ripened."

I nodded encouragingly. His gaze lingered on my mouth, and I fought the urge to chew with my mouth open. If he wanted to stare to intimidate me, then I'd eat like a cow chewing cud for a few moments.

"She needs a final sacrifice to fuel her ascent to godhood, and then she will challenge Marduk."

I nearly choked, which might've been karma for my pettiness. The napkin saved me as I spat the food into it, coughing. *"What?"*

Ilani had gone still as a mouse, violet eyes moving between us.

Raphael laughed. "Do you think she's content to be a servant when she could rule?"

"I'd never thought about it..." I was still trying to wrap my mind around it. Morgan was many things, ambitious, pitiless, powerful, but a step away from godhood? That was terrifying on so many levels. While the King and Queen were cruel, at least they were distant.

Morgan struck me as a hands-on manager. That quality, combined with godhood, gave me shivers.

"To give you credit for not considering the obvious, you're young and ignorant. She's had more than one reason to collect mages for these many years. Mages are a wild card, tricksy and they blur prophecy." He took a bite of his own meal.

The pasta didn't appeal anymore. I pushed the plate away. "Is there any way to stop her?"

"I'd do so gladly, if I were free." Innocence radiated from him, well suited to his appearance.

Ilani hunched down in her chair.

"Is there any other way to stop her?" The last thing I wanted was to free one evil in order to stop another if there were other options.

"Prevent her from consuming the sacrifice. Keep her from finding the seer for the Sun King—I believe that is Lily, one of the changing kin, somewhere in your hometown. How coincidental. All the players gathered in one convenient place." His smile would have dazzled me if I hadn't been worried out of my mind. As it was, I wasn't going to fall for it. And after the rage and threat earlier, he was all charm now. When was the other shoe going to drop?

I pulled the end off a garlic stick and changed the subject. What I'd seen also weighed on my stomach. "Why is this a place of punishment?"

To his credit, he didn't flinch or dissemble. "It was created that way, long before I came here."

"Then how do you rule it rather than being punished?" I set the bread down.

Raphael raised a brow. "Ignoring the assumption in that comment, I'm very powerful."

"Why are innocent people like Ilani here?" I couldn't help glancing her way. Her eyes were wide, and she looked ready to bolt.

"She's a special case. It's also not polite to talk about her in the third person when she's present."

"I'm sorry, Ilani." I spoke mechanically, not taking my attention off Raphael. "What about the humans here? Why do the mists exist, why do they attack some people and kidnap others?"

I knew the answer to that. I wanted to know if he knew.

The intensely blue eyes met mine, as if he were trying to read my mind. "The mist was conceived as a protection, I think, by my mother as she grieved. There are very few of my people left alive after the massacre of my kin, and our enemies wanted to be sure they were none. While I am trapped here, and my son was banished here as well, the mists were created to keep enemies from hunting us. I believe they have a basic consciousness...I'm not entirely sure why they seek people out and bring them here. I've never asked. My theory is they do that to keep me from being bored. I get destructive when I'm bored. And even a dominion can be fragile when I face ennui."

He destroyed dominions when he was bored? The man needed better hobbies.

The self-centered theory matched some of the facts, which would be funny if this conversation weren't so dangerous. "Who condemns all those in the barriered areas? Why do you hide them away?"

He steepled his fingers. I was worried that he was going to go on the attack, but he didn't seem to be running out of geniality just yet. "It depends. Some are delivered to me by old allies and enemies, with accounts of the crimes they've committed, and their punishment my choice. Others condemn themselves. I merely provide them with the torment they want. Only the worst are sent here, Ceri, and all deserve what I mete out."

"You'd say that regardless." He wanted me to believe that he was the good guy, and he wasn't going to achieve that by saying that he was drowning unicorns now, was he?

"True." His smile was bright enough to dazzle and didn't flicker for a second.

"Could you send the normal people home? Would Diego allow it?"

"Probably. But the mists choose well. Most who live here don't want to leave."

I called bologna on that one, but I'd allow that he probably didn't talk with the mists much either. Self-deception was powerful, especially if it allowed him to have something he wanted.

My eyes turned to Ilani, then back to him.

Raphael shook his head. "Not a topic to discuss at this moment."

"What about the people who bring supplies here?"

"Those who come and go aren't like the people who live here. They're descended from me, but without the majority of my abilities. Diego lets them go because they're his kin too." He considered, eyes calculating. "For the rest, Diego judges, decides who among those who come here are not fundamentally broken. The ones who are functional, he'll let pass the gate if I also permit them to leave."

"I see." The signal was clear. I needed his consent to get people out of this dominion. He'd already stated his price.

He gazed at me sardonically. "You're the only person here other than me who could potentially open a different gate."

Just in case I'd missed the implication. I decided to poke him a little. "Who made Diego the judge?"

A fleeting expression crossed his face, part brooding, part angry, a little amused. An odd combination. "Our parents. For all he's a prick, he's good at what he does, which is mostly keeping me here."

In the conversation we'd had previously, Raphael hadn't lied directly to the best of my knowledge. So if I let him free, the people trapped here could be freed too. That begged several questions, though.

Those in the punishment areas—who had condemned them? Could I judge innocence or guilt to potentially let them out? The kins were in no way fair when they decided punishments. Eternal torture didn't sit well with me either, given how some trivial offenses were punished by death in the kins. Possibly something as trivial as littering would warrant being condemned here.

But what if I was wrong, and a freed prisoner hurt someone?

My head throbbed. These were circular thoughts, leading me nowhere.

"Do you have documentation on those in the

cysts?" I'd fully admit that I was nosy, but anything that I could learn would help me learn.

"Ceri. It's not something you wish to read. I will swear by my name that none in those chambers are innocent, and all deserve punishment for *terrible* crimes. Compared to them, Una's butchery of human children was a peccadillo. That's why she didn't go into one."

My blood chilled. If that was true, I didn't want to think about what those people and creatures had done.

"Which leads me to the topic of the evening. I want you to use the technique you discovered to free me tonight. I have a task to complete, and you have shown me you can pierce the barriers here."

I only thought my blood had run cold before. "What is this task?"

"Not any of your business, Ceri. It began long before you were born, though it might end within your lifespan. Especially when you breach the barrier, and I walk free."

Not likely to happen. "I need to know." I folded my arms and gave him my very best *make them quiver in their boots* glare. It didn't work, because I was mortal, and he was very much not.

Anger shadowed the bright blue of his eyes. "You forget yourself, Ceri."

It had to be said, be he lord of this dimension or not. I'd promised help, and I'd given it. I wouldn't loose a terror on my world. I'd done all this to protect my world, and my world wasn't less important than that. "You're not the boss of me. Letting you out of here was not within the scope of our agreement."

Raphael rose and paced around the table to me, anger beating off him, so thick it was like being slapped. He could go from good humored to enraged in a moment...I hadn't known that. "Clever. What you seem to have forgotten is that you're stuck here for a long time, and I can make your life completely miserable."

Ilani bolted from her chair and ran out of the room. Poor girl, I had no idea why she'd been there, other than to show her how adults shouldn't behave to each other.

I got out of my chair, too, not wanting to be at a disadvantage.

I raised my chin, meeting his eyes squarely, refusing to show him fear. "Yes. But the time *will* end. I want to know the whys."

He circled me, lithe as a tiger, and about as friendly. He spoke in a conversational tone. "Instead, let me help you with some matters that seem to bother you. Your Nick? The reason why it took you so long to go to his bed? You don't want a trustworthy kind man, because you think in the end all you'll be is *his woman* and not yourself. You don't want a man who needs you, because you value yourself and your freedom before what any other human can give you. You don't want a man who loves you, because he might see all the lies you wrap yourself in."

Three times repeated, the magic shimmering around him. He spoke each word as if it were chiseled in the stone of reality. Each sentence hit like a punch, the more because each contained a kernel of truth.

I said nothing, though I wanted to protest. Giving him more ammunition would only let him know he'd struck home.

An unkind smile curled the well-shaped mouth. "Nothing to say?"

"Yes. I don't want to let you into my world. Especially not bearing the name Asmodaj—and ruling a place called Ha'al."

"You're smarter than I thought. Not that that would be difficult." He regarded me, still searching for some sign of weakness that I refused to give him. "You know of the leaders of the kins, what they do. Why don't I get a pass and they do?"

"Because you're an asshole." It felt really good to say, even if it did feel like hurling an insult at a childhood bully. "Because while you're pretty, you're empty. Like a doll. A really evil doll. Do you see anything in the mirror but a shell? Because I don't."

His eyes narrowed. "Now."

Movement caught my eye in the door of the kitchen. A lovely woman stood there, wringing her hands, nervousness in every line of her body and wide eyes. A lilim, most probably, she had the look. "What?" I snarled.

Sexual heat slammed through my body. Desire, exactly as lilim could force. The abrupt change was a flashback to the really bad times. Anger ignited within me, as strong as the lust, and I stared at him as my breath hitched in my throat.

Raphael smiled at me, smugness written all over his face. He purred. "No, really. I can make you very uncomfortable. Our agreement stated that I could touch you if you requested it. And it's not *my* power affecting you."

I could see exactly where this was going. And I wasn't going to allow it.

The magic crashed down on me like a tidal wave. She was very powerful.

I glared at her. She was pale as snow, shaking like a leaf. Dark eyes full of fear. Even with a brain over-amped with wanting, it was obvious she was doing this under coercion and didn't deserve to be attacked.

I walked forward, keeping my eyes slightly averted and my pace shy and slow as if I were fighting moving forward. He waited, arms crossed.

I got close enough and tilted my face back. He moved, his face closing with mine.

The second he came into range I punched him in the nose. I put my hips and my shoulder behind the swing and hit him as hard as I could.

Blood sprayed from his nose all over me.

I yelped. I'd taken enough self-defense classes to know it was a bad idea to hit the face with your hand. The face was hard and bony. They'd been right. I'd never hurt my hand like that before, pain radiating from my knuckles, but at least I'd hit with the right knuckles, the first two, and put my last two behind it. There was something to be said for that, wasn't there?

He stared down at me, blood dripping down his face, and burst out laughing. Out of all the reactions I'd been expecting, that wasn't one of them, and somehow it was just as frightening as him being angry. What had I just done?

I BLEW out a breath as he swaggered out, still laughing. The lilim woman had already bolted, her magic evaporating with her disappearance.

Dealing with Raphael was like juggling cats—even if they seemed happy with it, eventually you were going to bleed. Extreme power and randomness didn't go well together in my opinion. It made him terrifying, for all his attempts to be approachable.

A new definition of stress: strangling the urge to slap him because I knew he'd slap back twice as hard. That way lay scorched earth at the end of the fight. I knew the measure of our powers well enough now to know that I couldn't take him in a direct fight, but I could do serious damage if I went all out. Between the two of us, I was afraid that a third party was going to get hurt in the crossfire.

Today, if I could've guaranteed that Raphael was the only one who would've gotten hurt, then I'd have more than happily roasted him without a second's hesitation.

A part of me wanted to ask Raphael more about time and how this dominion interacted with it. But that would wait until our tempers cooled. Though he'd promised not to manipulate the relative time flow here, I hadn't known to specifically request being sent to a time in my dominion. Now I knew.

I drew in a long breath. I should probably go to Ilani and see if she was all right, but I was still terribly angry and didn't want to upset her further. Going outside was out of the question since the twilight had fallen.

That left messing with the television again or reading.

Standing in front of the TV, I connected to several more strands I'd seen Raphael use. Presumably they weren't harmful, so I'd experiment with several to speed the process. I hoped one of them could penetrate scrying defenses.

I really wanted to see Nick.

I formed his image in my mind, energizing the TV. The screen blurred.

The new strands pulsed, and diffuse emotions poured through me. Images flickered on the screen. One of the linkages tugged at my attention, like a child pulling on my sleeve.

Interesting. I yielded to the tug, letting the target of the scrying be directed by the television.

Cold duty, underlain by whiffs of anger hammered at my awareness. Instead of simply seeing the image on the screen, the strand tugged me into the moment, into the awareness of the target, as if it were a magical kind of VR.

I was Ceri. I was also Earl Smith, a fireman driving the truck and my coworkers toward a nightmarish fire, headed for residential areas. Sirens rang in my ears as I drove, heading for the call—a wood fire. Motion caught my eyes as the trees cleared above us before the turnoff.

A thick line of fire billowed across the road at the turnoff. I hit the brakes. The fire thickened as we skidded forward. What the hell?

I glanced up. A huge flying lizard thing above us, fire pouring from its mouth onto the road. Red as a candy apple. Like movie magic, only the fire had melted the asphalt and set the trees nearby on fire.

A dragon? Like in Game of Thrones?

I shifted to reverse and backed up. We had to get to the rest of the fire, but we were going to have to find an alternate route. Just had to outthink the giant flying lizard, call it in, and hope there weren't a bunch of drug tests waiting for me at the end of this.

I drew back, heart pounding. Earl Smith had seen one of the Great Wyrms, one from the dominion dominated by dragons. Its size meant it was ancient, its fire could melt steel, and it was smart. They were mercenaries, and they would never have gone there without a huge payment, or a favor from a powerful person.

I'd recognized the woods, having been in an accident there before. It was near Johann's house, and the forest was on fire.

I tried again, focusing on Johann's house. The screen went blank, and Johann's voice spoke in my ear.

Ceridwen. I recognize your magic. I do not permit spying within my home, even if I let it happen in limited cases on the grounds. I'm glad you're well. If I do not meet her again while I live, give my love to the purple eyed maiden in Ha'al. A tone of deep regret colored the mental words. The connection cut off.

Another tug. I wanted to resist, but I'd gained valuable information from that method the first time. I let myself be drawn in.

Frustration clamped me as tightly as my flight harness. Targeting for the A120 should be able to grab the hostile—it was bigger than a house, but it slid off whenever I tried to acquire it as a target. "I can't get a lock."

"Same, Rascal. Closer and engage with Sidewinders?" Legend, flying the other F-16, answered me.

"Yeah. Let's do this."

Even closer, the damned missiles wouldn't lock on. Fights should take place with miles between us and the target, but no, not me and Legend. We had to punch the damn thing and probably break our arms.

"Flyby with the Vulcans," I said. Getting hit with

20-millimeter rounds, the thing would know it'd been kissed.

The controls gleamed green and red and blue, and my gloved hands moved, pulling the trigger as I passed the large reptile.

The damn thing flew, I'd no idea how. That big, with the wings tiny in proportion to its mass, even if the wings were huge too. Physics was probably sitting in a corner crying, because I could certainly think of no justification for something that big being able to fly. We swept by, the rounds spitting and chewing on its hide as we passed.

It wasn't immune to them. Good.

I pulled up, sucked in a breath as one of the bogey's wings lashed out and clipped the tail of Legend's F-16. The tail disintegrated and the jet arrowed into the ground, smoke and flame slashing into the sky at the impact. Why hadn't he been able to eject?

I'm going to get you for that, you bastard.

"Pull back, Rascal. Scrambling F-22s. Get back to base." Central command came through loud and clear. I swore. I climbed and veered away even as the temptation to disobey and shoot the monster dragged at me. I wanted to kill it, my gut hurt with the need to hurt it ...

I pulled out of the rapport, panic lighting in my veins. Crixus. I needed to talk to Crixus. I left all the emotion and thought strands energized, only wanting to talk as fast as possible. This time I ignored the tugging and pictured him, concentrating as hard as I could.

When I touched his mind, he was calm. I didn't sink into his awareness, thankfully.

The picture focused around him.

Crixus was fully armed and armored. He stood near Johann's house. Other goblins crouched behind the low makeshift wall made of earth, shooting out against other forces. The focus shifted, and I could see they were comprised of a mix of goblins and daoine sidhe.

It looked like a war zone between them, deep holes ripped in what had been a lawn and surrounding trees, trunks lying shattered, holes gouged in the dirt, grass and standing trees burned and smoldering.

I pulled the picture back further, looking at it from above.

Was there something you needed, Chainbreaker? We're rather occupied at the moment. Crixus' thoughts and emotions were perfectly calm and razor focused.

"How long can you hold out?" I asked.

It depends on several factors. If she shifts the Wyrm to this location, defenders outside the house's wards will die. I can't answer as to the strength of the house's wards vs dragonfire. Assuming Morgan keeps using the Wyrm to kill humans to try to lure Johann out, we can hold indefinitely.

The image on the television showed Johann's house surrounded. In the enemy forces I spotted goblins, trolls, a younger dragon flying above—Morgan had pulled out all the stops. She wasn't bothering to hide anything from human authorities—at this angle I could see twisted and burned wreckages of fire trucks and ambulances. Smoke rose from the jet I'd just seen crash.

What was she thinking? Was she insane? She couldn't just unleash every magical creature in all the dominions in the human world. There were secrets that had to be kept, and she was putting all the kins in danger if she kept this up.

She did nothing without a purpose and a plan. This was all leading to a desired end, and I needed to thwart it. If Johann needed help, then they all needed my help.

Whatever it took. If she won, Jimmy and Dara would be slaves and Nick would die defending them.

I pulled out of the link, my heart slamming against my ribs, and ran for Raphael's study.

The door slammed open before I touched it. The room changed when Rafael was in it. Even with the presence of all the books, he dominated the room. He looked up at me, seated at the desk.

He set the pen he held down. He didn't seem the slightest bit surprised that I was here, and I wondered if he'd expected me.

"You've reconsidered?" No light of victory in his blue eyes, no sign of anger from the heated discussion, no sign of a bloody nose.

"Can you send me back in time to prevent the attack?"

"You've seen what's happening there then. Good. No, it's affected too many people, made too much of an impact. It can't be prevented."

"Can we cut this short to what you want in exchange for sending me there now? I also want everyone here to be restored to their home dominion *if* they want to be there." I didn't have time for this dance, not when we both knew I was here to make another bargain. A bargain had gotten me into this mess, and a bargain was going to get me out of it. Nor was I going to go small and nickel and dime myself—one bargain would cover all.

"Certainly. You will summon me to your dominion within a day of your arrival, punching a hole into this dominion if it is required."

That blocked many options. I'd find one. "If I die before I can summon you, then this agreement is void."

He regarded me and nodded. "Fair. You're walking into great danger. I will permit it if you agree not to seek death."

"Agreed. I want Ilani and Tatiana to go with me to my dominion."

A dry smile flickered on his face. "So it's time for that as well, in ignorance. On your head be it. Go."

He rose. "Fetch your fosterlings, I'll follow."

I bolted out the door and ran to Ilani's room, hammering on the door. She yanked it open, Tatiana in wolf form next to her, fur bristling. "We're going to my dominion. There's fighting there. Do you want to come?"

Ilani's face lit up. "Yes!"

She ran into her room and grabbed a knife.

Tatiana pressed against my leg and whined as Raphael walked down the hall.

He put a finger under Ilani's chin. "Farewell, child. Don't get yourself killed."

"I won't." She sounded very sure. I hoped she was right.

Raphael hooked a finger into the air above my head. Silver light ripped. He pulled it down all the way to the floor and the light hung in the air, looking like a glowing spider's web. A gateway we couldn't see the other side of.

"You will fulfill our contract, by your name, Ceri? Keep in mind you won't enjoy life if your enemy achieves godhead. Your lover is close to this spot."

"By my name. And you?"

"By mine."

I jumped forward, Ilani and Tatiana a breath behind me.

CHAPTER 13

THE NOISE and smells hit me, even though we stood among trees.

"Get down!" Nick's voice was urgent.

I dropped down onto my face, trusting him, grabbing Ilani on my way down. We landed in sticks and leaves and thorns, behind a log. Tatiana pressed against us, a growl vibrating in her chest.

Gunfire rattled through the space where we'd been standing.

I couldn't see Nick. If he was here, he was acting as a sniper. Which meant he—and we—would need to move after he took a shot.

As if in answer to my thought, a gentle tap brushed my ankle. Tatiana jumped.

Even more impressive, he'd moved to our sides without the wolf noticing.

"Ceri, my love. Why are you here?" Another moment, and he was next to us.

I glanced to my other side, where Ilani lay, eyes wide as saucers, no evidence of fear on her face, just surprise and interest.

"I saw the fight, and Crixus said you'd lose if she sicced the dragon on you, so I came."

"I'll ask how later. Morgan has a team of mages defending her. When I take the shot, would you try to hammer down the shields they have on our friendly daoine sidhe?" Irony colored his tone.

"Of course. Where is she?"

Binoculars nudged my hand. "Three o'clock."

She was partly obscured by trees, but I finally focused in on her and the tremendous amount of magic veiling her. She wore dark gray and black armor—rumor had it that it was dragonhide, taken from an intelligent dragon. Her famous red hair wasn't visible, tucked into her helmet, but the magic gave her away.

A roar thundered through the air, the Wyrm swooping overhead. I flattened to the ground even more, Tatiana burrowing into my side and Ilani rigid next to me.

Shouting drew my attention. I turned my head. People stirred at the door of the farmhouse, defenders parting as Johann walked out onto the porch. He walked confidently, not like a man who was walking out to face his death.

He held a huge sword in his hands.

"What's going on?" I asked.

"Morgan. This dragon is a message to Johann

telling him that unless he comes out and duels her, she's going to keep killing humans until he does. She knows she can't dig him out of his place of power, so she's taking advantage of the fact that he doesn't want her slaughtering cities full of people. I doubt Zanesville is still standing, to be honest, and she'll send the Wyrm to Columbus next."

"Can you...?" He knew what I was asking.

"No. I'd need a cannon, and time to prep. I didn't think she'd go insane, so I don't have any dragon slaying bullets premade."

"So the plan is to shoot her?" There had to be more.

"Yes, love. If you could keep your eyes on her?"

I examined the knotted ribbons of magic in the wards and protective magics gathered around Morgan. So many layers and interlocking wards—at least a dozen people powering it, people who were accustomed to working together. She took her safety seriously. I was only one person. I could unravel several wards—I was stronger than her mages individually—but this would be difficult.

Nick would know that. He made his own bullets, and I didn't doubt the one he'd loaded literally had Morgan's name on it. I was going to make it more likely he wounded or killed her, he wasn't depending on me to do it all.

We were a team, though he'd been ready to do this alone.

"I take it you found more family? I'm Nick, girl and

wolf. Pleased to meet you, and please stay down and don't break cover, or you will get killed."

"I'm Ilani. She's Tatiana. And this is very exciting. Is your world often like this?"

Nothing kept Ilani suppressed for long.

"No," I answered. "This is very unusual."

Nick breathed a laugh that I refused to acknowledge.

"Do you think Morgan will come out of cover?"

"If Johann accepts her challenge. Luckily, I don't work for Johann and have no allegiance or connection to him, so he can swear his people won't harm her in good faith. I've no doubt she's made similar arrangements. We'll see. Morgan's well aware of modern weaponry." Nick's voice was grim. "I'm not a fan of Johann's, but if she wants him dead this badly, I want him alive."

As if in answer to Nick's words, Johann walked out into the torn zone. "I'm waiting, Morgan." His voice was clear, his tone mocking.

She strode out. I began working on the wards, gently, fraying them, letting their power dissipate, trying to conceal what I was doing from the people maintaining them. It was delicate and difficult work.

"Let me know when you've done all you can," Nick murmured.

Morgan's and Johann's blades met. Johann's silver mail lay oddly on his paunchy form. There was no lack of strength or speed in his handling of the two-handed sword, no matter how out of shape he appeared. Given his true self was a tall elf broad as a barn, I had no idea why he was fighting in this form.

A flurry of blows later, they parted, neither of them showing wounds though both had connected multiple times. They were so fast—I hated to admit it, but faster than Nick, even. I couldn't even see some of the parries and hits clearly.

They met again and my blood ran cold, even as I picked at the defenses surrounding her. Johann seemed evenly matched in skill, but Morgan was the better defended and she'd managed to wound him, a trail of blood trickling down his outer right thigh.

Again and again they met, and I picked at the defenses, Johann picking up more wounds. Morgan was gaining the upper hand.

I wished I could work faster, but it was better to be sure. Johann would heal.

Nick lay next to me waiting, waiting, silent.

The last of the wards I could manage fell apart. "Now", I whispered.

Johann stumbled, and Morgan followed up on the thrust, putting her sword through his heart in one fierce motion. No.

I was surprised at how my heart lurched. Johann was morally gray, but still I didn't want him dead.

Nick took the shot.

Blood sprayed from Morgan's arm. I wanted to cry. The remaining wards still had the strength to divert what should have been a fatal shot. Energy fountained out of Johann and Morgan grasped at it greedily.

No, no, no…

The gem that I wore and had almost forgotten burned against my skin as the energy flying out of Johann shot to it, marking our location for all to see.

I couldn't see Morgan's expression, but her delighted body language turned to rage. She'd been denied his sacrifice, his soul.

And given the energy flowing here, she'd be joining us in a moment. Ruh-roh.

Morgan charged toward us, graceful, leaping over obstacles, her bodyguard a breath behind her. Blood stained her armor, bright against the black and gray, still running free. At least that would weaken her a little.

I threw some of my remaining strength into a ward against bullets as Nick and I rose. He left the gun where it lay, knives appearing in both hands. He'd be at a disadvantage against a sword, but he didn't tell me how to do magic, and I didn't tell him how to fight.

"Run, hide, we'll find you," I said to Tatiana and Ilani.

Ilani ran to a nearby tree, wolf next to her, and hid behind it. At least it would help block bullets if my ward failed.

"You move back too," Nick said. "I'll keep her off you."

I backpedaled, heading for a different tree than Ilani's.

Morgan jumped another stand of logs as Crixus and his troop of goblins moved to intercept her guards. Our friends and the rest of the defenders were doing their best to keep the other troops off us.

Nick glanced over his shoulder and grinned, flashing his teeth in a feral grin. "Looking forward to the rabbit you pull out of the hat."

No pressure. Though, I already knew what I was going to do. It was why I'd kept a reserve back. I'd sworn by my name to summon Raphael, and he and Morgan were not friends.

Call him now and let her fight a two-sided battle while I implemented the second half of my plan. I began the process of opening the portal to Raphael's dimension, boring the hole, ready to call his name once the way was open.

Morgan closed and Nick stepped into her path, and my heart climbed into my throat.

Concentrate! She'd kill him if I didn't get this open and fast.

I drilled at the barrier as I watched the two of them. Both fought dirty, and it seemed as if each of them were willing to take wounds to hurt the other. Unfortunately, Nick was in no way her equal.

Not unexpected. She'd had far longer to train than he. Nick was old, he'd said two millennia give or take when I'd pressed him. Morgan was *ancient*, active when civilizations first rose in the middle east.

The wound on her arm had evened matters, and Nick exploited it ruthlessly, targeting that side.

And took a heavy hit doing it. Every drop of blood he shed hurt.

Morgan was breathing heavily, far more exhausted than he.

Nick used that against her as well, feinting and making her work for each strike, tiring her out even further, frustrating her. Blood flowed freely on both. Morgan staggered. Still, I couldn't shake the feeling that it wasn't going to be this easy.

While it seemed an eternity, it'd only been some odd seconds. I connected to Raphael's dominion. I drew in my breath to shout.

The hilt of Morgan's sword slammed into Nick's temple, and he folded like a laundry rack. A mocking smile curved her lips and her mouth opened, no doubt to taunt me.

"Asmodaj, I summon thee!" I screamed it, the words coming to me, though it wasn't how I'd intended to say it.

The field went still as Raphael appeared next to Morgan.

"Why, hello," he purred.

She slashed at his throat, but he parried with a small knife, laughing.

Guardian? I pushed through the opening, maintaining it, searching for a flicker of the mist's magic.

I am very unhappy. Why did you let him out?

"I had to. But I've found a woman who'll keep him from being bored for a long time, who is as strong as he is. Could you fetch them both back to Ha'al?" I breathed the words as quietly as I could, hoping the two of them were too involved in the fight to hear me.

Yes, yes, I can!

Raphael hammered a blow to Morgan's head, similar to what she'd done to Nick, She staggered, and he disarmed her, grappling her.

"Our bargain is done. Come here, Ceri, now." His voice was like an iron chain wrapped around my throat, dragging me forward

One step.

The mist flowed out of the hole, gathering behind him and Morgan.

Another step.

A smile played on his face as he watched me. I threw more in the struggle, partly to keep his attention, partly to keep my pace slow. I didn't want to go to him.

Morgan kicked him, and he squeezed her. I heard a cracking noise.

I wanted to walk even slower. I fought to do just that.

"Thank you for the gift. I didn't bring you anything. But I have some ideas," he said to me.

The sexy menace never ended. I was within arm's

reach. Any time now, Guardian!

As if in answer to my thought, the mist pounced.

Morgan and Raphael vanished.

Shut the rift in the dominion wall; I have them both. He sent all the others away before he came. You're sure this single one will keep him from being lonely?

"Oh, yes." I stopped feeding energy to keep the hole open, and it snapped shut. It was done.

I fell to my knees, gasping.

That would never work again.

Nick stirred near me, and I crawled over.

He smiled up at me despite the blood on his face. "We make a fine pair."

"Is it safe to come out now?"

Bullets had stopped flying. Morgan's troops retreated, heading away from this place. I spotted the mages—they'd rallied by another of the daoine sidhe warlords in Morgan's army, but I wasn't sure of his name. A problem for later.

She and Tatiana picked their way over. The gem still burned, and when Ilani came near, it tugged in her direction.

I wasn't one to ignore a hint. "Ilani, cup your hands."

With a puzzled expression, she did so. I pulled the improvised necklace over my head and dropped it into her hands.

Her eyes widened, and she stared into it. The gem glowed, a burst of golden light, which continued rolling over us and the battlefield. As familiar as I was with the gem and the whispers and flickers of vision it held, I was still surprised as the light healed Nick's wounds.

He rose and we walked to Johann's body. Jimmy rushed forward to hug me, wiping away tears. I clasped my arms around him and fought the urge to cry. I wanted to hold on to him for hours... days. But that had to wait. I let him go, then he walked over to stand by Lotus awkwardly.

Lotus knelt at Johann's side weeping. It took a few minutes for her to stop sobbing. I clasped Nick's arm and gave her the time she needed to grieve.

Then she rose, eyes not swollen or red, because magic and nature wouldn't let her be anything other than beautiful. Her eyes—and mine—widened when they fell on Ilani, still holding the gem. Mine did as well, because the twelve-year-old had matured to a woman, tall and beautiful, albeit with Ilani's usual expression.

That would take some getting used to.

Lotus bowed. "You're his heir, then. The last of your people. For all the kindnesses your father gave, I will care for you until you're safe on your own."

"As will we," said the trolls laconically.

"Lady of the apsara, we should move him inside," Ilani said.

Lotus's shoulders slumped, and she nodded.

"Thank you. I'm Ilani, and I wish we could've met again while he lived." Ilani's voice had changed. She spoke a bit more slowly. "Thank you for bringing me here, Ceri." She turned and looked at the little wolf. "Let's go, Tatiana."

As Santo the troll carried Johann, the rest of us hobbled toward the house, dodging debris.

I moved to Ilani's side. "Johann left me a message for you. He said if he didn't see you again alive, to give you his love."

She swallowed. "Thank you, Ceri."

"Who's going to deal with the kins in Columbus?" I asked once we passed the doors. "Someone needs to do it."

"Nick Damarian?" Lotus said hopefully.

"No." His tone left no room for disagreement.

"Pryce, then." She paused.

A good choice. Though our requirements for the job were admittedly rather low. Pryce was powerful and not insane. Not exactly a glowing recommendation, but good enough.

"He's a dealmaker, and strong enough to enforce decisions, if he'll take it." Lotus rose. "I'll step into the next room and call him. Ilani, if you want to wander around and find a room, I'll see about it being gotten ready for you. Santo, could you start with cleanup?"

The troll turned to Ilani. "Does the agreement with Johann stand?"

"What was it?" she asked.

"We get to eat the other side's dead."

Ilani considered, then nodded with a canny gleam

in her eyes. "With all the other parts of the deal, too."

Santo laughed. "Smart. Hope Pryce isn't that smart when he takes over."

He left, and Ilani asked, "Are there computers here? Phones?"

Lotus came back into the room, still on the phone. "I'll contact some government agents that I know to see if we can come up with a story in case all of us want to come out."

I glanced out at the destruction that had been wrought, the wrecked ambulances and fire trucks that could be seen even through the windows. One hell of an explanation would be required to wave all that mess away.

Jimmy came over and hugged me again. "I called Dara and told her what happened here. She'll come tomorrow. She wanted to be here sooner, but all the roads are blocked, and Pryce is coming then too. She's at Pryce's house, but that's just to have one place for the bodyguards to keep safe, there's nothing going on that shouldn't be. I told her you'd call once you got some rest. Go to bed, Mom."

Then he turned to Ilani and gave her his phone.

Her face lit up. "Thanks!"

Exhaustion swamped me. Too much adrenaline was starting to take its toll. There wasn't much else that I could do at the moment.

"Do I still have a room?" I asked Lotus.

She nodded. "The same one. I'll get you a phone

later."

Nick accompanied me upstairs. He didn't speak, but he was right behind me even when I closed the door and pulled my shoes off. I barely had the energy for that and there was no way that I was going to change clothes, or even take my clothes off, but I had some manners at least. I wasn't going to sleep with my shoes on the bed. I wasn't a heathen.

"I'm not complaining at *all*, but why did you follow me? You must have a lot to do." I crawled under the covers. Thankfully, other than sweat, I wasn't overly disgusting from the day's adventure, so it wasn't as if the bed was going to be covered in soot and dirt, at least on my side.

Nick on the other hand... He kicked off his shoes as well, then peeled off his bloodstained shirt and jeans, joining me in the bed and gently kissing the side of my neck before he pulled me close and murmured in my ear.

"Because you make bad decisions when I'm not around, and I'm not going to lose you again."

We curled up side by side, his arms holding me tight as my eyes fluttered closed. At least this way, I felt safe. I knew that I was safe to sleep, because he was here with me, and he wouldn't let anything happen to me.

I had no idea how long I slept, but it probably wasn't very long. There was still light in the windows, and I wasn't much less tired.

"Better?" Nick asked.

"A little." Barely.

"Feel up to an important question?"

I wriggled until I was facing him. "Maybe, depending on the question."

He shifted, reaching to the floor and scooping up his jeans. He fished in the pocket, pulling out a small black velvet bag with a drawstring. A gentle tug, and the contents tumbled out.

A ring of pale metal, intricately engraved with twining vines of rose gold. The vines framed a large green stone, sparkling in his palm. It was lovely, and knowing him, he'd made it for me. One of a kind, like he was.

"Will you marry me, and come live someplace safe for a little while? Somewhere where you can help guide a bunch of stubborn people out of the Middle Ages?" His silver eyes were intent on mine.

"What about your nephew?" He'd attacked me and the others at Nick's home there.

He shrugged, body relaxed. "He's had his warning. If he comes by again, I'll kill him."

Nick wasn't human, and he knew his people. I declined to protest. If that issue were cleared up...

"Can I take people with me, oh ruler of stubborn backwards people?" I asked. I wasn't worried about the amount of time I spent with him since I was aging much more slowly now, thanks to what another mage had taught me.

I was tired. If we lived in his dominion, we were leaving Columbus in not-terrible hands. I just needed to make arrangements for the fetches, the goblins, the Kellers, my children... The list was long.

And supernaturals had been revealed to the world here. It was a pretty good reason to visit Nick's dominion, actually. "Can you adjust with the time differential between there and here, so a year there is a day here and we check in everyday here to make sure everything is going well?"

"Of course. However you want." Nick smiled at me. "I love you, Ceri Gault."

"I love you too." I kissed him. "But I'll love you more after you shower."

He laughed. "Join me?"

it'd been a while, but even grungy, he looked good. "Sure."

Hot water running, I looked at the soap and shampoo. "We have a choice of rose or jasmine. Which flower do you want to smell like?"

"My masculinity is up to either, but I like jasmine on you." He took the bottle and massaged the shampoo into my scalp. Heaven. I leaned back against him, enjoying the contact and the spray of warm water.

After rinsing my hair, I returned the favor, then started getting frisky.

"Many accidents in the home occur in the shower," he murmured against my mouth.

"Let's risk it."

NICK'S EXPRESSION of humorous resignation as he took me down the stone hall sparked wariness in my highly honed intellect. I trusted him with my life, but that didn't mean that I sensed trouble when he had that expression on his face.

"Where exactly are we going? The mist is supposed to be by, and I don't think it's a good idea to expose more people here to it." I felt it could be trusted, especially since we'd just gotten to the end of the first book, and it desperately wanted to hear the second. On the other hand, I thought it best not to expose Nick's people to something that might trigger their xenophobic tendencies.

"We're going to meet with one of the people who handles customs and arrangements for a large festivities." A wisp of humor made its way into his words, but I could still figure out what he was saying, even if the description was a bit odd. My eyebrows arched curiously. That was the last thing I'd have expected from him.

He'd led me to an unfamiliar section of his house. That wasn't unusual, since it was apparently the size of a small city, especially if you counted the part of it built into living rock, complete with tunnels. And lots of caves. I wanted to explore it more fully eventually, but I hadn't exactly had time yet.

"We're going to see a wedding coordinator?"

"Of a sort. There's a lot of customs here. I wanted to run them by you and come up with a compromise. Now that I have you in my grip, my pretty, I don't want you wiggling free."

I snorted. "I caught you."

"As you wish." His mouth quirked up on one side like I'd dragged the smile out of him.

We turned into a cave. Inside it was decorated as an office. Heavy wooden furniture, several shelves of books, a lovely desk, quill and ink and blotter, and a svartalfar woman. Her silver-white hair was braided and coiled like a crown, and she actually had faint traces of age on her face, which made me curious as to how old she really was. Nicholas was over two thousand years old, and he showed none of it. If she had wrinkles, even faint ones, she must've been ancient. It was a scary thought.

"Adalric." Her voice showed no signs of age though, low and strong. It was like honey and made me jealous. I wanted to sound like that.

"Custom keeper." They nodded at each other, and she showed no real deference to him. Interesting. "I plan to take this woman, Ceri Gault, to be my wife."

"And this will be an official celebration." She looked me up and down neutrally.

"Yes. But I've come to ask for some alterations to custom."

Her brows raised. "Which customs?"

Nick sat, indicating a chair for me. I sat down, curious about what exactly were the customs. He'd never seemed overly concerned with rules before, so why now?

"I was hoping you could run through them for Ceri and see which ones that she felt comfortable with and not comfortable with."

"You're going soft in your old age, Adalric." Amusement twinkled in the woman's eyes.

"Of course. If having some care for the feelings of the woman I wish to spend the rest of my life with is soft." Nick made air quotes with his finger to drive the sarcasm home.

She shrugged. "No screaming, no weeping, no bruises..."

I stared at her. Yes. I thought I detected a tinge of sarcasm, and I had. So many people in this dominion appeared to be deadpan snarkers.

"Well. Betrothed of the Adalric." Her eyes met mine, pale blue and intent. "To begin. Custom dictates that you and the Adalric be separated for a week before the celebrations commence, for purification. From gossip I've heard, you're already a mother, so you do not need to lay your maidenhood aside, correct?"

I nodded. This was not a good start, but I could deal. My kids were the light of my life, and it was far too late to worry about such an antiquated concept as my maidenhood.

"One could wish you were, but we deal with reality. That sets aside at least a day's worth of ceremony. To continue, custom suggests your dress be red, but any bright color will do."

I nodded again, like a bubblehead. It wouldn't be red, but I could do a bright color. Easy enough.

"You will need a sword associated with your family, preferably your father's."

My jaw dropped. "That might be difficult... He died when I was very young, and I have none of his possessions." Not that I thought he'd ever owned a sword, but I didn't know. I knew grandfather had an athame, but that was long gone.

"Do you own any blades?"

I shot Nick a sidelong glance. Suddenly, the long knife he gave me recently took on a whole new meaning. Somebody had been plotting. "Yes, I do have a blade. It's a knife though."

"That'll do."

"What does it symbolize?"

"The custom is to exchange it as a symbol of you

giving up your family's protection and entering your husband's family's protection."

Irritation shot through me. "What if I don't need protection?"

"It's symbolic. It isn't as if you're expecting to be attacked at your wedding." She spoke as if I were a child.

It was difficult not to snort. "I wouldn't know about that. And I don't need protection." Maybe it was childish, but we were also going to try to drag them out of the Dark Ages here.

"This might be one of the things that we need to discuss. Let's get on with the rest of it." Nick intervened before this could degenerate to a pair of two-year-olds arguing.

"Very well. You should wear a crown of flowers, which will be exchanged for a metal crown that comes from the Adalric's family."

Something fun; I could wear a crown. I nodded.

"You exchange rings."

Yay! Something familiar! Finally.

"A thrall is sacrificed, and a fir branch dipped in the blood, then sprinkled on you and he for luck and fertility."

I stared at her, a variety of words struggling in my throat. Mostly leading with hell no, and less friendly from there. Human sacrifice was never a basis for a good relationship. Beyond that, I was fully aware that I had terrible luck, and no amount of blood sacrifices would change that.

Nick said, "I think a sow, or a goat would be better. I haven't allowed thralls to be sacrificed since I took the position, Keeper."

She shrugged. "It's expected for a man of your rank."

"They'll have to learn to deal with disappointment."

"Can we skip being splattered with blood entirely?" I snapped.

"Another point for discussion," Nick said. "Go on."

Nope. No discussion there, even if he didn't realize it yet.

She shook her head. "There's a feast, which the entire realm will join in. Everyone is expected to get drunk."

I could pretend. Easy enough, since everyone else would be too drunk to notice.

"And you need at least six witnesses to the consummation of the marriage."

I burst out laughing at the audacity. Wait, what?! Once again, hell no from me.

A slight smile curved her lips at my reaction. "Is that another point that will need discussion?" she asked sweetly.

"Yes," I said around my chuckles. I didn't look at Nick. I didn't need to. Inside, he was laughing his head off, and I wanted to slap him for it. I loved him with all my heart, but he'd come into this knowing full well what the customs were and hadn't warned me in the slightest.

I leaned forward. "Yes. Let's talk about how were going to have to change these customs to accommodate the fact that I'm not a svartalfar, not from this dominion, and not going to have people watch me have sex."

A *year of preparation later...*

I looked out over the feast hall. A new structure, it stretched as far as the eye could see. So many svartalves, so many tables, all groaning under the weight of roasted animals and fruit and bread, with barrels of ale and mead at the walls.

Fetches and goblins had their own section. They'd already taken refuge in Nick's realm, when he went back out and invited them to stay here while Columbus and the world sorted out the fallout of Morgan's attack. It had eased the burden on Pryce as well.

Albrecht's family were separatists who'd left the dominion and wouldn't permit him to attend.

We'd decided on a different ceremony for my family and the others on earth, since the fetches and goblins had strained Nick's people to their breaking point, but Nick had surprised me with Jimmy, Dara, and Noir. They'd snuck them in, or maybe Nick had bribed someone. I wasn't sure. I was just glad to be able to look down the table and see my children, with Noir perched on Dara's shoulder, begging for scraps.

That little dragon was going to have to go to fitness camp or something. He'd been spending all the time I'd been gone with Drake and Katie. Katie'd been spinning off bits of chaos magic for him to eat and he had a little round belly now.

I couldn't believe how far we'd all come. Gone were the days of hiding in the shadows, terrified of anyone finding out my secret. My children were in more danger than before, yes, but they were fully living their lives. As they were meant to.

The crown I wore on my head was a confection of silver, gold and emeralds and rubies. It weighed a ton, but it was possibly the most gorgeous piece of jewelry I'd ever seen. I didn't have to keep it on much longer, since Nick showed no intention of getting drunk either. Many of his subjects are enthusiastically making up for his lack, however.

He turned and kissed my knuckles. "Shall we head up?"

I smiled at him. "Yes."

That was the one point that I'd not yielded on in the least. No witnesses to our lovemaking, not my kink. The compromise was the kiss we were about to share.

His lips met mine. I leaned into him, hands on his shoulders, his on my hips.

Cheers erupted around us.

He drew back, brushing a kiss on my nose, and said low, "I love you."

"And I love you. Let's move before the barbarian horde decides to accompany us anyway."

We ran up the stairs laughing.

MORE FICTION BY DAPHNE MORE

https://daphnekmoore.com/books

Midlife Mage

Unveiled

Unfettered

Set in the Midlife Mage Universe:

The Reckoning

Unwanted

Unrepentant

Unbroken

ABOUT DAPHNE MOORE

Daphne Moore has been a storyteller from her preliterate days. She writes them down now for those out of earshot. She writes what she loves—speculative fiction in all forms, with a seasoning of romance.

Read More from Daphne Moore

Visit her website for a free story.
www.daphnekmoore.com

MORE PARANORMAL WOMEN'S
FICTION BY L.A. BORUFF

Witching After Forty (Paranormal Women's Fiction)

A Ghoulish Midlife

Cookies For Satan (*A Christmas Novella*)

I'm With Cupid (*A Valentine's Day Novella*)

A Cursed Midlife

Birthday Blunder

A Girlfriend For Mr. Snoozerton

A Haunting Midlife

An Animated Midlife

Faery Odd Mother

A Killer Midlife

A Grave Midlife

A Powerful Midlife

A Wedded Midlife

Fanged After Forty (Paranormal Women's Fiction)

Bitten in the Midlife

Staked in the Midlife

Masquerading in the Midlife

Bonded in the Midlife

Fae

The Meowing Medium

The Meowing Medium (Paranormal Cozy)
COMPLETE SERIES
Series Boxed Set Coming Soon

Secrets of the Specter

Gifts of the Ghost

Pleas of the Poltergeist

An Unseen Midlife (Paranormal Women's Fiction Reverse Harem)

Bloom In Blood

Dance In Night

Bask In Magic

Surrender In Dreams

ABOUT L.A. BORUFF

L.A. (Lainie) Boruff lives in East Tennessee with her husband, three children, and an ever growing number of cats. She loves reading, watching TV, and procrastinating by browsing Facebook. L.A.'s passions include vampires, food, and listening to heavy metal music. She once won a Harry Potter trivia contest based on the books and lost one based on the movies. She has two bands on her bucket list that she still hasn't seen: AC/DC and Alice Cooper. Feel free to send tickets.

Printed in Poland
by Amazon Fulfillment
Poland Sp. z o.o., Wrocław